Incandescently

Incandescently

SYLVIE PARIZEAU

Incandescently
©2016 Sylvie Parizeau
By the Book, an imprint of :
www.sylvieparizeau.com

Library and Archives Canada Cataloging-in-Publication Data:
Parizeau, Sylvie
Incandescently: Book 1 of the Incandescent Series / Sylvie Parizeau

ISBN print : 978-0-9953240-2-2

Interior Design and Formatting by:

www.emtippettsbookdesigns.com

Prologue

Infinite darkness, the fury of the winds unleashed, sheets of rain and waves pounding mercilessly; I am numb.

Time ceases.

An impression of gray light eventually filters through my battered eyelids.

The capsized hull to which I secured my body harness is but a bit of flotsam, abandoned to the whims of the swirling waters of the Caribbean Sea surrounding me.

The graceful Thalassa, Primeval Spirit of the Sea, is no longer.

My sanctuary. Gone.

My soul cries out desperately to Liam … my Liam. And in the remembered warmth of his embrace, I let go as blessed unconsciousness finally welcomes me within its arms.

One

LIAM

I shove my body up if only to prove I'm awake. My bedroom is dark and new enough that it takes a moment to place where I am. For a split second, the terror of the dream follows me into reality. But then I remember.

Bar Harbor. Maine. My new teaching gig. I'm good.

Even so, the nightmare doesn't quite fade. My pulse still erratically beating, I take a steadying breath, and remind myself I'm safe and dry. No death grip on a fraying strap, no being tossed about on a raging sea.

As nightmares go, this particular one's a first. I usually relive impressions of traumatic memories of my own in a night terror, not conjure up brand-new ones ... but what I felt just now seemed way too real to be dreamed up by the weirdness of my brain alone. Yet, I've never been on board a ship like that one, much less hanging on a capsized hull in the middle of a wild sea storm.

A cold knot of dread settles in the pit of my stomach for absolutely no good reason. And I just can't shake the vividness of drenching sheets of rain and waves pounding on my back.

"Awesome," I mumble under my breath. *You're a new kind of crazy, man.* Which is saying something.

I groan into my pillow, cracking my eyes open. Guess I won't be going back to sleep any time soon.

The full moon shines down on me through the glass wall, its silver beams highlighting the sparsely furnished bedroom of the rental condo, and draws attention to the mess of clothes strewn about. Through the high window, I see that the nighttime sky has lightened, heralding a fast-approaching morning. *Good to know this torture is at an end.*

I let the soothing rhythm of waves lapping down the southern Maine seashore below shake the last of my disorientation, clearing my head of what's left of my weird dream.

Jesus, what a night ... I reach for the bottle of water stashed beside the bed, and a swift sharp pain jolts me. *Shit, that hurts.* The water bottle falls and rolls underneath the nightstand, sloshing.

I fumble with the light switch, eyes squinting when it clicks on. Large, angry red welts cover both my palms. *What the—?*

I blink, swallow, blink some more. The welts are still there.

My mind clamors for a logical explanation, and I run through the list of possibilities.

No wild partying the night before with possible gaps in my short-term memory. Nope, haven't done that since university.

Some sort of prank definitely gone just this side of too far from one of my GGS buddies? Not an entirely impossible feat considering our shared history, but sadly, in no way a viable possibility. Not with all five of them currently flung about to their own far reaches of the world.

At this point, my brain's just about ready to settle for a bloody spider. And so am I.

I search through my bedding, desperately foraging for a logical culprit, and find none.

Zilch. Nada. Rien.

The plot thickens while the list of suspects thins.

With a judicious blast of music, the alarm clock suddenly recalls me to the here and now, abruptly reminding me that if I don't hustle it up, I will be late for my first day of class. Students can get away with a tardy so easily. Faculty, not so much.

I hop out of bed and hurry through my morning shower, not bothering to shave. Scrambling back into the bedroom, I throw on a pair of jeans dark enough to pass for dressy. It will have to do since it's the only clean pair of pants I have left until I figure out a way to do laundry on my own.

Hmm, wonder if the need for clean clothes will be enough to make me regret the easy comforts of my usual hotel stays...

After another harried search, I grab the first collared button-up shirt that looks in decent enough shape to be worn in public.

Guess laundry needs to be higher up on my *To Do* list after all.

I tuck the shirt into my jeans with ease and stop mid-motion. I slowly take my hands out of my pants and, when I do, I stare in utter confusion at two perfectly healed palms.

"What the hell?" I say to the empty apartment.

The silence doesn't offer any answers. Go figure.

Running out of time, and refusing to dwell any longer on the bizarre red marks, I quickly grab my messenger bag and jog down the stairs to my rental car.

Thankfully I toured around quaint Bar Harbor all of last week upon accepting this professor gig, so I'm quite confident I'll keep to the right side of the road this time around ... *incoming traffic on the left, man.* Courtesy of the near miss my first day out that frightened the bloody everlasting hell out of me, my short drive to campus this morning is all-American, smooth and eventless.

A cup of straight black coffee sounds like heaven after the hellish night I've had, and I make a beeline for my next pit stop, The Blair Dining Hall— affectionately called Take-A-Break, or TAB for short, by everyone at the College of the Atlantic.

Caffeine fueled and with only a few minutes to spare, I fly through the back door leading to the amphitheatre allocated to my guest lecture series for the semester. Before I round the platform, I take a moment to slow down to a more dignified pace. After all, as of this morning I am a faculty member, sort of, but still ... might as well act the "honorary" part of it, and blend in.

I'm relieved to see that no other administrative personnel are here yet, so I guess I'm not as late as I thought. Maybe my jet lag, courtesy of my seven-month jaunt in Australia, is still messing with me.

I make my way to the podium and stash my notes, trying to appear busy and important. Like I know what I'm doing or, better yet, like I'm supposed to be here, doing it. Man, what was I thinking when I said yes to this guest lecture?

I feel about as qualified to be standing here as the kid in the back row with his cap pulled low over his eyes.

I rub the bridge of my nose, sighing heavily. Just means I'm better at playing the role, not much else. Oh, and I am a New York Times Bestselling Author—the words bounce around in my head. I inwardly scoff but it's too late to backtrack now.

As I wait to be introduced to the crowd, I discreetly look around at the freshman faces already assembled. What would I give to be that young again? At twenty-four, I feel ancient compared to these kids.

I check my phone, giving me something else to do besides standing there. Bad idea. I struggle to keep my face impassive without barking a few rounds of snickers as I scroll down the text messages I've received in the last few hours. My GGS buddies know me better than anyone, and even with some of them scattered to the outer reaches of the planet, they've all managed to text me well-wishes for today. P.O., enrolled in a grad program at MIT alongside Yann, even pokes fun at my luck of the Irish teaching hot coeds, stressing they're "do not touch," but reaffirming his willingness to fill in for me, phone numbers optional. Luck of the Irish indeed as, contrary to popular belief, the expression is meant to be ironic, so he's basically saying, *tough luck, mate, sucks to be you.* My GGS crew's witticism is impeccable as always. Lips quirking, I can't help but shake my head.

Officially known as the Goddamned Geek Squad by the end of primary school, as we all had skipped ahead one grade or two by that time, yet better known in our inner circle by its shortened version of GGS, it didn't take us very long to elevate it to Geek God Status by the time secondary school rolled in. Yeah, owning the nickname totally short-circuited the bullying from the older crowd, and the degrading intentions it originated from. One of the many "elite" joys of growing up forgotten in an all-boys boarding school near the Swiss/Italian border. The six of us were thrown together as roommates—and unlikely friends—but we quickly learned to ditch entitlement and outwit bullies. And, in the end, we bonded. Now, despite physical distances, P.O., Zac, Yann, Theo, Leo, and I are still the closest thing to family we have ever known.

My internal trip down memory lane is cut short by a slap on my back. I slide my phone away and turn into the waiting smile of the Dean.

"Good to see you, Mr. O'Shea," the tall and sprightly gentleman says. He doesn't pause long enough for me to respond as he rushes up to the lectern. Looks like we both have "last minute" syndrome.

A full retinue follows in his wake, and I'm left suddenly swamped by a round of I-can't-believe-it-and-so-pleased-to-finally-meet-you-in-person handshakes from various professors and whatnots wanting a piece of famous before my lecture kicks off. I paste on a plastic smile and shake and repeat until they wander off.

From behind the lectern, the Dean's disembodied voice, amplified by the excellent acoustics of the room, jovially drones an overly flattering list of all my accomplishments concluding with, "and so, without further ado, please welcome Liam O'Shea, author extraordinaire."

I take a deep breath. Cue me in.

A surprising roar of applause, chants, and whistles greets me. I put my game face on, making my way up in a fog. They're louder than I expected—or maybe it's the way the room echoes back at me.

For a second, I'm sucked back into the blur of my childhood media circus, and I grip the lectern with both hands, willing myself to calm down. A residual flash of pain from this morning's phantom welts startles me out of my flashback.

I rub my hands together absently until the pain fades, and clear my throat once, twice. "I'm deeply touched by your enthusiasm, and can only hope I'll live up to the sterling reputation Dean Hawkesbury just bestowed upon me. That was quite an introduction." I wink at him, and the crowd laughs.

I unhook the microphone and step in front of the lectern, casually crossing my ankles. Someone whistles from the back, and I banter a bit with the crowd in response, completely immersed in my public persona now. You'd never know by looking at me that I absolutely hate public speaking.

"Truth be told, I'm quite honored to have this unique opportunity to speak to the next generation of authors. The Indie phenomena can no longer be ignored and is revolutionizing the publishing industry from the bottom. The popularity of e-books is spreading far and wide and, contrary to what major publishers predicted, they're definitely here to stay. But the landscape of the marketplace is constantly changing. What worked for me as a self-published, best-selling author a mere two years ago is no longer applicable. New technologies are constantly challenging us to be more, and do more. Publishing is a brand-new world and yours for the taking..."

As I continue my lecture, rows and rows of eyes remain fixed on me, but I don't focus on them. I focus on the message itself. "Set your imagination free. Be intense, passionate about what you write. Go out there and concoct new sub-genres. If I were to sum up this new publishing era in two words? Endless possibilities."

My blood pumps wildly through my veins on the last line and the crowd applauds furiously. It's the same rush I used to get from writing, only it's shifted. Now, I'm lit up simply talking about writing. Instead of being pleased, the realization only depresses me. I haven't felt inspired to write in months. I'm still hoping this teaching gig will reignite a dying flame.

When the lecture hall finally empties, my previous high's already fizzled out. I'm seriously drained, but there's one more stop to make before I can call it a day.

The note left for me on the lectern is from the Dean himself. *Stop by my office on your way out.*

"Mr. O'Shea, come in, come in." Dean Hawkesbury scurries around his desk the moment I poke my head through his open door. The dean's towering figure of a man moving so swiftly is a bit startling. Next thing I know, he's standing before me with a hand outstretched, and I have yet to step inside his office.

My eyes narrow by a fraction. "Call me Liam," I say, accepting the firm handshake.

"We just got the news," he says with a broad smile revealing a row of crooked teeth.

"The news?" I ask, my shoulders tensing. Uneasiness seeps in. Did someone dig a little too deep into my past?

I watch Dean Hawkesbury's bushy, grey eyebrows shoot up at my dubious reaction, before he launches into a spiel. "Well, yes, the confirmation just got in, and we're all so grateful for your generous contribution," he says, still pumping my hand enthusiastically, his other hand cradling the handshake now. "You just propelled COA to the forefront of Twenty-First Century Academia."

My face clears. Looks like Theo finalized the tablets' subsidies, then. "I'm more than happy to contribute," I assure him. "Your Go Green mission statement is something I strongly believe in, no need to thank me." I extricate my hand from his, and discreetly shake my numb fingers back into working conditions.

His nervy hand clamps down on my shoulder instead. *Jesus.* "If you need anything at all for your seminar just ask Mrs. Pringle, our registrar. Anything at all."

"Just keep it simple, no fuss over me, that's all I ask." *Yeah, keep it all under the anonymous donor umbrella, please.*

"Whatever you say, and simple we can do, Mr.—Liam," he corrects reading my expression. I flash him a tight smile and make my escape.

Compliments on my "sooo inspiring" lecture du jour are slinging back and forth as I walk through the outer rim of the quad, but I keep my head down, making my way to the parking lot. One of the comments having to do with imagination let loose catches my attention, and brings me to a halt.

"Oh, look," one of them squeals, and I accidentally turn before I can stop myself, "it's him."

"Liam," they all shout, jumping to their feet.

I cringe inwardly and plaster my most charming smile on my lips.

Within seconds, a slew of beautiful, highly sophisticated women vying for my attention surrounds me, so yeah, the usual ... and every twenty-four-year-old male's ideal job environment. And yet, I can't muster one ounce of enthusiasm. Instead, I'm quite inexplicably drained of energy.

Maybe I'm coming down with a sort of flu I have been warned is making inroads into the college population. And by the look of this mixer, all males of the species were wiped out by it. Am I the only guy left standing?

"Ohmygosh. I can't believe it's you. I can't believe you're here," says the brunette jumping up and down in front of me, the rest of her ample attributes following suit.

I school my expression to something calm and collected. "Hmm, yes, quite unbelievable indeed and yet, here I am."

"Can you believe that, like, I just bumped into you? Like, wow," says a blur of sparkling pink shirt to my left.

"You're so famous, and I'm like your biggest fan ever," exclaims a busty blonde pushing her way through.

At the sound of their squealing voices, my exhaustion turns into a pounding headache.

In another lifetime, I'd be all over this All You Can Eat Buffet, but that's just it. I ate too much. I'm sick of it. I'm hungry for something different, not just filling but nourishing. Something I tasted a long time ago, and have craved ever since.

Éolie...

My heart takes a tumble just at the fleeting thought of her. My one and only bright light in a messed-up childhood. Long-lost love, a strange recurring theme of mine I've been grappling with my whole life. I sigh heavily. *Don't go there man.*

"—and, like, I keep your book, you know the one with your cute picture on it, like, right next to my bed you know, so that we already, like, sleep together."

Not in this lifetime. "How nice," I say, checking my watch.

A hand clamps down on my arm, and I grit my teeth, irked by the encroachment on my personal space. "Ooooh. It's really you, Liam," gushes a brunette built exactly like the first. I wonder if they're sisters. Or if even they can tell each other apart with the identical way they all lead with their cleavage, and toss their hair on cue.

Same old shit, different day.

"That's me," I say, not even daring to add, "in the flesh."

Mentally, I label them girl number one, two, three, four ... In no time I'm up to nineteen, and counting. Keeping tabs on their numbers keeps me on my toes. It's either that, or get caught rolling my eyes. I might not be up for a coed feast, but I'm doing my best not to be rude on my first day either.

"Wait, wait. I have one of your books with me," adds the most recent brunette. She digs furiously through her bag.

"I'm quite flatte—" I humph as she pulls out my latest title in hardcover and shoves it at me.

"Would you sign it, pretty please?" she coos, and I watch in consternation as all the others jockey for position, T-shirts at the ready.

"I'd be delighted to," I say by rote, my eyes glazing over. She bats her eyelashes at me, handing over a red lipstick.

Seriously?

"Whoa. You're so hot," she exclaims, her fingers lightly trailing down my wrist. I hastily scribble my name and today's date and shove the book back at her, lipstick and all.

Nope. I don't really feel all that hot ... Unless you count fever. My insides are burning up and it has nothing to do with the crowd of female attention.

"Hot? You don't say." I suppress a shudder, and not so subtly shove my hands into my pockets.

Way to go, man. So suave.

"It's, like, so incredible to meet you, Liam." another generic blonde says as she enters the fray, boldly claiming my arm, and shrugging off girl number who the heck knows, in the process. "Is it true what everybody says?" she asks.

And that would be?

I angle a brow. "Hmm, depends—"

"What's it like living in hotels all over the world?" she cuts in, grabbing my forearm.

Not as fun as it looks on paper.

"Well, it has its advantages..." *Like what?* I inwardly snort. *Laundry?*

I stall, still trying to figure out a way to bail out. The longer I stand here, the warmer my skin feels. I'm beginning to feel like a caged animal. Not in a good way.

"You're a bit hot, you know?" girl number ten says. Or is she number six?

"He's a whole lot. Just admit he's too hot for you to handle, *Mimi*." The blonde clone clinging to my arm aims a death stare at her classmate.

"In your dreams, Mikaela Minirelli," screeches one Mimi to the other Mi-Mi.

"Never met any guy too hot for me to handle," said Mimi scorns, breaking out of the death glare contest long enough to lay her hand lightly against my cheek, and I clench my jaw overcoming the urge to recoil. "No, he's hot as in feverish, feel him."

Half a dozen hands reach for my skin, and I jump back.

"I'll take your word for it," I say, holding my hands up in a defensive gesture.

And in lieu of graceful I make the most grateful exit ever. I can hear Theo's dry quip from here, "And not a single phone number, that's sick, all right."

By the time I make it back to my condo, I'm seeing black spots and shivering up a storm, giving more credence to the flu theory. Searching madly through the medicine cabinet over the bathroom sink, I knock over some toothpaste and a box of condoms in my haste to grab bottled salvation. And at last, I shake out a handful of aspirins, popping three in my mouth. *Jesus.* My teeth are rattling so much I can hardly swallow anything. *Shit.* I spit out the painkillers, gagging and coughing on their powdery residue, sticking my head under the tap instead. The water cools me and washes away the worst of my delirium.

By the time I fall into bed, it's no longer a theory.

Clearly, I am dying from the flu...

An hour passes. *Give or take an eternity or two.*

My phone blares with P.O.'s ringtone and I grunt into it, "Dying, man, call back later," only to realize I've let his call go to voicemail. I moan into my pillow, letting my phone drop onto the hardwood floor.

When I come to again, I notice the sunlight slanting much harder to the left than before. I don't bother turning over to glance at the clock. Time is irrelevant when you're dying.

Just as I'm resigning to my fate and have accepted with relief my forthcoming demise, every symptom stops. No more cold sweats. No more black spots. No more shivers. I sit up, cautiously optimistic.

No two ways about it. Not one iota of pain remains. I am brand new, as if nothing happened, and an eerie sense of déjà vu floods me. But I shake it off.

I'm in serious need of a shower, fresh sheets, and a head check, not necessarily in that order. I get up, peeling off my soaked shirt, and head for the bathroom.

Liam LiamLiamLiamLiam...

The angelic voice drifts through my mind and lingers, immediately slicing my heart in two at its soft familiarity. I stagger, coming to an abrupt halt.

Éolie.

No way. There's just no way.

And yet, what I heard cannot be unheard.

I wait motionless, as I will her voice to fill my head once more.

Right on cue, *LiamLiamLiamLiam* suddenly plays on my soul like a chanted prayer. So loud and clear my gaze sweeps the room once, wondering if it isn't being spoken aloud rather than only in my mind. But of course, that's the only way I've ever heard her. So, no big surprise, the room is empty. I rub my chest, feeling hollowed out.

Liam... she calls to me. Letting my head fall back, I close my eyes in remembered bliss.

Fragile hope rises.

I teeter between two realities. The one from my childhood, complete with a sweet voice in my head that's not my own ... and the one I've learned to accept as truth, that she's nothing more than a figment of my imagination, a result of years of enforced therapy. Suddenly, after some fifteen years of convincing myself, I can't quite decide which is real.

Her voice is silent now, and I wonder if I even really heard it at all.

I pace back and forth, only stopping once in a while to rest my forehead on the coolness of the wall. Éolie, my mind entreats her to come back over and over.

Dusk comes, and goes.

My shallow breaths are the only sounds in the quiet of the room overlooking the ocean below.

The silence in my head remains.

Hope shrivels, weighted down by seventeen years of no contact between us.

I pinch the bridge of my nose on a deep exhale. I'm ruined by a figment of my imagination.

"Just a wonderful coping mechanism your little brain cleverly engineered," my therapists back then were quick to validate, one after the other. I went through a trauma, after all.

I rub the jagged scar on my elbow. Éolie. So many reasons existed back then for a coping mechanism to even be necessary.

Not going there, man.

I resolutely step into the en suite, chucking my jeans along the way, along with any temptation to let my thoughts go back to that harrowing time ... Mysterious healings, a whispered voice, none of it does me a damn bit of good now. And I've worked too hard to let any of it resurface.

Instead, I pull a trick from my therapist's bag, and focus on the here and now. The things I can control, the actions I can take and the security, the promise in that.

And, right now, there's a shower with my name on it, and I fully intend to collect on its hot promises.

Two

LIAM

I spend the evening doing market analysis on readers' buying habits of e-books based on genre. Yeah, I know, my life is glamorous. But the spreadsheet I'm preparing takes my mind off the earlier part of my day, the crazier part.

My laptop screen chooses this moment to freeze up. I click a few times. Nothing.

"Great," I grumble under my breath, not sure when I last saved the document I've been working on. My computer screen blips twice, and goes black. What the—?

I'm checking the plug when my screen relights to P.O.'s ugly mug filling up the space.

I glare. Just great. I've been hijacked.

"Shit, man. That was awesome," he says, shaggy, light-brown hair sticking up every which way, his green-hazel eyes scanning lines of codes popping out on my upper screen.

Shoving my hands through my hair, I say, "P.O., for chrissake, get out of my laptop."

"Why? I just got in, man."

I roll my eyes just for the sake of it and blow out a heavy breath. No use arguing with this kind of logic.

"By the way," he says, "your Wifi connection's for the birds. It's full of holes."

"Obviously," I say annoyed. "Is that what you guys at MIT to do for kicks now? Hack into computers just for the hell of it on Wednesday nights?"

"Nah, we do it all the time," he says, unfazed. "Admit that my security team seriously kicks ass. Eight minutes to zap you out of cyberspace."

"I'm working over here. Go target practice your security breach protocols on someone else's computer."

"Already on it. Lucie's tightening up your security access codes as we speak."

"Lucie? What happened to Guinevere?" I ask, leaning back in my chair. Might as well get comfortable, who knows how long these updates will take.

"Guinevere? Dude, keep up, she's last month's flavor. I'm into Lucie now, supermodel GigaHot Lucie, and I can't get enough," he says, and I can practically hear him drool over the line. "Man, best performance I've ever had. She's my missing link."

My eyes turn skyward, but I can't help the small grin that curls on my lips. Only P.O. could fall in and out of lust with his computers and completely own it.

"Speaking of missing link, haven't heard from Yann in a while," I say.

"Me neither, and we share an apartment," P.O. deadpans. "MIT's full of math brainiacs lost in dynamic time warping. He's just being Yann," he says, shrugging it off. "What about you, Professor? All's good with your first week in honorary academia?"

"I'll tell you when I get there. Today was just a guest lecture," I say, stretching, trying to work the kinks out of my neck. "Regular classes start tomorrow, but I only have one class, an extracurricular seminar, on Mondays and Wednesdays. So, long weekends for me I guess."

"And when are you gaining back freedom?" he asks.

"Mid-November," I reply, but his eyes are intent on something off screen, and I wonder if he even heard me.

"Short semesters over there," he says distractedly.

"P.O.?" I ask, fighting a dull, gnawing ache of nostalgia centering on thoughts of Éolie, love, and family. And losing.

"Hang on, almost done with your upgrades." His fingers fly over the keyboard until, with the final stroke of a key, he looks up at me. "Done. Yeah?"

"Remember when we were kids at BIA and we dreamed about what normal would look like?" I ask. "Do you wonder about it sometimes?"

His brows dip until they connect in the middle. My stomach tightens, and I wonder if it was a mistake to bring it up. I blame my weird, disquiet mood for bringing back to the surface things that I've kept buried.

"What brought that on?" he asks after too long a beat.

"Mid-life crisis?" I reply, attempting to lighten the mood. I should never have said anything.

"Cut the crap," P.O. says, giving me a look. He knows me way too well.

"I don't know. When we got out of there I only wanted to travel, never settling in just one place ... But now, five years into it, I'm tired of it all."

"So that's what this is about." His expression clears. "Wearied by too many years of travels, huh?"

I relax back into my chair. This is a much safer conversation. And it means he won't press me about Éolie. The sweet angelic voice I heard in my head once upon a time ... My childhood love. He knows—they all do, and more, they believed it, same as I, up until I didn't dare to anymore—but it hasn't happened in so long, and I'm not quite ready to admit today was real.

"I guess I am, yeah..."

"Bet you're ready to grow some roots in a forest somewhere, like we always said we would," P.O. says, narrowing his eyes on me knowingly.

"Man, I forgot about that." I shake my head, offering a nostalgic smile. Me and my bedtime stories. "Knights on quests for freedom in the Enchanted Forest of Laure," I quote, taking on a dramatic bass tone that works much better now than it did at seven.

"Hey, who knows? Maybe you'll get to keep the mysterious fairy this time around." P.O.'s face turns all-knowing.

Yeah, right. Not likely. Éolie ... She's the fairy from my made-up stories—though I've never told the guys. Guess it wasn't that hard to figure out, though, at seven, she was the only thing I talked about. There's just no escaping her tonight.

"You think about it sometimes?" I ask. "Settling down somewhere, I mean?"

"Not me, man. I'm not ready for any of that normal shit yet. So many Lucies, so little time," P.O. says slyly. "But I'll bet you're ready for it."

"Not betting on something I'm not even sure how to get," I say, shaking myself out of my strange mood.

"Too bad, 'cause it's a sure bet," he says smugly, but I don't rise to the bait. Normal? Me?

"Okay, enough already. Get out of here."

"Hey, want some tips before I do?" he says, typing away, clearly entertained.

"It's not like I have a choice," I say sardonically.

"Go rock your professor shit; that's as normal as it gets for now," he says, signing off, just before my bottom screen lights up with a marquee that reads **"and send some hot students my way while you're at it."**

I snicker as I remember the crowd I barely escaped from earlier. *Done,* I silently tell P.O. *All yours. You're welcome.*

I resume work on my spreadsheet, or try to. My mind is no longer engaged in it. P.O.'s words taunt me. *I'll bet you're ready for it.* Hauntingly, the ghost of Éolie's presence whispers by. Am I ready for roots? A home? Love and family? What my GGS buddies and I have always labeled "normal." Is this what my restlessness of the past few months is all about? But my wish upon normal is so far out of reach it's not even funny. Not when the girl I want to share it with doesn't even exist.

Ever-present darkness. The bitter taste of fear, debilitating. Loud screeching and grunts from above make me cower in an even tighter little ball under the bed. Please, Dad, come and get me away from here, I pray over and over. I release a bloodcurdling scream as a gaunt hand with broken nails suddenly grabs me by the ankle and yanks me out of my hiding place.

My shoulders heave and I gasp, coming out of the familiar dark terror, looking wildly around the empty room. I am alone.

Some of the anxious tension in my gut uncoils as I realize it's only a nightmare—a familiar, nasty sort, but not real. No monsters from my past. She can't hurt me anymore.

Christ. I haven't had one this bad in years. Why now?

Nerves fried, I sit near the edge of the bed, forearms resting on my thighs, looking down. I run my hands through my overgrown buzzed-cut hair and brush it off, no closer to an answer.

Getting up, I plod my way to the kitchen. I need a drink and dreamless sleep, preferably in that order.

Unbidden memories swirl in my head as I realize where the dream left off. I woke just before I was about to meet Éolie for the first time. In the gloom of my kitchen, I uncap my bottled water, guzzling half of it.

"Ton papa il est où?" a sweet, tinkling voice had asked me in the dark. I close my eyes, her presence almost palpable once again.

At the time, utterly shocked, I had looked left and right brightening with involuntary hope. My eyes had only met darkness in that tiny closet, and a tug of my leg had confirmed my ankle was still chained to the ring bolted to the floor.

"Liam, ton papa il est où?" the very young voice had insisted, wanting to know where was my dad.

"Who are you?" I had whispered. "Are you captured too?"

"Capturée? Mais non… j'ai juste entendu ta prière dans mon coeur, c'est tout." Her angelical voice had answered that she wasn't captured, but she'd heard my prayer in her heart, and I instantly felt her light enfolding me in warmth. I remember asking her if she was speaking angel-speak.

My mouth twists up at the thought. I know better now. She talked to me in English afterward, or as she called it, mommy-speak, when she realized I couldn't understand a word she spoke in French or, as she called it, papa-speak. That was then. Je parle très bien français maintenant.

I'll never get back to sleep at this rate. I need to shake this off. I gulp the rest of my water.

—*LiamLiamLiam, please Liam ... I need you...*

I spew water across the tile floor, jarred out of my memories by the new dialogue playing in my head. My coping mechanism never needed me before, quite the contrary. Bloody hell, have I snapped for real?

Liam ... please be there...

This time, I'm wide awake as I'm yanked back into last night's brutal images of pounding rain and slashing waves, and spewed right back out. This is no dream. I stumble back, holding on to the kitchen island, coughing at the imagined feel of saltwater sloshing down my throat, filling my lungs. How's that even possible?

Liam? Thalassa ... can no longer ... capsized ... need you to know ... in my heart ... Liam, I wish ... I wish... I hear Éolie's disjointed speech loud and clear in my mind.

Heart rate all over the place, I clutch my head in both hands, pressing on my temples to the point of pain. Why would a figment of my imagination reach out in agony all these years later? I'm either completely insane or...

My whole body stiffens. My eyes widen in the dimness of the kitchen and I stop breathing. "She's real," I whisper. "This is real."

The moment I say it, I already more than half-believe it. And a new terror washes over me as I realize that if she's real ... Christ Almighty. So's the danger.

"Don't you dare give up now, do you hear? Tell me where you are, please, Éolie, I'll come get you!" My voice grows frantic and rings out loudly against the quiet. "Éolie-Jolie, tell me, I'll be on my way, just, please ... tell me." *Let me save you for once.*

My eyes dart between the shiny cabinets, the sink, the counters, the ceiling, hoping they'll offer an answer, but there's no voice. Only the distinct impression of a connection, and I can feel her. She's there, pressed against my thoughts like when we were kids, only this time, I have the vague impression she's saying goodbye.

The connection weakens.

Bloody hell. "NO. Hang on, Éolie, I'm coming to get you, you hear me." *I can't lose you again. I won't lose you again.*

Paralyzed with dread, I feel her slipping away into nothingness.

And just like that, I'm seven years old. I'm a scared, abused, worn-out mess.

And this time, there's no one to save me.

Three

LIAM

I gulp air into my lungs and brace my hands on the kitchen island, calming my racing heart. I remind myself I'm no longer a helpless little boy. I'm no longer a victim. I have control over my reactions. My choices are mine to make, and I get a grip.

I walk over to the study while texting the word **galette**, a code the guys and I came up with years ago upon leaving BIA, signaling an emergency video conference call, and send it out. After seventeen years of mending a broken heart, I know better than to face this alone. I need them, and I need them to believe as before, like I do now, that Éolie's for real. Not sure how I'm going to accomplish the last part, but I know I have to try.

I fire up my laptop and connect to our private line. Then I wait. The other six squares on my video screen sit empty until suddenly, one by one, they spring to life.

"You better have a pretty damn good reason to text **galette**, Liam my man," says a disgruntled Zac, running a hand down his tired-looking face, which is in stark contrast to the backdrop of banana trees rustling in the breeze screaming tropical holiday.

I can't blame him. Presently flying helicopters on a mission with *médecins sans frontière*, he's somewhere in the back boonies of South America. His strange enjoyment of mosquitoes the size of tennis balls is not to be messed with. Neither are spotty satellite connections. He's the last one to video call in after my text alert.

Other than Leo, but we've all counted him out for now. He's finishing up his doctoral thesis in agronomy at Cambridge, and the island in the middle of the Gulf of Guinea he chose for his field research is not exactly up to speed internet wise, or otherwise. So by the time my **galette** text alert reaches him, it might be days, even weeks, depending.

"Are you bored already with your last-minute decision to take a sabbatical in the States; what's with the text alert?" Yann asks, pushing wire-framed glasses up his nose, his bright-green eyes blinking owlishly behind them. "Man, I need to upgrade the prescription on these," he says, surprise clearly written all over him. Typical. Yann is more often than not surprised by the mundane details of life that eventually catch up to him, like regular eye checkups.

"Tell me again how long it's been since you left Perth?" Theo asks, his short locks of sandy-blond hair sticking out in a rumpled look none of us has seen him wear in quite some time. "You do know what time it is in Eastern Daylight, right?"

"What have you got to complain about? The four of you are currently in the Boston area now, enjoying the perks of civilization. You just had to roll over in your comfortable beds to answer the call," Zac grumbles, wiping his chiseled face with his tee.

"Please," P.O. scoffs. "We all know you love the jungle, Zac. The real one, not the concrete—"

"That's enough," Theo cuts them off in his most lawyerly voice. "Liam has fun lampooning us in his books but he never pranks, so the text alert is for real. What gives?"

I plop down on the swivel chair to prevent me from pacing the length of the study back and forth, suddenly wondering if this was such a good idea after all.

"It's Éolie," I finally say. "I heard from her. Tonight."

Silence. I double check to make sure I haven't lost the connection. But the line is still on, they're just frozen.

"You guys still there?" I ask, unsure. They're not even blinking.

Zac's the first to recover, and his tone is wary. "You're messing with us, right?"

"He's dead serious," Theo says, correctly assessing the pointed look I send in their direction. I don't joke about Éolie—ever.

"As a heart attack," I say.

It took close to two years, but once Berlinger International Academy's most esteemed in-house psychologist, Dr. Englehart, convinced everyone, myself included, that Éolie was, in fact, an idealized figment of my imagination, I couldn't even think, let alone say, Éolie's name without agonizing pain. For the longest time, I simply dropped her into my "don't go there" zone, and the guys have all respected the ban on all things Éolie. Fifteen years of it, no exception.

Until today.

So, I can't really jump down their throats for their current disbelief. But one thing's for sure. They know there's not a snowball chance in Hell I would, even remotely, think to use Éolie to prank them with. Because if there's even one tenth of a chance that what Dr. Englehart labeled as my coping mechanism is, in fact, a real life possibility, all bets are off.

"Okay then," Theo says, scratching the stubbles on his jaw. "Éolie. You heard from her?"

I can hear in his voice that he's trying to be open-minded. That's good. At least for now, I've got one of them on my side. And if Theo, our resident skeptic, is on my side, the others won't be too far behind.

"I swear Éolie reached out to me," I say, pulling at my hair with my free hand. "And ... I'm pretty sure she's lost in the middle of a stormy sea as we speak."

"And by reached out, you mean?" Theo asks, drilling me with one of his infamous staredowns. I pinch the bridge of my nose. He's a born cynic, I remind myself. That's just his personality, part of what makes him a good attorney.

"I mean, I heard her," I say, unsure how far to go with admitting her voice is still only in my head.

"Right," P.O. says, his brows shooting up. "And she's in the middle of a storm, lost somewhere at sea. So, naturally, she reached out to you now, after years of silence, because...?" His condescending tone grates on my frayed nerves.

My head tilts back, and I count to ten to calm the fuck down. Christ, what if I can't convince them?

I'll go at it alone, Éolie, if I have to. Just ... hang in there.

"You don't believe me. Fine." I make a sound at the back of my throat, almost a growl. "Then explain to me how a figment of my imagination, someone I supposedly made up to reassure me with, would suddenly throw nightmares at me out of the blue?" I ask, my voice increasing in volume to the point of shouting the last few words. My heart thuds in my ears.

"Unless she didn't," Theo says quietly.

My temper flares. "I didn't make it up," I say through clenched teeth.

"Liam, Christ. Listen. That's—" Theo shakes his head, remorse already taking over, but I'm too far gone for it to make any difference now.

"No. You listen," I snap. "You didn't feel any of it, goddammit. I did." My voice is low, a warning, but just as quickly my anger deflates, replaced by heartache. "The storm, the way her lungs—my lungs—filled with water ... It was way too intense. I tasted salt, for fuck's sake; she has to be real. It was never like this before. Not like this." I close my eyes for a brief second. "She's in trouble—" My voice cracks.

"Tell us what you need, man," Zac interjects, "and it's as good as done." His whiskey-brown eyes glint with determination as he stares the others down through cyberspace.

It doesn't take much else before they rally behind me, their hands coming up for a virtual fist bump. My breath swooshes out.

I swallow to clear the tightness in my throat and nod once, squaring my shoulders.

"I couldn't find anything just by Googling it. P.O., man, I need your computer genius to look deeper into the web for recent storm formations, missing sea vessels, search and rescue missions in progress, any information you can unearth on a ship called the Thalassa, got that?" I say, reading from the checklist I made earlier. But I don't even need to tick the items off; the guys simply jump into action.

"I'm on it." With that, P.O. signs off.

"As soon as P.O. comes up with more intel, I'll hone in on some coordinates. With any luck, I can come up with a pretty accurate area of search and rescue to concentrate on." Yann's mathematical brain's already gone off in search of algorithms.

"Sounds good," Zac says. "I'll check out some obscure regional maps I've got stashed. Search high-risk storm areas. Global wise what's your feel, continental, tropical, in-between?"

Zac may be a medical doctor fresh out, the ink still wet on his diploma, but for as long as I've known him, his passion for flying has always been a constant in his life. His stint in the jungle is his way to reconcile both for now. No one knows the globe like him.

"Tropical," I say without hesitation as I recall the feel of the warm rain pelting down my back. "Which, of course, narrows it down to precisely half the globe," I answer back with an edge of frustration.

"I'll put out my own feelers. We'll find her, Liam, I swear." Static takes over Zac's end of things, but I can still hear the parts he didn't say aloud. *"If she's real."*

"Zac?" I ask, but his line goes dead, and I know he's taken off already.

"Knowing him, he's probably drawing up a flight plan to volunteer for a rescue mission that has no destination yet," Theo says. "Liam, I want you to breathe. Just breathe. If Éolie's out there, we'll find her. You know that, right?"

If.

"Yeah," I say quietly. "I know, Theo."

We hang up, the thought left unspoken between us.

But I'm not worried about the "if" part. I'm worried about whether we'll find her in time.

I check the microwave readout. It's close to five in the morning here, but I can no longer contemplate sleep. I'm too keyed up. Adrenaline pulses through me to the beat of the torrential rain I know is pounding, maybe even right now, on Éolie.

Although I don't even know what she looks like, it's an image I can't get rid of. And not just because I gut wrenchingly loved her once upon a time. It's more than that. It's about returning the favor. She saved me. Physical presence or not, I'd be dead or God knows where without her. It's time I did the same for her.

Éolie, I pray with fervor, *just hang on. Help is on the way.*

Four

LIAM

An hour later, I contemplate the sunrise and stare at the view of the water from my living room window. Whitecaps unfurl as far as my eyes can see. The ocean's as changeable as my mood this morning. The wind is picking up. And Éolie's out there somewhere ... I pull at my hair.

Man, this waiting game is excruciating, shredding me up inside.

I slam my palms on the glass wall gracing the living room, no longer caring for its spectacular ocean view. Pushing away from it, I return to my pacing. I concentrate on putting one foot in front of the other, walking for the umpteenth time the condo's perimeter. I count backwards from one thousand, conjugate French verbs ad infinitum, nothing works. Even sleep deprived, my brain refuses to completely shut down.

I still fear. I still see. I still imagine.

Maybe I should go troll the net once more. Maybe a Google update miraculously occurred in the last fifteen minutes. Éolie. *Where are you?*

I round the corner and watch in bafflement my phone wiggling on the kitchen island counter. Bloody hell. I left it on vibrate, I realize as I lunge for it.

"Anything yet?" I say into my phone when I see P.O.'s face on my display.

"Maybe. Go open your laptop and check this out, man," P.O. says before hanging up. And I almost trip over my own two feet running back to the study.

I power on my computer and the screen lights up, already taken over by an invisible hand as my cursor clicks through to open a chat window.

"P.O.?" I ask into the built-in mic. For an answer, my cursor starts furiously typing some code lines seemingly by itself. I plop into the swivel chair behind the desk, and wait while P.O. does his thing.

A couple of hours. It only took P.O. a couple of hours to come up with the intel he's about to show me. Is this good or bad news? I shove my hands through my hair.

"Bad news first, man," P.O. says, still typing away.

Bad news ... I flinch. White knuckles gripping the leather armrests, I brace for impact. "Lucie's been crunching away, and we're dealing with five plausible spots of weather trouble on the globe's tropical oceans. I've checked in with transmissions via Coast Guard. They're being kept busy all right, but none of their distress calls have to do with a ship called the Thalassa."

"Christ. It'll be close to impossible to—"

"Yeah well, on the other hand, my Lucie did find the Thalassa."

I inhale a sharp breath as he continues, a sly grin pulling at his lips.

"It's officially registered with the Oceanographic Research Agency. And I sort of borrowed their security access code."

A majestic sailboat suddenly appears on my screen, running on the waves, full sails out, and P.O. zooms on its name. I release the breath I didn't know I was holding. For the first time since my stormy nightmare, I see some kind of proof that I'm not crazy.

The Thalassa does exist, or did. A shiver runs up my spine just as the AC kicks off.

"What else did you find?" I say, sitting on the edge of my seat, spellbound.

"She's a serious boat, for starters. We're not talking recreational sailing here, man. The Thalassa, Primeval Spirit of the Sea, is a high-tech, in situ research lab, privately owned," P.O. replies, clicking open the Thalassa's file that's just been transferred to my screen.

"In situ research lab?"

I live in the sea, her three-year-old self had told me, and my blood pumps wildly. This is it.

"Yep. The first few pages are a bunch of scientific mumbo jumbo and technical terms so, I'll just skip over to the very end," P.O. says and I watch while he remotely scrolls through the file on my screen. "In short, both Doctors du Maurier living on board have been conducting very hush hush studies for the past four years and—"

"Both?" I interrupt. "What do you mean both?" My heart stutters. Is it Éolie? She was three to my seven, so that would make her twenty. A doctorate this young? Possible, but doubtful four years ago, at sixteen. Where does that put her? Is she ... married?

"Calm down, man." P.O. darts a glance away and hesitates before finally answering. "Look, according to the paperwork, it's a husband and wife duo."

I brush it off, undeterred. Right now, all that matter is finding her and making her safe.

"Where, P.O.? Where are they?" I interrupt, heart pounding in my ears.

"Listen, even ORA's not privy to their whereabouts. Their research is listed as classified, and they've been working for the past year at an undisclosed location. Read the line right next to it though," P.O. says.

The cursor moves over, acting as a pointer, and I read the line he's referring to aloud.

"Automatic Identification System (AIS) XPNDR on board."

I lean back. "What the hell is that?"

"That's where it gets interesting," he insists and my brows bunch, uncomprehending and impatient as hell.

"I asked Zac's take on this. He says it's a very specific type of transponder. We might not know where the Thalassa is right now, but the United States Navy does."

Five

LIAM

Seven days crawl by where we dig up a whole lot of nothing. We still have no news, and it's driving me episodically bonkers.

P.O. tracked down the Thalassa all right—with a little help from the US Navy, although they didn't know it. According to the official manifesto, there was no sign of an Éolie on board. Before. During. After. I'm torn between relief and despair, especially considering both Doctors du Maurier—neither named Éolie, thank God—are presumed dead.

ORA has a way of stating facts in laconic bullet points.

- Thalassa PSotS: shipwrecked off the coast of Belize. Great Blue Hole area.
- Dr. Gilles du Maurier, Dr. Elin Hansson-du Maurier: missing at sea.
- Boat hull retrieved and stored for investigation: secured facilities, undisclosed location.
- Inventory of equipment salvaged: ongoing.

I read the status over, staring at the exact same words. Many times a day, each day. Willing new information to magically appear.

I'm spinning my wheels. Going through the motions. Showing up for my lectures. Dodging over-zealous coeds. Eating ... sometimes. The strange flu hasn't returned. Neither has Éolie's voice in my head.

I know I'm worrying the guys. They're not entirely convinced I'll find the answers I'm looking for. It's written all over their faces whenever we video chat.

I know they secretly believe that either way, it's probably too late. I can't even bring myself to say out loud that I feel this strange sense of calm sometimes, one that I can only describe as Éolie's Light, at least that's what I used to tell the therapist.

Now, seventeen years later, its welcomed and familiar warmth is pulsing in me, stronger day by day.

So I keep quiet. It would only increase their worry for my mental well-being.

For now, I just wait ... *and hope.*

Yeah, and how's that working for you, man?

I stare at the empty room, the quiet deafening.

I sigh heavily, pocketing my car keys, kicking my butt into gear. Might as well drop by my office on campus and finalize lesson plans, something I can focus on for the next little while ...

Six

ÉOLIE

The deafening sound of a jumbo jet taking off distracts me from my search of terminal E on the map, while I stand outside terminal C. I watch the plane climb up and wonder for a minute if I should even be here.

I've never seen so many people in one place. I look on, wide-eyed. All of the hustle and constant chatter and overly loud, disembodied voice announcements—it's enough to give me vertigo. I've been dropped in the middle of a busy ant colony. Every single one of them knows where they're going, how to go about it, what to do.

Except for me.

I take a deep breath. This crowd, the bustle, it's all normal. I'm standing in the middle of normal. This is what I want. I can do this. They're just like me, right?

"Ain't got all day, boy. Move." I'm shoved from behind. My Navy-issued duffel flies to the side, and I catch myself on my hands and knees on the rough concrete. I hiss in pain, and push to sit up on my heels. I watch with considerable dismay my bloodied palms self-healing in a matter of seconds.

"Hey, you good?" a voice asks. I startle, hastily hiding my hands behind my back.

"Oui. Um, I mean yeah. Yeah, I'm good." Head down, I answer straight to a pair of sneakers and frayed jeans standing some two feet away from me.

An oversized hoodie pulled low over my eyes limits my range of vision. But then again, it obscures my features, giving me a boost of false courage. I'll take false over none at all. I've been stared at enough at the Navy compound for the past few days. Might as well have the word "different" stamped on my forehead.

I get up, brushing my hands down my cargo pants. I stand on eye level with a scrawny chest with skinny arms that go on forever. A skateboard is safely tucked under one, and my duffel dangles from the other one.

I remind myself that anything I have of value, like my replacement passport and a brand-new debit card, are safely kept on me. He can take off with my bag, no big deal, I reassure myself.

But the teenage boy holds it up by its strap, offering it back to me. I reach for it and swing it over my right shoulder. "Thanks," I say.

"No prob, lil' bro. Gotta hate bullies," he says.

I glance up, surprised, but he's already riding away.

Not giving myself the chance to change my mind, I turn on my heels and resolutely walk inside Boston Logan Airport. *I can do this.* I repeat my new mantra, over and over, bolstering my self-confidence along the way.

Someway, somehow, I need to find Cape Air in this overcrowded, organized chaos the rest of the world calls normal.

A couple of hours later, I stow my duffel in the overhead bin of one of Cape Air's small regional planes, and self-confidence trickles in. I made it here. I sigh, encouraged, and buckle up in the window seat. My eyes transfix on the ongoing activities outside, my nose press up to the glass.

"First time flying?" a kindly voice asks. I didn't notice that the empty seat next to mine is now occupied, totally absorbed as I was.

The grandmotherly woman sitting next to me is dressed casually, wearing green slacks with a matching cardigan, and her quiet smile exudes sympathy.

"You could say that," I say, with a touch of sadness in my answering smile. I'm not sure flying unconscious, or hopping a ride in the cargo bay of a military plane, counts. I push melancholy away before it settles in, concentrating on the journey ahead instead. I clutch the folded piece of paper tightly in my left fist, sending a quick prayer.

"Don't you worry, we're in good hands." The older woman pats my arm a few times in comfort before adding, "I'm a frequent flyer on this weekend shuttle to Bar Harbor."

I'm touched by the simple gesture. I feel her positive energy pulsing through me, and I embrace it.

The small aircraft applies thrust and accelerates down the runway for takeoff and, suddenly, we are airborne. My breath exhales sharply, in equal parts of wonder and relief.

"You're from Boston?" I ask. Small talk. I'm making small talk. I smooth down the well-creased paper over my thighs. Maybe normal is within my grasp after all. My smile brightens.

"Heavens no, too big of a city for me, really. But I visit often," she says, eyes twinkling. "My daughter's a professor of medieval history at Harvard, and now my granddaughter attends as well. You remind me a little bit of her, actually," she says, tilting her head in my direction. "That one's always quietly watching. She's about your age too, and just as lovely."

I don't know what else to say, so I force a smile and turn to the window. I'm awed by this bird's-eye view of the land. It's mesmerizing. Until the plane veers to the right and we're flying over open sea. I swallow the lump in my throat.

"Thinking of enrolling at the College of the Atlantic?" she asks, and I whip my head around.

"How—"

She lowers her gaze. The piece of paper I unfolded with the college contact information is in full view. Taken in by new vistas, I forgot about it. I tenderly run my fingers over it. It's the only clue I have.

"No, not enrolling, just visiting..." *I kind of studied all my life really.* "I'm on ... a break from studying, I guess," I say, looking down at my new Keds. Wearing shoes instead of traipsing around barefooted is so strange. I want a normal life, but will I get used to it?

The need to confide in her, a perfect stranger, takes me by complete surprise. I can't help myself. Overwhelmed, I blurt, "I'm hoping to reconnect with this boy I sort of grew up with," *and love dearly. My imaginary friend.* "I hadn't heard from him in what seems like forever, and then I did and ... well ... a lot happened, and I saw—" *Uh-oh.* I need to pay closer attention to what I say. "Um. I think he might be there," I say in a rush. I look down, cheeks burning.

"But you're not sure." I shake my head, and she pats my knee. "Why don't you just call him?"

I wince. "I tried many times, but I sort of ... lost contact again." *And I don't know why.* "I keep trying, but I can't reach him, and ... and I have to make sure, so here I am," I say, forcing confidence into my voice.

My fingers splay on the glass and I let my index trace the contours of a cloud below us. "It's like I'm ready to come alive," I murmur to the vastness of the sky. It feels good to put it into words, even if just to myself. I glance down at the paper sitting on my lap and stare at the College of the Atlantic logo, a circle combining Human, Earth, and Water symbols, reading over their motto, now engraved on my soul. Life Changing. World Changing. *Are you there, Liam?*

I chance a peek at my involuntary confidante. Her eyes are shrewdly assessing me. "Dearie, I'd say you're ready to fall madly in love, but I think you're already there. And that's a pretty darn good reason to visit COA in my book."

I agree wordlessly but sigh on a deep exhale. "Maybe all of this is just wishful thinking on my part anyway," I say.

"Aww, sweetie, don't you go despairing on me. I like to think true love finds a way. Let's say he's there at COA, how's that feel?"

My soul ignites. My heart feels lighter. "It feels wonderful, actually."

Faded blue eyes lock with mine. "When the timing's right, you'll find each other, no matter where, you'll see," she says.

"When the timing's right," I murmur back. I take a determined breath and nod once. I'm ready to find out. And no matter what happens, I've joined the rest of the world. I've stepped out into "normal," and I'm determined to see it through.

"Do you know how far the local airport is from campus?" I ask.

Seven

LIAM

"But I'll show you a good—"

"Out," Mrs. Pringle and I say to the cougar wannabe.

In one of those quintessential stereotypes, the trench coat-wearing redhead turns up her nose at us, spins on her impossibly high heels, and slams the reception door on her way out.

I look up at a stain on the tile ceiling for a few seconds. Inhale. Exhale. The Dean thought he was doing me a favor giving me my own office next to administration and Mrs. Pringle, the registrar, as my assistant. But so far, it only made me an easier target for coeds and all other assorted females as well. Let's face it. Sweet, gullible Mrs. Pringle isn't exactly the best gatekeeper.

I rise and march through the open office door until I'm standing over the desk in the reception area. I lock eyes with the small, elderly woman seated behind it. "Mrs. Pringle, for the love of God, under *no* circumstances are you to let anyone in my office, or reveal my whereabouts to students, or *non*-students alike, at any given time," I say, leaning on my hands.

"But she not only swore she was your sister fresh off the plane for a visit, but that you insisted on picking her up over here. She even said to just forget she was even here, you'd be right over. Was I supposed to ignore her pleas?" she says, somewhat appalled and not one bit mollified.

I rub my temple feeling a headache coming on. "Yes, Mrs. Pringle, you absolutely do so. At all times. I don't care how prettily they plead, you ignore them all," I say. "Otherwise, the parade will continue, and I don't think you're prepared for the scantier costumes that are sure to turn up."

Finally, Mrs. Pringle has the good sense to look taken aback. "Mr. O'Shea. Are you telling me women parading in ... in ... less than their underwear is normal for you?"

"Afraid so," I say.

"Well, I'll be," she says, thin lipped and clearly scandalized at the thought. With her powder-blue twinset and pearls, tight gray bun and half-moon glasses, Mrs. Pringle wears old maid cliché with flair.

And she'd better get her gatekeeper's act together. It's the sole purpose behind assigning me this catchall office. I sigh heavily. Maybe I should rethink this whole stint in academia. What was I thinking? It's open season, and I'm a sitting duck on this small, private college campus. And for the first time in forever I can't just hop on the next plane, and forget about it.

Not to mention that by staying in one place, should the identity of my disowned father ever come up for scrutiny, the coeds ambushing me everywhere I turn on campus would become small potatoes ... Bloody hell. My personal life would once again be put under a microscope and my yearning for Éolie, for love, for normal, would be a moot point by then for sure.

Hell to the no. Not happening. I shake myself out of the unpleasant thoughts. Somehow, I'll see it through this semester and call it quits on academia. I am not cut out for this after all.

I step around Mrs. Pringle's desk and walk back inside my small, windowless office. My older sister. *Riiight*. She gave new meaning to coming out of the closet. I'll give her that. I inwardly snort, closing back the door, seeing all over again the shock on Mrs. Pringle's face at seeing the naked woman springing out of there. How the hell are they coming up with these desperate schemes? Not only was that woman old enough to know better, but my coming in this afternoon is spur-of-the-moment.

I plop back down on my chair and get busy compiling a detailed list of the fifty-eight students officially enrolled in my extra-curricular seminar. I whistle, impressed by their number. After all, we deliberately scheduled it at the insane hour of seven in the morning to help field out groupies. Or goopies, as Zac calls them. The thought briefly entertains me out of my funk. He might be on to something with that one.

I finalize my weekly lesson planner for the semester, update my agenda, scroll through my emails, all of which is done in under two hours. And I'm right back to nothing else to do but think, and wait. I shove my hands through my hair and push back from my chair, exasperated.

Searching for a distraction, my gaze lands on my brand-new staff lanyard, lying on my desk. Why not?

I grab the plastic key code card, shoving it, ribbon and all, in the front pocket of my jeans. COA is renowned for its marine biology program, might as well take advantage of it and dig around some text books in the library while here. With any luck, I might even come across some published articles written by either one of my Doctors du Maurier.

Decision made, and in no mood for female predators whatsoever, I open the last drawer to my right and take out the tacky baseball cap and cheap sunglasses I always keep on hand. I unhook from the coat rack a dingy hoodie, that may or may not have been dark grey in one of its previous lives, and pull it over my head.

I slip out my office door, cutting the light behind me, and am pulled short by a very startled Mrs. Pringle.

"How did you get in there?!" she shrieks, arms akimbo, blocking my way out.

Sliding down my sunglasses, I give her a look. "It's only me, Mrs. Pringle," I assure her.

"Oh." She sits back at her desk, totally ignoring me.

I shake my head on a deep sigh. If only she was as aggressive to intruders on their way in, rather than their way out.

"I'm off, Mrs. Pringle. Try not to miss too much," I quip, and she humphs.

Eight

ÉOLIE

The New England coast in early fall is spectacularly beautiful. Color everywhere. The beginning of red and gold mixing in the soft green of deciduous trees, the whimsical store banners of Bar Harbor's Main Street, their quaint, colorful buildings leading up to a pier and a marina, where boats offer daily cruises and restaurants, built on stilts, offer lobsters. No bright turquoise and blinding white sands and exuberant greens, yet I find the muted colors restful and the vibe of the small town peaceful.

I soak it all in, standing on the threshold of two worlds. Lulled by the familiar cry of the gulls, the briny sea air, and the crash of the waves nearby, I gain self-confidence along the way with each new step I take towards campus.

At the main entrance of the College of the Atlantic, I walk past a rugged, metallic sculpture of an impressive antlered deer. I find his stance intimidating with his head thrown back, mouth wide open as though warning me not to go in there. But I don't let it slow me down. My heart thuds. I'm near. I feel it.

The wind, my namesake and long-time friend, sings the sweetest song as it rustles lightly through the trees bordering COA's quad. The notes pass through the leaves, trailing a soft caress on my skin in greeting, soothing me.

I slide my duffel off my shoulder and let it drop to the grass. My heartbeats pick up. I've been here before through Liam's eyes but never like this, in person. Even then, I wondered if I'd only dreamed it all.

My gaze sweeps the common area, awed. It seems the only thing I didn't get was that campus sits right smack on the pebbled beach, ocean side. I stare enthralled at Kaelber Hall, the admissions office, and close my eyes, calling forth the images I caught before. I see once more its light-grey stone masonry, its many gables and chimneys, its leaded glass window panes, its covered porch. It seems like every details of these distinctive, elegant buildings are eerily familiar. And if so, it can only mean that I've done it. I've found him.

A huge smile blooms on my face.

My head falls back, and glorious sun rays kiss me with life, giving warmth. I spread my arms wide open and welcome it. Inhaling deeply, I draw out the moment. I survived both the rogue wave and the storm for a reason. To live. Alive, I. Am. Alive.

I hum in total bliss, and slowly reopen my eyes. My pulse leaps. I feel Liam. It's as though he's watching me. I'm electrified as I search for him, turning on the spot.

Students are spread out all over the quad, most classes done for the day. Some are group-studying, some are just lazing it out. Across the lawn, half a dozen guys are playing a pretty intense game of Frisbee.

Like the foreigner I am, I stand on the outside, looking in, the proximity of so many people still unsettling.

"Head's up!"

I hear the shout, just before I'm blindsided by something hard and fast barreling into my face. I double over and then crumple, yelping in pain.

Nine

LIAM

My stomach rumbles, reminding me that I skipped lunch. But I don't care. It's not the first time, nor is it the last. Nothing, not even food, tempts me away from the library right now.

Piles of marine bio textbooks are littering my little cubicle, hidden way back in some obscure corner of the library's ground floor. Pretty fascinating stuff, so maybe I'll get my inspiration back sooner rather than later. I take a few notes, roughly sketching a blueprint of fantastical undersea worlds set in some other galaxy. It keeps my mind occupied for a little while, anyway.

I stretch my tired shoulders, getting up to work some of the kinks out, and hear muffled shouts, catcalls, and laughter drifting in from the quad.

It seems everyone's out, enjoying the late-afternoon sunshine, and I could do with a dose of it myself after holing up this past week. I approach the nearest window, wondering if it opens, and yank the metal knob. Useless. Even straining, I can't get the side-hinged window to budge. It's not giving an inch, probably painted shut many times over.

I take in the scene, bracing my hands on the upper window frame. A pretty extreme game of Frisbee is causing the ruckus. I watch their antics, shaking my head. They're showing off, and by the glances they keep throwing, they're trying to impress some girl dressed in cargoes and an oversized hoodie standing close by. She's a lost cause if she didn't take notice by now, boys.

My gaze rakes her petite form, and I absently give her the onceover, until she tilts her head up, letting her hood fall off, and I see her face. I inhale sharply, stunned by a direct hit to the solar Plexus. Holy...

I straighten. My pulse leaps. The sheer sensuality of her blooming smile takes my breath away. As I watch her, she opens her arms wide, her radiant face turned up to the sun, and I'm struck by the notion that I'm witnessing a life celebration. My gut tightens, and heat instantly floods me. Jesus, I've never felt such a strong pull before ... But it's there. Without knowing how or why, I can almost *feel* the girl's warmth slamming into me.

Her eyes slowly reopen and she looks right at me. I stagger back and feel half-insane, wondering if she can sense me the same way. I'm pierced by her otherworldly gaze. My logical self knows she can't possibly see me through the one-way tint, but the rest of me swears she does.

Suddenly, Éolie's comforting Light starts pulsing in me stronger, brighter, warmer than ever before.

Blood pumping wildly, I stare transfixed as the exquisite girl on the quad gracefully turns in a circle, as though searching for someone.

My shallow breaths turn ragged. Could she be...? Is it possible...?

I hear the shout seconds before I watch her go down, felled by one of the idiot players' wild throw.

Christ, no. I push away from the window and take off at a run.

Ten

ÉOLIE

My hand comes over my injured cheek and ear.

I curl up, folding into a tight little ball, forehead resting on the grass. In a matter of seconds, I hear running footsteps, heaving breaths, and then I'm surrounded. I'd give a lot to melt back into the anonymity of my hood just about now. My arms are covering my head as best as I can, and I pray it's enough. My thick blonde braid tumbles down around my shoulder and I hear exclamations of surprise.

My heart's in my throat. I should never have come. Should never have braved civilization. They'll see my weird. Even worse, I'm healed already.

"Holy shit, you all right?" one of them asks.

Another cuts in before I can answer. "Josh, you ass. You almost killed her."

"She fell for you, all right. Killer moves, man," says another, and the first quickly silences him.

"Shut the hell up, Erikson. Hey," the one they called Josh says, leaning close. "I'm really sorry about that. You all right?"

One of my hands slowly reaches for my hood, pulling it back up. I open my eyes. Hesitant, I sit back on my heels still cradling the side of my face, hiding my smooth cheek. A red-haired guy with a dimpled chin, lots of freckles, and sparse stubbles, presumably Josh, squats on the ground in front of me. The others are standing around, hands on their hips, or arms crossed over their broad chests, waiting. I lower my gaze, cheeks burning. I don't know what to do or say, I just want them to leave me alone. I bite my lip.

"Let me see," Josh says quietly, and I look up in alarm. His gaze is entirely focused on my hand still covering what should be the abused area as he reaches for me. I shake my head, recoiling, and my hood falls away once again.

"I swear, I only—" he peers up into my eyes, and his words cut off. My face is suddenly exposed from up close. Murmurs go up around the group. "Whoa, she sure is a looker," I hear from the third friend—the jokester.

I furrow my brows. *A looker? Is that slang for seer? How can he tell from my eyes?* This is so not good, I wince.

Josh blinks and looks away as red creeps up his face. "What I meant is … I wasn't trying to…" Josh still doesn't manage to finish his sentence.

I rub my hand briskly over my cheek, and lower it as naturally as possible. Like the blow I received was nothing more than a startling stroke. No one else seems overly concerned. I push myself up off the ground, hoping they'll leave if they see I'm okay.

But no one retreats.

There's a blur of six or seven guys towering over me, closing in on me, suffocating me. I back away.

"Hey, could have sworn bonehead here hit her pretty hard," one says.

"Rad, no marks," says another.

"Sure, you're okay?" Josh asks, still hovering close.

"Hey, haven't seen you around before—"

"Callin' first dibs—"

The jokester gets elbowed hard. "Dude, you're such an ass—"

I hold up my hands, trying to ward them off before I start to hyperventilate.

"What's your name?" Josh asks.

"Rose. Je m'appelle Rose," I repeat for good measure. Hiding behind my other name's second nature by now, my security blanket. And after years of using it, I don't even hesitate to offer it up. "Je ne comprends pas très bien ce que vous dites. Je ne parle pas anglais. Je suis … Je suis attendue déjà…" I babble, pointing in the direction of Kaelber Hall over my shoulder, still backing away from them. I'm not exactly proud of the little white lie dipped in lots of grey around the edges. But pretending I don't speak English is the only thing I could think of quickly to keep them at bay. Improvising is clearly not one of my strong suits. But using French as a buffer seems to have thrown them off enough. None of them respond.

Finally, Josh blinks and seems to come alive again. He bends at the waist, hand out towards my duffel. "Lemme get that for—"

Eyes bulging, I dive for my bag and shake my head vigorously over and over like a crazed person as I tug on it.

"Okay, okay." Josh hands it back to me, and I grab it roughly. "No need to panic." He holds up his hands, letting me go.

I don't waste any more time. Heart pounding, holding my duffel up close to my chest, I almost run up across the lawn and up to the steps in my haste to escape. "See you around, Rose," I hear him say, and the rest of them chorus the same.

No one follows me, and I say a few *merci mon dieu* under my breath, truly grateful I'm left alone.

I dash up the steps and inside before any of them can change their mind and try to join me. Inside, I come to a stop and struggle to get my bearings. It takes my eyes a few moments to adjust to the darkened foyer. It's weirdly quiet in here, especially coming in from the noisy quad. Too quiet, in fact. Maybe everyone's gone for the day already? And maybe it's just as well, a small part of me argues. After the way things just went outside, a little more time to adjust might be best.

"No. Get a grip. You've come this far," I mutter to myself.

I slowly count to five in my head and square my shoulders. *I can do this.*

I take a quick look around, orienting myself. The walls are painted a soft eggshell white and kept bare. Of the three doors opening up to the high-ceiling vestibule only one is left open, but it's on the other side of the vast expanse of black-and-white checkered tiled floor. The two other doors closest to me, labelled Dean C.S. Hawkesbury and Kaelber Conference Room, are closed tight.

I leave my duffel tucked out of the way on the inside corner, and much too soon or not soon enough, I can't tell anymore, I'm standing in the open doorway of the Registrar's office to my right.

I peek in.

The large reception area is overtaken by plants. The walls are painted a soft yellow, and the pale color pops out with framed nature and undersea world posters. Besides a huge, L-shape desk, a sitting room boasts inviting armchairs anchored around a coffee table crammed with brochures. It's quite welcoming, and in stark contrast to the minimalist entrance hall.

Reassured, I breathe a little easier.

A petite, grey-haired lady is busy filing away a huge pile of documents at the back of the room. Should I knock, just walk in, or wait to be summoned over? I'm not sure how to go about this so, I wait. I fidget around. And wait some more.

I sigh. What's the worst that can happen, being eaten alive? Or spit right back out? I knock lightly on the door frame to make my presence known.

"Dear me," the sweet-looking woman says, turning on a small gasp, her hands fluttering about. "You're so quiet, child, I didn't hear you there."

I send her an apologetic smile, and swallow hard, my throat suddenly dry.

"Can I help you?" she asks, peering at me over half-moon glasses.

I wet my lips. "Oui ... I mean, yes. Yes, you can help me," I say, my face brightening. "I'm visiting from ... out of town. I'm looking for one of your guest lecturers, Liam, a childhood friend of mine—"

"You know Liam?" she interjects, eyes narrowing to slits.

She knows him. My eyes fill up and I blink moisture away. Liam, I did find you after all. Overcome, I nod beaming.

"Liam," she repeats forcefully.

She abandons her filing to prop her hands on her hips and shoot me a glare. "I just bet you think you do," she says.

Slack-jawed, I watch her turn from amiable to an evil-eyed Medusa, petrifying me in two seconds flat.

Eleven

ÉOLIE

"**N**o, he doesn't know I'm visiting. I came straight from the airport. But Liam's my best friend. Truly," I vow, staring at a polished name tag that reads Mrs. Eleanor Pringle, Registrar. "I swear to you."

I cross my fingers she won't quiz me on the details—like, for instance, his last name. *See, I'm the girl in his head and he's the boy in my heart, and we sort of skipped formalities...*

I wince, like that would go over well.

She clucks her tongue. "You girls think you can pull the same tricks on me more than once?"

What tricks?

"Mrs. Pringle, please, can I at least leave a message for him?" I plead.

She purses her lips, giving me a sour-faced look. "Sure, I can put yours with all the others," she says, giving me a pointed look.

I shake my head and my brow dips in confusion. "Others?"

"You thought you were it?" she asks, her voice oozing sarcasm. Her lips thin, disapproval stamped all over her face as she points to a wastebasket overflowing with balled-up papers. "Want to know how many girls left messages claiming to be Liam's long lost best friend? I'll tell you how many. Twenty-eight," she snaps, leaning over her desk. "And that's just in the past week alone," she mumbles, holding her forehead.

Did she just say Liam has twenty-eight best friends? My mouth goes slack.

"What's wrong with you young women these days; don't you have any self-respect?" She slaps her hands on her desk, and I startle. "It's unseemly. You're turning this place into a zoo," she rants.

I cover my mouth and take a step back, then another, all the while keeping her in my sights.

"Why you think his being handsome and famous gives you permission to jump all over him is beyond me," she mutters, and I honestly don't know if she's talking to me or herself, but then her words dawn on me.

I stagger back. "He's ... famous?"

"Well, that's a new line all right," she huffs. "Next, you'll tell me you've been living under a rock all your life?"

Not exactly, but close enough. I cringe.

"I'll give you that," she says, eyes narrowing as she studies me like I'm some sort of unresolved enigma, and I swallow uncomfortably. "You're not the usual type."

I have no idea whether that's a good thing.

She gets distracted by a commotion beyond, by the entrance hall, and her eyes dart past me. I'm no longer the sole recipient of her gimlet-eyed stare, and my shoulders slump in relief.

Her head cocks to the side as we listen to the fast-approaching sounds of heels clicking on the tiled floor, mixed with some high-pitched voices arguing heatedly. I watch her spine grow rigid. *Uh-oh.*

"The Mimis," she grumbles under her breath, throwing her hands up. "Like I need this."

The Mimis?

I turn in time to see two beautiful girls stride in. They could be twins with their matching blonde hair, same sparkly clothes, same ... everything. They're walking with the same brand of confidence perfectly balanced on short skirts and high heels. I stare in fascination. They're my exact opposite, but the epitome of what I imagine is sophisticated cool. Maybe even normal in a place like this.

"Liam's meeting me here, Mrs. Pringle. Go do whatev," the first blonde sneers with a flick of the wrist in my direction. "With whomev."

Liam? My eyes widen and an uncomfortable knot forms in my stomach. *Is this Liam's type?*

"You're such a liar, Mimi. Admit you're making this up," the other one all but shrieks. "Liam doesn't even know you're here."

"Please," the allegedly lying Mimi snarls. "I saw him earlier on campus. We talked and he told me it's me he's into, not you."

And they start screeching...

"Says who?"

And shoving one another.

"Says me."

"Mais c'est quoi ce délire?" I say to no one in particular, stupefied.

And I realize to my horror that they're fighting over possession of ... Liam? And that they didn't so much arrive as a pair as race here, one against the other.

There's just no way I can do this.

I recoil, wondering suddenly if Liam is the kind of guy who encourages this. What if I have him pegged all wrong? My chest squeezes tight. I only have my visions to vouch for him after all ... and until a few minutes ago, I wasn't even sure they weren't just some wishful dreams of mine. On that last thought, fleeting images of the Forest of Laure swirl back in, whispering through my mind once more. Liam. Unconditional love. A place to belong. A family of my own. Normal.

No. It can't be that bad. The pull is just too strong, it wouldn't steer me wrong, right?

The twin Mimis are still going at it. I've seen enough.

But with their catfight blocking the exit, I'm trapped.

I fake an interest in the bulletin boards lining the wall near Mrs. Pringle's desk, just wanting to fade into the woodwork, when a notice for an early morning, twice-weekly, extracurricular seminar catches my eye.

I inhale a sharp breath. The name Liam O'Shea, honorary professor for the Department of Writing, Literature and Publishing, leaps out at me.

I bite my lip. Could this Liam O'Shea be my Liam? He did weave some pretty wonderful bedtime stories, once upon a time ... long ago.

My thoughts spin.

Mrs. Pringle shouts above the melee. "You are not on Mr. O'Shea's list of approved visitors! Out with you, I've had just about enough!" She cracks a ruler on her desk and I almost jump out of my skin.

Liam O'Shea. My heart thuds in my ears. Fighting my growing excitement, I can't suppress the tiniest of smiles from curling on my lips.

The two other girls push themselves out of Mrs. Pringle's office one shove at a time, glaring at one another.

I dart my head between them and Mrs. Pringle and glance down, taken aback by her stony expression. She seems to be taking it in stride. Is this type of animosity and behavior expected then?

A bit at a loss on how to proceed forward, I let my gaze wander, and it lands on the bulletin board. I quickly look down. Monday morning, seven. It gives me two days to acclimate, and blend in somehow with the regular students attending a certain Mr. O'Shea's seminar.

I can do this.

"You as well, out," she says, and my startled gaze locks with Mrs. Pringle's. "Don't you give me that wide-eyed look, it won't work, young lady," she huffs, and motions with her head.

I stop on my way out on a sudden thought.

"What now?" Mrs. Pringle sighs heavily behind me.

I turn in the doorway. "What's Liam famous for?"

Twelve

LIAM

I finally reach the middle of the quad what feels like an eternity later.

I catch my breath, hands on my knees, looking around. *Where is she?*

"Man, those eyes. I've never seen the likes," I hear one of the Frisbee players say. "They're freakishly beautiful."

"Hey, Mr. O. What's with the running?" Tim or Josh, can't remember which is which, asks.

"Want us to play interference with The Mimis for you again?" the brown-haired one snickers and I choke. The name's gone viral on campus, but then again, I'm not their first kill that's for sure. Still wheezing, I say, "Not this time." *Thank the fuck.* "Where's the girl?" I ask baffled, turning on the spot.

"Which one, sir? There's about a dozen looking your way," the red-haired one in the Tim-or-Josh duo asks.

"The injured one, where's the injured one?" I ask, my gaze frantically scanning the lawn now. Christ. Should have jumped through the damned window; she can't just disappear, can she?

"Oh, you mean Rose? Nah, she's not injured." The brown-haired one shrugs it off. "Just a little shaken for a minute there, that's all."

"Rose?" I repeat, dumbfounded. Her name is Rose?

"Yeah, Rose. But I can't say it the same as she did, she pronounced it differently. She's our newest foreign transfer, and with her looks? I'm betting she's Swedish," the red-haired one says over-enthusiastically, high-fiving the other one, and my hackles instantly rise. "She can't speak a word of English, but I'll teach her *everything* she needs to know," he says lewdly, pumping his fists with a knowing smirk at his friends on the other side of the quad, earning a few catcalls and loud whistles.

Lips thinning, I cross my arms, raking him with freezing contempt. "Is that the way you treat vulnerable girls on campus?" I ask, making them both flinch at the steel in my voice.

"It's, huh ... no ... I ... was just fooling around," he stutters, his entire face turning a bright red, closely matching the color of his hair. "I meant no disrespect, sir," he finally mumbles, brushing the back of his neck.

"Keep it that way," I say through clenched teeth, silently adding, *or you'll have me to answer to.* My jaw ticks. Jesus Christ, they're just boys being boys, man. They're bragging over nothing just for the sake of it. I need to calm the hell down. What's with me?

"Yo! Josh, Tim, you comin', or what? Ain't got all night," one of the boys yells from several yards away. He waves a Frisbee at them for emphasis.

"In a minute, Erikson, chill!" the brown-haired one yells over his shoulder as said Erikson saunters over. "Hey, we better get back. See ya on Monday, Mr. O."

"Yeah, Mr. O. See you around the butt crack of dawn," Erikson hoots.

"You're such an ass." Tim-or-Josh slaps Erikson upside the head.

"Have a nice one, sir," the other one says bashfully.

The boys run off and I just stand there, for who knows how long, dying a little inside. Rose. And here I thought she could be...

Man, a student. I have officially reached a whole new level of messed up. I need out of here. I can't breathe.

I turn on my heel and stumble across ... the two Mimis.

"Liam!" they squeal in unison.

Christ. Give me a bloody break.

As per usual, they appear out of nowhere ambushing me, cooing, oohing and aahing, clearly having made up after almost coming to blows over me that first morning. Now, they cling like two poisonous vines as I sleepwalk my way to the parking lot.

Numb, I don't even have the energy to shake them loose.

Fuck my life.

Thirteen

ÉOLIE

Keeping my head down, coming out of Mrs. Pringle's office, I'm turning the corner of Kaelber Hall, ocean side, when a squealed "Liam" and loud giggles make me stop dead in my tracks. My heart stutters to a stop, and kick starts again.

I duck behind some shrubs growing by the side of the building, and chance a look at the quad. I've seen his handsome features so many times in my dreams I'd recognize him anywhere, but seeing him now, in the flesh ... He takes my breath away, unprepared for this grown-up version of him in all its warm physicality. Hair the color of rich black coffee adorably falls every which way, as though tugged on repeatedly by restless fingers, and dark and sexy stubble define a face chiseled to perfection. A man's face.

Liam's really and truly standing on the other side of the building. Looking down, hands on his hips, seemingly lost in thoughts.

I can walk up to him. My heartbeats thud in my ears. *I can do this.* But before I can even put one foot forward, he turns on his heels and all but falls into the arms of ... the squealing Mimis.

The very welcoming, very beautiful, very handsy Mimis.

Well ... they're no longer fighting over him, there's that.

I gasp and slap my palm over my mouth, squatting low to the ground. I'd even go as far as say they've become the best of friends in the last few minutes. They're all over him.

Their oversized breasts and their hands brush up his chest as they lean their heads on his shoulders, giggling, confident in their welcome. And why shouldn't they, they know this mating game, I don't.

And from here, it seems he likes their attention. A lot. He just stands there, sandwiched in between them from what I see. Lapping it up for all I know.

I'm so out of my element.

I lean back against the stone wall for support, breathing hard, folding my arms around me.

When I glance back up, I'm probably having heart failure as I watch them disappear in the opposite direction, glued to one another.

I blink, thrown by this sudden dose of reality. In my gratitude for surviving twice over, I didn't really think beyond coming here.

What did I expect? For Liam to be waiting for me? To just walk up to him and say, "Hey, remember me? I'm the girl who hung out with you inside your mind for months when you were a boy. You thought I was your guardian angel but in reality, I'm a freak with a strange gift of telepathic communication that somehow only works on you." And that he would what? Instantly know it was me, and kiss me blind?

My mouth turns down as I look away, knowing quite well that deep down, I sort of expected all of that and more. But now that the moment is upon me, it seems a tad extreme as far as expectations are concerned, shared connection or not.

My eyes fill up, tears threatening to spill. I brush them away with the back of my hand.

Ugh. "Get real," I chide.

I don't know how to do famous. Worse, I don't even know how to do normal. I'm a freak, one of a kind, probably my own species by now...

I sit by my duffel and hunch over. Chin propped on my raised knees, I fiddle with the shoelaces of my brand-new shoes.

Looks like the timing's all wrong, and I'm too soon. *Or too late.*

My gaze strays down the beach, and I listen to the waves crashing rhythmically on the rocky shore. I stare at the horizon, caught off balance by the strange mélange of familiar and remote the ocean evokes in me now. I can never go back there. *I don't belong anywhere anymore.* I sigh, feeling sorry for myself, and hating it.

Chin up, Éolie. You want normal? Make it happen.

"Only problem is, I'm out of my element here," I murmur.

Or am I? My head whips up. What if I've been approaching this all wrong? I stare at the receding waves, clinging to the familiar sight like a life raft.

"I've been doing bio research all my life, observing wildlife in situ," I say under my breath. "There's not that much difference."

'Discovery of a new subspecies within the genus, human, and the gender, male. Famous.' I'd have put on record in my Log Book aboard the Thalassa.

"Liam O'Shea, you're hereby put under observation." I perk up somehow at the idea of treating this like any other scientific project I worked on. *And come Monday, I'll dive into your natural habitat to study your mating rituals and note anything worth emulating.*

I nod once, and push myself up off the grass.

And just like that, I'm back on familiar ground.

Fourteen

LIAM

Monday morning, I feel like death warmed over, and probably look like it too, as I unlock the lecture hall and students start filing in. Some in far worse shape than I am, which is to be expected for seven in the morning on a Monday. Not that it makes me feel any better.

I make my way over to the lectern and shuffle some papers around, trying to appear busy so no one can guess I'm a complete and utter mass of nerves inside.

Logically, I know what a long shot it was, that beautiful girl on the quad on Friday being my Éolie, but I'd hoped. Christ, the pull from the library was just so strong. I tilt my head down and clutch the lectern just remembering it.

That leaves me with a Rose dilemma. Big time.

Fuck. I run one hand down my face.

Wildly attracted to Rose, a student. Madly in love with Éolie, a phantom.

Way to go, man.

A frisson runs up my spine and my entire body stiffens. A familiar feeling ribbons through me—Éolie's Light—pulsing warm, strong and bright.

"Bloody everlasting hell," I curse under my breath, running my hands through my hair in frustration.

I cross my arms and stare hard at the rows upon rows of students. If there's one good thing about the early time slot it's that everyone keeps quiet. And suddenly, I want nothing more than to begin—so that I can finish up and get the fuck out of here.

"Good morning."

I unclench my jaw. Fortunately for me, this isn't a regular class and there's no actual teaching, it's more about honing writing skills in a series of ad libitum projects the students will be challenged with.

"If you've read your syllabus, and I'm sure you all did, you know by now that last week was just a warm up for what's to come, so we'll dive right in and let the challenges of this extracurricular you signed for begin for real. Today, I'll put your short story skills to the test. In two thousand words or less, I'd like to read about your most significant childhood memory," I say.

Goddammit, did I just say childhood? I glance down at my notes. School. I was supposed to say most significant school memory, I grit my teeth.

Might as well admit I'm obsessing here. I forge ahead, and lay down the rules and objectives of today's writing assignment, my usual inscrutable mask on. "I want to see your creative thought patterns, so you'll give me handwritten copies by the end of class."

My gaze lands on a small hoodied figure sitting in the back, and our eyes lock for a fraction of a second. I'm knocked sideways, recognizing their dazzling shade of pale aqua in an instant. I catch my breath, and pray I won't lose all composure.

Rose. She's here.

The class gets to work.

I refuse to look again in Rose's direction. And fail by a mile. To my dismay, my eyes keep straying her way, but she never looks up again. She's intent on her pen moving over her notebook. She's bent so low, her expression is obscured, but the translucent color of her eyes is burned into my mind.

I have to see her up close.

The rest of class passes in a blur. Tight jawed, I keep my gaze fixed as much as possible on my laptop screen, but the article I downloaded might as well be written in Swahili. I don't understand a word of it. All I can think of is Rose. Rose who'll soon be coming down, turning in her assignment.

Will our hands touch? Will she look me in the eye? Will I...

Will I what, man? She's a student, for chrissake, I sternly remind myself.

Fat lot of good it does, I almost laugh in self-deprecation. Her student status be damned; heat shoots up my groin and I'm sporting a semi just at the thought of seeing her up close.

By the time I've wrapped up, dismissing everyone else, she still hasn't approached. I look up as the last assignments are handed in, and find her seat already vacated.

I pack up fast, barely shutting my laptop off before stuffing it in my bag and hauling ass out the door. Outside, I search for her in the crowd of students, but she's nowhere to be found.

The following day finds me bright and early on campus. And to be perfectly honest, I don't even have a really good excuse to be here.

I'm torn between avoiding temptation of the Rose kind, and looking for it.

I end up in the library for the better part of the morning immersed in research, or trying to be. Not because I want to be here, but because it's a legit reason to be on campus on my day off; much more respectable than searching for a strange girl I may or may not be obsessed with before ever meeting her.

By the end of the day, I haven't seen a lick of Rose, and I'm well on my way to earning a new reputation of eccentric reclusive. The title fits my current mood.

Back at the condo, I change into a pair of comfortable old sweats and take a moment to contemplate the sun setting over the ocean. Éolie-Jolie ... Are you out there?

Not a single Light flare-up today. I look away, sighing heavily as I walk out of the bedroom. And not a single Rose sighting either.

Jesus Christ. How does one recover from emotional whiplash?

I pour myself a glass of red wine, sipping but not really tasting anything.

Sitting on the coffee table across the room, mocking me, yesterday's large pile of writing assignments awaits. I sigh and dig in.

It's not long before I'm absorbed in the task. I read, comment, grade. All in all, I do make a serious dent in the pile. I have to say that bland subjects are, more often than not, a great way to see true talent at work. And I must admit, I'm pleasantly impressed so far by the creativity and diligence applied by my students on this first assignment.

I flip open the next one, scanning quickly. I reach the second paragraph and my heart stops ... and jump starts as if jolted by a thousand watt defibrillator.

Why do you keep saying I'm an Angel? I'm no angel. I've no wings, I looked. Angels have wings, and I live in the sea, Liam, not in the sky. I'm just Éolie. Your Éolie.

The whispered memory passes through my mind.

I read on, fast becoming undone.

According to the story, the little girl who lived in the sea was born with preternatural sensibilities or, if I prefer, with some natural human abilities weirdly enhanced. Intuition, healing, visualizing, reaching. And like any other human abilities, like healing a cut finger, all of which aimed at oneself, but for one overwhelming exception. A little boy captured and kept hidden by some Wicked Monster. And for a strange and unexplainable reason, one night, her little soul heard his heartbreaking cry for help, and in a pull much too strong to resist, she simply answered it. A pull so strong, a connection so big, it fused this little girl's heart to this little boy's and from then on, she could heal him as she would herself, even at a distance, from his daily abuse. And so it went between them, friendship born of their magical ability to communicate telepathically. Over the many months that followed, they became inseparable. Deep devotion grew between the two until—

"Bloody hell," I breathe.

Light in Darkness. Éolie. I hover between incredulous shock and all out euphoria. Held under her spell once more, I read on.

—until the night the little boy's Monster showed the true depth of its depravity. The Monster let loose on a rampage of unbridled beatings, the fury of which neither of the children had seen before.

I have to pause so the flow of memories can take their course and leave me be. That night, my mother's wrath...

It was, unbeknownst to both of us, my last night of captivity in the abandoned motel lot I was kept hidden in for more than five months. I was to learn much later that my biological, crack-addict-former-beauty-queen mother overdosed and died that night. The commotion she caused in her hallucinating drug rage, though, thankfully frightened a few passersby into alerting the authorities of shady doings. I was thus saved. Twice.

All those bloody doctors and their examinations. Even confronted by the fresh, inexplicably healed scars, they dismissed everything I said as nothing but the incoherent imaginings of a traumatized little boy. I never heard from Éolie again.

Why did you disappear on me that night?

Riveted by the story, I read on. According to the looped handwriting, on that fateful night, while healing the little boy's extensive injuries through their mysterious connection, the little girl slipped into a deep coma only to awaken more than a year later, once again completely healthy.

"Christ, Éolie," I gasp out loud, scanning quickly now, desperate for more answers.

As she got older, the little girl thought often about the blue-eyed, dark-haired little boy, Liam, she had seen through her mind's eye, but she could no longer link with him. All along, she was led to believe in a made-up friend. One conjured up specifically to soothe away her solitude, a by-product of her unusual circumstances as the strangely gifted daughter of two seafaring, marine biology scientists. As she grew up, her imaginary friend, Liam, accompanied her everywhere on her many journeys, sharing her life at sea. His existence tucked safely away in her dreams and memories. Until some ten days ago.

I flip the page over as if possessed. And right there, the most beautiful words in the universe dance before my eyes. Validation, confirmation, intractable proof.

> *Mille fois merci, Liam.*
> *You saved me back.*
> *Éolie du Maurier*

I'm overwhelmed. Completely, utterly, overwhelmed.

Éolie's real.

And there was only one new face in the crowd...

I glance down at the class assignment I'm holding up to my face with shaking hands.

A certain Rose by any other name may have a lot to answer for.

I've no idea how she slipped into class yesterday, but I pray she does it again tomorrow.

Fifteen

ÉOLIE

Tight schedules are such a foreign concept.

From l'Hôtel de la Mer, a lovely seaside hostel near campus where I booked a room last Friday, I'm running up the beach, late. I increase the pace of my jog, hoping I'll still make it to this morning's seminar on time.

I'm paying for too many late nights in a row reading a certain Mr. O'Shea's very engaging SciFi saga, Eiloe. Immersed in the intricacy of Liam's strange new worlds in distant galaxies well into the early-morning hours for the past several nights, what was bound to happen, happened. I overslept.

Absorbed in my thoughts, I almost run into the double doors already closed. Guess my subtle entrance is shot now, and the stealth observation mission I'm on is probably just as compromised.

I lean in and rest my forehead against the cool metal, catching my breath. Should I read this as a sign? If I go in there, nothing about my entrance will be stealthy. I remember the short story I slyly handed in on Monday via the boy two rows up. Now that I've given Liam proof that I do exist, I'm not sure I'm ready to find out right this minute if it's too soon, or too late, for us to meet in real life.

I could leave, I tell myself. A clean break now will make it easier to leave Bar Harbor tomorrow ... or the day after. Or never. I straighten, shaking my head at the impossibility of walking away from here. From him.

Liam. I'm pulled forward by an urge stronger than me.

I struggle to discreetly open one of the doors. It's stuck. I push against its heavy spring resistance with both my hands, grunt with all my weight and, even then, I barely manage to yank it clear. I dart through the small opening, hurrying before it closes again.

The door clicks shut behind me with a resounding clap of thunder. In the stadium-style lecture hall, dozens of pairs of eyes swing my way, but I don't see them. My knees go weak as I'm instantly pinned down by the intensity of his stare from the lectern below.

My breath catches. Liam.

So intent is his gaze upon me that I feel the searching stares of some of the students wondering what they're missing out on. Flustered, I keep my eyes lowered and my head bent, sliding in an empty seat right next to where I stand. I plop down on it, knees shaking, and hunch my shoulders, attempting to make myself even smaller.

No one speaks and the silence drags into awkwardness. I must have broken a Thou Shall Not rule I know nothing about by coming in late.

My lips are dry, and my heart beats too fast in my throat. I fuss with the hem of my cobalt-blue hoodie, plucking at a thread.

A few coughs across the rows are heard throughout. I breathe a silent sigh of relief when Liam relents, and turns his attention back to the students at large.

My eyes still downcast, I listen to the inflection of Liam's smooth voice as he explains the details of today's writing assignment. Gone are Monday's clipped tones, replaced by deep and mellow ones. His unique accent, more pronounced today, envelops me in its auditory caress and unwittingly awakens all of my senses. My skin tingles all over, and my mind turns sluggish. I squirm, flushed to the roots of my hair. Is it any wonder I can hardly make any sense of the instructions given out? Something about the natural world and an essay consigned the old-fashioned way...

I honestly do try, but it's of no use whatsoever. Giving up on making sense, I sigh, closing my eyes. I'm ready to lose myself in my very own Liam concerto for the next couple of hours or so, when everyone around me suddenly erupts into action. My eyes fly open, and my brow dips in confusion at the flurry of activity.

I watch in dawning comprehension with a pinch of panic thrown in the mix.

Everyone's picking up a pen and hardcover notebook handed out by Liam, before they disappear outside.

I gulp, and lower myself in my seat. *Can I do this?* I bite my lip. *Just walk up to him ... ready or not.*

I stare for so long at the back of the chair in front of me that when I chance a peek, even the swarm of girls clustering around Liam's desk is thinning out. I'm fast running out of options.

"Could Ms. Éolie du Maurier come forward, please?"

Liam's clear and precise tone slices through the lecture hall, temporarily stopping all movements.

Stunned, my eyes whip up and instantly lock with his.

Everything else around me fades into nothing. For all I know, we might as well be the only two living beings left on the planet. I fall into deep indigo eyes, as familiar as my own. Blue, blue, bottomless indigo sea-blue eyes that are now solely intent on me.

Wide-eyed, weak-kneed, I swallow and push to my feet.

One by one, the other students cast confused—then curious—looks my way as they slowly file out.

For a fleeting second, I hesitate, uncertain how to proceed. Everything about him is such a strange blend of intimate and aware, yet full of unknowns.

But then he extends his hands, inviting me in, and my heart flips and my feet make the decision for me. I reach the bottom step of the risers and run past the last few stragglers on their way out, straight into his arms.

"Liam," I whisper. I'm almost unable to believe I'm finally here, in this exact moment. My face inescapably buried in the crook of his powerful chest, I inhale him into existence.

Sixteen

LIAM

Uneven heartbeats slam against my ribs. I wasn't sure she would even answer to the name when I called it, but then her head had whipped up and she'd stared at me, and I knew. I almost lost it when she paused, terrified she was going to turn and bolt.

But then she'd stepped into my arms.

Time slows to a stop, everything else fades and only Éolie remains.

In that moment, I am lost ... and found.

By the sweetest miracle possible, I am holding tangible proof of Éolie's existence in my arms. Her face buried deep in the crook of my chest, I can hardly take it all in.

I reach out and slowly lower her oversized hood, a blurry glimpse no longer enough. The moment the hood is gone, I know that nothing I saw or lived before prepared me. I'm rendered mute, our eyes locked in wonder.

Her eyes are truly amazing, their color extraordinary, and I willingly sink into their pale and unusual sea-green depths.

Seeing her from afar the other day did not begin to do her justice. She's glowing from within, youthfully fresh and wide-eyed. Silken, light-blonde hair held back in a simple braid perfectly frames her lovely face, highlighting just so, her delicate high cheekbones and her full, parted lips.

Éolie's elemental beauty leaves me reeling.

Her clear gaze pierces through my many layers of defenses as though mere gossamer veils. I should feel exposed, vulnerable, and I never do vulnerable, at least not since I was seven years old. But for the life of me, I cannot even summon one familiar reason to stand protected and blessedly detached.

"Éolie..." I grab her and hold on tight, unable to bear even the smallest distance between us. I can feel her trembling in my arms—or is it me trembling in hers? "Say my name again," I entreat, close to undone.

"Liam," she breathes, and I close my eyes, wonderstruck, heart cracked wide open by the sound of a voice I've been waiting my whole life to hear out loud.

Thrilled, I whirl her around in a circle before setting her done, the both of us suddenly grinning like loons. I laugh, out of sheer joy.

"LiamLiamLiam," she intones aglow, leaning back into my arms. "I've dreamed of you all my life please kiss me blind," she says all in one breath and I ... stop breathing.

Did she just ask me...?

Seventeen

ÉOLIE

I hear Liam's sharp intake of breath.

Oh mon dieu.

"Please tell me I didn't say that out loud," I say, burying my scalding face into Liam's chest.

Liam chuckles lightly. "Éolie?"

I shake my head and tighten my hold on his waist, burying even deeper into the folds of his shirt. It smells of the ocean on a clear windy day, and of something else all Liam, a clean warm musk that makes me feel tingly all over.

He brings one hand against my head, cradling my cheek close to his heart. I feel the rapid rise and fall of his chest—or is it mine? He dips his head, and his breath tickles my ear. Goose bumps travel up my skin at lightning speed, and a strange, delicious sort of shivering centers low in my belly.

Warm lips lightly trail down my face to the corner of my mouth where they whisper, "I want to kiss you blind. So bad." Lethal words and lips that spread liquid fire. I have no clear idea what to do with either.

He tips my chin up and brings his hand back up to my cheek, cupping it. "Don't think I won't," he says, his thumb stroking my bottom lip, and my pulse leaps out of my throat. "I've waited a lifetime. I won't stop at one kiss, promise." His smile is slow, creasing his cheeks, bringing out his dimples, and I forget I'm supposed to breathe. His voice rumbles, deep and magnetizing, "But it won't be here, or now, my little Rose."

He straightens up, leaving me reeling and light-headed.

"Rose—?" I murmur in a daze, still looking at his mouth. How could he possibly know of this pseudonym? But then something else suddenly dawns on me. *I won't stop at one kiss, promise* ... I crash back to Earth.

"I've never been kissed. I don't know how. I might be bad at it. And I'm not the Mimis, that makes me not your type. I'm not normal. I shouldn't be here. It's too soon and you're—" I stop spewing words, and stare in shock at the wrinkled blue shirt in my hands. I smooth the fabric over a lean, muscled, stock-still torso, heat creeping up to my hairline. "—famously you," I conclude, squeezing my eyes shut in utter embarrassment.

I brace myself, waiting for him to laugh or make fun or tell me I'm odd—but he doesn't.

His hands never leave my waist as he stares, shaking his head.

"The Mimis? You've got to be joking, right?"

Eighteen

LIAM

Watching Éolie leave earlier on, so that we could meet back privately at l'Hôtel de la Mer after class, was, hands down, the most difficult thing I've ever done. It took everything in me not to bolt after her, and ditch my students. Let's just say, class was dismissed in record time.

I debated on the drive over whether or not to call my GGS pals with the update, but deemed it too soon. I'm not ready yet to share the news with anyone, nor am I ready to heed the friendly warnings that are sure to come next. First, I need some time alone with her myself. Face to face. Without interference.

I park and cut the engine, my nerves wound up tight, half-afraid I imagined her or worse, that she won't be here, waiting for me.

I swallow to wet my throat as I step onto l'Hôtel's deck, a beautifully restored Victorian-era mansion beach side. Even with my limited local knowledge, I know that L'Hôtel de la Mer, reminiscent of Old World charm, and its distinguished, older gentleman owner, are quite the landmarks in this town. And I can vouch for it. I practically live on Monsieur François's cuisine, an edible poem in itself. Just a few blocks over from my condo, I readily admit to succumbing, every possible chance I get, in fact, to the lure of exquisite meals served with a delicious side ambiance of *je ne sais quoi*.

All of which makes me more than happy that Éolie booked a room here.

Not only is she close by, but I know that she's in a safe environment.

I immediately spot her sitting near the door at one of the small bistro tables of Le Petit Café, the hotel's bistro, and my breath swooshes out in unabridged relief.

Éolie's just a few short feet away. All of the tension and impatience I fought earlier disappears. I blink to be sure she doesn't move. She's no mirage, no delusion. She's here, just like she said she would be.

She's unaware of my arrival, utterly captivated by her surroundings, keenly watching a young family of four enjoying a late breakfast a few tables over. I watch her watching them.

Her expression is lit and I have to shake myself free of the sheer beauty of her face—a real-life version that is so much better that my own concocted fantasies.

Éolie.

She looks up just then, and her radiant smile electrifies me on the spot. She pushes back from her chair and meets me halfway and I can't help myself, I sweep her up into my arms.

"You're here." Delight rings clear in her voice.

Warmth spreads in my chest. Along with primal needs that boil into singular words—more like commands. *Mine. Take. Possess.*

"Éolie-Jolie, you both compel me to feel and scare me to death," I murmur, inhaling the fresh clean scent of wind and sea on her skin.

I set her down slowly and she takes a step back, wide-eyed, blushing, and I grin, totally charmed.

I hold out my hand. "Want to go for a walk?"

Without a single hesitation, Éolie takes my hand and something snug unfurls deeper in my chest.

In a quick move I didn't see coming, she upturns my hand, and I watch, entranced, as she presses a tender kiss to my palm.

"A walk sounds good to me, but didn't you want to talk over coffee?" she asks, pulling me along.

"I'm not sure coffee is such good idea right now." I'm enough of a live wire as it is. I can't sit down, not just yet. "I need to do something … anything," I say, unashamedly gawking.

"Then by all means, Mr. O'Shea, let's go for a walk on the beach," she says, beaming.

We step off the hotel's deck and for a beat or two, angry rap music blares as a lone jogger, his sweat-darkened hair plastered to his skull, runs by us. He does a double take and whirls around, checking her out, and I shoot him a look. He gives me a "not my fault she's a hot piece of ass" shrug, before taking off in the other direction. *Glad you know what's good for you, man.* I unclench my jaw, letting my gaze sweep up the beach. Not much traffic on this middle of the week, "cloudy with a chance of rain" Wednesday morning. Apart from an older couple beachcombing, it looks like we have this entire stretch to ourselves. You won't see me complaining.

"I know it's just a walk, not a proper date or anything—"

"It's absolutely a date," she cuts me off, looking me in the eye, and I lose my train of thought. "It's my first ever, so you're not allowed to say otherwise. It's against my rules."

Her eyes glitter mischievously, belying her serious tone.

"Well, seen that way," I say. "By all means, mademoiselle du Maurier, this is a date." I chuckle under my breath.

Up until my unplugged brain finally registers. I tug on her hand, pulling her to a stop.

"Wait, wait, wait," I say. "Hold on."

She tilts her head to the side, and her thick braid of sun-kissed blonde hair tumbles down her shoulder. Christ, she's so gorgeous. How am I to concentrate on anything?

"First date, ever?" I ask, my eyebrows shooting up.

Never been kissed, never been on a date ... Hard to believe at the sight of this larger-than-life, exquisitely beautiful specimen before me. "How's that possible?" I ask, dumbfounded.

She quickly looks down, her arms folding around her waist.

"It's easy enough, au contraire," she says in a small voice, barely audible above the sound of the waves crashing down on the shore.

I stare at the graceful curve of her bended neck, and her drooping shoulders.

"Are you pulling my leg? Éolie, come on. Look at you," I say. *You're so beautiful.* "Is the entire world populated by idiots?"

She looks back up, a look of pure consternation darkening her features. "I forgot it's too soon," she says, her hands coming up to cover her mouth, and is that a wet sheen of tears glazing her eyes?

"Too soon for what?" I ask, growing concerned.

"Forget it. Let's just go for that walk," she blurts, turning on her heels.

"No way. I'm not joining all the other idiots that went before me," I say, overtaking her. "Make no mistake, this is a date." My heart starts hammering with apprehension; is she getting ready to bolt out on me? "I'm just blown away it's your first ever, that's all."

"Well don't be," she says, coming to a halt. "Here's the thing, Liam, there are no idiots. Not one. There aren't that many boys floating around in the middle of the ocean," she says, shaking her head in a self-deprecating kind of twitch. "Real ones, I mean," she quickly amends then groans, red creeping up to her hairline. "Can't you see I'm nothing like what you're used to?"

I look down at the simple khaki cargo pants and cotton shirt she wears, her clear skin free of makeup, her glossy blonde hair, windblown and begging for my fingers to untangle the tangles framing her cheeks. Everything about her is sweet. Pure. My heart pings. "For the record, I'm glad you're nothing like what I'm used to," I say truthfully.

"Who's pulling my leg now? Come on, you're you," she gestures, flushed and clearly embarrassed, "and I'm ... me. I've never even been kissed. I know it's just another layer of weird on top of my weird." She picks at her long sleeves, her fingers curling over the hem before crossing her arms over her chest.

Her words tear me in half, clear down the middle.

I tip her chin up and look her in the eye. "Éolie, it's me you're talking to, remember. The boy who needed you. The boy you saved. The boy who's known you all your life. You're special. I don't wish you to be anyone but you, *ever*. You hear me? It's against *my* rules."

She shoots me a smile that turns her from gorgeous to flat-out devastating. And I know right then that amazingly weird has always been my type.

Nineteen

ÉOLIE

You're special, he just said. I don't think I've ever been special to anyone. Weird, yes. Special? No.

Moist, briny sea air fills my lungs, and the shrill cry of the gulls claiming the perfect catch blend with the rhythmic sound of the waves crashing. And, suddenly, I want nothing more than to steal that moment for just a bit longer.

I grab Liam's hands and say in earnest, "You must have a bazillion questions, I know. I have loads of them myself, and so many answers to give you, I hardly know where to start. But ... would you mind terribly, if we shared a time-out on this walk-date? Just us two. In the here and now. Nothing else."

"A time-out? Wow, that brings back memories, big time. We had so many of those, enchanting ones that took me away from my gruesome reality back then, remember?" His forehead drops to mine, and his breathing grows ragged—or is it mine? My hands splay on his chest, and I let his warmth seep into my palms, seep into my very soul. His arms enfold me.

"I do remember, every single one of them," I breathe, hugging him close. "I think I need a short time-out if just to absorb the reality of you, here, physically, beside me, doing something perfectly mundane normal people take for granted. Does that make any sense?"

"It totally does. I'm in," he says, kissing the top of my head. "So? How about a walk? Just us two." He flashes me a boyish grin, full dimples out, turning me to mush, before he holds out his hand.

The wet sand is packed hard beneath my bare feet. In our wake, our footprints are washed up here and there by the receding waves I laughingly try to outrun. Coldness seeps through, numbing my toes.

I feel Liam's joy flowing through me, bleeding into mine, sharpening even more the moment. I walk backward for a few steps, smiling at him as he trails behind me, the cuff of his rolled jeans already soaked.

I give up trying to outrun the waves and run back to him instead. Reaching up on the tip of my toes, I lay a quick kiss on the corner of his jaw. "Thank you for this," I say.

He stops and stares into my eyes, shaking his head. "I owe you so much more than an hour's walk on the beach..." His voice wavers and trails off at the end, and the back of his fingers comes up, brushing down my cheek. His gaze drops to my lips. My skin tingles, releasing a slew of butterflies fluttering about in my lower belly. And I revel in it.

I'm ignited, awakened at long last. I'm overwhelmed. Alive.

Trembling fingertips gently trace the contours of my cheekbones, my eyebrows, mapping their way down to my chin, up to my lips where they stay for a brief moment.

I watch his eyes darken to the point of pain, and I know our time-out is over. And I'm okay with that. He searches my eyes, and I silently give him the go-ahead. "I felt you, you know, during that storm ... I didn't save you back. I tried though. So hard. The only information we could come up with on the Thalassa came from ORA, and it's not much. Éolie, there's simply no trace of you anywhere out there."

"I know," I say, looking down.

"Why couldn't I find you?" he asks, tipping my chin up.

"Because when it comes to no existing traces of me out there, you're right, there's none," I say quietly.

Liam sits, tugging me down with him, running his arms around my waist; he nudges me, scooting me in closer so that I'm sitting between his outstretched legs. "Why is that?" he asks again. He leans me back onto his chest, strong arms sheltering me.

"It's from way back," I say, my gaze straying to the ocean. The overcast sky dulls its surface to a pewter grey today. I lick my lips, my mouth suddenly dry. "When we met, I was not much older than a toddler really, so I didn't know any better. So I spoke to you and you to me—all through our minds. To me, my weirdness wasn't out of the ordinary. Everybody talks, everybody heals, right? I didn't question any of it or try to hide it. Nor did I understand the impossibility of those gifts. But my parents did. And they knew what would happen if I were discovered. They were terrified I'd become some permanent lab rat, or worse. Let's just say, my cabin was more often than not the confines of my entire universe when we had to dock someplace populated. But they were so right," I say, my gaze fixed on the horizon. "Their fear became my fear soon enough."

His arms tighten around me, offering quiet comfort, and his chin dips on top of my shoulder. "What happened?"

"I ... became this medical prodigy overnight when I simply woke from my coma at the hospital. And I hadn't done any odd things yet, except show unusual brain scans. Tests upon tests," I sigh heavily. "All of them fascinatingly abnormal. Neurologists from everywhere suddenly descended upon me wanting a peek inside my brains, and my parents had to practically kidnap me to get me out of there." My eyes close, inhaling the cool breeze from the ocean, tasting of the familiar, comforting smell of the brine. And my gaze, with a will of its own, strays back to the ocean.

My toes dig into the coarse sand; a new sense of self spreads within me, leaving in its wake, peacefulness. And I know it's the beginning of goodbye. To both my parents and the ocean. It's like it happened in another life, and maybe it has. "They kept me hidden for my safety from then on. I've lived on the Thalassa all my life in remote corners of the world."

Liam's entire body stiffens at that last remark.

"Christ, you're saying you lived isolated, hidden on board a boat, all your life?" he asks, spinning me around.

I push away from him and rise, needing to compose myself. I wade through the shallows at the water's edge. Liam follows on the beach at a more sedate pace. I watch with some envy a young mother with two toddlers, playing in the sand, building a castle. I love hearing the sound of their belly laughs as I draw near.

This is what happy sounds like. One day, it will be me, I vow. And I swear that not a day will go by without my babies knowing just how much they are loved. One of the little girls looks up as I walk past, and waves at me. I wave back and blow her a kiss over my shoulder, delighted.

I let Liam catch up to me.

"It's not nearly as bad as it sounds," I assure him. "I've lived close to nature all my life, a life full of wonderful discoveries and freedom," I say, filled with gratitude, for that part at least. "When we had to go into towns or villages or interact with the world, we used Rose as my official identity, my avatar of sorts."

"So that's where Rose comes in." He shakes his head, the ghost of a smile playing on his lips. "Lucky for us, you won't have to worry about her now."

My face scrunches up, and I come to a halt. "What do you mean I won't have to worry about her? And how do you know about Rose, come to think of it?" I ask, curious now, as he never did answer me on that one. Not that I blame him after I subjected him to the worst case of talk-out-loud babbling I've ever had right after. I wince, remembering.

Liam catches a stray lock of my hair between his fingers staring at it. "Last Friday, on the quad, I saw you go down and when I asked about you, some students of mine told me you were Rose, COA's newest foreign transfer."

"The Frisbee players?" I say on a sudden realization. "You were there? And I missed seeing you?" I frown, thinking back. I really took a good look around before being hit and I could have sworn Liam was nowhere in sight. But I felt him though.

"You looked at me straight through the one-tint library window, piercing me with your eyes," Liam says, brushing my hair behind my ear but the wind picks it right up.

"So I really did perceive you near, didn't I?" I perk up; maybe our connection is rebuilding.

He raises a brow, giving me a pointed look. "I did feel something too. Big time, Éolie. And for the record, after going through four days straight out of Hell thinking I had it bad for a student, on top of worrying about you, I'm thankful you're one and the same. And that you're okay."

"Oh," I say, wide-eyed. Rose really did a number on us. I mean, I did. We could have met that much sooner.

"Yeah, *oh*." He tugs on my hand to resume our walk. "So, Rose kept you out of official databases," he continues after a minute or two, giving me a light squeeze, and I nod.

"And for good measure, in front of others, we all pretended Rose was mute and, well ... not all there, lingering traumas you see."

He grabs my arm. Indigo blue eyes searching mine fill with sorrow. "They made sure you didn't really exist to anyone."

I look away, breathing in the air redolent of the sea. "I'm solitary by nature. But now, with my parents gone, I'm not sure if my being different made me so, or if I would have preferred it that way anyway. But either way, Liam, I don't want your pity. I've never been lonely," I say, my gaze returning to his. "I had nature, the ocean's wide-open space, my studies ... and I had you." I smile softly.

"Bloody hell, Éolie." He exhales, bending low to rest his forehead against mine, chest laboring. "Did they know about me?" he asks. "I mean, that we could communicate."

"Sort of ... I talked to you nonstop, remember?" I whisper.

"It's the only thing that kept me sane throughout," he murmurs, and my heart splinters on the memories.

"Even afterwards, I never stopped talking to you. Whether you could hear me or not, I was always there for you."

We stare at each other, fast becoming undone.

He pulls on my shoulders, drawing me into his strong embrace, and we share a comforting hug.

"What do you mean by sort of knew about me, then?" he asks after a while. His eyes search mine, and his hands come up to cup my face.

"They never acknowledged that you were real," I say, and his mouth thins. "They played along, humoring me in my games of make-believe. Probably thought you were an imaginary friend I made up to keep me company while they worked. But I knew differently. I saw you clearly in my mind's eye, felt you. You were completely there next to me. Until I woke up a year older at the Melbourne Children's Hospital, and suddenly you weren't there anymore ... and make-believe was never the same ever again." My eyes overflow with tears at the memory of losing him.

"I missed you like crazy for the longest time afterward, Éolie," he admits, his thumbs brushing away my tears. "It rips me apart just thinking about that last time," he whispers. "Christ, you lost a whole year of your life because you saved mine. And to know that caused you to fall into a coma ... I'm so sorry—"

My fingers come up and press down his lips, shushing him. My gaze drops and locks on them, warm yet firm underneath my fingertips. My pulse picks up.

"Don't ever be sorry for that. I'd do it again and again and again," I say emphatically. "And I want you to stop thinking right this minute that you cost me a year of my life, because it's just not true." *I stayed with you the whole time your first year at boarding school,* I almost say ... But I'd rather we clear all the other questions we have for now before raising others that are sure to come with that shocker.

I'm not ready to stir that stew right this minute, but I will. Someday soon, I silently promise, hoping that when I do, he won't freak too much. "The only thing I'm sorry for is that I never did it ever again. Link with you that is, until the storm," I say softly. "I tried so often but could never make it work."

He drops a kiss on my fingers, taking hold of my hand. I lift my head, and he fixes me with thoughtful eyes.

"Any idea why the storm brought it on?" he asks quietly. He laces his fingers through mine and squeezes my hand, pulling me alongside him as we resume our walk down the beach.

"No. Well, nothing definite anyway." I sigh. "I wish I'd come with an instruction manual." I sigh once more, and Liam gives me a sidelong glance. "Even now, I know next to nothing about what triggers any of it. I tried and tried hundreds of times since. It's as though without dire circumstances thrown in the mix, I just can't reach out to you."

His eyes flicker past me to the ocean, and then back. "Jesus," he mutters under his breath. "I think you might be on to something ... But I'd rather not put it to the test if you don't mind."

"Me neither. I like safe and sound just fine, and I'm nowhere near ready to test that do-or-die theory." I shudder.

"Agreed."

He pulls me into his arms and I willingly surrender to the moment, hugging him close to my heart. I am safe and sound. And so's Liam. I feel compelled to touch him in some form or other. It's as though I need this physical contact to reassure me that he is flesh and blood. Real. I breathe him in. Will I ever get used to it?

"Who do I need to thank for saving you, and finding me here?" he asks, leaning back, gently brushing strands of fly-away hair from my face.

I smile all the way, pointing my finger at him.

"Me?" he asks, eyes narrowing.

"You."

"You completely lost me there ... There's just no way, Éolie. If it were up to me, I would have done it sooner—and bloody well remembered it, I'm sure." He grabs me by the shoulders, staring into my eyes. "It drove me nuts, not knowing, just waiting. I swear I would have done anything to get to you."

"But you did," I say. "And twice over at that."

"Twice—? Me?" he repeats.

"You." I nod a few times.

He raises an eyebrow, and I search the turbulent blue of his eyes.

"The moment I reached out, you answered my call. I felt you in my heart, in my mind, just like before. It's the strength and hope you infused me with that kept me alive long enough to be rescued. So it's you, Liam, who saved me," I say, giving him a heartfelt hug. "It's all on you."

"Jesus, you're undoing me," he replies, crushing me to him.

Eyes closed, pressed against his powerful chest, I listen to Liam's thudding heartbeats until they slow down into a steady pulse. A few barks pop our bubble, and we retrace our steps back to l'Hôtel, nodding a greeting in passing to the middle-aged man walking his dog.

"And how did I manage to lead you here, to me, without my knowing?" Liam asks after a beat, clearly baffled.

"It's a bit ... bizarre how you did it," I say softly, absently fiddling with one of my shirt's buttons.

Bringing us to a halt, he tips my chin up and his eyes run over my face, heat washing over my skin. "I'm more than intrigued now. Please, tell me how I did it so I can keep on doing it," he encourages with a smile, and I lower my gaze, praying he'll keep an open mind.

I take a deep breath and look at him. "Somehow, I don't think you'll want to keep on doing it ... It was happening to me but I wasn't me." My eyes search his, and a bemused look appears on his face. "Have I lost you?" I ask, unsure. He stares at me a second longer than awkward.

"Not sure, but keep going. So, it wasn't you, but it was happening to you."

"Exactly," I agree, relieved that he understands what I'm trying to say, and doesn't question it so far. The rest of it is not as weird. Well, not any weirder than this. "At first, I didn't know I wasn't me. And in retrospect, some of it is kind of funny," I say, reflecting back on my complete bafflement at the time, wondering why I was being hit on by so many women. "I was delirious by then, barely there, and I kept hallucinating, or so I thought, bombarded by strobe images, sensations, and sounds. I received compliments on my inspiring lecture, and there was a blur of women crowding me on this beautiful quad, but my gaze kept straying over their heads, staring at Kaelber Hall with its College of the Atlantic logo. And a few squealed your name pressing on me, or you, and that's when I knew—"

"I didn't catch a strange flu ... *You* are my strange flu." Liam takes a step back, blinking.

"It made you feel sick?" I exclaim. "I'm so sor—"

"You're not really going to say you're sorry, are you?" He pins me with a direct look, and I shake my head somewhat sheepishly. He dips his head and whispers close to my ear, "Good. Because no matter how sick it made me, I'm not sorry. At all."

And a delicious sort of shiver runs down my spine, distracting me. I close my eyes a brief instant, savoring the new rousing sensations.

"So? That's when you knew you weren't you, but sort of me ... And then?" His gaze drops to my lips.

"And then—" His fingertips trail down my neck, lingering right where my pulse leaps in a new haphazard rhythm. "—I was drifting in and out of consciousness, calling your name, reaching. And then I blacked out until I woke for real. When they released me, I knew I had to come and see. To make sure. So, here I am."

"Here you are."

His eyes run down my body slowly, and his breath grows shallow. Mine follows. He leans in, inhaling me, lingering in the crook of my neck. I sigh in pleasure, tilting my head back. I am lost in these new sensations, where nothing else exists. He groans deep in his throat, and wraps one arm over my back, holding his other hand against my head. Leaning me back, his lips nibble their way up my neck to the curve of my jaw, and my shallow breaths turn ragged. And I swear, in that instant, I feel the earth shake beneath my feet.

"Ewww, gross," holler a few dozen, matching-T-shirt-wearing preteen boys, making loud smooching noises as they run past us in a tight pack, effectively startling me out of this earth-shattering moment.

And just as suddenly, Liam scrambles away, cursing under his breath.

"Boys, that's enough," one of their coaches huffs as he brings in the rear. "Eleven, and they think they know it all," he says wryly as he jogs by us, a sweat-slicked soccer shirt clinging to his muscled back.

"Jesus," Liam says, scrubbing a hand through his hair. "Give me a moment to cool off here, and bring it down a notch."

"Why?" I ask, mystified. "I liked it." And that's putting it mildly. *Again please.*

"Argh ... Éolie, that's not helping," he says, walking backward straight into the surf, keeping me in his sights. "Holy freaking shit, that's cold!" he exclaims, stopping knee deep.

"Are you cooled enough to answer me, now?" I ask him, letting the receding sea foam tickle my toes.

"If you really need to know why, First Date Ever," he says, like it explains everything. "It won't do," he adds, correctly reading my blank look.

I make a mental note to add this new information to my Log Book under the topic Strange Rules and Regulations Governing Mating Rituals.

"It won't do? Why?" I ask, my brow dipping.

"Why, she asks?" he says, face upturning to the sky, hands on his hips. "Because as a first date ever, mauling you in public like an overeager teenager just won't do. And you were two seconds from it happening, in case you're wondering." He drills me with an intense look.

I stop breathing, trapped by his burning gaze, indigo eyes drinking me in. And I just stand there at the water's edge, mesmerized.

"And your first real kiss sure as hell won't take place somewhere public. It won't do either. The way I feel? I won't be able to stop at just kissing, Éolie ... Be warned."

"Consider me warned and ready." My gaze strays to his lips, and my body tingles at the remembered feel of them, warm and full as they trailed up my neck, and a small whimper escapes from deep within me.

"Don't—Christ—" Liam stumbles back, arms flailing, and almost falls in. The incredulous look on his face is so comical I let out a peal of laughter, and it deflects our libidinous mood into something more playful.

"Bloody hell. I'm either obsessing here, or I haven't cooled enough yet, not sure which." He shakes his head on a small chuckle. "I never had any problems controlling my reactions, ever ... What are you doing to me?" he asks as he wades back towards me. "I'm bewitched."

"Oh, good. I'm not the only one." I plant a quick kiss on the corner of his lips, the same lips forming the 'O' of his wide open mouth. "Does a First Date Ever include lunch? I'm starving."

Twenty

LIAM

Great. We've been back at Le Petit Café de l'Hôtel de la Mer for less than ten minutes, and already the pimply busboy, a teenager all feet and hands, has dutifully refilled our water glasses three times. If Éolie so much as take a sip, he pops up.

"Thank you," Éolie says to him, before looking down, brushing a stray lock of hair behind her ear.

"We're good," I tell him pointedly.

The boy gives me a tight nod but has the grace to turn beet red as he shuffles away. Realigning bread plates perfectly aligned, and fussing with cloth napkins already folded to perfection at the next table over. A water pitcher at the ready. Jesus.

Guess this place needs some more late-lunch clients to keep him busy elsewhere. It's almost two in the afternoon, so the regular noon-hour lunch crowd is rather thin now. But as though conjured up by my thoughts alone, a group of seven business associates in impeccable charcoal-grey suits walks in, and commandeers several tables in one corner. Alleluia. That should do it for the next little while. Now, where were we, here? Ah, yes.

"You can ask me anything," I say, arms folded, leaning over our little bistro table. A blushing Éolie bites on her lower lip. I shift in my chair reminding myself, once again, that she's never been kissed. I swallow. Hard.

"Anything?" she ponders, drumming her fingers on her lips, leaving me envying, of all things, fingertips, and aching for a taste. The soft music playing, the conversations, the cups clanking in saucers, everything else fades, and only Éolie remains. Hell, at this rate I'll internally combust before I even get to the kissing part. *Slow down, man.*

"Favorite color?" she asks me straight-faced, but her aqua eyes dance with something akin to mirth.

"Aaah, the favorites," I tease, the hint of a smile playing on my lips. "You're really going there?" I ask.

"No ... not really," she says, shaking her head on a small laugh. "Unless you tell me yellow's no longer your favorite."

Yellow. The happiest color I could think of at seven. It's the color that came to mind whenever she talked to me back then. My mouth quirks up. We used to play "what's your favorite" for hours on end, and it used to drive me nuts; she changed favorites every hour or so. Me, not so much. I always came up with the same answers. It drove her nuts, I recall fondly.

I lean in just a couple more inches. "Right now? It's turquoise. Ask me again in an hour," I say, and her eyes grow wide before she lets out a peal of laughter. "Shocking isn't it?" I rest my elbows on the table and prop my chin up in my hand.

"More than shocking. You've always been the steadfast one in your favorites, even as a little boy. I was the one discovering new ones every few hours at the time, if I recall. Have you been corrupted by a three-year-old. Should I worry?" she asks and I smile, enjoying this.

"No worries. Yellow is still in my top ten favorites."

"Dieu merci. I thought I'd led you astray for a moment there," she says, letting her shoulders sag playfully.

Oh, Éolie... "You can lead me astray. Anytime. Anywhere," I reply, watching her blush anew.

"Why do I get the feeling we're not talking about the same thing anymore?" she asks, her arms crossing over the table.

"Because we're not," I answer, leaning closer, my heart pounding. *I'm held under your spell, Éolie.*

"I wouldn't know how to lead you anywhere," she says, her eyes darting to my lips.

"Oh, you'd be surprised," I murmur, and her gaze whips up.

"What about girlfriends?" she asks artlessly.

"What about them?" I lean back.

"You're ... famous with lots of them. Ever had a serious one?" she asks, rearranging her silverware, suddenly avoiding my gaze.

I look at her for a long moment.

It's time for some damage control. The very worldly version of Liam O'Shea she built up in her mind, the Mimis incident helping along, is not who I am. Well, not anymore, and not for quite some time now.

"By serious, you mean for more than one night, right?" I ask, and my fingers steeple in front of my mouth.

"Huh ... something like this, yes." Her head tilts to the side and her fingers still.

"Definitely no girlfriends. Not ever," I say, my eyes never straying from hers. "But there's a first for everything." She releases a breath, and I grin.

"Do you believe in love at first sight?" she asks softly.

As of now? Absolutely. "Do you?"

"Ask me again in an hour," she retorts with a small, secretive smile, her sharp wit delighting me to no end.

"Fair enough." I lean closer, drawn by her tender gaze, and I get lost into warm, wondrous sea-green eyes.

"Are you ready to order, Mademoiselle Éolie?" Our assigned waiter clears his throat and I look up, thrown by his overly friendly voice and the way he says her name. Not only does his timing suck, but the question's clearly addressed to Éolie, and only her. The athletic-looking, dark-haired, twenty-something guy is leaning much too close to my liking, practically bent over her shoulder. The young busboy falling all over himself to get to our water glasses earlier on was pretty mild compared to this. I narrow my eyes.

"Oh. Sorry. I'll have ... um." She quickly drops her gaze to her unopened menu sitting there, and she scrambles to open it.

"We're not ready yet," I say, raising one eyebrow, staring him down.

"My apologies, sir," he says curtly. "I'll be back shortly."

He leaves our table but not before casting a sidelong glance at Éolie.

"You know him?" I ask Éolie as he hovers nearby, fussing with salt and pepper shakers on empty tables, soon joined by the pimply one holding on to a fresh water pitcher. They keep casting looks our way. Awesome.

"I don't really know anyone. I usually eat in my room. It's the first time I'm eating downstairs, why?" she asks, looking up over her menu.

"How did he know your name?" I ask, my eyes following his every move.

"Oh. Everyone here calls me by my name. And I can't thank them enough for that. You've no idea how much it boosts my confidence hearing it out loud. Booking a room here, it's the first time I've publicly used my given name, and it's something I swore I would fearlessly do from this point on," she says with a beguiling smile, before looking back down at her menu. "I don't know how they memorize us all, though, but they go all out to make you feel welcome."

"I'll just bet they do," I say under my breath.

"Sorry, were you asking me something?" She looks back up, guileless, and man, I just can't go there with her. That guy's not worth shaking her newfound confidence in the world.

"Favorite dish?" I ask the first question that pops into my head, opening up my menu without even glancing at it.

"Ugh. Tough question if ice cream doesn't count," she replies, eyes twinkling.

"So, we're back to favorites?" I can't help but grin.

"Looks like it," I say. "For now."

She puts down her menu, folded arms leaning in. "Any dish as long as what's in it never had fins, claws, legs, or hooves before it came to my plate."

"Well, it's not like you're a fussy eater now, are you?" I say, voice low and amused. Guess my sushi favorite won't make it on her Top Ten, I inwardly grin. I cross my arms over the table. "What's a guy to feed you?"

"That's two questions, but I'll let it pass," she answers in a playful tone of voice, "just this once."

She gestures, half-smiling, and I cock my head to the side. "Ask me what's my favorite food instead, and you'll know what to feed me," she whispers into my ear.

Leaning back, lit from within, she smiles, and I stare. Her smile fades, and she stares. My eyes drop to her parted lips.

"Compliments of Monsieur François, Mademoiselle Éolie." We both startle and look up as the dark-haired waiter from Hell plunks down a platter of sliced fruits that could probably feed a small village, or two. I narrow my eyes at him, and he smirks.

"It's so thoughtful," Éolie says. "I could live on fresh fruits alone." She beams up at the poor chap who stumbles back under impact. And it's a lot nicer than my method for sending him stumbling.

Still smiling, she slides the platter over to me. "What would you like?" she asks.

"You," I murmur.

The hotel's deck is deserted by now. Everybody's back inside getting ready for supper, but I'm not hungry for food.

We never ran out of silly questions and sillier answers. Nor, for that matter, simple questions and simple answers. For instance, I learned a few quirks of hers, like studying Latin, and botany despite being in the middle of the ocean, or that her morning routine includes yoga stretching ... And, she may have learned that I conjugate French verbs to help me defuse tight situations or that I can go for long periods of time on little to no sleep.

By tacit agreement, we skirted around the boatload of hard questions still hanging there, needing some form of respite from our emotionally charged morning. And still the afternoon flies by.

I love this ease, this instant bonding and familiarity we have going on. It's as though I've known her all my life. But then again, I have.

There's a new chill in the air and Éolie's folded arms press close to her body. "Come on, let's get back inside before you catch a cold." I rise and stand over her.

"I'm good. I'd like to stay a little longer and watch the sunset," she says.

"There's still about an hour until then. Come here," I insist, pulling her up from the red Adirondack. I briskly rub her back, transferring some of my warmth. "I'm sure I left a couple sweaters in my car, let's go get them."

"How come you're not even cold in your shirt?" she pouts.

"Curse of the hot-blooded male," I say, waiting for her blush, and she delivers right on cue, eyes downcast. My insides melt.

She soon rolls the sleeves of one of my sweaters we found in the car, but the sleeves are too wide and fall right back down again. It's adorable, the way it dwarfs her. I run my eyes down her toned little body, taking my time. Doesn't take much effort to imagine her in nothing but my sweater hitting her mid-thigh, one silken soft shoulder bared, and suddenly, adorable becomes sexy as hell and I get lost in the fantasy.

She looks up and her eyes darken, a shadow passing through. My smile fades.

"I don't want this day to be over," she says, grabbing me by the waist, holding tight, and I close my eyes, returning the embrace.

I'm caught in a tornado, emotions flying high and low. I'm all over the place. I don't know what the hell's happening to me, but I know what she means. "I'm afraid I'm dreaming you and I'll wake up and never recover from that dream," I murmur.

She takes a step back and her expressive eyes grow solemn. "No dream," she whispers. "I promised to *live* if I ever survived."

Tears well in her eyes and spill over, slaying me. She brushes them away on the sleeve of her borrowed sweater as she walks over to the steps leading down to the beach, sitting on the top one. The wind whips strands of her hair and the golden light of dusk haloes her as she stares at the horizon.

"Our retrieved intel from ORA doesn't mention any survivors on board, just the recovery of the wreck," I say after a moment. It's a question that's haunted me for a while, and I finally feel grounded enough to ask it.

"I wasn't officially there," she explains. "My parents made sure my name never made it into the official log. Not even as Rose. I've been a classified item within a classified mission. Protection, they said."

"How did they manage that working for the US Navy?" I ask.

She shrugs but it's more of a stiff jerk. "You'd be surprised the demands they give in to when you're the only qualified scientists already cognizant of half the answers they're looking for to begin with, let alone equipped and willing to research the other half of it."

My chest aches at the sadness and loss in her voice as she speaks of them.

I sit beside her, my arm coming round her shoulders, pulling her close to me.

"What were they like?" I ask quietly.

"Driven, by the ocean," she says softly. "They had each other and one little oops ... me. A glitch in their otherwise dedicated lives to marine biology research." Her voice is candid, without any trace of rancor. And I stiffen, my hands fisting at the idea that anyone could ever view Éolie as a mistake. "Don't get me wrong, they had so much compassion for all living creatures that, in their own roundabout way, they cared deeply about me too. But unraveling the many unsolved mysteries laying deep within the oceans was like a fire in them, the sole purpose of their lives." Her eyes glisten with unshed tears.

I squeeze her shoulders. "And you never did fit comfortably in the equation, did you?" I murmur.

"No. I didn't. But we made do," she says, a sad look passing through her eyes. "Do you know what the worst part is? We weren't even supposed to be there when the storm hit ... But they'd just had a major breakthrough, something solid after years and years of speculative research, so there we were, so enthused we didn't even notice the squall rolling in on us. They were swept away by a rogue wave ... and I survived." She nods a couple of times, silent tears over spilling. "I survived."

"You never had the chance to say goodbye, did you?" I ask.

"No," she murmurs, staring out to sea. "But I accepted it. You can't live close to nature all your life, or for that matter, do dangerous dives routinely, and not acknowledge that death is part of the deal," she adds in a choked voice, lips trembling.

Éolie shivers, and I'm wrecked against the tide of her flashback. My own chest constricts painfully, and I gather her trembling body into the shelter of mine. "You're here now," I whisper. "I won't let you go." *I can't let you go.*

"Promise?" She wipes her face dry on my sleeve, and I press her close to me.

"Promise." I kiss the top of her head, suddenly feeling on top of the world. I want to be with her, absorb her into my life and have her absorb me into hers. And I get lost in yet another fantasy. Love. A place to belong. Family. Her, with me. Could this kind of normal be within my reach?

My palms grow sweaty and I rub them dry on my thighs, unaccountably nervous all of a sudden. "Do you have any loose ends to tie ... with the Navy?" I ask, swallowing tight, heartbeats in my throat as I wait for her answer.

She contemplates the sunset on the horizon, turning the evening sky into a burst of orange, red, and pink. "No. I'm never going back to the ocean," she says.

I breathe out a long sigh, blindsided by the overwhelming relief.

It's happening, man. Normal starts here.

"Just watch me," I vow under my breath.

Twenty-One

LIAM

We huddle close on the steps of the deserted hostel's deck well past sunset, skipping supper altogether, thanks in part to our late lunch. And I could stay there all night without complaint. But, I can no longer ignore the signs. Even loathe to let her go, I'll have to. I can see plain as day that Éolie's delicate features are drawn taut with fatigue. Her eyelids droop and flutter closed once every few minutes, and she fights it, blinking them open.

"Let's call it a night, you look pretty done in," I suggest, kissing her temple. I can't seem to help it. I need to touch her in some form or other, if just to make sure that I'm not dreaming her.

"I hate it, but you're right. I'm about ready to drop," she says, sounding a bit despondent, and I'm right there with her.

"Come, I'll walk you to your room." I pull her up against me, and she offers no resistance, holding in a yawn, or trying to.

"I would have liked nothing better than to stay up all night and talk, though," she says on a yawn, trudging back inside. "Raincheck?"

"Absolutely. Expect me back bright and early tomorrow." I follow her up the stairs and down an elegant hallway on the third floor.

"Promise?" Anxious eyes rove over my face.

My fingers curl tightly around her shoulders, and I pull her towards me. "Try and stop me. Bright and early, Éolie, promise," I vow, kissing the top of her head, and she sags against my chest, nodding once.

"Okay, this is me," Éolie says, pointing to the last door. The old-fashioned key jangles into the lock, and the door to her hotel room squeaks open. I swallow. She's exhausted and so innocent—and exhausted...

I brace my hands in the doorway, taking a look around. I frown, unsure this even qualifies as a bedroom. This room is just about the size of the walk-in at my rental condo. The white and azure theme is somewhat nautical, with a wallpaper border of stylized anchors, following along the wainscoting on the walls. There are a couple of pillows and a folded duvet on a white-painted wood chair near a French door leading to a small balcony, ocean side. There's a US Navy duffel, propped by the foot of the single bed shoved against one wall, and in the opposite corner, an antique bureau with mirror stands, covered in ... sticky notes? And they're filled with a now-familiar-looking, loopy handwriting. I shake my head at the quirky sight, and can't help a small grin. It fades quickly though, when I take another look around her tiny room.

"You good here?" I ask concerned. "Because if you need anything. Money, food—"

Éolie puts a finger on my mouth, leaning her slender torso against me, and to my dismay, the semi I've been sporting all day swells to full mast just at the feel of her small breasts pressing in on me. Bloody hell, what's with me? I've never been in a state of perpetual arousal like this before. Just an innocent touch makes me want to jump her. I need to get the fuck out before I do.

"Éolie, you good?" I ask again, needing the reassurance that she is before I head out.

Her gaze stays transfixed on her finger and I shush, pulse picking up. "I'm good. Call it occupational hazard, but all of my parents' creatures were well provided for. Don't worry, I'm fine," she insists, leaning away.

Good to know one of us is, 'cause I'm not. My erection painfully strains, constricted by my jeans. Eyeing the small bed, I grit my teeth, battling thoughts of the two us twisting up the sheets twelve ways to Sunday. *Not happening, man.* Don't forget that she just went through a lot. That last thought makes me refocus on my latest concern for her. It works wonders. I shrivel up in no time. L'Hôtel booked her in a damn closet to live in for chrissake.

"I asked for the smallest room possible; it comforts me," she says, looking straight at me, her gaze slicing through as though reading my mind. And for a split second, I wonder—

"Can you read other people's minds?" I ask, unsure whether I like the idea or not, but she shakes her head, and I'm more relieved than I expected. "When we talked as kids, were you reading mine?"

"You mean like in the quad, when you got sick of me being you?" she quips.

"Jesus, you were sort of being me there, weren't you?" I brush the back of my neck. Is it getting warm in here?

"Sort of, or pretty close to anyway. Pretty crazy, right?" she says. "But I wasn't all there so ... I don't think you need to worry too much. I don't intend to make it a regular occurrence."

"Good to know, I like you just fine when you're all here," I say on a swoosh of breath. "And when we were kids?"

"I'm not sure. I was so young. I felt some of your emotions, some of the times ... like all the strong peaks. But for the most part, it was just us sharing a silent conversation." She shrugs. "What I'm sure I felt, though, is the warmth of your essence, like a physical imprint, pulsing bright inside of me. If describing it that way makes any sense to you."

"Yes, it does, I felt it too," I say, thrilled by the notion that we shared this added layer of connection even more that our psychic conversations. "I used to refer to it as your Light ... And I have been feeling it again, pulsing high and low, since the storm. In fact, it's what kept my hopes up, even when we couldn't find you."

"Since the —and you still feel it?" she beams the question, and I nod. "Maybe I'm getting better at being weird, who knows?" She perks up, and I crack a smile. She's adorable.

"So, now that we met in real life, the actual question is, can I read your mind, or better yet, do it on purpose?" she wonders, growing still, her otherworldly eyes unblinking. And my eyes grow wide at what she's undoubtedly picking up from my one-track mind and wholly inappropriate thoughts right now. Shit.

She lets out a peal of laughter. "I'm messing with you. I don't know what you're thinking right now, honest," she says.

I lick my lips, my mouth suddenly dry. If I lean by a fraction of an inch our breaths will intermingle, our lips will ... She yawns behind her hand. *Jesus, man, keep with the program here.* No jumping her bones. She's done in. I'm done for. I stumble backward in my haste to put some distance between us, and end up half sprawled on the small bed an arm's length away from the door.

I inhale a sharp breath through my nose. Her scent permeates the closed space, something untamed like the open sea, sweet like vanilla, and sultry like the deep caress of a warm summer's wind. I'm getting high on her and if this night is going to end even remotely gentlemanly, I need to go. Now.

She steps around me to reach her duffel, and I exhale, scrambling back up. I have to brace myself on the door frame for support, weak kneed. "Tight space," I mutter.

"Staff calls this room the monk's cell," she says, unzipping her duffel. "But I call it the perfect hideaway." The last part is said on a breathy sigh, her face taking on a faraway look.

The back of my head thumps on the door. I bloody well won't stop if I let loose and kiss her; I'll vaporize. I can't tell if she realizes how affected I am, but now she's moving around, fidgeting with her pillows and the blanket, and I know we're both full of frayed nerves at how alone we are in here. Even so, her exhaustion hangs about her like a scarf, and I can see how fragile she still is. I'm so screwed. She needs to be tucked in bed, to sleep, and I want...

"Please don't go yet," she pleads softly. I straighten from my slouch, trying to figure out how to respond.

"Éolie..." I hesitate a beat, then nod. "I'll stay as long as you need." But I can't think of anything except her and me naked. I push away from the door, the floor creaking underfoot.

"Would you mind staying until I fall asleep?" she asks softly, her request punctuated with another yawn. "It won't take very long, I'm halfway there."

"I ... don't mind..." I gulp, pulled under by the landslide of erotic images the last few words just evoked. I'm in so much trouble.

My eyes sweep the place, searching for a quick distraction. There's the bed, the bureau and oh, there's the bed again. My eyes finally land on all the sticky notes, and I do a double take.

"Mind if I read?" I ask, crossing over to the Post-Its mural.

"Says the guy afraid I'll read his twisted thoughts," she deadpans. "By all means, read away, my own." She rolls her eyes as she takes out a small toiletry bag and a white garment before zipping up her duffel, and putting it back on the floor.

Eye rolling, really? This may be just the distraction I need right now. Bring it on.

"Twisted? Me?" I humph, crossing my arms. "Says the girl who spins a new twist on twisted by putting her feet up to the back of her head in a pretzel yoga pose, and does it for fun. Repeatedly."

"Says the guy who eats raw fish for pleasure." Her face scrunches. Guess the marine biologist in her is still unimpressed by my favorite dish, sushi. I'm hard pressed not to laugh, enjoying this.

"Says the girl who studied Latin for the heck of it," I say. "Who does that for pleasure?"

"Says the guy who conjugates French verbs for no reason."

I chuckle low. "Yeah, that's pretty twisted all right," I concede, looking down, mouth quirking up one side. *But then again, learning angel-speak gave me reason to believe, deep down, that you were real all along, Éolie...*

She walks past me, pulling my sweater over her head along the way, letting it drop to the floor. I swallow, heart thumping. She's undressing? Right now? Here?

"Go for it, Liam O'Shea," she says on a lilt.

"Come again?"

She motions with a grand sweep of her arm ... to the mirrored bureau. "I'll be right back," she calls over her shoulder, and I just stand there slack jawed as she steps out of the room.

I shake myself out of my trance. "Can't be the perfect hideaway without an en suite now, can it?" I ask the ceiling, hands on my hips.

I don't waste any more time. Beyond curious, I read the first of the colorful mosaic of Post-Its.

> Better three hours too soon
> Than a minute too late.
> -William Shakespeare

Hmm, I scratch my jaw ... interesting. To take or not to take in context to this morning's outburst about being too soon, that is the question. She'll never be too soon to my way of thinking, in any case.

Logic will get you from A to B.
Imagination will take you everywhere.
-Albert Einstein

"Well, well … What have we here?" I say, charmed to find the opening quote of my first-ever self-published book.

Love is composed of a single soul
Inhabiting two bodies.
-Aristotle
What if?

"Éolie," I murmur, struck by the notion, seduced by the thought. Aris, my good man, what if indeed.

The next one is unfamiliar. I frown, trying to place it.

vérifier horaire de trains
– Montréal

Why does she have a note to check train schedules to Montreal? Is she leaving? Already? That won't do. Shit. How much time do I have to convince her otherwise?

Ugh! Just because you can doesn't mean you should
Eat three bowls of ice cream for breakfast
Take hot showers five times a day
Flush the toilet more than once

Bloody hell. I find it both poignant and hilarious, and I've this peculiar warmth twisting my guts as I read through her sticky notes. But it's nothing compared to the punch in the chest I get from the next one over.

My fingers reach for it of their own volition.

"You stayed."

I startle and spin around, shoving the note into my jeans pocket.

"That was quick, I … I…" I clear my throat. Wearing a white eyelet cotton nightdress, she's hovering in the doorway, and light spills out, framing her in angelical halo. So fitting. For me, she'll always be part angel. Locked away in the deepest recesses of my soul, the luminous presence of her spirit kept darkness at bay.

"Thank you so much for staying," she says on a worn-out smile, swaying a bit. And before I can recover my wits and reply with something as inane as "no need to thank me," she literally drops down on the bed, planting face down, not even bothering with the blankets.

Another déjà vu hits me as I gently tuck her in. I have done this in my mind so many times before. I was seven ... and the feel of her was so real back then, I could have sworn she was cuddled next to me, each and every night.

"Je t'envoie de beaux rêves," she mumbles drowsily, breathing a sigh against the pillow, already more than half asleep.

I kneel on the floor next to her, getting lost in the memories she just unleashed. No mere sweet dreams, sleep tight, type of wishes, no. Not Éolie. *I'm sending you beautiful dreams,* she'd say instead every single night when I tucked her in. And, true to her words, breathtaking images of green hills, lush forests, valleys, and streams straight out of her magical kingdom, the Forest of Laure, would play in my head as soon as I closed my eyes, sweeping me away from my real-life nightmare at the time .... setting fire to my imagination. And when I lost her, it's my *Tales from the Enchanted Forest of Laure* I weaved at night, inspired by those images, that kept me this side of sane.

Soon, her breaths are even and her eyes closed.

"*Je t'aime...*" I hear her voice whisper softly in passing through my mind. Unsure I heard right, overwrought by a wealth of dizzying emotions, I stare and stare some more, stroking her braided hair in a gentle, tactile lullaby, breathing her in.

"I love you too," I murmur into the quiet of the night.

I punch my pillow for the umpteenth time and bury my face in it, tight jawed. Christ above, I'm truly obsessing. A persistent picture of Éolie, sexy as all get out in her demure nightgown, forms anew in my mind. Only, this time, she's standing in my bedroom doorway, face glowing as she walks up to me. "I'm ready to be tucked in," she'd say, pressing in on me. My hands would slide down her abdomen and hips, cupping her bottom, lifting her up, wrapping her legs around my waist...

The generic ring tone of my phone blares, jerking me from my fantasy, and I wrestle with the sheets, diving for it. The alarm reads two forty-five, *not good* my brain screams as I sit up on the edge of the bed. Did something happen to one of the guys? Apart from COA's administration, my buds are the only ones who have this number. But then again, didn't I program a different song for each? What's with the ring tone? Did it reset itself? Caller ID's blocked. A wrong number? My mind is spinning a hundred miles a minute as I pick up the line.

"O'Shea," I say.

"Son?"

I flinch, hearing the gravelly voice on the other end.

"I'm no one's son." I press end, hanging up. Reeling, I shove one hand through my hair. Of all the voices I expected to hear on the other end, his was the very last. Some seven years since we last spoke, and it hasn't been long enough as far as I'm concerned.

I growl into the empty room, pacing. "I disowned you. You're forsaken, disallowed, repudiated, what's not to understand." I curse him under my breath. Christ, that man is so far removed from normal, and from everything I aspire to be, it's not even funny.

The phone dings a text alert. Bloody hell. Here goes. I pinch the bridge of my nose. What time is it in Los Angeles anyway?

Sean: Heard you're in the States. It's been a while.

"And we were doing so well too, why break such a perfect seven-year record?" I glare at my phone.

Sean: Son.

Sean: Let's talk Eiloe.

"Let's not," I say, bristling at the name of my series from his mouth—or thumbs in this case. He wants the rights to it. That much I know. And he wants them bad if he's willing to try by himself, his army of minions having failed these last few months, and it leaves a sour taste in my mouth.

Me: Not selling. Lose the number.

I resist the urge to hurl my phone at the wall.

Forget sleep, I need air. I step out onto the balcony, turning my phone off before another text can come through, and throw it on the chaise longue. I brace my hands on the rail, head bowed.

But it's of no use. My peace is gone. I slap my hands on the railing, stirred up by the one person I try to avoid at all costs.

Sean Elliot Pierce. A-list actor. Movie mogul. Toxic Prick of the first order.

My *ex*-father.

I close my eyes, and my head falls back as I fill my lungs with cleansing, briny sea air. I hear the waves crashing on the shore and a gentle breeze whips through the darkness, raising goose bumps on my bare chest.

I reopen my eyes and search for the Little Dipper and Polaris, the North Star, its brightest star, and locate it almost immediately in the clear night sky. My gaze zeroes in on it. I don't even second guess myself as I make the exact same wish I made a lifetime ago.

A wish seventeen years in the making, goddammit all.

All bets are off now that I've found her.

Love. Belonging. Home.

No more wandering, no more hiding behind my aloneness. With Éolie in the picture, normal is finally within reach.

Mine for the taking. *And I will.*

I march back inside, grab the first pair of jeans and sweater on hand, and dress quickly. Taken from last night's viewpoint, three in the morning is technically bright and early tomorrow, like I promised her, isn't it?

I peel the Post-It off the door, the one I grabbed before Éolie could see, and re-read it on my way out.

> One day, I am going to wake up,
> roll over on my side,
> and kiss the love of my life
> good morning

I vow to make this one a truth for her, if it's the last thing I do.

Twenty-Two

ÉOLIE

I hear Liam from afar ending a phone conversation in a curt tone. I sit up, eyes and ears alert. But all's quiet, and I'm alone. No Liam. I must have picked up the chime of a phone from one of the two other bedrooms on my floor somehow, and spun it into a dream. A quick glance at the digital clock shows that it's two forty-six in the morning.

I slept so much better and so much longer this time around. Maybe I'm getting used to staying inside, landlocked, and I'll finally get back to my full eight hours of sleep soon. I smile in the dark, encouraged by the five hours I managed to grab before waking.

I swing my legs out of bed and my feet land on something soft and woolly. I bring the sweater up to my nose, inhaling Liam back to life. I already miss him. And the faint trace of his scent on this sweater makes me yearn in a way I never did before yesterday's face-to-face. I pull his sweater over my head, smelling its collar before smoothing it over.

"Guess it will have to do for now," I sigh.

I step outside on my little balcony and prepare my nest, bundling up to my neck in the thick duvet. Propped on my two pillows, I watch the night sky.

At the equator, when I looked straight up, the stars would fly past me all night long, sweeping me around the circumference of the Earth, right along with them. This far up north, I can see Polaris, the North Star, who gives both the illusion it is fixed up there in the sky and that stars are slowing down in their spin around its central point. I stare at Polaris for a long moment. I'm looking at what's little more than a cosmic coincidence for this one star to sit right over the North Pole, almost exactly at the point around which the Earth rotates and yet, there it is.

A Lodestar.

Love. Family. Home. Roots. A central point.

"The Forest of Laure," I whisper into the night.

I smile and close my eyes, thinking of Liam's *Tales from the Enchanted Forest of Laure*, the ones he made up at boarding school. Already a superb story teller at seven, he used to spin nightly tales of adventures, cleverly using as a backdrop the images I've had of this place I called the Forest of Laure, and that I had shared with him. And that first year at BIA, unbeknownst to any of them, I was there, all curled up by Liam's side, avidly listening to his bedtime stories. Full of fierce dragons, powerful wizards, and noble knights on quests for freedom, wanting to come Home, searching for love and family, searching for one little lost fairy I know to be me. And according to Liam's wonderful stories, Home, also known as the Normal Kingdom, exists somewhere in the Enchanted Forest of Laure ... waiting for us to reunite. And, fiction or not, I long for it all, I realize, more than ever before.

A rustling sound in the bushes below gets my attention. I grow still, intently listening. I hear twigs snapping in quick succession. There's something down there, and it's foraging big time. I mentally check my balcony's access, and relax back. Unless that critter has wings I won't be mistaken for food.

What about claws .... I sit up straight. Can a bear climb wood siding? I get up on my hands and knees, crawling up to the railing, head poking out.

"Éolie?" Liam whispers.

"... Liam ... what—?" I say, lowering my voice.

"I'm coming up, stand back," he says.

"Are you nuts? I'll come get you," I say, growing quiet as he starts to climb up to my balcony. Heart in my throat, I watch his rapid progression and I scramble back as he hoists himself up my railing, landing in a crouch besides me. I exhale on a huff, my hands covering my galloping heart.

He takes me by the shoulders, his chest heaving, piercing me with an intense look. "I don't ... want to ... be separated ... ever again," he pants, catching his breath, taking mine away. My mouth falls open. I'm not sure I heard him right.

"I'm applying for the position, Éolie," he says, sticking a note on my chest, right over my heart, his burning gaze never once straying from mine. I look down ... at a familiar lime-green Post-It, recognizing it instantly. My eyes whip up.

"That's ... You ... It's—" I stutter, overwhelmed, unable to fully process what he just said, half afraid that, maybe, I'm reading too much into this.

The back of his hand comes up, tenderly stroking my cheek in a gentle brush. "For once in my life, I want more, way more," he affirms, and I melt into this big fat vat of compote de coeur. Tears pool in my eyes, and I quickly look up to stem the flow, blinking them away. Polaris twinkles back at me like crazy through my watery eyes. "More?" I murmur.

"More. I want to live, Éolie. With you. I want you to wake up next to me, and kiss me good morning, every morning. That connection we had, I want it back, in flesh-and-blood normal. Just say yes and stay, don't go. We'll take it as slow as you need, I promise you. Just ... stay with me," he urges me on solemnly, warm fingers brushing strands of hair away from my face.

Flying. Standing tall at the bow of the Thalassa, soaring over waves, arms stretched up to the sky. Here and now, I am flying away, soaring high on the same sensations of weightlessness.

"Stay with—? Liam," I say with wonder, my thoughts spinning.

"Éolie? Are we on the same wavelength right now? You in?" His beautiful indigo eyes are darkening to midnight-sky blue, intently watching me, waiting.

"In," I say just before leaping into his arms.

Sitting on my balcony, I rearrange the duvet around us, snuggling close to Liam as we wait for sunrise, and a more decent check-out time. He holds his hand palm up, and I press mine into it until energy hums through our joined palms. Such strong hands he has and yet, they're not overpowering. *Safe*, I feel safe.

"You have the hands of a poet warrior," I say, marveling at the difference in size.

"Poet warrior?" he asks, amused, long lean fingers curling over mine. "Yours are fairy like..." he replies, voice trailing off.

Fairy? Once more thinking of Liam's *Tales from the Enchanted Forest of Laure*, where, once upon a time, his imagination turned me into a fairy on a nightly basis, I almost groan out loud. Angels, fairies, I'm decidedly uncomfortable with being likened to mythical creatures. I'm weird enough for real as it is.

"Should I worry when you grow quiet like this, right in the middle of what you're saying?" I ask, upturning my head, and his gaze collides with mine.

"No worries. It happens regularly when I'm on to something, plotting," he says, the hint of a smile playing on his lips.

"Oh. That's reassuring. And I'm the weird one, right?" I squeal as a finger pokes my side, and I promptly slap one hand over my mouth to hold in my outburst. He tickles me some more, and I squirm out of his arms and start crawling away, and he follows.

"Shhh ... I don't want to wake anyone this early, it's rude." I lower my voice, hands held up, my back pressed to the railing a few feet away.

"I'm not the one squealing," he chuckles just as low. He sits back against the wall, motioning me over.

I shake my head, fighting a laugh.

In a swift move I didn't see coming, Liam grabs me by the ankles and slides me back to his side, and I yelp in surprise.

"We need a few ground rules here," he says, straight-faced. "Rule Number One: Thou Shall Not Stay So Far Away." His face softens. "Stay; I'll behave."

"That's rule number two?" I ask blithely.

"Not even close to it." His mouth quirks up on one side, revealing my favorite dimple. "I'll tell you when we get to Rule Number Two." He kisses my temple.

"You should know I'm terrible at rules, and I don't want to mess up," I say on a more serious note.

"Not possible to mess up, Éolie." I feel his gaze like a hot touch, and it gets to me. "It's a favorite rule of mine," he says, lifting me up on his lap, and my heart melts.

"Promise?" I ask.

"Promise."

He strokes my hand with his thumb back and forth, and my heart melts just a little bit more. He glances down to where his fingers touch mine then back up, with a speculative glint in his eyes.

"What are you thinking about?" I ask quietly.

"How I could be soothed like nothing else, by either the sound of your voice, or the sight of those beautiful green hills rolling as far as my eyes could see," Liam replies, staring at our linked hands. "The Forest of Laure, Éolie. All those breathtaking images made of forests, valleys, and streams that played in my mind whenever you fell asleep ... You were sending them, weren't you?" he asks, searching my eyes.

I nod a few times, looking into his eyes. I feel his energy pulsing in me and The Forest of Laure shaping up to come true, and my heart thuds in my ears.

"When we met? That's when I first started to get these impressions, and these images of this place I called the Forest of Laure started streaming in my mind, like constantly during the time we stayed connected." My fingers stroke down his cheek in a feather-light caress.

"Are they ... foretelling? I mean, is it a real place?" he asks softly.

"I wasn't sure before, up until I saw you last Friday," I say, and his eyes brighten.

"And now?" he asks.

"Now, I'm pretty sure that's what they are, a glimpse of what could be," I whisper, glancing down at our interlaced fingers.

He tilts my head so our eyes meet. The soft look in his makes my heart turn over.

"Could be, or will be?" he asks.

I struggle to find the right words. "If the pattern from last week holds ... I'd say, could be, until we make it so, it will be. And somehow that forest I saw when I was little connects to us, to what could be, I believe," I say haltingly.

His eyes are the warmest blue I've seen so far, and his voice drops so low I can barely make out his next words. "Remember what we used to wish upon?"

Pulse pounding in my veins, I nod. "Yes. Something we'd never had and yearned for. Something I still yearn for," I whisper, and watch a look of wonder light up his face.

"A place to belong with someone I love, you ... I've never forgotten our wish, Éolie."

"Neither have I. It's still my number one wish," I say, holding my breath.

"It's mine as well. Our normal is out there, Éolie. The Forest of Laure ... I want to live that," he says, nodding his head. "With you."

"Me too," I exhale softly.

"We'll just have to make it happen then. Deal?" he asks, dropping his forehead on mine.

"Deal."

The sky lightens up to the east.

And I'm ready for this new day to begin. In normal.

Twenty-Three

LIAM

After breakfast, I unlock the front door and let Éolie enter first. She takes a few tentative steps forward before unexpectedly stopping, and I plow right into her. I drop the duffel, and grab her just before she plummets down.

She spins around, hands fisting in my shirt. "This room alone is like twice the size of the Thalassa—" She breaks off to suck in a shaky breath.

I crush her to me, cradling her head. "Hell, Éolie. We can crash in the walk-in for all I care." My gaze sweeps around the open layout of the top-floor condo, and a painful knot forms in my stomach just at the thought of her panicking. She won't bolt, will she? "It's rented for the fall semester, but I can look for something else—"

She straightens her spine. "No. I can do this," she murmurs, and I release a breath. "Show me your space," she says, pushing away from me with a look of determination.

I show her every nook and cranny, discovering them myself as I go along. Not because I think she wants to see it but because I want her to belong. Here. With me.

Those extraordinary eyes of hers look on with wonder, shyly taking everything in. She brushes a finger over the sleek lines of the white sofas, she marvels at the gas fireplace, the stainless steel appliances, and the shiny, dark granite countertops. Trusting me in full measure, she makes me feel ten feet tall.

I almost skip the bedroom altogether, my emotions obviously not as settled as I might have liked. You promised slow, Liam. Time to deliver.

"A balcony!" she exclaims, going straight for it. I hover in the doorway, watching.

"It wraps around, with a view on all three sides," I say.

"It's almost like living outside. This whole wall is made of glass?" She turns back to me, her face lit up. "Can I sleep here?" she asks, waiting with parted lips.

Lips. Kiss. Taste. Touch. "I ... yeah, sleep there, here..." What am I saying? Man, my ears are ringing.

"Do you have some extra pillows and blankets for me?" she asks, admiring the view from the glass wall. "You're missing out with your bed way over there, you know. You could be sleeping à la belle étoile every night," she sighs breathily. "Minus sand fleas," she adds over her shoulder, eyes twinkling.

I swallow to wet my throat. A little something I hadn't considered yet, now dawning on me. "I ... don't think there's any," I manage to say.

"Fleas?" she asks, amused.

"Extra blankets. Pretty sure there's no fleas," I say, struck stupid. Turning back to the view, her hands come up and splay on the glass. I could walk over and pin her front against the wall.

"We'll have to share the bed," I croak. Nice, man. Slow, you said.

"I don't mind if you don't mind. It opens?" she asks, bending, fingers searching for an opening. I blink at the sight of her tight ass bent over. My pulse skips off the charts.

"Aaaah ... open ... sure, yeah. Do. Open," I choke. Don't get me started on what I'd like to open, I may not recover.

"Where's the door?" she asks, groping around, brows furrowing.

"Away from here." I scramble out, and make it as far as the back door on the other side of the open floor area before I suddenly realize that Éolie's no longer with me.

I quickly retrace my steps to the bedroom and find her standing in the middle of the room, wearing an utmost surprised look on her face.

"That's not normal ... is it?" she asks tentatively to the room at large, her eyes darting between the bed and the floor.

And that's when I take a real good look around.

I draw in a breath. "Shit."

She's right. I don't think it's anywhere near normal.

But in my defense, my mind has been otherwise occupied lately, pushing laundry down the To Do list.

Way down.

"Obviously," I say, eyeballing the mess of dirty clothes strewn about all over the goddamn place.

Twenty-Four

ÉOLIE

I glance around Liam's bedroom. Or what's left of it. Noticing for the first time mounds and mounds of clothes scattered all over, I stop in my tracks.

I hesitate, unsure if Liam's attempting to set a record here. And if so, it's either a record for the most extensive wardrobe ever, or a record for how many days without laundry a human can possibly get away with. It's a pretty awesome sight.

"Shit," he mutters, rubbing the back of his neck, gawking at the piles on the floor as though they magically appeared out of nowhere.

"Would you like some help with your laundry?" I ask hesitantly, gesturing in the general direction of the mess.

"Laundry. Yes. I'm all for laundry." Liam perks up, crossing over. "Let's do this laundry thing."

Brilliant. "Um. 'Kay ... Show me how," I say, and he darts his head toward me.

"What? We *both* don't know how?" he asks, shaking his head.

I roll my eyes. "No washing machines on sailboats." I grab handfuls of clothes. "So, wait. You've never done your own laundry?"

"Huh, that would be a no," he says, scratching behind his ear. "Hotels, remember. I never knew room service was such a hot commodity until I rented this condo, in fact. Guess I've never been completely on my own before."

"Well, then, today marks the very first day of your hotel living emancipation," I declare with conviction. "How hard can this be?" I ask, determined to conquer once and for all any mundane chores of normal day-to-day living.

Liam snorts, and motions for me to follow him. He leads me to a laundry room at the back of the kitchen.

"You asked how hard? On a scale of one to ten, I'd say a twelve," he says, opening the door, and I think he's only jesting.

Guess he wasn't.

From the doorway where I stand, I'm left staring at two front-loading stainless steel appliances, one of them with its thick, round porthole door yawning open. That thing could swallow me up, and I'd fit comfortably inside its mammoth-sized drum.

"We both don't know what we're doing?" I ask, making sure.

"Yep. That sums it up," he says wryly.

We dump our armful of clothes inside and then study the dials of the space module's washer dryer combo together. A central one with seven different core cycles, nine push buttons with sub-cycles, each with five different settings to choose from, as wide ranging as allergy cycle, sanitation cycle, steamed cycle, and anything-in-between cycle. Except for the one I'm looking for. The clueless cycle.

What we need to program in order to start a wash is mind boggling. Apparently, Liam agrees. Beside me, he, too, stands motionless in front of the giant machine.

"And there's no instruction manual?" I ask.

"Nope."

Just then I notice a push button on the bottom left corner that reads *Delay Wash.* "Hey look, we have Abort," I point, snickering. "See? If all else fails, we'll be okay." I pat him consolingly on the back.

"Hey, don't mock the Laundry Gods. They eat socks and shrink your underwear when displeased," he says, his voice low and amused.

I snort. "With the loads and loads coming up, they'll be screaming, enough already."

"Damn straight," he chuckles, and his full dimpled smile flips my stomach. He flicks a finger on my nose, and goes back for some more clothes.

I blink. And follow suit.

"Jesus. It's really a lot, sorry." He sighs, looking at the piles left to haul. "My mind has been elsewhere, and it seemed easier to just order a bunch of stuff online, and forget about it."

"That's one way of taking care of it, I suppose," I say, grabbing another handful of clothes.

"So, what did you do? With your clothes, I mean?" he asks.

"We didn't wear any."

The look on Liam's face is priceless.

"Come again?"

"Any soap?" I ask, scanning the empty shelves above the machines, but Liam stares back at me with a vacant look. I almost give in and crack up. Instead, I blink and try my best to look completely and innocently serious. I brush past him, pretending not to notice all the lewd fantasies that are playing out for him right now.

"Soap?"

Twenty-Five

LIAM

"It's huge," Éolie says half an hour later, and I choke.

"It'll take us hours," she adds, and I almost hack up a lung, right there in the middle of the entrance.

"Probably more," I finally manage, thumping my chest with my fist, earning a wide berth from the next wave of shoppers. *Get your mind out of the gutter, man.*

"I think we should observe them first, and see how they go about it," she suggests, and I can only shake my head at the scientist in her. But like hell am I going in there without some props. I grab a cart. The wheels screech slightly but it's better than those tiny baskets in the corner. I push it through the front door with Éolie close beside me.

"Attention, incoming shoppers, for the next five minutes—" an overly loud announcement informs us about a five-percent discount on who knows what.

"It's like watching piranhas feed," she gushes, growing wide-eyed at the flurry of activity the announcement generates around a huge bin near the cash registers.

"I'll protect you. Come on," I say, chuckling low.

She stays focused as we stealthily follow natives in their natural habitat, hunting down food in the grocery store in town. I chuckle under my breath, watching her studiously watching them, utterly charmed.

"They just throw plastic packages in their carts without even glancing at them, frowning for the most part. Is it me? Do they look like they're enjoying this to you?" she asks, a frown etching into her face.

"Well, you're frowning too," I say. "You enjoying this?" I ask.

She gives me a look, and I cough behind my fist to hide my grin.

"They make haste then fret at the checkout line. I don't get it," she says, her face scrunching.

"They don't get it either," I agree, and she lets out a peal of laughter. I smile, loving the sound of her laughter.

"It's so different from open air markets where whole villages meet and greet. It's another universe," she ponders the matter.

"I'm with them, who wants to meet and greet over frozen pizzas? C'mon, we got this. We'll find laundry soap, and get the hell out." I stride away, reading the overhead panels. "Aisle Twenty-Five, Detergent. See? Simple." I congratulate myself, waiting for her to catch up to me. With a grand sweep of my arm I let her pass, and I follow.

"Simple, right." She nods, sassing me, eyeing the insane amount of choices we're facing head on. My mind bowls over the overstocked aisle of detergent. There are hundreds of them, give or take a few dozen.

"I'll go to the other end, and start reading labels from there. Hopefully, we'll meet back somewhere in the middle," she says over her shoulder. "See, simple."

"Hold on. I've a better idea," I say, my eyes narrowing on the colorful display. "What's your favorite color right now?"

"Indigo blue." She shoots me an impish look.

"Is that so," I say, perusing the shelves until I find exactly what I'm looking for. "Indigo blue. See? Simple." I hold up the appropriate-colored bottle up triumphantly.

She raises her hands over her head. "Yes. We so got this." She chuckles, eyes lit up.

"Anything else we need in here?" I ask, ready to take on the world.

"How about some fresh fruits?" She grabs the front of the cart, pulling me in.

Minutes later, Very-Organized-Éolie is completely immersed in shopping. I inwardly groan, holding up a small bag for her as she squeezes a plum lightly between her fingers, testing its firmness. No sweat. I discreetly readjust.

"Since we managed to figure out laundry detergent, how about cooking supper?" she asks, delight echoing in her voice.

"Cooking? Like no bistros, no take-out, no room service, like left to our own devices cooking supper?" I ask, rubbing my chin, unsure if letting me loose in a kitchen is such a good idea.

"Exactly that kind of cooking supper," she says, and her face fills with excitement as she grabs the cart. "Heads up, though. Aboard the Thalassa, food was merely fuel to go on. We never cooked, and more often than not, we were quite satisfied with ration packs, you know, to the point. And something tells me you didn't do much cooking, either. So, we both don't know what we're doing once more. Shall we give it a try?" Her head tilts. She waits, daring me.

Challenge accepted. "Bring it on," I say, crossing my arms. "This place is full of frozen meals in case you haven't noticed."

"Frozen dinners are cheating, not cooking." She crosses her arms in turn.

"And what will we cook if we can't have meat?" I ask, challenging her.

She holds her hands up in a little gesture of surrender. "Okay, you have a point. You'd think after a lifetime of guts and gore I'd be immune, but just the thought of voluntarily eating those dead specimens is way too much," she says on a shudder. "I've been thinking vermicelle aux petits légumes croquants," she exaggerates her French accent, fluttering her hand. "It's on Monsieur François' menu at L'Hôtel, and it's really good. Bonus, it looks like it'd be simple enough to do, so we could start with that, non?"

"Great. Vegetable pasta." I fake a long suffering sigh. "C'mon then, let's go hunting rabbit food down the next twenty-seven aisles."

She rolls her eyes. I smirk, and she swats my arm.

"Start hunting right here. Are there any vegetables you don't like?" she says, selecting broccoli.

I make a face. "Want me to make the list of those I like, it'd be quicker," I suggest, and she whips her head around.

"Oops. Guess, we'll cook something else." She puts the broccoli back on display.

Bloody hell. There's this overflow of feelings spreading in me like rapid fire. No one ever cared enough to ask me what I liked or didn't like before, never mind taking it into consideration. That simple. Blindsided, I blink away a surprising excess of moisture in my eyes. Too much dust in the air?

Turning around, I swallow, regaining some form of composure. "I, huh ... No need to change menus, I like some," I say, picking a handful of bell peppers, carrots, and onions and bagging them. "You can add potatoes and zucchinis to my short list," I add. "I tolerate all the others." I hand over my loot.

"Got it," she says, eyes luminous and soft, and the warmth in her voice conveys that she really does. Get me.

An hour later, I'm crying buckets. Éolie's crying buckets. And I wonder what sort of insanity made me think I should cook anything, especially with onions. I start whacking the offending vegetables quickly with my knife in a bid for freedom. But I've only made it worse. *Shit.* Tears track down my cheeks, my eyes burning.

"Jesus Christ. It's too much, Éolie."

I look up through tears and fumes strong enough to wipe out the meanest playground bully, and find Éolie holding onto the kitchen island for dear life. She gasps for breath, convulsively crying ... Laughing herself silly. And there's not much else I can do, but join in.

It takes us a little while to tame our hysterics into chuckles. And then, finally, into small hiccups. I don't think I've ever laughed so much. My jaw hurts like crazy.

Éolie grabs me by the shirt and wipes her face dry on it, and takes an immediate step back.

"You must have rolled in onion juice, you reek." She blinks back tears, and her nose wrinkles.

I lean forward and sniff my shirt. Whoa. Man, the stink kills, and my eyes water all over again.

"That's it. No more onions. Done." I grab the whacked-up remnants and drop them forcefully into the sink, where nothing happens.

A slender torso arches into my back, and I still. A graceful arm reaches out from behind me. "Non-reusable wastes were compacted on the Thalassa," she says near my ear, "at the touch of a button." She flips a switch on the wall. Onions à la down the drain, brutal.

I turn sideways leaving her some space, but she deliberately bends over me instead, reaching for the wet kitchen rag by the sink. The temperature of the room spikes by ten degrees, and my pulse starts to race. She straightens so very slowly, I stop breathing. She leans away and starts scrubbing the counter. And the moment's over before it even started.

I brush one hand down my face, reminding myself all the reasons why I can't proceed full speed ahead. Not this time. I check the pan simmering on the stove instead.

"How do you know when it's cooked?" I say, poking the blob.

"Your guess is as good as mine." She makes a face, her nose wrinkling in disgust.

The saying's right. We cooked up a storm. Every available counter space is either smudged with vegetable goo, or taken over by dirty pots and pans. The glass smooth-top range is smeared from the many overspills, and the melted stuff is kind of cooked solid on the surface, permeating the room with a god-awful burnt smell that's quite unappetizing. I lean a shoulder on the fridge.

"There's no way we're eating that stew," I say decisively.

"I'm with you," she responds in kind. "And here I thought you couldn't really burn water." She eyes one of the skewed pots.

"I've got surprising skills," I reply before I can catch myself. Yoga pants are sexy as all hell on her, and I debate sticking my face underneath the cold water faucet. Her innate sensuality is killing me here, and I have to remind myself every few minutes to take it slow. Her innocence and my prurient thoughts are on a collision course.

"Tell me about it." She shakes her head, leaving me wondering if she heard my inner dialogue here. Man, if she could read my mind just now...

Shoes and socks long gone, she goes to sit cross-legged on one of the counter stools. "I really thought we'd breeze through cooking after laundry. It's harder than I thought," she says a bit despondently.

I cross over, bracing my hands on the island's countertop. "Hey, it's no big deal. I'll introduce you to the many joys of take-out. What do you say?" I bend down at her eye level.

She bites her bottom lip, tempting me to leap across the island counter and soothe the little hurt with my tongue. Instead, I shove my hands through my hair, and lean back against the opposite counter.

"Would you mind eating at L'Hôtel de la Mer?" she asks tentatively. The public outing offers me mercy from the singe of my sizzling thoughts, so I jump on it.

"Nope, don't mind at all," I say as I make a beeline for the door, grabbing my set of keys. I'm already out the door before I realize my need to cool my jets left Éolie behind, and that I'm standing outside all by my lonesome.

I walk back in, and find her sitting on the floor putting on her socks, diligently tying her shoes. My mouth quirks up, and my heart turns over at the adorable sight.

"I'd like to ask Monsieur François, the chef and kindly owner, if he'd give me a few pointers over the next few days," she says, standing up. She pulls my sweater over her head, smelling the collar before smoothing it ... She's pulling me under. "I'd really like to master a few basics. You've no idea how long I've dreamed of sitting down to home-cooked meals, prepared with care and thought behind them," she says, her expressive eyes full of yearning.

I just stand there, poleaxed. She has no idea how long I've dreamed of the same. It all sounds so ... normal. Home. Anchors. And I realize that in the space of two days together, Éolie has become my anchor. I hope she never plans on leaving. She'd have a hard time doing it alone.

The small dining room at L'Hôtel is crowding me in tonight. I feel our blond-haired waiter's eyes covertly following Éolie's every move. He's another twenty-something guy, and he's been hovering all night near our table, grating on my nerves. I absently listen to the conversation taking place between Éolie and Monsieur François, fiddling with my coffee cup.

"Mademoiselle Éolie, je vous attends sans faute lundi matin." Monsieur François bows his regal head, chock-full of snow-white hair, confirming their cooking lessons next Monday morning.

"Thank you so much, it really means a lot to me," she beams up at him, glowing.

There's a thud and small grunt, and I turn, seeing our red-faced waiter straightening an upturned chair at the next table. Where a lone middle-aged man, I vaguely remember seeing somewhere else, sits motionless, his fork suspended in mid-air, the both of them gaping at Éolie.

The dining room's conversations die out for a moment, and then slowly resume.

"Are you all right?" Éolie asks, concern clouding her eyes.

"Yes," they both answer at the same time, and her head tilts.

"Totally fine," the waiter assures her, before scrambling towards the kitchen.

"Well, that settles that," I say under my breath. This place employs a shitload of eligible males tripping over themselves to get Éolie to notice them.

Monsieur François looks on, fingers tapping on his mouth. "I'll probably have a slew of volunteers lined up for the breakfast shifts, begging for kitchen duties on Mondays and Wednesdays once it gets out you'll be here," he says, clearly entertained.

"Awesome," I growl through clenched teeth, a surprising surge of bright-yellow lava pooling in my guts. Monsieur François gives me a sidelong glance. I know. I know. *Calm the fuck down, man.* Protectiveness is one thing, but possessiveness is quite another. I loosen my fists, brushing my hands a few times on my thighs to relax my fingers. I breathe through my nose, willing myself to shift gears, and curb down on the jealous streak I didn't know I had ... Jesus.

"I'd want to listen in too if I worked here," Éolie candidly says, genuinely pleased. "I don't know how to thank you for your lessons."

Monsieur François chuckles under his breath, giving me a light pat on the shoulder. "And she only has eyes for you," he says low, clearing my dessert plate. I nod, my chest expanding. *He's right, she does. The rest is up to you, man...*

"Mademoiselle Éolie, you're delightful, as always, but truly, there's no need to thank me, it's my pleasure," Monsieur François says, lips tugging up on one side as one of his age-spotted hands takes her plate. "I'll be there Monday morning, every step of the way, don't you worry," he adds, and we share a look of understanding. "Besides—" this he says to her, "—it will give me a chance to reminisce about my good old days teaching at l'Institut de Tourisme et d'Hôtellerie du Québec, and talk your ears off about Montréal."

"Montréal?" I ask him, the question popping out, remembering her note to check train schedules.

"Montréal is just a little something we share, n'est-ce pas?" He winks at Éolie, and she shoots him one of her lethal smiles. "Allez hop," Monsieur François says, giving our plates to one of the busboys. "Bonne fin de soirée vous deux, full moon out tonight, enjoy," he finishes on one last wink, wishing us a good evening.

"He's so kind, and we get along so well," Éolie says, watching him stop by a few tables on his way out, wishing goodnight to the few remaining patrons.

I'm relieved to know Éolie will be well looked after here, on her own, while I'm on campus. But to be perfectly honest, I'm even more relieved that it's by Monsieur François' grandfatherly figure, and none other.

"So what's with Montréal?" I ask her, my curiosity piqued, and her eyes dart back to mine.

"Believe it or not, both Monsieur François and I were born there, funnily enough. Although I was just a few weeks old when we all got back on the Thalassa, and I never really visited, Montréal happens to be our very own little French corner of the world," she says, eyes shining. "And I've always wanted to go back, and take in the sights. I don't know why, but it's like a pull."

"Really?" I ask, plans already loosely forming in my head.

"Really. The couple of times we went down the St. Lawrence Seaway, we stayed on the Thalassa in the Port of Montreal, and that's about it."

"Then we'll have to do something about that once the semester's over, and go to Montréal," I say, covering her hands with mine, and she beams up at me.

"I like the 'we' part," she replies softly, "even more than the Montréal one."

"I like that you like," I say, leaning in.

It's not that I was unhappy before now, I realize, it's more like ... I wasn't really happy either. Not like this. And I find it addictive. And as I watch the look of pure joy spreading over Éolie's face, I vow to put it there as often as possible.

"Would you like some more coffee or green tea?" our waiter asks, bursting our bubble. Éolie looks at me questioningly, and I shake my head.

"Not tonight." She smiles up to him, and he stills. "But thank you for offering."

I walk over to Éolie, and put my hand on the small of her back, guiding her towards the exit, and our walk back ocean side.

My head dips, and I whisper in her ear. "Your beams are lethal."

Confusion flickers on her face. "My beams?" she asks. "What are you talking about?"

"Haven't you noticed?"

"Noticed what?" she asks.

"Nothing," I say.

"And I'm the strange one?" She shakes her head, taking my hands into hers.

"You're so lovely," I murmur.

Twenty-Six

LIAM

Back at the condo, I watch as she unzips one side of her duffel, revealing neatly folded clothes. So Very-Organized-Éolie, I note with a private smile. I'm absurdly pleased to know that little quirk of hers.

Selecting her demure white cotton nightdress along with her small toiletry bag, she shyly points to the en suite bathroom.

"You don't have to ask for anything, not here, not with me," I say.

She shuts the door behind her. The shower comes on, and it takes everything in me not to follow her inside. Pinching the bridge of my nose, I debate going for a dip in the ocean.

Je suis, tu es, il est, nous sommes, vous êtes, ils sont. Que j'eusse été, que tu eusses été ... such an idiot. The bed.

I push it against the glass wall of our bedroom, satisfied she'll be able to nest in comfort near the great outdoors. *Our bedroom.* My mind splinters on the thought. The water shuts off, and shortly thereafter the door reopens.

I frown. She looks completely done in, even though it's not even nine yet, exhaustion once more tightening her delicate features. She's usually so vibrant that's it's easy for me to forget that she just went through a lot, and that she needs to recoup her energy and take it easy.

"Come," I punctuate with a soft kiss on her forehead. "It's lights out for you, young lady." I gesture to the bed and her lips part, mapping her delight.

She gives me a warm hug. "I know it's too early for you to go to bed yet, night owl that you are, but ... could you stay with me until I fall asleep?" she asks, holding on.

"I'm not going anywhere," I whisper against her hair. "I'll hold you all night. I won't let go." *Every night if you'll let me.* My hands gently stroke her face as I search her eyes. Balancing on my forearms, she gets up on the tip of her toes and she deposits a light kiss on the corner of my mouth, lingering for a second longer.

"Tuck me in?" she asks and I nod.

My heart pounds in my ears as I arrange the covers around her. Fingers of one hand splayed on the glass wall, eyes on the night sky, she whispers, "Je t'envoie de beaux rêves, Liam." I brush my lips on her forehead, and she settles down, burrowing deeper underneath the comforter, and just like that, she's fast asleep.

I turn off the light and undress, reluctantly going through my own night ablutions, downsizing them to a bare minimum.

My eyes search but there's no trace of her anywhere in the bathroom, and I'm suddenly afraid she's not really here, with me. I put on some sort of pajama bottoms, not bothering with anything else, hurrying out.

I slump against the wall; she's still there, abandoned to deep slumber. "Éolie, please don't let go of me," I whisper into the night.

I lie down next to her, as quietly as possible. Unable to resist, I gather her close to me, my front to her back, careful not to wake her up. To my delight, she snuggles closer. For the first time ever, I am not repulsed by the intimacy of sleeping with someone. I welcome it. I tighten my arms protectively around her.

Overcome by gratitude, I'm suddenly slammed by the notion that maybe, I too, finally belong.

For the very first time in seventeen years ... I promptly fall asleep.

Twenty-Seven

ÉOLIE

I rouse from sleep. A ray of early-morning sun shines down on me, and I stretch my arms over my head and smile, welcoming the day, rejuvenated by a full night's sleep. I open my eyes quickly, breath catching. Liam.

I turn on my side and there he is, sound asleep. I exhale and smile anew. Propping my head up on my hand, I stare, pulse picking up. Lying on his back, one arm thrown over his head, bare-chested, covers bunched at the waist, he takes my breath away. And I'm tempted to let my lips explore the hard planes of his chest and toned abs.

My breaths grow shallow, my skin turns hot, and I've this new itch I don't quite know how to scratch. But I resist the urge to touch him; he looks so peaceful. I sit on my heels, carefully rearranging the blankets around him. He stirs slightly but settles again. His handsome features are more boyish-looking in repose, more vulnerable in sleep. I prop my pillows up against the glass wall, hoping it will prevent the rising sun from waking him too soon.

On bare feet, I make my way to the middle of the bedroom as I search for my duffel. With the bed propped against the wall, it looks even larger and it's a bit intimidating, but it makes for one great open space. Perfect for yoga asanas. I grin. I can't seem to stop grinning at every little thing this morning, feeling lighthearted. And I love this silly, in-love version of me.

I'm startled out of my thoughts by a loud, imperious banging on the front door. I scramble out, checking one last time that Liam's still sleeping before quietly closing the bedroom door. I hurry over. On top of the strong, staccato beatings is a muffled shout, definitely male, and vaguely familiar. "Liam, open up, man." Without thought, I swing the door wide open, with equal urgency.

"Zac?" I cry out incredulously. "It's really you," I beam, hugging him. "Flying for real now?" I say, taking in his flight suit.

"What the f—" he gapes, just sort of frozen there, with one knuckled hand still raised. So I grab him by the arm, leading him in. It's surprisingly easy. I pull, he mindlessly follows.

"He's got a girl in there?" I hear another man say from behind Zac.

"No way."

"No shit."

"Oh. Theo. Yann. P.O." I exclaim, noticing them now that Zac's no longer filling up the entire doorway. "Look at you all ... I can hardly believe it," I babble on, still unbelieving.

I greet them all over again. I hug them once more. I kiss cheeks, right and left, my face still stuck on beaming. I'm that happy to see them all here. They're still close friends after all this time. That first year, they welcomed Liam into their inner circle at boarding school with such generosity of spirits, never letting go. And for that simple act of kindness, they'll always hold a very special place in my heart.

"Where's Leo?" I finally ask. And that's when I notice, like really notice, that they're all still frozen there. Oops. I forgot. My eyes grow wide, and I slap my hands over my mouth.

"Christ, Liam's gone off the deep end," Theo says, blanching.

What?

They huddle near the door to confer, either unconcerned or unaware that I'm standing right there, behind them. And that I can hear everything they're saying.

"C'mon, chillax. It's just a morning after, no biggie," Zac says.

"No way that one's a book bunny," P.O. says.

A book bunny?

"There's no fucking way he'd bring one up to his lair. He rented all three units of this condo complex just to avoid the company," Theo says, scowling. "She's not a book bunny. She's way worse."

Worse?

"How'd she know us?" Yann mutters, and I practically hear gears grinding in his head.

"He caved in, that's why. She's that Rose chick, he must have told her about us," Theo rants, shoving his hands through his hair. I inwardly cringe. There goes Rose again. "Fuck. Look at her. Is she even legal? What's with him? He knows better."

"He lasted longer than I would have," Zac says, crossing his arms, propping one shoulder on the wall, smirking.

P.O. slaps him upside the head. "Zac, get out of the jungle for a few. The girl's standing right there," he says. He turns to me. "Don't mind them, they were raised by wolves. Where's Liam?" he asks.

"He's still sleeping," I say. "And he needs it."

"I'd need it too—" Zac grunts, elbowed by Theo.

"Stop it. You'll wake him up, you're *way* too loud," I whisper forcefully.

They squint at me as though I just spoke Martian.

Snickers make the rounds anyway. I cross my arms and narrow my eyes, waiting them out.

"What he needs is to get his ass in here, pronto," Theo says, scowling anew as he starts down the hall, and I run past him, blocking his way.

"No," I whisper furiously, bracing my arms on either side of the corridor's walls leading to the bedroom nook, preventing him from stepping out of the main room. "He's exhausted, leave him be."

The bedroom door bangs open and I nearly jump out of my skin. "What's with you?" Liam blurts, pulling a grey tee over his head. "It's not even bloody six in the morning. What are you doing here?"

"What's with us? What's gotten into you?" Theo says vehemently, pointing to me.

Liam ignores him, taking me by the shoulders, searching my eyes. "You all right?" he asks, and I nod. He drops his forehead to mine, breathing out a sigh. "I got worried with you gone," he says, gentle fingers brushing back tendrils of loose hair behind my ear. I hug him tight, breathing him in. His full lips are warm and soft as he deposits on my forehead one of the most adoring kisses ever. And my stomach flips.

He gently spins me around, keeping me close to his chest, arms encircling me protectively as we face the pack.

"Guys, meet Éolie," he says, gesturing with his arm. "Éolie, the guys."

Not a muscle moves—except that their jaws open even wider now as they stare back at me.

His GGS pals are fully, completely, utterly frozen in shock.

Every single one of them.

Twenty-Eight

LIAM

I look at Éolie, stunning in her state of disheveled, and in all honesty, I can't really blame them for being thunderstruck. Long, curly tendrils of white-gold hair escapees from her once neat braid, give her a sensual air of tousled.

"Zac!" I exclaim, noticing him propped beside the front door. "You what, just flew the Piper straight out of the jungle to pick them up?". His current thrill might be flying helicopters, but the twin-engine Piper Comanche is Zac's pride and joy, and we rarely find one without the other.

Zac comes out of shock ahead of the others, as per usual. As our resident adrenaline junkie, his nerves are probably pure steel by now. "Don't mind me, I'm just the getaway pilot," he says wryly. "Did I heard right?" he asks, locking eyes with me.

I keep my arms secured around her, and I just know I'm grinning like a loon. "You did. She's Éolie," I manage to say. "And Rose." They continue to stand as stock still as salt pillars, spread out in the large open floor room of the condo, the same astonished look washing over all four faces. "Éolie, I don't know what they're doing here so early, but these guys are my—"

"Blood brothers. Zac, Theo, P.O., Yann, and Leo's missing," she says simply.

"Did you introduce yourselves already?" I ask, furrowing my brows, looking between her and them. The guys give me the same weird look, then stare at Éolie.

"Christ, Liam. Did she just drop out of the sky, or what?" Theo exclaims, and I give him a look that says *later*. "Éolie ... and Rose? How is that possible?" he asks, worry lines forming across his forehead.

"It's a long story," I respond, dropping a kiss on top of Éolie's head, and her hands curl over my arms, squeezing lightly.

"Is that why you couldn't call to tell us you found her?" Yann asks, frowning.

"Hey, c'mon. Gimme a break. I had other things on my mind the last couple of days," I reply, my voice tighter than usual carrying across the room, annoyed by his peeved tone. "Besides, she found me."

"Explains why you never answered your phone." P.O. crosses his arms over his chest. He turns to Zac. "Tell me again why we worried about him," he mutters.

My phone? When was the last time I even saw that—?

"Shit." I stride over to the back door, yanking it open and stepping onto the balcony. My phone's still lying on the chaise longue, light dew pearling on it. Thank god it's only late September with pretty mild temperatures at night still, or I'd be holding an ice cube for sure right now. I wipe it hastily on my sweats and turn it back on. My screen lights up, looking none the worse for wear as it displays the date and time, and then, finally, my notifications. I've thirteen missed calls, and just about twice the same amount of unread text messages. I scroll quickly as I make my way back inside, where the others wait. I delete all messages from Sean, not bothering with them, and hastily read through the others. The guys took turns calling and texting, their worry growing more pronounced over the last twenty-four hours. Bloody hell.

"I forgot about my phone being turned off outside," I tell them, holding it up now as proof. "I had no idea my going off the grid for a day or two would cause so much worry," I add, rubbing the back of my neck.

"You can't be half as surprised as we are right now, man," Theo says.

I sigh heavily. After some ten days of ongoing, constant communication over our mass manhunt for Éolie, my silence would surely be worrisome. And I realize I owe them more of an explanation. "Sean called the other night, and I almost smashed the damn thing," I say, shoving one hand through my hair.

"Sean?" P.O. repeats, his surprise shifting instantly to concern.

"Christ," Zac curses under his breath.

I can feel Éolie's confused and curious gaze on me, but I don't look over.

"He wants those rights pretty bad then to bypass everyone, and go straight at you," Theo says, narrowing his eyes, and I pinch the bridge of my nose.

It's way too early in the morning to think about the prick without at least a few cups of something strong. With that in mind, I head for the coffeepot. Now, I just need to figure out how it works. "He can want them for all I care, not selling, the end." The rights to Eiloe, my inter-galactic saga, pronounced Halo and derived from Éolie's name spelled backward is my own universe, and are not for sale and never will be.

"What'd you expect, that he'd just forfeit?" Yann huffs. "The arsehole did make Most Abominable Father of the Year what, eight consecutive times?"

"Yeah well, we're not sixteen anymore," P.O. says, eyes intent on me.

We all share a look.

Éolie crosses over to me, eyes growing concerned. "I'll let you discuss whatever He-Who-Shall-Not-Be-Named did this time around with your GGS pals."

We all stare at Éolie. "How do you know about us, let alone about GGS?" Yann asks, eyes entirely focused on her now. "It's fascinating. Not only are you for real, but we didn't know Liam when you two met. Did you know that?"

Éolie nods.

I still. "You really know them?" I ask.

She nods.

"Talk about irony, she knows me, man," P.O. says under his breath. Not being able to find even one trace of her is a first for P.O., and I know it pinched his ego hard. He yanks a counter stool from the kitchen island, and straddles it backward. "How's that possible, Éolie?" he asks, confusion written all over his face.

"Who cares, P.O., she's here now." Zac says, propping his shoulder on the kitchen wall next to him. "Éolie, you're some sort of legend in our group. Own it."

"Well, legend or not, she knows us, and I'd like to know how. Éolie, let's hear it straight from the source," Theo says, leaning one hip on the kitchen island, crossing his arms. "What's the story?"

"I need to sit," she says in a small voice, folding down right there on the floor by the glass wall facing the kitchen.

"Éolie?" I ask, unsure, crouching down in front of her. I take her hands, and she feels a bit clammy. And she's as white as, well, her nightgown, and I don't like it one bit.

"I don't feel so good," she says, closing her eyes. "I've a touch of hypoglycemia that's acting up. Just give me a minute, it'll pass."

"Zac," I say as calmly as I can, my worry growing by leaps and bounds.

He takes one look at her before turning on his heels, coming back seconds later with a bottle of green goop juice. "Whoa. Fresh fruits and organic wheatgrass juice in your fridge, man? Your condo came with room service spa edition, or what?" he asks, eyebrows shooting up.

"We bought them at the grocery store in town," Éolie says quietly.

"Grocery—?" I hear Theo choke, and a fit of coughing and muffled thumping follows behind me. I cut them a narrow-eyed look over my shoulder, and they hold up their hands.

"Your blood sugar levels are probably low," Zac says, crouching down in front of her, going into medic mode, offering up the bottle of juice. "Drink up, and we'll take it from there."

"Thanks," she says, drinking up, her colors returning. I narrow my eyes on her, and she shrugs, shaking her head. "I heal more quickly than normal, but it doesn't mean I'm on turbo boost all the time, or that I cure all symptoms by myself," she explains to me.

"Got it."

And I swear I'll stock up on fresh produce from now on, and I'll make sure she eats, and I'll make sure she hydrates properly, and I'll check the pharmacy, and I'll ... breathe through my nose. I've never had anything to lose before, and the flip side of that coin is suddenly scaring me shitless. My heart hammers in my chest and she puts one hand over it, the warmth of her palm seeping through my tee, calming me.

She sits straighter, facing us all.

"I know you all know about me, but..." she states the fact quietly to herself. She fidgets with her fingers, swallows and takes a few deep breaths. "It's just. I'm not sure how you'll take how I came to know about all of you."

She brings her knees up, demurely pulling her nightgown over her legs. Her arms fold around her bended knees, her chin coming to rest on top, and she stares at the floor, worrying her bottom lip. She looks so young and vulnerable. My chest constricts.

"Éolie, whatever it is, you're safe with us." I tip her chin up.

"You are," Theo vows, and the three others chorus. "And even though Leo can't be reached for now, we'll vouch for him as well."

"I know. It's not that, I trust you," she says, her limpid gaze sweeping past me to the four of them. "But you'll have to keep an open mind, and so will Leo once he learns." And we all share a look, nodding back at her.

She clears her throat and starts over. "For you to understand, I need to go back to the awful night that vile woman almost succeeded in killing Liam. I had a difficult time healing him through our connection like the other times. Everything was happening too fast, and his injuries were ... extensive," she says, swallowing hard. "I became hysterical as I felt his life force weakening into nothing." Her fingers come up and gently trace the jagged scar on my elbow. The only injury that remained partially healed when I got rescued. I take her hand and bring it up to my lips, dropping a kiss on her open palm. She cups my cheek, her hand radiating heat. I lean into it, and close my eyes.

I'm lost in a collage of long-ago images and sensations. Coming in and out of pain, shattered limbs, bones sticking out, my shallow breathing, the Monster passed out beside me, and then, Light. Blue Light.

"It just happened, don't ask me how. I projected out of my body, and simply healed Liam with the touch of my ... glowing blue fingertips," she says, her eyes brimming over with turbulent emotions, transfixed on my scar. "My body stayed behind, in a state of coma, and I couldn't find my way back to it for the longest time." She glances down at the floor then back up at her rapt audience. "So ... I was sort of there with all of you, during Liam's first year at boarding school."

Holy Mother of God.

"Sort of there, how?" Zac asks, elbows leaning on the kitchen island.

"Well, not physically, but I could see you all, feel you," she explains. "Sort of on another plane," she adds with a wry smile at Zac. His lips upturn in the ghost of a smile.

P.O. wears an arrested look, and Yann's face lights up like a thousand-watt bulb. And knowing him, he's probably getting all worked up over some quantum physics phenomena.

"Coma? For how long exactly?" Theo asks, unblinking, bringing me out of my thoughts and back to reality.

"You stayed with me that whole year, didn't you?" I guess, and her eyes dart back to mine. I bring one hand up to her face, stroking her cheek with my thumb.

She leans into my touch, nodding, and her eyes grow luminous. "Yes ... practically attached to your hip, actually. And then I came back to myself. The connection broke."

"I'm not batshit crazy. I really did feel you at times," I say, recalling with fondness our nightly adventures in The Enchanted Forest of Laure. All my other quests afterwards were never quite as intense as the ones I cooked up that first year.

"Mortal. An infestation of little girl's cooties?" Zac says on a sly grin.

"At three, girls don't have cooties," she deadpans.

Zac chuckles under his breath. "Yeah, guess not." He takes a hand and scrubs it through what's left of his dark-brown hair, as he likes to shave it in a buzz cut more often than the stubbles on his face. "But man, Éolie. Boys at seven? Living in a pack? Must have been a hell of an eye-opener for a little girl."

"You have no idea," she replies feelingly, a small grin tugging at her lips, but we all more or less wince on her behalf.

She heaves a sigh of relief. "I'm so glad you're taking it so well. I wasn't sure you would."

"You're kidding, right?" Theo says drily. "We all grew up with Liam, here. Your story is garden-variety compared to any one of his."

"I'll take that as a compliment," I say, pulling Éolie up off the floor. "But if you must know, the Forest of Laure backdrop I used for my *Tales from the Enchanted Forest* is all on her, compliment of my little seer here."

"Wait, you mean she sent you all those story ideas?" Zac turns to Éolie before I can answer. "On that first quest I was turned into a lizard. How could you?"

"Don't look at me." She wiggles a finger in my direction. "I had no say at all. I was literally in the middle of nowhere that year."

"Hey, not my fault, man. You couldn't spell *wizard*." I reply, holding my hands up, and we all end up snickering.

"Anyway," Éolie says, walking over to the kitchen island. "All I did was share the images that came to me. This place I saw. I can't claim any ownership of the enchanted part of the forest nor its tall tales; it's all Liam's boundless imagination that sprouted those."

"Boundless. Don't we know it," Theo deadpans, and I smirk. I really did a number on them more often than not.

"This forest place you saw, you mean as in visions?" P.O. asks, and she nods bashfully. "Awesome."

"So? You really did heal Liam with some kind of connection you two had, didn't you?" Zac asks her, quietly awed. "Can you do that with anyone?"

"No, I can't. Except for Liam, when we were kids, that is," Éolie says, looking down at her hands. "My body's self-healing responses are abnormally quick ... I was born that way."

"This is seriously cool. What was it like when you were with us?" Yann asks, his usual stern features coming alive with barely contained excitement as he plops down on a kitchen stool next to P.O.

"You mean being there, but unable to act on it?" Éolie says, hands bracing on either side of the counter. "Pretty frustrating. But all at once, incredible, amazing, enlightening for a three-year-old. I soaked up knowledge with you guys, like really way ahead of my time. I could read and do sums when I finally woke up, you know."

"That's pretty cool. Any other interesting things you learned?" Theo asks, scratching his jaw, giving me a sidelong glance.

"At seven? Man, not what you're thinking—" I say and the guys snicker.

I roll my eyes.

"You mean besides thirty-two wacky excuses not to wash behind your ears, Theo?" Éolie says knowingly.

He lets out a short bark of laughter. "I forgot how creative we were," he replies, still chuckling. "Zac, in particular."

"Me?" Zac snorts. "The only thing I did was run like hell in the other direction at shower time."

"Yeah, you did, naked ass bared," P.O. says, and we all start laughing.

Man, so many memories. Éolie's bringing out the seven-year-olds in all of us.

"Remember Herr Vorberger, and Yann's way too many 'studies show' excuses?" I recall, seeing all over again our dorm supervisor's dour face, and stiff posture. We never could sway him. "Yann never made it far either."

"I wonder why?" Theo says sarcastically.

"Beats me," Yann says, his lips twitching. "Studies show that having germs festering behind your ears is actually beneficial to some individuals."

"And clearly I'm not one of those who benefits. I do need to wash behind my ears," Éolie says over her shoulder, amusement bleeding into her tone. "So, I'll take that as my cue to go shower and dress, and let you guys have at it." She presses a quick kiss on my cheek and saunters out.

My eyes follow her down the hall. Man, I love that girl.

P.O. busies himself with the coffee maker. He lives on the brew, or for the brew, hard to tell sometimes. While the other guys listen, I recount Éolie's appearance on campus; was it only a week ago, last Friday? And the series of events—dare I say unfortunate—that led me to believe she was Rose, a student … And I put them up to speed by outlining the rest. And, somehow, it grounds me a bit more in this new reality. For once, my reality's enchantingly better than my imaginary worlds ever were. Thrilling and terrifying all at once. I get a new line, a new paragraph, a new chapter, but no rewrites on the manuscript of my life.

"Éolie's for real. Would Dr. Englehart have a cow over that one, or what?" Theo says, a wicked grin forming on his lips.

"Don't remind me. He couldn't get that I was way more upset over losing Éolie than by the events themselves," I say, remembering BIA's uppity therapist I had to see for two long years. "I didn't fit into any of his neat little boxes of denials."

"True dat," Zac agrees. "How does it feel knowing you've never been batshit crazy?" The condescending idiot pats me on the head, and is quick enough to back off before I can grab his arm to, quite literally, get him out of my hair. He laughs, and I scowl as I come up empty-handed.

"What's next for you?" P.O. asks.

"Aside from not letting her out of your sight, he means," Zac deadpans, shoulder leaning on a wall with a steaming mug from P.O.

"Yeah well, god knows when I'll be able to do that without wondering if I dreamed her up. I'm still integrating that she's for real," I admit, amazed all over again.

"Remember our search for the Normal Kingdom?" P.O. says, going for a fist bump with his free hand, and sliding me a coffee with the other. "I'll bet you're getting there, man. Just like we swore we would at seven."

"We did, didn't we?" I stare off, thinking of the pact the six of us made once, long ago, in the dead of the night, in our room at Berlinger. We were Knights of the Laure driven by our search for the Normal Kingdom, better known as Home, straight out the Enchanted Forest of Laure. Little did I know Éolie would be a real possibility in my future back then. But how I wished for it though. "I want it all. Love. Family. Normal. With her. That much I know," I say with conviction. "But I'm still working on it, and it's by the seat of my pants." I shake my head.

"And something tells me you'll be busy with that for the next little while," Theo says wryly, motioning to Zac. "And that you don't need us cramping your style."

"Well, now that you mention it," I reply, giving them a pointed look.

"This is your pilot speaking," Zac says in his best commercial airline voiceover. "We're leaving at the gate Late Blooming Liam, boarding flight to the wilds of Boston's night life as of now." He gestures at the others. "C'mon, boys. I'm ready for take-off. Let's hit the sky, time's a wasting." He struts out the door.

"Yeah, get to it, man. I want to copy your notes when you have it all figured out," Theo says, clapping my shoulder. "Say bye to the missus," he adds, chuckling under his breath, following Zac.

"Send a postcard when you reach Normal, man." P.O. backs away, fingers snapping a sharp salute.

"Do you think Éolie could give me a rundown on all of her abilities for analysis?" Yann asks, his eyes already glazing over as he undoubtedly calculates quantum leap's equations.

I stare him down, crossing my arms.

"Try and prepare to die," I utter one of our old gaming Calls to Arms, and I'm only half-jesting.

Realization passes through his eyes, and I see the exact moment it connects to everything I just briefed them on, pertaining to Éolie's slip under radar.

"Christ. I was ready to put her under a microscope for a minute there, wasn't I? Sorry, man. Sometimes, I even scare myself with my thought process," he says, eyes bulging, pulling at his hair, giving him the look of a mad scientist. And I can't help it. I chuckle under my breath.

"MathMan, shut your brains off for a few. Go. Get. Girls," Zac says, coming back in to pull him out.

"Yeah, think I need it," Yann says.

Zac motions with his head, backing away.

I turn.

Éolie's standing on the other side of the room. Truly alive, incredibly safe and sound. A fully-grown, beauty-infused Éolie, no less...

I hear the click of the door closing at my back.

"They left ... early." She drops her eyes to my mouth, wetting her lips.

"Yes," I reply, my voice growing husky.

She brushes a stray lock of hair behind her ear with nervous fingers. "Do you want to go back to bed?" she asks, her voice tentative, a flush rising from her neck to the root of her hair. Her eyes drop to the column of my throat, and then flit back up to mine.

"Do you?"

My heart leaps in my chest. The rest of me? Stiffens to hard steel in an instant.

"I just want to kiss you. Like really kiss you," she says, biting her bottom lip, driving me half-insane with barely contained lust. But I need to make sure she knows what this means.

I lean back against the door, hands tucked into the front pockets of my jeans, and stare.

"Éolie, you'll have to be the one to stop when you've had your fill, because ... I won't. I want you, bad." I shake my head. This might kill me. "I promised as slow as you need, and you're still recovering—"

"It's morning now. And I've had a pretty good night's sleep. The first since the storm. I don't need slow right now. I need you."

"You sure?" My eyes are fixed on hers, burning my message across the room. Éolie's gaze now firmly trapped within mine, I slowly straighten.

God, her eyes are telling me all I need know.

And Late Blooming Liam suddenly has some catching up to do.

Twenty-Nine

LIAM

Sweet Lord, yes. Desire brightens Éolie's deliciously blooming features, a delicate bud about to unfurl. Mine.

My heart's just about ready to come out my chest as I cross the room and reach for her, hands trembling with anticipation. I frame her delicate face, trying to memorize her utter exquisiteness as she leans into my touch.

Éolie's eyes, full of innocent awe, follow the gentle press of her fingertips on my lips, unhurriedly tracing their contours as if mapping her way to treasures unknown. Unable to resist, I press an ardent kiss on a passing finger, and her lips smile, full of wonder.

I slowly lean into her, and breathe her in.

I savor the honeyed flavor of her skin as I kiss my way from the curve of her jaw to the back of her neck. "What was it you asked me to do? Oh, yes. Kiss you blind," I murmur close to her ear, holding her up to me. She clings, exhaling on a soft moan. My lips, with a will of their own, lightly press on hers once, twice ... then again. Her lips soften in welcome to mine, melting into me. Her innocent delight shatters me.

I willingly let her explore, setting the pace. Sultry, divine, addictive lips seek mine then retreat, experimenting. She sighs, pressing closer still, implicitly seeking more.

Then and only then, do I allow myself a slow run of my tongue along her lower lip, eliciting another breathy sigh that has my already shaky control teetering. My first taste is not nearly enough.

My body hums, pulsing with life. My lips tease hers, gently nibbling, then intensely nipping along, enticing Éolie to follow and take, before I go insane with lust. *Take, Éolie, take.*

On a moan, Éolie's mouth suddenly crashes into mine, gifting me with its delicious reward. She devastates me. Tongues coalesce in a dance as old as time, infusing lust. Passion ignites.

I cup her bottom and lift her up and she instantly locks her legs around my waist. "Éolie, just say when and I'll—" I try to speak between wild nibbles on her neck, willing myself to slow down, willing myself to stop, but I can't, not just yet. Head thrown back, her mewls are overriding my control, keeping me on the brink.

I deposit her gently on the bed, fully intending to untangle myself and put some distance between us, but she holds on to my neck and I'm yanked until I crash over her. I reflexively roll, bringing her on top of me, taking the brunt of our fall.

"I want to feel this with you, all of it," she breathes, tugging on my tee, her small hands brushing up my back, and I roll her underneath me, pinning her down.

"Éolie," I whisper in the crook of her neck. My pulse hammers. I'm trying to slow down, to savor her and this moment, but I need this, need her, need us, too much. I want to take her, claim her, make her mine. I want to cover every inch of her skin with my mouth.

"Liam…" she whimpers, her body heedlessly rocking into mine, and my control snaps.

Clothes are shed in a flurry of limbs, but the sudden touch of skin against skin calms our earlier furor down to a simmer. Endless, languorous explorations of hands and lips ensue. Every caress, every movement, turns excruciatingly slow.

Until her mouth crashes down on mine again, on a deep-throated moan.

In no time at all, Éolie's artless sensuality whips my desire back into a white-hot pulsing. I press her hard against my rigid shaft and she naturally arches into me.

Exhaling on a groan, I let loose on my urgent need to consume her whole.

"*Je t'aime, je t'aime, je t'aime,*" Éolie's internal shouts play on a loop, my mind inscribing on my heart her heartfelt mantra as she comes apart in my arms. And this time it's not a whisper in passing. I hear it loud and clear in my head. And I have a hunch we're re-connecting when riding on strong, emotional peaks.

"I want you to let go, with me," she says, bringing her lips up to my chest.

"Oh, I will," I whisper.

Éolie's pristine beauty is strikingly enhanced by this new tousled, contented look. A look I intend to see often. She is magnificent in the throes of ecstasy.

My lips and tongue hungrily tease, nibbling kisses along her neck in a caress meant to arouse her all over again. She lets out a low whimper that whips my blood up a notch.

My seeking mouth trails a string of slow kisses along her honeyed skin. She stirs on a soft moan and arches against me.

I kiss her neck and then the swell of her breast, dropping my mouth to the erect bud of her nipple. My tongue slowly circles, then greedily suckles on one tight bud, then the other. She gasps and arches her back again, and waves of heat floods down my thickening erection, making me twitch.

Tongue and lips pursue their voyage of discovery downward, trailing down her taut belly, over the swell of her hips, reaching her core. My tongue latches onto the little nubbin of my final destination, in turn lapping, laving, sucking on it, and she lets out a startled cry, and bucks. My hands firmly anchoring her, I let go and devour her into all-out bliss, her high, keening cries an aphrodisiac, arousing me to fever pitch.

My heart trips and slams in my chest. "Look at me, Éolie," I say, and she slowly opens her eyes, their light aqua bleeding into a darker blue full of unleashed desire. "You're mine. I'm making you mine … deeply, completely mine…"

I slide forward into the tight, wet heat of her body. My eyes clench shut. So wet, so tight … I pant as I force myself to stay still as the walls of her sex adjust, embracing half my length. A trickle of sweat tracks down my back.

"*Yours, yours, yours,*" she chants in my head and I throb, half-sheathed inside her warm pulsing core, her incantation leaving me insane with want.

My limbs are shaking, I feel so raw and primal. Ready to take and plunder and yet, I loathe to inflict any kind of pain.

She mewls, mindlessly thrusting upward, pulling me in deeper. "Yours," she whimpers out loud, both undoing me and giving me the fortitude to breach her in one quick thrust, her quivering muscles pulling me forward until I'm lodged as deep as possible.

"Liam," she cries out, her breath coming in sharp pants. I bury my mouth in her hair to silence my own cry.

My body's in sensory overload, unable to move quite yet or process this level of intense sensation.

"More, yours, please," she breathes feverishly.

"Mine," I grit, my forehead pressing into the crook of her neck as I thrust into her once. And I almost lose it, letting the massive wave of pleasure break over me.

She gasps and shudders, and her ankles slide up my legs and lock behind my back, but if anything, I swell harder. Her Light pulses bright in me, asking, demanding, needing, pleading, all at once, to fall over the edge with me.

Bodies moving as one, I let myself be pulled into a place of worship. And when Éolie soars, rocketing over the edge of bliss, her Light splintering into thousands of sparkling fragments, I follow her ecstasy right over, echoing on ... and on ... and on...

I'm overcome, blindsided. Underneath me, Éolie's cries fall silent.

Still joined as one, we lay quietly, catching our breath. And I willingly lose myself in this moment, eyes locked on my eternity.

Éolie gently threads her fingers through the damp hair sticking on my forehead, brushing it away. "Are you okay?" she asks softly, and I feel my lips curl up, and a low chuckle escapes.

"You're stealing my line," I say, bracing above her on my elbows. "I'm more than okay. I'm blown away. Wow ... just wow." I take a deep, shuddering breath before rolling to her side.

"It isn't always like this?" she whispers dreamily, her face soft and mellow. And I brush a light kiss on her lips then lean back to look into her eyes.

"No, not even close, Éolie-Jolie," I say emphatically, the small endearment I made up for her when we were kids slipping out without forethought. At one time when we talked, she used to qualify everything and nothing with the word "jolie," meaning pretty in French.

"You used to call me that," she ponders, her index gently tracing my lips, and I kiss it reverently. "No one else ever did."

"I'm glad Éolie-Jolie, it's ours … And I'm sorry all at once that no one else gave you little endearments," I say, possessiveness and protectiveness tugging me in both directions.

"Please don't be sorry," she says quietly, searching my eyes knowingly. "I had you."

I prop my head on my hand, my fingers trailing along the soft contours and silken textures of her cheeks, and jaw. "Then I won't," I declare. "Seriously though, are you okay?"

"Way better than okay," she says, eyes full of wonder again. "What you said about being blown away … Does it mean I felt your rapture on top of mine then?"

"I don't know about you, but I certainly felt yours, and it's awesome." I brush my lips on her forehead, stunned anew by the intense pleasure that released into my bloodstream, almost to the point of pain. "I heard you in my head, you know, when you were…" I trail off, letting the half-formed thought sink into me before voicing it.

"When I was? Lost in the moment, and found in you?" She hums softly, eyelids closing.

My heart flips. "Yeah … that." I kiss her temple. I cradle her head in the crook of my neck. She threads her legs through mine, resting one hand over my chest, cuddling close. I close my eyes, savoring the feel of her, snuggled next to me. "We may be linked by shared pleasure as well, you know, and not just by do-or-die circumstances."

Her hand brushes in a slow back in forth over my heart. "I liked your shared pleasure," she says softly, languidly. "But I'm not totally convinced. We'll have to test that theory again later," she adds with a sly grin.

"Oh, we will," I say. A slow grin forms on my lips, and her fingertips brush over them. I take her hand and drop a kiss on her knuckles before bringing it to rest over my heart. I don't think I've ever felt this contented before.

"Why am I sleepy and you're not?" she asks drowsily, and I pull the comforter over us.

"Shhhh. Sleep," I say, tenderly cuddling her close to me. "Just means I did it right."

Her breaths grow even, and her hand goes slack.

"I love you, Éolie-Jolie," I whisper.

Thirty

LIAM

I glance at Éolie one last time before slipping out the bedroom, leaving her quietly napping. I need to refuel, or there just won't be any round two when she wakes. And that won't do.

I'm wolfing down fresh plums like there's no tomorrow, which can only mean I'm hungrier than I thought, when I receive a quick, warm hug from behind.

"So, that's where you are," Éolie says. She reaches around and grabs one of the last plums before sauntering over to the fridge.

"Missed me, did you?" I ask in an appreciative tone of voice. "How long have you been up?"

"Just long enough to miss you," she sasses me right back.

"It's just a quick pit stop." I raise a brow, crossing my ankles, delighted to no end by all that she is. "I'm refuelling for round two. We have a brand-new theory to put to the test, remember? I figured every couple of hours, in between napping time, should do for a start."

"Oh? You're planning on turning addictive?" She raises a brow, challenging me, but her lips spread into a slow, sensual smile.

"Yep. That's the plan." My lips quirk up in a shameless grin of my own.

"Do your worst," she says, looking at me through her lashes.

"I'll do my best," I vow, cocking my head to the side, and she shakes her head at me. My gaze rakes her. I couldn't keep my eyes from roaming even if I wanted to.

Her hair's unbraided, and I see the full glory of her blonde tresses hitting her mid-back for the first time. She's wearing my sweater, and from the looks of things, not much else. I swallow, hunger for food forgotten.

She takes a bottle of carrot juice out, uncaps it, her lips open and ... *I'm in so much trouble.*

She puts her bottle down, reaching for strands of hair, already halfway through braiding them before I can stop her. My sweater moves up a few inches, baring her upper thighs. And I decide, who am I really to tell her how to do her hair?

"Speaking of worst, can I ask you something?" she asks, leaning on one hip against the cabinets, worrying her bottom lip with her teeth. I watch in helpless fascination as she bends sideways to pick her bottle up. The small movement leaves my sweater with no other choice than to strain and stretch, losing the battle and sliding off her shoulder.

"Anything..." I say; my mind is in a haze, pulled under by the live fantasy standing in front of me.

"What's worse than a book bunny?" she asks out of left field.

"...A crowd of book bunnies?" I answer without thought, and she gives me a look.

Okay, seriously. How's my brain supposed to process anything? I mean, look at her.

"You're even more cryptic than Theo. That's all you've got?" she says, upturning her eyes. Her hips lean on the sink cabinet as she washes her fruit, and I may or may not recover from the sight.

"Oh, I got plenty," I reply, taut and ready again.

Her luscious lips open and pearly whites take a bite of her plum. Then a flash of pink tongue comes out to lick the running juice. She stands before me, totally clueless about what she does to me.

She swallows her bite. "Plenty of what, book bunnies?" she asks with a mischievous glint in her eyes.

Wait. What's with the book bunnies thing? I blink, trying to clear my head enough to catch up to the conversation. Clearly, we're not on the same page here.

"What brought that on?" I ask, taking one step closer.

"Theo said I was way worse than a book bunny, earlier on, when he first saw me." She shrugs, and takes another bite of her fruit.

"Just goes to show Theo knows jack," I say, making a mental note to tell him off next time he calls. "Let me show you..." My stare is hot as it roams her skin in the second before I launch into motion, closing in where she stands wedged against the counter. My fingers curl around her ass, and I pull her to me, my hard-on pressing into her. Just when my lips are nothing but a whisper away from hers, I turn my face slightly and graze her cheek against my own. And I wallow in her shortness of breath.

"Show me?" she whimpers low.

"How far off the mark Theo is," I murmur in her ear. Pulling her up to sit on the counter, I anchor her between my legs, bending down, breathing her in. Her hands brace on my shoulders, and her head tilts back, coming to rest on the upper cabinets, giving me unrestrained access to her neck. My lips nibble on her skin as I pull her hips to the edge of the counter.

"Book bunnies are pieces of fluff. They're not even close to the intensity we have going here," I say, my thumbs circling on her upper thighs. "Intimate relations are my new favorite," I continue in between little kisses up her jaw, "and I'll show you by how much."

She moans low in her throat, and I grind her into me. "You have no clue—" I'm suddenly hit by my own cluelessness ... *Shit.*

"I'm such an idiot." I straighten, trying in vain to feel taller than a two-inch worm. *Man, I suck at this caring thing.* I forgot about condoms, and I never ever do. What does that say for me?

"What...?" Éolie blinks, eyes glazed over.

"Éolie ... I—" My suave side is quite unimpressed with my eloquence. Which is quite deflating. "I really lost it ... I never even thought about protection," I finally manage, rubbing the back of my neck, wincing. Bloody everlasting hell and back, we're in a pickle of my own doing. I take a step back, and shove my hands through my hair. "I'm so sorry."

"Protection? It's too late," she says, dazed, grasping me by the shoulders.

Yeah, don't I know it, I almost say but I'm not quick enough. "I told the Navy I was reuniting with the love of my life so, they shot me."

"They *what?*" I cry out, my thoughts running in all directions.

Brows suddenly clearing, she bursts out laughing.

"Sorry. Sometimes I think in French, and my brain wires are caught in the crossfire when English comes out," she finally says. "I meant I received a contraceptive injection, and it's good to go for the next three months."

A slow grin forms on my lips.

"So, no worries," she murmurs, staring at my lips, wetting her own. "I'm yours for the taking."

I brace my arms on either side of her, bending at the elbows. I slowly lower my lips to her ear, stopping short of kissing range. "Éolie? I plan to take. And take," I whisper, drinking in her sharply drawn breath.

Thirty-One

LIAM

Conventional time is losing all meaning. The weekend flew by. We mostly stayed in bed, talking, cuddling, making love, lazing, only coming out for short walks through Bar Harbor once or twice a day, mainly to eat.

By Monday morning, it's a toss-up as to who's the most addicted. We can hardly keep our hands off each other.

I pick Éolie up and swing her over my shoulder. She squeals as I walk back from the en suite where I caught up to her.

"No, stop." She swats my back, hiccupping on contained laughter as I head for the bed. "We'll be late. And it's for my first cooking lesson ever—cheese omelets, Monsieur François mentioned the other night—so we can't. And don't you have class at seven this morning?"

"Excuses, excuses. It's not even close to six yet, we have time," I growl, putting her down. On the other hand, come to think of it, it could have been my stomach that growled.

"No, we don't. You have no idea how long it took me to finally get up," she says over her shoulder. "It's hard to leave a warm bed this early. I deserve a medal. You're the best cuddling partner I've ever had."

"I'm the only cuddling partner you've ever had," I say, watching her enticing backside saunter away, before following her into the en suite.

"So? You happen to be the best," she replies smoothly, reaching for the hem of her nightgown. "And besides, there's no food in here. Aren't you starving? Cheese omelet at Monsieur François' anyone?"

"You had me at food. Go shower already so that we can get to it," I say, playfully thwacking her butt with a towel, before closing the door behind her. We'll never leave the place otherwise. I shake my head, half-tempted to stay in anyway.

We head out within minutes and much too soon to my liking, breakfast is over at Monsieur François's, and I'm standing in the back doorway of L'Hôtel's kitchen, kissing Éolie goodbye.

She grabs me by my coat, angling her head for one final aching kiss, and a restrained moan builds in my throat as our tongues meet. "You were so right. You're addictive," she groans, before pushing me out the door.

"Told you so," I say cockily, reluctantly backing away. "You sure you don't want me to pick you up here?"

"I'm sure. I'd rather walk beach side to campus anyway before our new round of grocery shopping. I'll meet you there." She leans on the partially closed door. "See you soon."

She blows me a kiss on her fingers, and I catch it with my hand. I gamely open my coat, and carefully stow the kiss I caught in my inside pocket for safekeeping. I feel like a complete cheeseball but I can't help myself. She chuckles, shaking her head at me, and I decide the idiotic gesture was worth it.

"See you soon," I say, but I don't get a move on until Monsieur François's kitchen door closes with a soft click.

Mind occupied by pleasant thoughts of her—mostly pleasant thoughts of her and me naked—I unlock the door to my assigned amphitheater just a few minutes before seven.

"Someone sure got some," I hear one of my students mumble in passing.

He catches me listening in and reddens, but I just chuckle, shocking the hell out of him. "Some? You know nothing, man," I say under my breath.

I switch on the lights and walk down to the lectern, getting busy preparing the last of today's lecture. Students filing in are either getting used to the hour, or a storm is brewing. They're rowdier than usual, I absently note. I open my laptop, and laugh out loud.

Don't mind me I'm just a little side note
who'll stick around until class ends.

I unpeel the note, and laugh at finding another one underneath it.
You peeled me off?

To my amusement, I find another one underneath.
Please keep me.
See, I've this soft spot for the teacher.
Miss him already.
xxx

I pocket the first two, and stick the third one on the upper corner of my screen, keeping it within my sight. I check my watch, still four hours to go before we'll meet back outside Kaelber Hall. Maybe I'll swing by L'Hôtel instead, surprising her by ditching my self-imposed office hours after class ... I sigh, quickly changing my mind. I don't want to cut into her time with Monsieur François.

When my focus returns, I land in the beginning of mayhem. Whoa. Students are jumping up and down the aisles, reaching across seats, stretching to see their friends' phone screens or reaching for their own, squealing. Something gone viral caught their attention at the wrong time, wrong place.

"Okay, everyone, recreation's over. Time to settle down," I call out, but no one pays any attention.

Putting my fingers to my mouth, I whistle long and clear. The sound reverberates in the abrupt silence as all movement stops. "Phones off, *now*." I cross my arms, staring them down. Well, that certainly did the trick. They scramble to their seats, but they're still buzzing with a weird sort of energy. "Okay, let's get you hyped on this new project instead," I say, uncrossing my arms.

I'm met with a chorus of groans.

"We'll do something with a little twist," I continue, writing with a stylus on my screen, the PowerPoint slide appearing to all.

The narrator gets on an elevator and presses "Lower Level." The elevator

descends, and descends. When it finally reaches the bottom, he finds himself...

"You'll be writing two chapters based on what I just wrote, no longer than four thousand words, no shorter than two thousand," I say, earning me a few more groans.

"Where's the twist in that?" one of them asks.

"Glad you asked. Bear with me, it's coming. For the next four weeks, I'll be giving you the next prompts. You'll use these to build the story in increments of two chapters due at the beginning of each class." Crossing over to the front, I lean back on the lectern, bracing my hands on it, crossing my ankles. "In the notebooks I distributed last week."

Murmurs greet my announcement. "That's right. No World Wide Web coming between you and your imagination." I look them over. "Oh, and by the way? The main reason they're hardcover and not spiral? No ripped-out sheets allowed. You don't like what you wrote, cross it out, but it stays, do over's unlimited. Revisions and rewrites are part of the interesting journey you're embarking on, and I want you to keep a visual on it."

A collective grumble ensues. I wonder how long it's been since these kids were forced to write with a pen rather than the tips of their fingers.

I catch the eye of the kid who questioned me earlier and send him a smirk. "Now for the twist. At the beginning of each class, you'll pass the notebook you had to the next person sitting to your left," I say to my now captive audience. "At the end of this project, we'll share the results and we'll go through steps to self-publish the experiment."

Aaah. Self-publish ... magic word. Satisfied, I watch them hop to it. All but for three girls huddling near the back, furiously whispering, checking their phones and pointing at me. Their heads are bent close as they seem to argue over something. I narrow my eyes. Noticing it, they end their conversation and start writing.

My skin prickles. An unpleasant feeling washes over me.

When class ends, I pack up quickly and head for my office across the quad. I'm stopped five times by admirers—several of which aren't even enrolled in my writing class.

The last one is bold enough to yank me to her, propositioning me with what's supposed to be the best blow job of my life, one that will ensure I'll never forget her. "I'm ready to do anything you want, anything you say, anytime. So keep me in mind," she cooes coyly, running her fingers up to my chest, dropping a note into my shirt's collar.

Bloody hell. Is it me, or are they getting bolder? I fish the note out, and hand it over.

"Not interested," I say firmly, but she doesn't take the hint, pressing it back into my hand with a lewd run of her tongue on her lips. "No, means no." I manage through clenched teeth, squishing the note into a ball, shoving past her.

"Okay, ladies, get to class," an aging professor says to the small crowd following me, and they immediately disperse.

"Thanks," I tell him, rubbing the back of neck as a new lump of tension forms there.

"Saw you the other night at Monsieur François's," he says, clapping my shoulder, and I recognize him now. "I'd keep to myself too with that young beauty on my arm, and guard her well."

"I intend to do just that," I tell him, relieved that Éolie isn't due here for another couple of hours.

"It must be hard to stay incognito being closely related to such a celebrity," he says on a commiserating sigh, walking past me.

"Closely related to—What?" I choke. Surely, I misheard. But the man's already disappeared around the corner.

I run up the steps to Kaelber Hall.

"Mrs. Pringle," I say storming in, "I'm unavailable for the next hour." I slam my office door shut and lean on it, my chest heaving.

Calm the fuck down, man.

He'd never willingly do it, risk it all over again. I give myself the pep talk.

I drop my messenger bag on my desk, and do a quick search on my phone. I blanch and drop into my seat, landing with a hard thud.

I read the article, picking out keywords like a flashing neon sign. The longer I read, the harder my heart pounds.

I've just lost all semblance of normal.

Sean Elliot Pierce, what have you done?

Thirty-Two

LIAM

"Can we do something? I need damage control, man," I say, pacing my small office while Theo curses under his breath over the phone line.

On my desktop computer, the browser displays the article everyone's clearly been whispering about all morning. **The Apple Doesn't Fall Far. Ever wondered why Liam O'Shea, world-acclaimed author of Eiloe, the phenomenon book series everyone raves about, closely guarded his past life? Well, wonder no more.**

"From what it says here, he sprouts a load of crap. How proud he is of your phenomenal success as an indie, and now that you've proven yourself, it's time you be brought back into the fold, and blah, blah, blah," Theo says, clearly reading from the same garbage I did.

"Fuck that," I snap. I bang my head a few times against the wall, exasperated enough to give my budding headache a legitimate reason to stay.

Theo is quiet for a moment, and I know he's wading through article after article. Sean really went all out, as usual, so no big surprise there. From the limited results I allowed myself to scan on my phone's news feed, every major media outlet is covering the thing today.

"Not looking good for any kind of damage control," Theo says finally. "I don't even have a solid grip on any breach of confidentiality here. He spins it around like the sweetest fairytale, and with no libel, we'll be overruled, man."

I pull at my hair. Christ ... After seventeen years of burying me deep into oblivion—of cutting the cord—he's gone and announced me to the world like a fucking newborn. A proud papa deserving of a cigar—to the entire free world. Normal, or whatever semblance of it I'd hoped to achieve, is gone.

"This is so fucked up. I never really thought he'd willingly and publicly claim me back as his son," I say, thinking back on the time immediately following my rescue, and all the sympathy I garnered, eclipsing his grander-than-life parade in the media. He'd enjoyed it for the first two seconds—then he'd hated me for it. Despised how easily I usurped his spotlight, bringing forth my permanent exile to Berlinger International Academy in order to regain his media throne. "Even if he doesn't know that I know about the files, he paid gazillions, for chrissake, to have me disappear into the sunset at Berlinger."

I breathe through my nose, willing myself to calm the hell down.

"You still won't use the copied files even now?" Theo asks, referring to the "mbrón dhaid" files, some pretty messed up secret ones, P.O. discovered by accident, hacking into Sean's computer system one night just for the heck of it when we were sixteen. Well, mostly for the heck of it, give or take a virus or two.

"I know P.O.'s no longer in any danger from them, but I'll never shake loose of the controversy shit storm if I put it out there. I want normal, Theo. Away from all this."

Inside, I'm still boiling with fury, but the words I give Theo come out in defeat. Because we both know there's no winning. When it comes to dealing with Sean, I always feel like I've lost.

Theo's pause says he gets it. "I'll shake things up on my side, see what his legal advisors are up to, and I'll get back to you. Stay on the down low as much as possible and if anyone approaches you, on the record or off, it's no comment across the board," he says.

My promise to obey is drowned out by some sort of commotion taking place outside Mrs. Pringle's office. I hear shouts. And the high-pitched screeches I hear are clamoring my name, and getting louder by the minute. Dread fills me. Knowing Sean, he's probably cranking up the fans to the next level by offering some kind of wild prize for cornering me. And, hopefully, it won't be me on a platter.

"Will do. Got to go, man," I say loudly, ending my call with Theo as I remember Éolie and our meeting on campus. I can't hide in here and leave her to fend for herself through all of that.

I dig out my dingy disguise, an old baseball cap and oversized faded black hoodie, oil stained and frayed in a few places, and cheap mirror sunglasses, praying it will be enough. I grab my bag and cross it over my shoulder as I head out the door, searching through local numbers for L'Hôtel de la Mer, and start dialing. I don't want Éolie anywhere near campus right now, not with this. She's already uncertain enough with just me. This kind of crowd would definitely freak her out.

Like sharks circling...

"Mr. O'Shea, you're ... you're ... you're the son of *the* Sean Elliot Pierce..." a breathy-voiced Mrs. Pringle swoons, almost running me down as I come out of my office.

Christ almighty, so it begins. "Not anymore," I say, darting around her and not bothering to look back.

I listen to the sound of the line ringing in my ear as I hustle into the main hall and toward the exit. Mrs. Pringle's voice fades behind me just as someone picks up.

"Bonjour, L'Hôtel de la Mer. My name is Donovan, how can I help you?"

"Monsieur François, s'il-vous-plaît," I ask, exaggerating my French accent in the hopes no one recognizes me by my voice alone underneath my flimsy disguise.

"Monsieur François? Hold on."

I take a quick peek around the next corner to make sure the coast is clear. Goddammit. The Hall is filling up with girls. First things first, I need out of here. My boarding school upbringing is finally giving back something useful. Stealth in-and-out missions? I got this.

"Monsieur François speaking."

"Is Éolie still with you?" I ask, my voice quiet but urgent.

"Who's this?"

"It's Liam, Monsieur François," I say, turning to face the wall to let five over-excited girls pass me by. I tug on the lip of my hoodie out of pure habit as it's already hanging as low it goes, topping my baseball cap. I push down on the bill of the cap in the hopes it will shadow my face completely and shove the mirror sunglasses up my nose.

"She left some twenty minutes ago," he says, and I let out an expletive. "To meet you, I believe," he adds as if that solves everything. I curse again. "Is everything okay?"

"No, but I'm working on it. Thanks." I press end, and read the text I just received from Theo.

Theo: Get your ass out of there NOW. A post went up. The role of a lifetime in Sean's next blockbuster to the first girl who takes a selfie with you. Offer ends... today. Heads up. The sick bastard gave your location at COA. They're going wild, man.

No shit, Theo. My heart starts hammering with apprehension. I have to get Éolie out of here. I know from past experiences that it doesn't take a lot of fans for a swarm to gain momentum—and turn rabid.

I charge around the corner and into the throng, cutting through the incoming crowd. Head down, I weave in and out until I reach the top of the steps leading down to the quad, growing frantic. Someone's arm snags on my shoulder and my hood falls back and I make a grab for my baseball cap, but not fast enough. The girl next to me does a double take. Shit.

She grins, and the girl besides her screeches.

Double shit.

I shove the cap back low over my eyes and hastily pull the hoodie back up, but it's too late. I scan the faces that are, one by one, all fastening their eyes on me.

Éolie. I have to find her. Now.

"Liamliamliamliamliamliamliamliamliamliamliamliam..." Voices buzz in my ears in a panic-inducing rhythm. I dodge left, and push my way through while I still have a brief window of opportunity, the end of the line not yet au fait as to what makes the front of the line whirr.

In a bid to gain a bit more time I shout, "He's inside Kaelber signing autographs for the next half-hour." Girls start jostling each other, half wanting in, half wanting out. Should keep them occupied for the next ten minutes, at least.

Quickly scanning the surrounding area, I spot Éolie standing out of the way to the side of the building at our rendezvous point. Bloody hell. I see red. The Mimis are manhandling her into a corner, shoving her around. I hop over the railing halfway down the stairs and land on my feet. When I get close to the Mimis, I catch their accusations and my fury builds.

"It's so our business, you lying bitch. Mrs. P. ordered the three of us out that day, but we saw you cozying up to Liam in town this weekend," one Mimi yells, shoving Éolie anew, and she stumbles back. "You're poaching on our territory."

"What are you talking about?" Éolie's arms curl on herself. "He's not a thing—"

"Here's the *thing*, you slut. Why don't you go back to where you came from—"

I quickly grab the wrist of the other Mimi before she can bitch slap a dazed Éolie, bringing it back down slowly, but firmly. I hover protectively in front of her, facing the two girls with a death stare, that's probably lost behind the mirrored lens I'm wearing. I growl deep in my throat.

The first Mimi takes a step back, then another.

"Why don't you kiss my ass, freak," the one Mimi I prevented from hitting Éolie hisses before going for me. I block the blow and hold her fast while she struggles.

"Assault on a teacher is a criminal offense. And I'm pretty sure they don't offer plastic surgery in prison," I say, my voice low, warning. "Now get the hell out of my sight."

"Oh, it's Liam in disguise," they coo, and cry out, motioning wildly with their phones, shrieking like banshees, reversing the flow of traffic, zeroing on us. *Shit.*

"Come on." I grab Éolie by the arm. We make a run for it in a desperate bid to reach the faculty parking lot, and the relative security of my car.

"Liam, what's happening?" Éolie asks, already winded and flushed.

My jaw tightens as I realize her run in with the Mimis probably already freaked her out and now the crowd—

"I promise I'll explain. Right now, let's get clear of this mess," I say, still running, still holding on to Éolie, helping her keep up with my longer strides.

"Once we get to the car, I want you to drive straight out of here," I instruct her, not even slowing down, struggling to take my car keys out of my coat pocket. My mind is spinning, going a mile a minute sifting through my options for getting Éolie safely back at the condo. I'm ready to jump out of the car if need be, and face the crowd if it comes to that. I just want her safe.

We make a sharp right into a very narrow passageway between Environmental Sciences and Human Studies. We abruptly stop running, just about ready to cough up our lungs, and flatten ourselves up against the wall of Human Studies, the irony of which is not lost on me.

We're barely concealed as it is from the hordes of hysterical females, and I'm praying for them to pass right by, hopefully leaving us free to reach the parking lot and my car. I try again to pass Éolie the car keys, but she shakes her head, and shoves them right back.

"If you ever need ... to dock your boat ... in gale winds conditions ... I'm your girl, but a car? Not happening," Éolie pants out, and it's not quite in the way my fantasies dictated all morning, either.

"Hell," I mutter, palming the keys, and dragging Éolie along as we both run for the car.

Thirty-Three

ÉOLIE

"It was quite brilliant really, P.O. and the rest of the guys sending them off on a wild goose chase to the next town over with bogus sightings." I hop on a flat boulder, and balance on it.

Rather than risk the crowded parking lot, we're trekking back to Liam's apartment through the woods. And I'm held under the spell of this mixed hardwood forest, immersed in northern trees and native plants I only ever saw in textbooks.

We're walking under a lush canopy lit by the late-morning sun and brilliant autumn colors. The moist, nutrient-rich soil supports a diversity of mature deciduous trees, like maples and oaks and beeches, and ground covers, like moss and ferns, my favorites. A faint trail meanders in between august, century-old maple trees, and ferns, turning a rich russet brown at this time of the year, are in sharp contrast to the lime green, mossy boulders dotting the way.

Green, gold, orange, a dash of red dappled by the sun, the pungent smell of the first falling leaves ... After the pushing around, the noise, the rush, the crowd, stepping into such calm is like stepping into another world. A safe one.

Ahead, Liam is turning in a circle, scowling at his phone in between mutterings about GPS apps that are for the birds, which makes me wonder if he knows the way back to his condo. Clearly, he's still stressed out by what just went down on campus as, tight-jawed, a muscle ticks on his cheek. I don't even think he heard my comment just now.

"Jesus. I can't even find my way out of the woods with a GPS app," Liam grumbles under his breath, shoving his phone away, fondling with something on his watch, turning this way and that.

"Can I help with something?" I ask.

"I got this," he scowls at his watch. I decide to let him have his space for a moment. I shade my eyes with one hand, squinting, taking note of the sun's position and the dominant wind's direction.

I wiggle my legs to limber them, unused to this sensation of muscle fatigue. I'm discovering the hard way that being toned by years of yoga, swimming, diving and sailing doesn't make that much difference when running for your life after almost dying at sea.

I shift my weight to my right foot while reaching back to find the inside of my left ankle with my left hand. Keeping my body facing front, I begin to lift my left foot and leg while extending my right arm straight forward, until I find my standing backbend. I breathe five times, and repeat on the other side.

Liam's waving his arm back and forth, entirely focused on reading his watch.

Near my feet, I discover baby ferns unfolding straight out the moss covering the other side of my boulder. I bend down, inhaling their fresh and green aroma capturing the elements of the forest. I stare at the delicate fronds, fascinated, trying to identify if they are *Adiantum Pedatum*, northern maiden ferns, or Common Polypody, rock ferns. My fingers extend to stroke one and, in the instant moment, a vision comes to me, pulling me inwards.

A small foot trail, the width of a wheelbarrow, poetically meanders on and invites me in farther for a short walk, ferns abounding come spring time. Up ahead in the shade of mature maple trees, an apricot yellow house with cranberry-red shutters appear out of a breathtaking meadow, a gurgling brook running nearby into a field of wild flowers.

"Christ, Éolie. You okay?" I hear Liam from afar. I'm coming back disorientated, my shoulders seized in a death grip. I fight a bout of dizziness, and blink into concerned dark-blue eyes. My gaze sweeps around.

Forest.

I'm back in the here and now, in Bar Harbor, where we're trekking to Liam's apartment by way of the woods, avoiding his overwrought mob of fans. I remember the stress and chaos of it, but in the wake of the vision, I only feel utter peacefulness.

"You went stock-still, unblinking, not even breathing ... I thought you'd collapse," Liam says, holding me up so I don't fall off the boulder. "You okay?"

I nod.

"What happened?"

"I saw a house in a forest full of ferns," I whisper. *A yellow house, our house.*

"Does that happen often?" he asks, and I realize he's gone as white as a sheet.

"Define often?" I say, wincing.

He takes a few steps back, shaking his head, shoving his hands through his hair. "I'm putting you at risk in more ways than one with my shit," he mumbles. "We need out of here. This way."

He motions in just about the opposite direction we need to go to get back to his condo.

"We're going back to get your car?" I ask, unsure.

He gives me an incredulous, *are you for real*, look. Which my whacky, but untimely, sense of humor finds comical given our circumstances, but it's not like now is a good time to swap quips, judging by the firm set of his mouth and his level gaze.

"We're that way then," I say, pointing in the other direction as I hop down from the boulder.

"Whoa, there, hold on. My compass points..." He re-checks his watch. "Christ, now what? It points North in just about every direction." A deep scowl darkens his features as he waves it around.

"It's not standing on a flat surface," I say, grabbing his wrist before he pokes himself in the eye. "And even then, I wouldn't trust my life on a watch compass, in spite of being a Swiss-made one. It needs to be calibrated every time you sneeze. Cool watch though."

Liam grumbles something about Zac and losing a dare that went wrong in Zurich.

"Zurich's a long way from here, so trust me. We're that way." I pull on his arm and stop, standing absolutely still, ears alert.

"You heard something?" Liam asks, eyes scanning our immediate surroundings.

"Yes, and they must be pretty near," I say just as the sound grows louder.

"Fuck," he let out. Something dark flashes in his eyes, and before I know it, he spins me around, backing me up against the rough bark of a huge sugar maple tree's trunk. Liam's body bends over mine, his hand coming up to cover my mouth, warning me to keep silent.

I point my finger up to the sky, and we both look up in time to see highly vocal Canada Geese migrating back South for the winter, flying in a crisp V formation. His shoulders sag, and his hand slides down, coming to rest at the base of my neck.

"I'm going to have a heart attack right here in the damn woods," Liam mutters.

"Did you know they mate for life?" I ask, desperate to change the subject when I see the tension in his downturned mouth. "And that they can live up to thirty years," I say, amazed, watching them disappear overhead.

His palms come up to cradle my face. "Éolie-Jolie ... I'm so sorry."

"What's to be sorry about?" For a split second, his gaze darts down to my mouth, lingering there for no longer than a heartbeat, before flashing back to meet mine. His jaw clenches and the muscles in his face tightens, resolve written all over it.

"Too many damn things," he finally admits, his forehead dropping to mine. "But for now, we need to get you back to the condo as soon as possible."

He holds out his hand, and I hug the Acer Saccharum tree goodbye before taking it. "It's so beautiful in here," I say quietly, walking away. "There's so much to observe and learn from."

I'm yanked to a stop. "You're not coming back in the woods by yourself," he warns, searching my eyes.

"Are you reading my mind?" I ask, my sense of humor tickled by the thought.

"It's written all over you." His mouth turns down, and the air turns thick with tension.

"Worried I'll end up in Vermont?" I tease to defuse some of the tension.

"No, I'm not worried you'll end up in Vermont. I'm worried, period. You're at risk, and you don't even know by how much. Please, promise, Éolie," he says, and I flinch at the quick, panicked look crossing over his features. I know the crowd here likes to fangirl over him, but today was different. I want to ask why, but clearly talking about it now would only make things worse for Liam.

"Then I won't," I assure him, losing the smile, crossing my heart so he'll know I'm serious. "If it's that important to you. Promise."

"You don't understand. I've lost—" he sighs heavily.

"What is it?" I ask, giving him a tender kiss on the corner of his lips, concerned by the heartbreak I see clearly etching on his face.

"I can't just now," he says, shaking his head. "We'll talk once we're out of the woods."

He takes the lead, and we walk the next mile in silence. And the next.

We trudge back inside the condo shortly before one in the afternoon, Liam still uncharacteristically taciturn.

"Well this has been a very interesting experience, and by far the strangest form of human behavior I have ever witnessed," I tell him, taking off my socks before I let myself fall back on the bed. Our long trek through the woods might have helped contribute to my exhaustion.

"This is nothing compared to what's coming. I'll be tracked down and followed in my every move. You trusted me, and I lost the normal we were aiming for."

I sit up. "Liam?"

He hasn't moved one iota since I took off my shoes and socks. He stares at me from the doorway. Neither coming, nor going.

"I'm so sorry," he says. "This is all my fault. I shouldn't have exposed you to me. I didn't mean to—" He beats his forehead a few times on the doorway, muttering under his breath.

"It's about your mob of fans? Surely it will blow over, no?" I ask mystified.

"You don't understand."

"Then make me understand."

He makes a sound at the back of his throat, almost a growl. "They're *not* my fans. They're *fans of famous*," he cries out, pacing the bedroom. "He feeds on them, Éolie. He employs an army of people to feed the public with these concepts of him. He's been doing it so long, he probably believes it himself. And God forbid they stop listening. He just buys them off. He pays them to pay attention. He probably owns half the tabloids by now, and who knows how many paparazzi."

"Who? Your father?" I ask, concerned.

His features harden and he whirls on me. "Don't call him that. He never was," he says, and I watch the muscle tick in his cheek. "Before the abduction and you and I, my childhood was one long-ass reality show where he played the part of perfect daddy until he tired of it. I didn't have nannies. I had stylists and publicists. And no matter how fucked up I'll sound saying this, being abducted turned out to be the best thing that ever happened to me ... I had you, Éolie-Jolie." He turns to me with sorrowful eyes, and mine fills up. "I had you, and you saved *me*."

He thumps his fist on his chest once, over his heart. "I lived to tell the tale and he hated that I took the limelight away. But the thing is, I thrived away from him. And now? For whatever sick reason, he wants me back in *his* spotlight. And he'll do something to fan the flames anew every single day, and I'll be dodging hyped-up fans and paparazzi for all eternity ... and I'll have to—" he swallows, looking down at his feet. He then takes a deep breath, squaring his shoulders.

"You'll have to what? Tell me," I insist, and he looks away.

"Let you go," he says, tugging on his hair.

"Liam? You cannot be serious." He is.

"I'm worried sick—" His jaw ticks, and he stares off over my head.

"About me? Don't. I'll be careful," I say.

"You won't be able to. Not with the shit storm coming, it's—" He exhales loudly.

"What if he doesn't really want you back into his life?" I ask, clearly seeing the yellow house in my vision, feeling its peacefulness all over again. It has to be real. I trust that more than ever. What Liam is saying can't be true.

"At this point, it'd be a miracle."

"Miracle or not, I'm staying with you. You're not responsible for that crowd's behavior," I say.

"But I am!" he cries out, crossing the room in powerful strides.

"How do you figure?" I ask, jumping out of bed, meeting him halfway.

"Don't you see? Sean's name linked to mine brings the worst kind of fame. Crowds everywhere, no privacy. And all of them foaming at the mouth at the sight of you, someone permanent on my arm, and I can't let it happen. Sean ... it's ... pretty bad. At seven, I didn't know how bad, and you were the only thing I talked about. And now, it's putting you at risk big time. If he so much as learn you're for real, he'll destroy you bit by bit every goddamned time I sneeze wrong to make sure I keep up with him. And if I pretend indifference, hell, he'll probably destroy you, period. Your pick, but either way, you're in danger." He shoves his hand through his hair. "And as if that wasn't enough, I've just dropped you into a fish bowl with thousands of sharks circling. You've been sheltered from humans your whole life ... It was thoughtless and dangerous of me, and I'm sorry—"

"Don't decide for me, Liam," I warn. "I was sheltered from human company, not from human nature," I point out, and his eyes darken searching mine.

"You forget what I saw when we were kids. I couldn't even fully comprehend how such ugly could be done to a little boy. I wanted to be able to take you away with me and I just couldn't—" I choke, swallowing the lump that forms in my throat, eyes watering at all of the resurging emotions.

"And you're losing sight of the fact that I grew up on the Thalassa, doing marine biology research. So trust me, I've seen it all!" I cry out. "I was there, on site, preserving what was left of natural habitats in the aftermath of humans, saving some marine wildlife, watching others becoming extinct at the hands of careless, greedy, and cruel humans."

I give him a look that dares him to argue and he rubs a hand down his face, uncertainty churning in his eyes.

"Life is full of the ugly and the beautiful. I choose beauty. To see beauty, to spread beauty, to be beauty. There are so many wonders to witness and live out there, and Liam? Just so you know. You *are* one of them," I say, "and I want to be with you no matter how ugly the rest of the world gets."

"Éolie, I ... I just want to be with you too..." he says in a choked voice, stepping closer. "You've no idea how much I want to ... When I'm with you, I see beauty everywhere. You *are* beauty ... But I'm scared shitless I'll bring you to harm—"

"Don't be afraid. Let go. With me."

I close the remaining few inches between us. "Believe, Liam. Both, that we'll find a way around Sean, and that we'll find our way to the Forest of Laure."

Chests heaving, we stare at each other for a beat, just before our body's slam together, mouths crashing.

Thirty-Four

LIAM

"You're free now. Go on," Éolie warmly says, bending low in the back doorway before opening her cupped hands.

"Christ. She'll be eaten alive by all the sharks waiting for me out there," I murmur.

"I can scare sharks away." She spins to face me, with her hands planted on her hips.

"Really?"

"Really."

"Says the girl who frees house spiders." I exhale, and run my hands through my hair, my guts twisting.

"What are you not saying right now?"

She knows me well.

"Maybe ... it'd be best for you if you stayed far away. You could go visit Montréal like you wanted to?" I manage to suggest, my voice gruffer than usual, avoiding her gaze.

"Not without you. We just had this conversation. We're not having it all over again. There are seven weeks left to your semester at COA, and we'll take it from there. I'm not going anywhere. You're stuck with me, so deal," she says.

Bloody hell. Wondrous aqua eyes are staring me down, entreating me. How am I supposed to say no to that? Especially when I long to say yes. Éolie, here, with me? Indefinitely? Of course I want that. But with Sean in the picture, I'm just not sure it's doable. Not forever. If he learns that she's for real...

No. I can't let that happen.

"Éolie, he can't find out about you, so you'll be stuck in here all day. And everything we long for is up in the air now. Are you sure about this?" I ask one last time, holding my breath.

Her gorgeous eyes grow soft and luminous in the special way they do when she looks at me, drawing me in. Her stare moves over my face, full of strength and support, and she nods once without hesitation. My heart practically hammers out of my chest. This is it. Point of no return. I'm selfish enough to want her here, with me.

I breathe out, giving in. *Please don't let me fuck this up.*

"We'll need ground rules," I say.

"Absolutely," she agrees with enthusiasm.

"To be followed at all times, Éolie. I'm serious," I warn.

"I know I said I'm not good at rules, but write them down and I'll be on it, coach." She snaps me a sharp salute. I raise a brow, crossing my arms. "Seriously, you'll see. Don't worry so much."

Her confidence is endearing, and my heart lightens a bit. There has to be a way forward for us, somehow. But forever is not on this afternoon's menu. Right now, it's almost two o'clock, and food is our top priority.

"You'll have to be on it preferably *before* we set foot outside to get some food," I say.

"Huh ... *before* is stretching it a bit thin, work in progress here, and starving. Maybe take-out?" she asks.

"Too risky right now with my face plastered everywhere, and fans avidly looking for me, thanks to Sean's crazy postings," I sigh heavily. "And I don't want you opening the front door either, or standing in line at a counter. I'm not willing to take any risk as far as you're concerned."

"What about before now when you had take-out? Won't the delivery crews that came here rat on you?" she asks concerned.

"Not possible. I never had any take-out delivered here. I always picked it up at the counter before."

"Wow, you're good at this stuff," she says, clearly impressed.

"Yeah, well, I've never taken my privacy for granted. I enjoy it too much." I brush a hand down my face. "Enjoyed it, I should say," I add bitterly.

No one knows where I'm staying yet, the leases here are under my management company's name, but I know it won't take long for Sean's people to figure it out.

"We'll find a way, and you'll enjoy your privacy again. I swear," she says, giving me a warm hug. And I revel in it for a few moments, closing my eyes. I'd like to share in her optimism, but I'm nowhere near that place. "So?" she says, leaning back. "I guess that leaves us with cheese omelets and frozen meals to live on from now on."

"Yeah, something like that ... Even though I don't particularly relish having the list of what I buy at the groceries posted on websites. Not to mention being accosted everywhere I turn." I frown, and she wrinkles her nose.

"What if I go instead —" I give her a look that says *over my dead body*, and she holds up her hands, conceding. "What if you're disguised?"

"It won't make any difference. Once we're under siege, disguised or not, I'll be followed from here," I sigh. "For now though, I'd like to buy a few more hours of calm and not risk being recognized, so I'd rather go to a trustworthy source for food. And the only person I know around here that possibly fits the bill is Monsieur François. I'll call him, and we'll see how it goes."

"Sounds good to me. So, we bundle up and walk up to Monsieur François's back door, knock and beg for food," she says, striding to the bedroom. "Surely you've enough clothes in here to mummify us under several layers."

"And what, pretend we're zombies out on the town," I joke, following her, dialing L'Hôtel's number. "We need to stay nondescript, and blend in."

A desk clerk answers, sounding bored. I ask to speak to Monsieur François, and wait for him to come on the line.

"Zombies? Really? That's the first thing that would come to people's minds?" she asks.

"You'd be surprised at the kind of apocalypse that waits out there," I mutter.

"Okay, well you're the expert, choose our weapons," she says.

While the hold music plays in my ear, I select hoodies, sunglasses, and baseball caps. A moment later, I briefly outline the situation to Monsieur

François on the phone and, thankfully, he's sympathetic and more than understanding, although I get an earful for worrying him with my erratic behavior on the phone earlier today.

Thirty minutes later, I think we're ready to give it a shot.

"Remember—" I begin.

"Rule number one, stick to you like gum on a shoe," Éolie says, "which by the way is gross. Rule number two, never show my face. Rule number three, never engage. Rule number four, don't stop no matter what," she recites while I finish pulling her two different hoods up.

"Well done, cadet." I push the bill of her baseball cap down. "Let's do this."

All's quiet on the home front and we walk up the beach unnoticed, until we reach L'Hôtel and, suddenly, the only thing separating us from a pack of paparazzi is a low cedar hedge. There's about twenty of them.

Shit.

They're already in Bar Harbor, and they sure know where I hang out, thanks to Sean's usual due diligence. The hope I could get away with a few more hours before they descended all over town goes down the drain. Éolie takes a step back and gets behind me. One of them gives me the onceover with something like suspicion in his eyes.

We probably have too many layers of clothes on to be completely inconspicuous.

Time for Plan B, deflect the attention by hiding in plain sight. I grab her by the waist and, angling my head, I take Éolie's mouth in an all-possessive, heart-stopping kiss. Her lips and tongue are kissing me back, giving me her all, and I'm hard pressed not to get lost in the moment. A covert glance sideways proves it's nowhere near enough to put us in the clear as one short guy aims his long-focus lens at me, alerting the others. They start calling my name, testing me, but I don't react like I'd like to, which is run like hell in the other direction.

I briskly rub her arms down, and Éolie goes with my cue. She feigns being cold by folding on her herself, keeping quiet. I casually swing my arm over her shoulders and strut past them, guiding her to the Hotel's deck on the other side of the building, all the while speaking German. Granted it's Swiss German and it might give me away, but I don't think these guys will know the difference, or that I was educated at Berlinger for that matter. In any case, within earshot, I lewdly suggest going straight up to our room to warm up before supper. My hand comes round the small of her back, gliding down to cop a quick feel, and Éolie blushes right on cue, correctly reading my tone and gesture.

"Nah, foreign tourists," one paparazzo grumbles to the others, putting down his long-focus lens camera. I sigh in relief.

We step into the common room by the deck's entrance where Monsieur François waits for us.

"Come," Monsieur François says, opening a side door leading straight into the kitchen's stockroom. We follow him to the very back, and he unlocks another door marked private. "We won't be disturbed in here. I'm afraid I can't trust my lads not to tattle on you," he adds with a discreet head motion towards Éolie, and I nod my understanding.

I'm sure some of them would like me to stay out of the way, busy elsewhere, giving them another shot at Éolie. *Not on my watch.*

We step into a small office space.

"There's a pack of paparazzi loitering in the parking lot," I say, shifting us. I run my hands around her waist, nudging her so that we both face Monsieur François. "Campus must be hopping with them by now."

"They know where you hang out, that's for sure. We've received dozens of inquiries about you already, since you called me," Monsieur François replies, his eyes narrowing in thought. "But I think I have the perfect solution to your predicament," he adds with a twinkle in his eyes.

"You do?" Éolie asks, her head tilting to the side.

"What if I came to your place once a week instead? I mean, who'd suspect an old man like me coming and going, right?" he asks Éolie, his whole countenance brightening. "I'll bring down food, we'll have our cooking lessons and a grand time, non?"

"You'd do that?!" she exclaims, all but jumping into his arms, hugging him, and I'm about ready to do the same. "Oh, merci beaucoup."

"Are you kidding me? You're doing me a favor." He winks at me over Éolie's head. "Have you forgotten that I promised to talk you ears off about Montréal and my good old days teaching at l'Institut? I'll never get a better opportunity to do it than with you as my captive audience, non?"

"I'll never be able to thank you enough," I say, giving him a firm handshake.

"Allez, none of that," he answers back with a light shoulder clap. "From what I heard you say on the phone, you must be famished by now if you haven't eaten anything since this morning's omelette." He points at something behind us. Two covered dishes are waiting on a credenza to one side of the desk.

"I've brought two plates, filet mignon and baked potato fresh off the grill for Monsieur, and penne à la marinara for Mademoiselle," he says, and my stomach rumbles.

"Enjoy. I'll be back shortly, and we can iron out the details," he says with a head bow before walking out.

We dig in, practically inhaling up the meals.

"We'll be okay," Éolie assures me when we're finished eating. She laces her fingers through mine, her thumb stroking me in a soothing back and forth caress. "You'll see. We'll get our normal, one day soon. Promise."

I can't buy into her optimism yet, but at least, I breathe more freely for the first time since coming out of class this morning. And it leaves me clear headed enough to deal with the fallouts and campus, or what's left of it for me after today. And plan ahead.

Thirty-Five

LIAM

There's a nip in the air tonight in sharp contrast to this morning's balmy temperatures, and I'm wearing my thick leather bomber jacket, covering a black hoodie. Éolie is safely tucked away at the condo, I remind myself every few steps.

An emergency meeting has been called with members of the Board of Trustees, Dean Hawkesbury, as well as Mrs. Pringle as COA's registrar, to discuss today's events, and security measures I'd like for them to implement. My car is still parked on campus, and the forty-minute walk beach side, underneath a star-studded sky, listening in to the waves crashing on the shore, keeps me calm as I'm readying to run the gauntlet.

The quad is flooded with paparazzi, Dean Hawkesbury warns me on the phone. No big surprise. "I'm walking by the college pier as we speak," I say, letting him know that I'm almost there, as previously agreed.

The minute I set foot on the darkened quad, paparazzi stick to me like white on rice. I keep going, aiming for Kaelber Hall straight ahead, staring down to avoid being blinded by flashes going off like strobe lights.

"Sean Elliot says—" Questions are fired up at me from every direction, but I tune them out as much as I can.

"What's it like—"

"Can you confirm—"

"Is it true—"

"What about—"

"Tell us—" I hear the shuffling of feet, and the whir of the cameras as they keep up with me, but I don't look up.

At Yann's suggestion, my *"No comment"* comment plays on a loop on the small digital recorder I use to consign ideas I frequently have on the go. I hold it up over my head, and my sense of humor perks up, finding it hilarious to hear the ring of exasperation both in their tone of voice and their line of questioning. Guess you won't get a rise out of me tonight, boys.

Dean Hawkesbury's waiting for me at the top of the stairs, and we hurry inside. He locks the door behind me, talking a mile a minute while ushering me into a small conference room to the left of his office.

"Liam, I'm glad you made it," Dean Hawkesbury says. "We'll be having a mandatory student assembly tomorrow morning. This type of harassment is not condoned here, and there will be consequences if there's a repeat performance." He stops to take a breath and I nod once, taking my seat.

Mrs. Pringle's already seated, and she gives me a brief nod of acknowledgement before glancing down, hands folding and unfolding on the conference table, looking uncomfortable. And I wonder if she's embarrassed by her unusual gushing all over me earlier on this morning.

Aside from Mrs. Pringle and Dean Hawkesbury, three others are seated as well. I'm facing them, but no one makes introductions. I wait, feeling the tension from them. I wonder if this is the part where I get fired.

Huh. I've never been fired before. I sort of want to just know what it's like.

One of the three strangers does not bother to wait for introductions. "Such a cute baby boy you were, the spitting image of your handsome father. I looked for you on TV and magazines all the time. You're wearing fancy contacts and dying your hair now, is that it?" I'm asked point blank by a ninety-something relic, wearing more red lipstick on her teeth than on her lips.

"You're members of the Board of Trustees, I presume," I say as I steeple my fingers, cocking my head to the side, refusing to comment on the fact that she has it ass backwards. Stylists used to bleach my hair blond and make me wear contacts to lighten the hue of my blue eyes to glacier blue, matching Sean's, feeding his overblown ego by having his very own Mini-Me tag along. My face stays impassive, but I have to fight not to shudder at the memories.

"We wanted you to bring visibility, but this is ridiculous," the middle trustee says. He may be balding and just shy of eighty, but he sits erect and his sharp grey eyes are silently taking my measure.

"I agree," I say, shrugging because he's right.

"Howard, your dentures are clacking; it's driving me nuts. Either take them out or shush your mouth," the relic says, cupping her hand towards her right. I watch the middle trustee, Howard, pull out his dentures, dropping them in front of him on the conference table. "Satisfied, Ha'iet," he says, crossing his arms, giving her what I'd call a peeved look. And I realize I can no longer take him seriously.

I hope he's not the one firing me. I don't want to laugh in his face when he tries to make an "f" sound.

"For now," Harriet replies, her blue-veined hands folding prim and proper on the table.

Dean Hawkesbury's patting his forehead with a handkerchief. "They were the only trustees available on such short notice," he side mouths.

The third one squints at me from behind the thick lenses of his black framed glasses. "John Dougall," he says in a grating tone of voice. "I was here in '69 at the opening, and I haven't seen this much ado about nothing since '74 when Harriet here, swore she saw Elvis eating lunch at TAB's, and even then," he huffs.

"You're full of it, Dougie, it was '72." Harriet snorts.

"Three years before '77 makes it '74."

"'72!"

"'74!"

"Order."

We all startle at the deafening sound of a ruler cracking a couple of times on the table, and turn as one to look at Mrs. Pringle. "Elvis is not on tonight's agenda. I believe Mr. O'Shea is," she says, lips thinning.

"We're truly sorry it completely got out of hand," Dean Hawkesbury says.

"Not your fault, mine for being here," I reply.

John Dougall clears his throat loudly a few times as one of his thin, wrinkled hands comes up to realign his checkered bow tie. "*I think* it'd probably be best for all concerned to end your seminar right away," he says.

"It's your call," I say. "And in the end, I'll respect your decision." And it isn't until the words are out of my mouth that I realize I don't actually want to be fired after all. Despite everything, what's happening in that classroom is pretty fucking amazing.

Before they can hand me my walking papers, I stand up, hands leaning on the table, looking at each one in turn. "Let's not ignore though that I have this bunch of talented students coming in at seven in the morning for an extracurricular they really work hard at. *I think* I owe it to them to tough it out for the next seven weeks. I agreed to this meeting to outline a proposal, not to quit."

John Dougall chokes, hacking up violently, and Howard slaps him forcefully on the back a few times.

"That should clear your mind right up, Dougie," Harriet says.

"What's your proposal?" Dean Hawkesbury asks, leaning as far back from Dougie as he possibly can.

"We need to limit access to the grounds, or students will be harassed by packs of paparazzi relentlessly," I say, straightening. "I'll hire out a security firm to guard the perimeter for what's left of the semester. It will do as far as thinning them down at least."

I look at Mrs. Pringle. "My students will need a specific identification card, starting now. Without it, no one enters my lecture hall, clear?" She nods. "Can you have them ready and distributed by Wednesday morning?"

She brings forth a small box full of laminated cards already matched with my students' enrolment list. I raise an eyebrow, impressed, and she gives me a tight smile.

"Duplicates of their student I.D.s printed in red instead of blue," she says. "I thought of it after this morning. I'll be there at the door, and I'll check mark each one."

"In the meantime, we think it's best you limit your campus presence outside of your seminar's hours," Dougall adds.

"Fair enough," I say.

"Your seminar's schedule is a God send in more ways than one, considering,"

Dean Hawkesbury considers, rubbing his jaw as if never really intended to sack me, and I wonder if he's thinking of my donation in the form of digital tablets upon my arrival. "Most students are either still sleeping or at TAB's eating breakfast so early. There's not much activity on campus before eight."

"If we don't limit access to the grounds as much as we possibly can, you'll be surprised by how much activity you'll have on your hands by four in the morning," I say, pinching the bridge of my nose, thinking of Sean's idea of giveaway prizes. "So I'm clear to give them the green light?" I ask.

They all nod, Dougie grunting his approval with one last slap on the back delivered by a smirking Howard. I guess it makes for a unanimous decision.

Outside the conference room, I speed dial P.O. "Green light but we need that security team here in the next twenty-four hours. I'll let your contact speak with Dean Hawkesbury to coordinate the details. He'll be able to answer any questions he has on campus specs."

"On it."

Dean Hawkesbury goes to his office to take the incoming call, and I'm left with the denture brigade. Time to go.

"So? Up for a diversion while I slip out the back?" I ask, shrugging back into the bomber jacket. My black hood pulled low over my brow, I palm my car keys.

Howard puts his teeth back in. "I'll give them a speech on dignity from the Hall's balcony," he says, stepping out, and I shake my head watching him walk tall and proud down the corridor. I almost want to stay to hear that speech.

"Whoohoo! Let's do this." Harriet rubs her hands together, almost sprinting out, and John Dougall follows in her footsteps, whining all the way.

"Harriet, it's undignified. Keep your clothes on, you hear me. Harriet, stop it. You can't be seen running around in your underwear like you did at that protest in'70," I hear from somewhere down the hallway.

"Guess I'll see you at tomorrow's assembly then," I say to Mrs. Pringle, backing away.

"'68!" Harriet yells.

"'70!"

Mrs. Pringle upturns her eyes, nodding once before rushing out, her ruler held in a tight fist.

"Meeting adjourned," I say to the empty room, snickering at what I unwittingly unleashed as a diversion. In between Mrs. Pringle disciplining any unruly paparazzo with a rap of her ruler, Harriet running around the quad in her unmentionables, a complaining Dougie hot on her heels, and Howard hollering from the balcony about dignity ... Yeah, for a very brief second there, I almost feel sorry for those paparazzi guys.

Almost, but not quite.

Thirty-Six

LIAM

This morning's students' assembly went better than well, I reflect. I unlock the front door to the condo only to be tackled by a small bundle of curves in all the right places, jumping into my arms. Holding onto my shoulders, her legs locking around my waist, Éolie kisses my face all over.

"That's one hell of a good reason to speed home," I say, cupping her bottom and leaning back to search her face.

"How did it go?" she asks, her expressive eyes searching mine.

"Better than I thought," I say, kissing her forehead. "The student council apparently held their own meeting last night, and they had a signup sheet prepared already for security patrols. And a lot of students signed up on it before leaving, volunteering to patrol alongside my hired crew. And I'd say the rest of the lot was kind of shamed into compliance."

"Told you," she says, face lit up, climbing down, and I'm mourning the loss of her legs wrapped tightly around me. "Come and see." She tugs on my hands, and my eyes widen as my gaze sweeps the space.

"Whoa. You've had a busy morning," I comment. The kitchen island counter has two colorful place settings in front of the bar stools. A chocolate cake is cooling, and the smell in here makes my mouth water.

Éolie's fairly bouncing with happiness as she opens cabinets left and right.

"We have spices and dry goods. Aaand..." she opens the refrigerator, "all sorts of yogurts and cheese and fruits and, well, you can see it's loaded up." She takes out a covered bowl, closing the door with a swing of her hip. "Aaand I've cooked up my very own recipe, under Monsieur François's directions," she says as she puts down the bowl in front of the place mats.

"Had fun?" I ask wryly.

"Loads. Cooking is a chemistry experiment," she tells me with gusto. "And I know how to read recipes now." She throws out her arms dramatically, "I have power."

I can't help it, her joie de vivre is infectious. I sweep her up into my arms, my mood lightening.

"You need to go sit down for this." She pushes on my elbows, squirming, and I tighten my hold.

"Lucky for you it smells better than good in here, and I'm starving," I murmur in her ear before letting her go. "Or you'd be the meal."

She blinks. "Hold that thought," she says, pointing a finger at me, and I grin wolfishly, closing back in.

"No really, hold it," she insists, backing away. "It's historic. It's my first ever cooked-up meal. You have to tell me if it's any good," she entreats, putting on oven mitts to take out two plates, and my growling stomach wins the debate for now.

"Careful, plates are hot," she warns, and I stare at mine.

"You grilled chicken breasts?" I ask, poking it with my fork to make sure I'm not hallucinating.

"Nope. Pan seared in a drop of olive oil with lemon, dill, and sea salt. Monsieur François says it's one of your favorites." She drops a quick kiss on my temple. "And my pièce de résistance, salade de poivrons doux au romarin, since they're on your short list of veggies," she says on a lilt, spooning into my plate mixed strips of red, orange and yellow bell peppers. And bloody hell, the aroma drifting out of that bowl is mouth-watering.

"I liked the mix of colors," she goes on. "I think I'll name this one Maine's Caribbean Sunset. Pan seared in olive oil and rosemary, left to marinate a few hours in the fridge with the added touch of Monsieur François's special ingredient, which believe it or not, is maple syrup. Pan searing was this week's technique if you're wondering." She comments non-stop, spooning some into her plate, a plate heavy with what looks like roasted tofu cubes.

I stare, my hand coming up to cover my mouth.

"Hey, no worries. It's nothing like the blob. We tasted it, and it got the go ahead of Monsieur François, swear," she says, growing concerned.

"You cooked meat? For me?" I say, and for some unexplained reason that gets to me.

"Of course it's for you," she replies, her nose wrinkling in distaste before she shrugs. "It's no big deal. Just because I won't eat meat doesn't mean you shouldn't eat what you like, non?" she says like it's evident.

I'm rendered speechless.

"Before you get your hopes up, I won't do bones, innards, or carcasses," she informs me, shuddering once. "But hey, as long as I can't identify the body part, I'm totally okay with cooking it. Boneless or filleted, bring it on. They come wrapped in those cellophane packages everyone was throwing in their carts the other day, did you know that? So, dig in," she says, offering me back my fork, her head tilting.

I take a tentative bite. I vow here and now, I'll find cardboard tasty if it comes to that, but I don't even have to pretend. I'm blown away. "Whoa, it's better than good," I say, impressed by the flavors bursting in my mouth. I savor each bite, and her blooming smiles are the biggest I've seen so far.

I force Éolie to join me for all but the chicken and our plates are empty again in no time, and we're on clean-up duty.

I'm struck by the simple gestures of everyday life we're currently doing as a couple as we put away the last of the cleaned plates, and the quiet joy that comes with it. The outside world can wait, for now I'm wrapped in a peaceful bubble.

"Want to take a nap?" I ask slyly, and I watch her eyes grow wide before she dashes down the hall. I follow at a more leisurely pace.

The bedroom door's closed and Éolie's splattered all over it, blocking the way in. "Before you go in there, on a scale of one to ten, how attached are you to your thirty-four pairs of jeans?" she asks, and I raise one eyebrow.

"You counted them?" I lean one shoulder on the opposite wall facing her.

"Is that a trick question?"

"What do you think?"

"I'd plead the fifth, but I'm Canadian."

"A fat lot of good it would have done since I'm Irish." I straighten. "Should I worry?" I casually lift my arms, bracing them on the upper door frame.

"Maybe ... not?" She bites her lower lip.

"Define *not*," I say, my voice low and amused, leaning closer.

"Not ... now that we have laundry?" she says, wincing as she opens the door from behind her, and I gawk at the sight that greets me.

My jeans are strewn together on some kind of bright blue rope that looks suspiciously like the old internet cable from the study. They run the whole length of the glass wall, anchored out on the solid ones on either side, blocking the view of the ocean. "What's with the jeans mural?"

"Okay, don't freak out," she begins, and I brace myself. Whatever comes next, I have a feeling I won't like it. "After you left, there were a bunch of guys on the beach and they weirded me out. They kept looking up at our building, and then they left, and I know we're on the third floor and it'd be hard for anyone to see inside, but I got to thinking that maybe someone could climb up the balconies, and there's no curtains anywhere in this apartment; it's really opened up to the beach and the ocean, did you know that? Ugh. Of course you know that. So, anyway, maybe you'll start a new trend of one-sided sun bleached denim afterwards," she blurts the long-assed sentence in one breath. I stare. "Please say something."

One hand scrubs down my face. "Christ, I'm so sorry about all this."

"Thank God you're not upset about the jeans." She sags against the door.

I gape.

"I don't give a flying f—" I blow my cheeks, and breathe through my nose a few times. "How will you fare in here with the blocked-up view to the outside world, no contact with nature," I say, looking at the mural, my chest pinching tight at the thought of caging her in.

"I'm used to closed-in space much narrower than this. I'd be happy camping in the walk-in," she replies, motioning with her arm.

"Not good enough, for chrissake." I shove my hands through my hair, pacing the room. "I didn't even think about that. But you're absolutely right that you'd be at risk going out on the balcony, or just looking out the windows." I groan in frustration. "I'm—"

"If I hear you say you're sorry one more time, I'll ... I'll..." She huffs and puffs, advancing on me.

"You'll?" I raise a brow, challenging her.

"I'll make you eat tofu," she threatens, poking a finger at my chest.

"Aww man, Éolie. I feel so bad, without me you'd be free to—"

"Deal with it already, and stop thinking about sending me away. Can't you see I'd miss you more than I'll miss nature, which will still be there when the crazies are over? And they will, Liam O'Shea, trust me on this one. And how do you figure I'd miss coming and going, something I'm not even used to yet, anyway," she cries out, shaking me by the shoulders. Or trying to.

"Éolie ... the crazies are just starting." I sigh heavily, wishing I could share in her optimism. I gather her in my arms, embracing her.

"You're vibrating!" she yelps, jumping away. And the look on her face is so comical it momentarily brings me out of my funk.

I pull my phone out of my front pocket, waggling my eyebrows at her, and she shakes her head, rolling her eyes.

"O'Shea," I answer.

"*What* the hell, man."

"Leo!" I exclaim, and Éolie gestures that she'll leave me to my conversation. I motion back, mouthing, "I'll be in the study."

"What's up?" I ask him, surprised to get a call. Implanting new strains of cocoa beans in the back boonies of São Tomé Island off the coast of Africa, he should be out in the fields taking notes at this time of the day. And to my knowledge, he's still short a couple of months before he can call it quits, and wrap up his doctoral thesis at Cambridge.

"You're asking me—? Are you high on something? I had to trek four hours to get cell reception, I've this missed **galette** text alert dated back September 12, and by the way? You're the *only fucking thing* the villagers could talk about this morning, courtesy of our weekly Monday nights, world news reviews, playing in the village square. Sean made sure you're just about the hottest topic out there and congrats, you're their fairytale news of the month. *That's what's up.* What the bloody hell happened, man? You good?"

With a deep breath, I tell Leo everything as quickly as I can. By the end of my summary, I'm not sure who's more stunned. Guess it's a toss-up. My ugly mug has been plastered all the way down to São Tomé? Man, it's official. I'm cursed; it will never end.

Leo grunts, and I can practically see him dragging one hand through his shoulder-length brown hair, pulling at it, and his gold-brown eyes upturning to the sky as he thinks through what he'll say next. I shake my head, sighing. Knowing him, he's probably searching through his extensive collection of clichéd sayings for *the perfect one* he'll use on me for this doozy I just dropped on him.

"Let me get this straight. Éolie's for real, and from what I can surmise, she's happy as a clam at high tide staying on the down low, you've got seven weeks of house arrest ahead of you with nothing else to do but play desert island with her and … your problem is?"

Thirty-Seven

LIAM

Lying on my side, head resting on my bended arm, I stare. My fingers come up, gently brushing away a stray lock of hair from her forehead. Éolie stirs at my touch.

"Good morning, love," I lean over and whisper in her ear.

It's been a month since Leo's phone call spun me around. A month of "I told you so's" ringing in my ears thanks to his response to my woes. Who'd have thought I'd find a desert island in the midst of a media zoo? I'm enjoying the hell out my house arrest conditions, and testing the paparazzi's patience with my apparent non-life. I have come to treasure so many specific moments in the new normality of my days. But right here, right now, in the exact moment Éolie slowly wakes and becomes aware of me, beaming me up with happiness, is by far one of my favorites.

Éolie trails little kisses along my jaw and journeys up my chin, whispering along the way that waking up next to me is her first "happy" of the day. "C'est mon premier Bonheur du jour," she says with tenderness. Being in love's a potent brew with which to start the day.

I kiss her passing lips.

"Class this morning gives you first shower privileges," she says, lying down on her stomach, propping up on her elbows.

"And you know what my answer is, right?" No way am I missing out on her morning routine. I like my front-row seat and the first class view, thank you very much.

"Why do I keep asking?"

"Beats me. C'mon, you. Go. Get."

I prop my head up on my hand, my eyes following her. By now, I don't need a drop of caffeine to wake me completely. The sight of Éolie's backside peeking from underneath one of my shirts does it for me.

She comes back in a few minutes later, securing her wet hair into her customary braid. Her fitted white cotton camisole and matching boy shorts trimmed in lace give me peeks of soft skin and curves as she walks through to the middle of the room. She sits on the floor, uncapping her body lotion, and the fluid motion of her hands stroking her skin to satiny opalescence keeps me rigid at attention.

She gets up to stand straight on her left leg. Bending her right, she places her right foot on the root of her left thigh, palms joining in front of her as she slowly brings her arms up over her head in something called the tree position. She closes her eyes and breathes five times before repeating on the other side. And for the next fifteen minutes or so, she goes through a series of yoga asanas. Watching the sensuality of her moves, and the suppleness of her body, mesmerizes me all over again.

"Breakfast in five," she says, wearing one of her impish grins, waving her hand in front of my face. Great. She startled me out of my fantasy just as I was getting to the good parts.

"Got to love school mornings," I mutter under my breath, getting up.

I smack her butt as I walk by, and she yelps. I turn, backing away, holding my hands up. And my mouth tugs up one side as her eyes narrow on me. "I'm weak, what can I say."

I walk out of the condo with my hood pulled low, primed to run through the usual gauntlet of paparazzi, but there's no one out there this morning. I flatten against the wall, peeking around the corner making sure I won't be ambushed. No one.

I get in the car and drive over to campus, unsettled. I'm freaked out by their absence. It's ludicrous to think they've simply overslept. They've been camping on my doorstep every day for a month, rain or shine, and I certainly won't presume they got tired of me out of the blue. My heart pounds as I realize something bigger must have caught their attention. The question is, what, where, and who? I swallow, uneasiness taking root.

At COA's main gates, I lower my window. "Anything unusual to report?" I ask the security guy on post.

"All's quiet, sir," he says, letting me pass.

Yeah, that's the problem.

During class, I can't seem to string two coherent sentences together; my mind keeps going over possible reasons for the sudden disappearance of everyone. A quick search on the Internet yields nothing more than the usual outlandish speculations over my refusals to meet up with Sean. One of the latest posts on a popular site mentions that I'm secretly preparing my spaceship for a return journey to the world of Eiloe to arrange our upcoming reunion, the whole according to a reliable source. Good one.

My students don't seem to fare any better than me, focus wise. No one's writing. Some are staring off, head propped on their hand, but the majority of them are fidgeting in one way or another. I see pens tapping, knees jiggling, feet bouncing, hair twisting...

No one seems to be able to concentrate on more than two words at a time, so guess I'm not the only one unsettled by the strange calm before the storm vibe.

My uneasiness grows.

"Okay, guys, that's it for today," I say a bit before eight-thirty, setting them free half an hour early. "See you next Monday," I say as I gather my things, shoving them in my messenger bag.

Students clear out in a nanosecond.

I put my coat on and cross my bag over my shoulder, walking up the aisle, ready to get the hell out of here. Who'd have thought I'd find paparazzi camping on my doorsteps normal to the point of worrying by their lack thereof? No office stopover today. I'm still freaked out by their sudden desertion this morning, and I can't seem to shake the feeling that it's not a good thing.

I push the door of my lecture hall open and step right into ... my very own version of the apocalypse.

Chartered busses with license plates from all over the East Coast are processed through by dozens of crews talking into headsets, wearing a distinctive black shirt, their way-too-familiar bright-silver film company logo jumping out at me.

Frozen on the spot, I watch them drive by me one after the other, their colorful banners boasting slogans the likes of "We Want Eiloe Trilogy Movies" or, "Enough. Give us Eiloe in theaters."

My pulse jumps in my throat.

Fuck me sideways.

It's a takeover.

My shock is quickly wearing off and reality seeps in. I need to find out if his Former Greatness himself is here. I'd like to tell him where to get off face to face.

Still staring at the ongoing parade, I'm tapped on the shoulder. I whip my head around, and two of Sean's suited-up gorillas wearing shades are motioning me to follow them.

"We found him, sir," one of my gorillas says into his mouth piece.

"Well, aren't you accommodating? And to think I was looking for him. Lead the way," I say sardonically, and they brace on either side of me.

The quad is transformed into something resembling a three-ring circus complete with a stage and giant flat screens overhead, proof that what Sean wants, Sean gets. "And all in under an hour," I say to my watchdogs. "Impressive," I say drily.

They usher me over to Kaelber Hall, and everyone clears away from us in a close reenactment of the parting of the Red Sea.

"Well, look who's back," I mumble under my breath as the paparazzi's flashes are going off non stop, and I see spots. Sean must have tipped them off he'd be coming in this morning, which explains why they weren't waiting for me, for once. "His Highness must be close by."

Once inside, my two very well-trained gorillas stand at attention, keeping a firm hold on my arms, by all appearances preventing me from interrupting whatever's going on in here. When my eyes adjust and I no longer see white spots, I see him. Perfect as usual, the picture of an airbrushed model from where I stand some thirty feet away, his chiseled features too well-preserved. Guess fifty is the new twenty.

He's holding court in the foyer, a gaggle of professors standing there agog. Dean Hawkesbury is not faring any better, clearly just as impressed as the others. And Mrs. Pringle is about ready to expire from apoplexy judging by the purple color of her complexion, just from the close attention he's paying her.

"So, tell me, Eleanor. I may call you Eleanor, right?" he says, head cocking to the side.

"Yes, Eleanor ... I'm Eleanor," she stutters as he steps closer to her, and she squints at him through her half-moon glasses. "You ... you're ... you ... Mr. Elliot, you look just like Robert Redford up close," she blurts, trembling fingers coming up to cover her mouth, and I fight not to roll my eyes.

"Eleanor," he says, bending at eye level. "It's *young* Robert Redford *who happens* to look just like me. Oh, and that mauve twin set and pearls I must say, simply sublime on you." He kisses her knuckles, and Mrs. Pringle swoons. I roll my eyes.

"You're right. Young Robert Redford happens to look just like you," she says in dazed tone of voice.

"Of course I'm right. Now where were we? Ah, yes. Eleanor. My son Liam's office is in here somewhere from what I understand? Show me."

"What the hell are you doing?" I ask from the other side of the foyer. "Ever heard of the word disowned?"

"Ah. And here's my prodigal son," he announces to his audience.

"We need to talk," I snap, my eyes intent on him. "Alone."

"By all means, let's talk," he says, something like a triumphant glint passing through his eyes. He looks around as if searching for a space, and Dean Hawkesbury trips over his own feet opening up the small conference room.

I walk by him, motioning with my head. "Lose your dogs."

He gives them a silent command, and they step back.

I let him pass, and slam the door shut, leaning on it. Well, this is going to be interesting, if the victorious expression on his face is anything to go by. I school my expression into impassivity, but on a scale of one to angry, I've shot straight past seeing red and landed on blood boiling.

"Think you can pressure me into signing over those rights by making me star in your freak show outside?" I ask point blank.

He looks at his manicured nails. "Yes, actually," he says in a bored tone.

"Think again. Eiloe's not yours to take, and will never be made into a movie," I reply.

"That's where you're wrong. Your Eiloe is multi-billion adoring fans, movie material," he says, one shoulder coming to rest on the wall. "And you'll sign." He gloats, crossing his lanky arms over his overpriced dark grey suit, crossing an ankle. "Live, actually, in about oh, sixty-eight minutes or so," he adds, checking his Rolex, buffing it with his cuff, re-checking it, nodding satisfied.

I let out a snort. "In your dreams."

He looks up the ceiling, shaking his head. "Liam, Liam, Liam," he sighs in a desolate tone, a technique of his I know quite well, and it grates on my nerves, as always. I cross my ankle, shoving my hands in the front pockets of my jeans, waiting him out.

"I've just read an interesting report on my way over," he casually drops; his fingers' steeple in front of his mouth, and he looks me over. "About a young woman named Éolie. Such a lovely, unusual name, don't you agree?" he asks.

My breath hitches, and my hands fist in my pockets, heart thudding.

"I seem to recall there was an elusive Éolie in your life, once upon a time, one you couldn't stop talking about. And wouldn't you know? An Éolie did stay in Bar Harbor a few short weeks ago, a *delicious* beauty by all accounts. Funny coincidence, no?" he says, knowingly.

I slowly straighten from my slouch. My pulse picks up, and I struggle to keep my features devoid of any other reaction.

"She's not been seen since she checked out of a little beachside hotel. One of your favorite local hangouts, it so happens. I think she's still around. What do you think? Picture this, son. A treasure hunt, a too-good-to-pass-up worldwide search for your mysterious Éolie, your stories come to life—"

I lunge for him, slamming him against the wall, forearm resting on his windpipe, applying pressure, slowly but consistently. He stands on the tip of his toes, his face graying.

"Where did you learn those moves—?" he chokes.

"What? Didn't think I learned my lesson? You disappoint me, Sean. It's not as if I'd think trusting bodyguards should be enough, right?" He narrows his eyes by a fraction. I stare him down, maintaining just the right degree of pressure of my arm and my body to keep him immobilized, and I watch him struggle to maintain eye contact without flinching.

"Listen up, and listen good," I hiss. "You'll forget about her. You'll erase any traces of her. And you better start praying it works, 'cause anyone so much as breathes her name out there, and something called the 'mbrón dhaid' files will be all over the place before you can blink."

His eyes widen briefly at the mention of the files, but his expression just as quickly shutters down. "You lie," he spits, his voice coming out hoarse as I reapply a bit of pressure. My eyes never stray from his.

"Am I? Let's see. How's this for a movie synopsis? Actor-God engineers his son's abduction to spike up his declining ratings, and it works wonders across the board. The whole world prays with him, and the public's smitten all over again. It's a WinWin. Only, there's an unexpected twist in the plot. His son survives against all odds. Slighted Actor-God can no longer play the role of his lifetime, 'mbrón dhaid,' or grieving father in Irish Gaelic, as the script explained. Should I continue?"

"You have no proof," he sneers.

"Try me. Download time estimated at point six seconds to all major media, starting with your Jumbotron out there," I say, my voice is low, warning, and he makes an incredulous noise. My whole body slams into him, applying more pressure, and I lock my arm on his throat, shifting a little to pick my phone up with my other hand. Sweat starts to dot on his already pale face, but his eyes are cold as fuck. "At the press of my speed dial, Sean." I hold my left arm away, and lock my thumb on the keyboard, my gaze never once leaving his.

"Go ahead, I dare you. People will believe what I tell them to," he rasps, but uncertainty plays across his reddening features.

"Yeah, I know, but it will be too late. The controversy will have killed your persona," I say, sliding my thumb, unlocking my phone.

"You're not ready to put anything out there. You hate limelight. I call your bluff," he taunts. I raise one eyebrow.

I hold up my phone. "Activate. Voice. Recognition. App," I command into the speaker.

"Bing Android Voice Recognition App Activated. Hello, Liam," my phone replies.

His eyes bulge.

"Speed dial six," I say.

The computer begins the auto-dial. "Speed dialing six—"

"Hold," Sean chokes out, darkly scowling. "What do you want really?"

I press end, heart pounding.

"Should be easy enough. For you to forget I even exist. Leave me and mine alone, or I won't hesitate to unload the truth," I say.

He stares at me, my gaze is unwavering.

"Deal, or no deal?" I ask.

He remains quiet, glacier blue eyes coldly gauging.

"So be it. Just remember, this was your decision," I say, dead serious, sliding my thumb, unlocking my phone once again.

"Deal," he says, eyes going devoid of any emotion.

It takes everything in me not to slump in relief. But still, I don't let go just yet.

"How did you find them? I destroyed any proof—" he begins, but I squeeze anew, interrupting him, relenting a bit on the pressure after a few seconds.

"How we came upon them is of no matter. I do have copies of the files secured with me and with friends, that's all you need to know," I say, finally letting go so abruptly he almost collapses.

He straightens, tugging at his collar, and I back away, suddenly disgusted at sharing the same air space with this man.

"She's just a girl. You could be adored by billions of fans, live on eternally for posterity. I don't get it," he says, a bit of color returning to his face.

"Not surprised, you never did get me," I answer back, headed for the exit, "or the concept of love."

I watch the helicopter take off, soon becoming a small dot on the horizon. Tamping down on my giddiness, I walk up to the makeshift stage, a cordon of Sean's security people opening up a corridor.

"Focus, man, this is your last public appearance before disappearing into an elusive writer recluse," I say under my breath. I inhale, exhale, concentrating on my respiration. I climb up the four steps and my image appears live, magnified by multiple screens behind me. I walk past the backdrop of wannabe Eiloe movie posters, chairs sitting empty behind a long table wired with microphones, picking one up along the way.

Screams, shouts, flashes non-stop, questions yelled right and left bombard me.

I feel Éolie's Light pulsing warm and bright, pulling at me, calling me inward. Images immediately form in my mind's eye, bringing peacefulness in chaos.

Éolie walks through a meadow full of wild flowers in bloom, surrounding a yellow house with red shutters nestled deep in the lush forest and somewhere, close by, a brook gurgles ... Liam, come and see. Her face lit from within, she waits.

I stay right there at the heart of the lush Forest of Laure, blocking everything else away as I address the masses.

"Something came up and Sean Elliot Pierce had to leave, so guess it's just you and me," I say. "No suspense, Sean and I agreed to disagree, and I'm confirming that no movies will be made of Eiloe. Ever."

The crowd boos.

"Before you all get up in arms and boo me off till kingdom come, know that it's a personal stand, one I took at a very young age, and not by any means a reflection on the movie industry as a whole. So even though I'm touched by your show of appreciation and your enthusiasm, I can't let it sway my decision."

"It's been rehashed everywhere the past few weeks. So, yeah, at seven I was abducted, the details of which are irrelevant. What is still relevant today, and will still be relevant tomorrow, is that I was saved by this little spark that fired up my imagination, giving me the means to escape to a better world, a better place, a better time, giving me strength, breeding hope, inspiring me, freeing me. The stories that have swirled in my head ever since are written down first and foremost to spark one's imagination. My way to pay it forward, if you will."

I pause, closing my eyes for a brief second, gratitude filling me up.

"There are more than a hundred million Eiloe versions out there, mine, yours, theirs, thanks to everyone's imagination, each one unique, each one irreplaceable. Don't ask me to limit Eiloe, confining it to only one for all eternity. It's not so much that I won't, it's more like I can't. I owe it to me, I owe it to all of us to keep it alive only in the imagination. Endless possibilities. Ours for the taking every time we open a book. So what are we waiting for? Go read about it. I'll be right there alongside you. Safe journey home, everyone."

The rhythmic sounds of clapping, cheering, and whistling bring me back to the here and now, but I pay it no heed. I step off the scaffolding and my hired crew appears, surrounding me as they part the crowd. Flashes go off, and I don't even mind now that I see an end to it.

"Can you get me out of here," I yell to the closest security guard over the crowd's roar, and he signals me with his thumb up.

I'm on a high, feeling lightheaded, feeling lighthearted.

I'm coming home. The Forest of Laure calls to me, waiting to be lived, for real this time. I believe.

Thirty-Eight

LIAM

Back at the condo less than an hour later, I park and cut the engine. "Let's do this," I say under my breath as I open the car's door, and step out. I stand there for a beat or two. No one's jumping out from the bushes, no one's yelling questions, no cameras are flashing, nothing.

I sure won't take for granted that's the end of their crazies, but for now ... I can feel the nip in the air, smell the briny sea air, and hear the sound of waves crashing on the shore, and I welcome back the sensations and the freedom of being that comes with it.

"I'll take it," I say out loud.

I've lost seventeen years of pressure off my chest, a weight I didn't know I carried until it came off. I run up the steps, and unlock the door to our shared flat.

No Éolie-Jolie to greet me.

"Honey, I'm home," I call out playfully.

Silence.

"Éolie?" I call out once more, walking over to the kitchen then the study.

I sprint towards the hall, my worry spiking directly to panic, my thoughts scattering in unwanted directions. What if...?

I exhale, and my shoulders sag in relief. She's curled up in bed napping, and I know just what's missing in the picture. I shrug out of my coat, pulling my shirt off, chucking my jeans along the way, ready to join her in slumber for the next few hours, my previous adrenaline rush fizzling out. I dive into bed, spooning Éolie from behind. The moment my arms surround her, I'm zapped, sucked inward by her Light.

A wide-open window ... a warm summer breeze ruffles my hair. The fresh aromas of the forest after a rain shower overpowering.

I'm sitting behind a rustic kitchen table, its wood scratched and mellowed out with the passage of time. The room I find myself in must have been originally designed to be part of a covered porch judging by the yellow wood siding on the anchor walls, complete with slanted ceiling, painted wood plank floor, half-walls, and low windows, but is now converted into an L shape study, nestled in the woods.

Piles and piles of books and research material are spread all over, and I recognize my usual creative madness messiness. A side door squeaks. Éolie—not the version I embraced in bed just now, but another, softer version if that's even possible—comes out on the other half of the wraparound porch, her arms full of something that I can't clearly make out from this angle. She carefully holds onto a squirming bundle as she lets the old-fashioned screen door clack closed on her butt.

I lean as far back as I can in the chair to get a better look.

Holy Mother of God.

She's cradling a ... toddler? She rocks him gently from side to side, singing a sweet lullaby, and I recognize one of the melodies she used to sing to me when we were kids. Thinking about it makes my heart tumble.

She kisses the top of his short, light-blond curls, one hand tenderly rubbing his back, and the little dude nestles in the crook of her neck, sucking his thumb, completely abandoned.

I'm held spellbound. The nurturing vision sticks, and goose bumps travel up my arms. I don't make a sound, afraid to break the spell.

Éolie spots something outside, and stills. The little guy's head whips up. "Come and see the rainbow, quick," she calls out.

And my quiet spell explodes as, from somewhere inside the house, a stampede shakes up the rafters, followed by high-pitched squeals. And one, two, three, no wait ... make that four. *Four* children pop out of the house, oohing and aahing on the porch, right along with Éolie. The baby claps his hands excitedly cooing at them all. I study them while they study the sky, and I couldn't care less about a rainbow—a sight that pales in comparison to watching Éolie be a mother. The little one falls silent, resting his head in the crook of her neck. Slowly, his lids droop until, finally, they shut as he drifts off.

Éolie murmurs something to the children before she heads back inside with the little dude drooling, slumped on her shoulder, out for the count.

"Rose u're it u're it u're it," one tiny little girl with light-blonde hair, and familiar-looking sea-green eyes framed in dark-brown eyelashes, squeals, jumping up and down in front of another, slightly older little girl. This one a darker blonde with vivid indigo-blue eyes...

"Am not, you didn't touch me, Sophie," Rose says, skipping away toward the two stairs leading down to the yard. Beyond a patch of clover is a meadow thick with wild flowers and, beyond it, the sound of a brook gurgling close.

"She's only three, Rose. C'mon, give her chance," an older boy says, blocking Rose's escape. And Christ almighty, he'd be the spitting image of me at age seven, right up to the messy mop of dark hair and the dimple on his chin if it weren't for his striking, pale-aqua eyes.

"Come, Sophie, let's catch Rose together," says another boy, and I do a double take. There's another one identical to me ... I mean to him...

Holy shit.

"That's cheating, Sébastien," Rose cries out upon spying one of the twins bending low, offering Sophie a piggy back ride. "And Nicolas is blocking me, it's against the rules," she pouts, stamping her foot and crossing her arms.

"Pfft, I don't follow any of your rules, Sorceress. I'm a Dragon Lord, Guardian of the Laure." Nicolas raises a brow, and looks her in the eye. "I'm protecting all of you. That means you too, Knight of the Laure, like it or not. So, you coming?"

Sébastien shoots him a look, and they strike up a silent conversation, rapid-fire expressions crossing back and forth between the two. Sophie jumps down from her ride in front of Rose, and the twins take off, disappearing into the undergrowth surrounding my study.

"If I can't be a 'nitelor' like Sébastien, then I wanna be a 'dragonlor' like

Nicolas, not a fairy," Sophie pleads, watching the boys disappear into the forest.

"You're too small," Rose replies, putting her arm round Sophie's shoulders, her gaze tracking the boys.

"Am not, I'm bigger than Mathieu. Let him be the fairy," Sophie wails.

"Awwww, Sophie, don't cry. Mathieu's my little firefly, he can't be both," Rose says, hugging her close. "And when dragons cry, it puts out their fire," she explains, bending at eye level.

"I forgot," Sophie sniffles.

"If you don't want to be a fairy anymore, I'll change you into a dragonfly for now, just until you're big enough. How's that?" Rose says.

"A dragonfly." Sophie's eyes light up her face as she jumps up and down, arms flailing all over, cute as a button in her daisy covered dungarees and skewed pigtails.

"Fairy Fairy Dragonfly *be*," Rose incants, wiggling a sparkly miniature wand she took out of the side pocket of her navy-blue cargo shorts, her long braid swishing down her back.

"I'm a dragonflydwagonflydwaagonfly," Sophie singsongs underneath my windows.

The upper half of her face suddenly pops up, little fingers gripping the windowsill, wondrous sea-green eyes looking straight at me. "Come and see, Papa."

And I fall head over heels. Chair and all.

Thirty-Nine

LIAM

I hit the floor beside the bed with a dull thud. *Jesus.* I get up on my elbows, taking stock. I'm back in the condo's bedroom.

Éolie's face appears above me on the bed, surprise written all over, wondrous sea-green eyes looking straight at me, and my heart takes another tumble into déjà vu.

"How did you end up down there?" she asks, blinking.

"I ... fell..." I stutter, distracted by the instant replay streaming in fast forward in the back of my mind. "I don't understand how any of that happened. I just embraced you, and you sucked me into this ... this vision," I say, amazed all over again.

"I did? Like just now?" she asks, scooting over as I crawl back in bed next to her.

"You had the cutest toddler on your hip, and you were all watching a rainbow and..." I stare off.

"You were there?" she asks, and her face lights up. "Wow, this is so cool. I wonder how I was able to just pull you in like that, I didn't even see you."

"I watched from my study," I say, propping on my hands, dazed anew. "We're having *five* kids?"

"That we know of," she deadpans.

"Holy shit." My arms fold under me, and I almost end up sprawled on the floor once again. I dart my head towards her. Propped on her stomach, her chin comes to rest on her hands, and her face grows soft and luminous as she looks down on me. The lit-up face of an angel.

Even so, the truth of what I saw, and what she just said, hits me square in the gut. "Éolie? Seriously? More than five ... really?" I ask, astonished. "How's that possible?"

"Not my fault. You're that *virily* potent, just saying," she says, batting her eyelashes. And I can't help it. I laugh.

"Virily, indeed." I open one arm, and she instantly cuddles next to me, one hand coming to rest on my chest. Propping her chin on her bended arm, her index finger absently traces imaginary infinity symbols on my left pec. On the other hand, it might be an eight for all I know.

Bloody hell. "Please tell me your vision's not upgrading to eight right now ... I need way more time to keep up," I say, half-groaning. Her gaze collides with mine.

"The possibility of them freaks you out?" she asks quietly.

I caress her forearm in a back-and-forth stroke, getting lost in thought.

"It's not that, not really," I muse. "But I'm still reeling, I guess. I never really saw myself as a father. Not that clearly anyway. I know all about fucked-up fathers, but nothing about what it is that makes a dad a great one. What if I fuck up and mess them up?"

"We'll mess up, sometimes. I'm sure. But mess them up? I don't think so. I won't let you for one, and you've got your heart in the right place for two." Éolie's fingers curl over my arm and squeezes lightly. "And they seemed pretty well adjusted in the vision we just shared, non?"

"They were all so ... happy, carefree, *living* their childhood. That moment, that glimpse, it was beautiful, Éolie-Jolie. Have you seen it before?"

"I've had these moments with you, or with them, nearly all my life," she says with a faraway look, her cheek coming to rest on my chest. "For the longest time, I thought I was projecting in my dreams what I wished for, or wished I could have had myself. But you do exist. So, I guess they probably do too, somewhere down the line. The only thing is..." her voice wavers. She sighs, and her breath tickles my skin.

"The only thing is?" I urge, gently sweeping the tip of her braid on her nose.

"I don't know how it will play out ... Life happens, and I'm not an exact science. From what I understand, what we see are possibilities, not reality. And yet, as silly as it sounds, I'd be heartbroken if anything happened, and they couldn't be..." She sighs once more. "I'm not sure if I feel blessed or cursed for having seen."

I kiss the top of her head. "Come here, you," I say, bringing her on top of me. I cradle her cheek close to my heart, rubbing the small of her back in slow, gentle strokes underneath her camisole. Soothing her soothes me, and we remain quiet for a little while.

"I really want to meet them," she says, her voice barely audible.

"Count your blessings then, I've been told I'm manly potent," I reply cockily, and she smothers a laugh. Ah. There's my girl. I flip her underneath me, and place my hands beside her head.

She comes up to deposit a soft kiss on the corner of my lips. "Thank you for this," she says, her eyes smiling anew.

"Anything else that I should know that you know?" I ask on a teasing note.

"Let me think," she says, growing entirely too serious, her otherworldly eyes turning inward. Holy hell. Guess the bloody joke's on me. I straighten and wait. And wait. And wait. The space of a few heartbeats. An eternity.

"Why am I suddenly nervous about what you're not saying?" I ask, eyes growing wide.

"You should be, absolutely—" Éolie starts to reply, but abruptly comes to a halt. I do as well. Brain, heart, lungs, horny thoughts, everything halts, bracing for impact, ready to keel over at the next reveal. "—relieved to know that no, I don't. Have anything else. Forest of Laure, yellow house, five little kids, you know as much as I do," she says, shooting me one of her impish look.

I let out a pent-out breath, and toss my head back. "Good one," I manage, nodding. "Enjoy. You won't pull that trick on me twice."

"I'm sorry," she says, biting her bottom lip in a vain effort to contain laughter. "You should have seen your face, though."

In a quick move, I flip her over and straddle the back of her thighs, shifting suggestively. I cup her bottom, then lift it up. She inhales sharply, burying her face in a pillow. My grin turns wolfish. My lips trail down her shoulder blades, coming to rest for a quick kiss at the back of her neck, and she shivers. I slowly straighten, one of my hands loosely twisting her braid in my fist.

"Well, look what I caught. And I'm not letting you off the hook. You're mine now."

She moans softly, pushing into my erection, and I swell harder.

I groan, rolling my hips into her, spreading her legs wider. And I give myself over, completely caught in the moment.

"I love you," I say, just before I set out to show her.

Forty

ÉOLIE

As we lie in bed after our impromptu love session, Liam is decidedly buoyant as he retells what went down earlier on campus with Sean, and I have this tingly feeling in my chest, one I get when things are about to change in rapid succession. But for now, I revel in the warmth I see reflected in his eyes, and his dimple peeking out the corner of his mouth every few minutes.

"You did it." I kiss Liam all over his face. "Checkmate."

"Checkmate, hey. Nice. I like that. Yeah, I believe he is. I really do. Sean's out of my life and you're safe from him now," he says, nodding a few times, a joyous glint in his eyes. "You were so right, Éolie-Jolie, the crazies will end soon."

"Told you." I waggle my eyebrows, and he laughs.

"Know what this means?" he asks, his entire face lit, and the joy I see in his bright-blue eyes draw me in.

"No, what?" I ask, indulging him.

He props his head up on his hand, and a slow smile creases his cheeks. "It means we can begin to plan ahead. How about a road trip to Montréal for starters?"

My eyes grow wide. Hugging him, I cry out, "I'd love to."

"There's only three weeks left to the semester, means I better start planning now." He hops out of bed, shooting me a toothy grin. He pulls on sweats before strutting out of the bedroom in long-legged strides.

His head pops back into the doorway. "Oh, and by the way? The search is on." He winks before popping back out.

"Wait, what search?" I ask, thrilled to see him in such high spirit.

His head pops back in. "You, me, five kids in a yellow house. So the way I figure it, it stands to reason the Forest of Laure you showed me way back when, is out there, waiting for us somewhere. But right now? I'm off to plan our trip to Montréal."

I jump out of bed and pick Liam's shirt up off the floor. I put it up to my nose for a brief second, inhaling him, before putting it on.

"A trip to Montréal and a search for the Forest of Laure," I say, twirling on my toes, beyond happy.

From the beginning, I felt deep in my bones that the crazies over Liam's father would end eventually, even when Liam himself had pretty good reasons to doubt it. We can finally rejoin the rest of the world. Come and go as we please. Montréal though? Montréal's still up in the air since I've always had this strange pull towards it. So I don't rightly know if it's meaningful or wishful, but ever since Liam first offered to go visit with me, my gut is no longer quietly pulling in that direction, it's screaming, tugging, jumping up and down, and right now the surge is electrifying me. I'm coming home; I feel it, I can almost taste it.

My stomach rumbles. We skipped the noon hour with all of these revelations, and I'm famished, I suddenly realize.

Putting this energy overflow to good use, I prepare tossed avocado chunks, walnuts, cubed Bosc pears, shredded cheddar cheese, and dried cranberries in a sesame dressing, snacking on it as I go along, stuffing myself up to the gills.

I make a quick grilled cheese sandwich to go with my side dish, and bring it down to the study with a cup of strong black coffee, sliding the plate on the desk, in front of a focused Liam.

He startles, leaning away from his laptop, glancing down at the meal as if wondering where it came from. "Talk about stealth haute cuisine, I didn't hear anything. I thought you were napping," he says, angling a brow rakishly. "Worn out."

"We worked up an appetite. Hungry won over worn out," I reply.

"I'll take it," he says, his voice thick with amusement, wrapping one arm around my lower back. "I like you hungry even better than worn out."

"Then you're out of luck. I'm neither, right this minute." My fingers naturally thread their way into dark silky locks, smoothing his mop of messy hair. "But I figured you might be hungry." His lopsided grin tugs at his lips. "What were you reading that got you so absorbed?" I ask, dropping a kiss on top of his head before glancing over at the computer screen.

"Theo just sent me Sean's official press release, and he's not only endorsing my wishes for Eiloe, but he spun it around and he's asking fans to respect my privacy from now on, or else..." he says, taking a sip of his coffee. "I'm savoring."

"To freedom of being," I say, lifting my hand and we high five on it.

"End of semester in one word. Montréal." Liam sighs happily, digging in, his plateful fast disappearing.

"Ask me any questions about Montréal," I say enthusiastically, plopping down on the chair by his desk. "Like, for instance, did you know that it was first called Ville-Marie? Or that in 1535, Jacques Cartier simply climbed up Ville-Marie's mountain and named it Mount-Royal, or, according to Monsieur François's preferred theory, Mont-Réal in old Occitan French, thereby taking possession in the name of François 1er, Roi de France. And basically, that's all it took. Incroyable non?" I say, bringing my heels up on the seat, and my arms fold around my bended knees.

"Monsieur François's didn't kid around. Jesus, he really talks your ears off when he's with you," Liam comments, entertained, polishing off his meal.

"I don't mind really. I find it endearing," I say fondly. "The minute he gets here, he turns into a closet historian let loose. He's like a fountain of knowledge spewing out wacky facts. The way he talks about it? You'd swear those were the days, and we missed out on Jacques and his brilliant real estate development strategies."

"Any one of those facts more recent than the Renaissance by any chance? You know, something we could use, or do?" he asks absently, re-focused on his screen, typing away.

"Tons. Loads," I reply in an even tone of voice, and he peeks at me over his laptop. "We're just not there yet. But ask me again next Monday, I'm sure I'll have better material for you." I shoot him a mischievous look, but it's lost on him. He's suddenly sitting on the edge of his seat, clicking like mad.

"Éolie? Curious here. The Forest of Laure? Is it actually a name from a real place?" he asks, eyes glued to his screen.

"Um ... Good question. I think it naturally came to me, but I can't say from where, I was so little, why?" I ask, pulled up short by the question. I watch a grin slowly spread from ear to ear.

"Because I just typed it into the search engine for the heck of it, and I got more than eight million hits."

His eyes dart, reading quickly, and his smile stretches even wider, full dimples out, and I forget I'm supposed to breathe. Pulse picking up with a portent of things to come, I get up and walk over to his side.

"Check this out," he says, pulling me onto his lap. As he scrolls down, breathtaking photos appear one after the other. Green mountains rolling as far as the eyes can see, ski resorts and picturesque villages nestled in valleys within forests so lush I can practically smell the evergreens and hear the melting snow coming down in torrents, gorging up streams and lakes. I'm shocked by the eerily familiar vistas. It feels as if I've been there before.

I start reading the article Liam downloaded from a travel blog, a bit too floored to comprehend much at first, but when the dots connect...

Les Laurentides, it reads, 'along with its stunning natural beauty are also a delightful year-round destination for getting outdoors, whether it's for cycling, hiking and white-water rafting in the summer or skiing and dog sledding in the winter. The resort area begins at Saint-Sauveur-des-Monts and extends north to Mont-Tremblant. Beyond, the region turns into a wilderness of lakes and forests best visited with an outfitter. To the first visitor, the hilly areas around Saint-Sauveur, Sainte-Adèle, Morin-Heights, Val-Morin and Val-David up to Sainte-Agathe-des-Monts form a pleasant hodgepodge of villages, hotels and inns that seem to blend one into another—all of this to be found in less than a couple hours' drive from downtown Montréal, traffic allowing...'

"Liam ... the Forest of Laure ... it's real," I breathe softly, heart rate wildly beating. "It's happening."

"Damn straight," he says. "When the semester ends, we're going home."

Forty-One

ÉOLIE

It's Monday, and as soon as Monsieur François leaves the condo after our cooking lesson, I start scribbling into the Log Book my latest findings under **The Forest of Laure Research**, regarding our transportation under the tab **Experimental Set-Up / Phase One**. I write down, "ditch the train, ditch the bus, seven hours by car, no brainer" into the comments section.

According to the maps I pored over, Bar Harbor is not that far from Montréal, but we would have to detour to Boston or New York first to go there by train. And, well, forget bus hopping with the amount of luggage we would have to carry around. *So many clothes, so little space*, I write down in jest into the margin.

So I guess renting a car from Montréal is no longer an option either, and I cross a line over it, scratching it out. Looks like we're driving from here.

With Liam at class and my cooking lesson over, I slip earbuds in and turn up the volume on Liam's iPod. Within minutes my ears are ringing from Liam's heavy metal rock playlist. I switch to classical music, getting lost in Vivaldi's *Winter* as I write some more comments into the Log Book.

A minute later, someone grabs me from behind and I yelp, craning my neck, and relax when I see that it's Liam. He whirls me around in a circle before setting me down, and I drop the notebook on an exhale, trying to reattach my galloping heart. I yank the earbuds out and turn to face him. "You're back!" I cry out the obvious. "Had a good class?"

He slides off his messenger bag onto the counter and shrugs his coat off, leaving it to hang on one of the kitchen stools. "Let's just say campus is almost back to, well ... the usual," he says, a sardonic smile twisting his lips. "Enough said on that, how's the Going Home playlist coming along?" he asks, kissing my forehead, and I offer him one earbud.

"Aaah. Vivaldi's *Four Seasons.* I knew it'd be either classical, Celtic, or Gregorian," he says, gamely bumping his shoulder into mine, giving me back the earbud.

"Hey, I grew up on CCG's and whales' songs. Consider yourself lucky I decided to mix it up. How do you make it play without the earbuds?" I ask, fiddling with it.

He hooks his iPod to his computer and sets it on the kitchen island as I retrieve my notebook and put it back on the counter. Vivaldi's *Spring* fills the air with its allegros and powerful solos, and I hum contentedly.

"For your info, I've added Stan Getz, Dave Brubeck Quartet's *Take Five,* and some Michael Bublé too," I boast, hopping on a stool.

"Man, Yann will get a kick out of that. He drove us all bonkers with jazz at one time. It's the only thing he'd listen to, and eventually it grew on all of us," he says, mouth quirking up one side. And I quirk mine too, writing "expand playlist with some more jazz" under **To Do**, adding "and thank Yann too."

"Hmmm, so you like the violin, huh?" He scratches his unshaved jaw, his sexy stubbles distracting me. I prop my chin on my hand as he crouches in front of his laptop and quickly goes through his titles, selecting one. "Let's try some of this."

He folds his arms leaning on the counter, cocking his head, waiting. Soon, we hear throughout his laptop speakers the sound of a guy's self-assured footsteps echoing in what seems to be an empty studio, intriguing me. And before long, I'm swept along by some pretty awesome violin playing.

"What was that?" I ask, spellbound.

"Coldplay, *Viva La Vida,* in a rendition by German virtuoso David Garrett. The guy plays crossover rock violin to help introduce people to classical music," he says, winking. "Which is funny in its own way. Just you wait. I'll get you to cross over to rock." His voice takes a turn towards smug as he struts over to the fridge, selecting a bottled drink.

"Play it again," I request, the music's energy still coursing through me.

"Knew it," he says with a chuckle, putting the upbeat solo back on, shaking his head at my antics as I dance my way through the piece, with arms above my head.

"I love this! And that makes you now officially in charge of the playlist for the entire road trip," I say, plopping back down on the stool, adding it to the Log Book. "Just go easy on me. No heavy metal solos please. For now it's an acquired taste I haven't acquired yet." I wrinkle my nose.

"Not a problem. My taste in music is pretty eclectic, so I've tons of other stuff in there besides that," he says, a smile lingering on. "So? What's it to be, train, *bus torture*, or car?" he asks, uncapping his bottle of cranberry juice, chugging it down.

"Car," I decide. But now, it means we'll need a bigger one than his current rental car, a small cabriolet. My estimation for the cargo space required for Liam's luggage alone? Mind boggling. The guy has more jeans than is acceptable for any one human being to own.

"Highway or back roads?"

"Highway to Montréal, and back roads from there?" I suggest, biting my lip, pleating and un-pleating a paper napkin I used for a fruit snack earlier on. I silently add, *but to do so, we'll need a car a bit bigger than a sardine can.*

"No bus rides anywhere in there, *thank you god*," Liam quips, looking up the ceiling, saluting with his drink.

"Like that wasn't a given." I roll my eyes. Liam dropped enough hints over the last few days that bus travel was the very top contender on his least favorite ways to travel.

"That's because you love me, right?" he says with an overly cheesy grin.

"That's more of a strategic decision, actually." I stroke my chin, deciding to tease him a little.

"Oh?" he says, one eyebrow angling up.

"Do you have any idea how much luggage you'd have to carry around just for your clothes? I'm not even sure they'd let you ride on the bus," I snicker, and Liam leans back on the counter, crossing his arms.

"Cute," he says drily. "Want to travel light?" he asks, hands coming down on the counter, slowly leaning in, stopping a breath away from my lips, and mine hitches. "Ditch the suitcases, we'll keep clothes optional." He straightens, glints of mischief sparkling in his eyes.

I give him a dry look. "You're so *cute*," I volley back to him.

"I know," he says, a slow smile creasing his cheeks. He ducks, and my bunched-up napkin ends up sailing over his head.

"Ditch the jeans, Éolie, it's no big deal." He straightens, chuckling low.

"No way. I grew attached," I say, "we just need more cargo space ... Your car's kind of too small." I wince, sitting on my hands to stop myself from fidgeting, waiting.

His eyes narrow in thought. "I'm not driving the tin can I rented over such a long stretch of road with you in there anyway, that's for sure," he says. "Let me see what I can do."

He picks his laptop, flicking the tip of my nose on his way over to the study, and I let my smile spread from ear to ear.

Forty-Two

LIAM

"Let me get this straight. You bought your first car ever, online, and a Volvo at that, after years of drooling over them, and it's ... a cross-country *station wagon*?" Zac says, scrunching up his sweaty face on my video chat screen, the frame split between his mug, Theo's, and Yann's.

I stretch back, lacing my hands behind my head. "Yep. One-clicked a car."

"Did I miss something between now, and then? What happened to the vintage sports convertible Volvo P1900 you swore you'd get if you stayed in one place long enough?" Zac asks pointedly. "The one I wanted to drive."

"Life happened and besides, I've big plans for that station wagon involving Éolie and driving," I reply, completely unfazed. "Have you checked its security specs on the link I sent?"

"Hey, could have been a minivan," Theo deadpans, and I almost flip backwards.

"Get over it, Zac. It's a *Volvo* station wagon, what's not to like?" Yann says, eyes downcast as he reads something on his own screen— "with the rear seats up, there's a very usable nine hundred forty-two litres of cargo space in the back, fold them down, and you open up two thousand forty-two litres of space. Quick math here, dude. Do you know how many pairs of skis, or kayaks, or mountain bikes, or rolled down sleeping bags, and yeah ... well, whatever goes with that—" Yann cuts off, ears turning fire engine red.

"Fine, you had me at skis," Zac gripes, swatting a few mosquitoes buzzing around his face. "Please tell me it's red. The car. Not Yann."

"Forget red, man. I'm blending in. It'll be the most epic, bland color there is," I sigh contentedly. I ordered it twelve days ago, asking for the first available one for shipment here with Canadian specs. I'm thinking dirt brown, beige, or possibly silver grey from the pictures I've seen on the web.

"Who'd have thought." Zac shakes his head, a sly grin forming. "It's bloody working. You're really turning out to be normal," he says, uncapping a bottled water and guzzling it down.

"Getta outta here, you arse," I retort, throwing a paper clip at him, and he doesn't even flinch.

"When's lift off, now that Academia's freed from you?" Yann asks.

"Just waiting on the car's delivery, due here on Thursday." I check on the status to see if it's still on target. "Lift off expected in two days from now. So, Friday, early morning, boys."

"Holy shit," Theo exclaims, eyebrows shooting up. "Did you check Quebec's road regulations?"

Zac, Yann and I share a "what the f—" look.

"If I read the government website correctly, you're not only allowed studded winter tires from October to get this, May, but it's kind of recommended," Theo says aghast. "Christ, Liam, that's *eight months* out of the year."

Zac snickers. "You may drive a respectable Volvo station wagon, man. But hey, it's a studded one."

"That's one long-ass winter, dude." Yann whistles low.

"That's one long-ass ski season, dudes. With loads of après-ski," I say smugly.

I smirk, watching their sold on looks popping left and right, all over my screen. Skiing will do that to the best of us, and the après-ski speaks for itself, no comments.

"Bloody good point," Theo says, blinking.

"Aww, man, talk about dehydration. Now I'll drool over snow on top of sweating twenty-four/seven," Zac says, wiping his face on his tee. "Heads up. I want out of the jungle for winter break. Go find me a ski lodge getaway, stat."

Forty-Three

ÉOLIE

The only thing left to check mark on my To-Do List Thursday night is to go load up the car. Except for a few last-minute odds and ends for my duffel, which will double as an overnight bag for light travel, much to Liam's enthusiasm, everything's packed and ready to go.

I grab my coat, putting it on with knitted cap and gloves, fairly bouncing down the steps. By now, Liam should be finished with the Volvo guy.

Turning around the corner to the parking lot, I stop in my tracks. Liam's hands are braced on top of the car, his fingers beating in a staccato. "I didn't even know they made red station wagons," I say amazed. The car is a beautiful shade of metallic red.

"What are the odds, right?" he asks tilting his head up, eyeing the twilight sky. "The only one available for express shipment with the required specs is a *bloody red one*," he says sardonically.

"Don't listen to him, you're not *that* red." I pat the car consolingly. Blame it on my upbringing if you will, but I can't help but look at our car the same way I looked at the Thalassa. To me, they're not only marvels of engineering, but also something close to a breathing, living organism with its own personality. Companions, if you will. Well okay, a sailboat is probably closer to it than a car, but I don't care. "What's wrong with red anyway?" I ask Liam, mystified.

"It's a look at me froufrou color for a serious car," he grumbles. I turn, looping my arms around his waist, giving him a quick, comforting hug.

"Not that it's much of a consolation, but I like that's it a quirky color for a serious car. It gives *Odyssey* a surprising edge, adds a certain je ne sais quoi, sort of a dangerous flair to her seriousness," I say, down pulling his dark beanie over his brow to lighten the mood. He gives me a wry look.

"Odyssey? We're not naming the car on top of it."

"On top of what? Red is a fun color. It's got wild flair. Seriously. It's cool."

"Hear that, *car*," he says, darting his head towards it. "She likes you a bit wild, better deliver on your security specs, or I'll see red, got that." Odyssey beeps her assent, hatchback yawning open, and Liam lower the tailgate.

I hop inside the cargo bay, delighted to note its utilitarian size.

"Red-Dee to load up, captain," I say, giving Liam thumbs up.

"You're such a dork." He shakes his head, hands on his hips, a tiny upward twist forming on his lips, and I inwardly grin.

"Takes one to know one," I retort, jumping down.

"No comment," he says, pulling my knitted cap over my face. "Stay down here, I'll bring the bins over."

I stack the last of our eight color-coded plastic bins marked, jeans, jeans, jeans, sweaters, buttoned down, tees, underwear/socks, and bed linens, alongside Liam's regular suitcase filled with a selection of everyday clothes, snapping closed the vertical cargo net.

Liam locks Odyssey and holds up his hand, and I skip over, lacing my fingers with his. "We're all set for tomorrow morning, first light, Éolie-Jolie. Are you ready to call it a night?" he asks.

I nod, inhaling the cold briny sea air, letting it fill my lungs, memorizing the feel of it until next time.

"You really made Monsieur François's day, earlier at l'Hôtel, by refusing to say goodbye," I say, a soft smile tugging at my lips as I shrug my coat off. We went over there one last time to have supper. "I know you've heard me say it too many times already, but when you said to him, 'see you soon, same time next year,' well, it really got to me," I sigh, happy. "Bar Harbor holds a special place in my heart." I stand on tippy toes, brushing my lips to the corner of his jaw in a tender kiss.

His warm hands come up to frame my face. "Ditto. It's where you materialized," he says, brushing a strand of my hair, smoothing it back behind my ear, and, my heart melting, a crooked smile blooms.

Trailing the back of his fingers down my jaw, leaning in, our lips connect. My heart thuds in my ears as one of his hands splay at the nape of my neck, and the other at the small of my back, bringing me up flush with his hardening body. And I moan as his tongue slide inside my mouth in a possessive, heart-stopping kiss.

The waning moon crescent smiles down on us one last time through the glass wall as we let our bodies speak of love for the next little while, stopping time along the way.

Forty-Four

LIAM

The following morning finds us on the road by sunrise. The car handles like a dream, and I don't even have to figure out where we are; the dot on the screen does it for me. A match made in heaven.

"Turn left onto US-2, entering Vermont, twenty-three miles until Severance Hill Road," the smooth GPS system directs, momentarily taking over the surround-sound system.

"According to the little dot moving up the screen, we're less than an hour away from the border. Would you rather pit stop for a late breakfast in Vermont, or an early lunch in Québec?" Éolie asks, lowering the volume on Supertramp, Dreamer, currently blasting in the car.

"We're crossing over," I say, hyped by the drive. I feel the car's sporty responsiveness like an extension of myself, which I didn't expect in a boxy station wagon.

"Turn right to merge onto I-91 North towards Newport, thirty-five miles until exit Twenty-Eight," the computerized voice says. And for the next thirty-five miles, I let the music seep into my soul, as one with the car, the road, the universe, life. Beside me, Éolie's face is practically pasted to her window, fascinated by everything she sees.

"Exit Twenty-Eight, slight right onto US-5 North Vermont 105, Derby Center, zero point two miles."

The instructions are coming faster; we're getting closer.

"Turn left onto Beebe Road, entering Canada in three point one miles."

Éolie and I look at each other for a split second, eyes growing brighter.

"Turn right onto Canusa Street, Québec Route 247 Sud, destination on your right, three hundred forty one feet," the disembodied voice instructs on a final note, before shutting down.

I park the car on the right end side of Canusa, a residential street opening up to a small, paved square, flanked by a rectangular, red-brick building, where US and Canadian flags are flapping themselves silly in a borderline crazy salute, interspersed with a few Québec Fleur-de-Lis ones. A simple parking barrier gate at the end of a semi-circular drive is the only thing apparently closing the border.

If I look to my right, where I'm parked, I see a neat row of white houses, A-shaped and proudly proclaiming to be on American soil by sporting the flag. If I look to my left, I see an equally neat row of white houses, A-shaped and proudly proclaiming to be on Canadian soil by sporting the flag. And both sides have front-lawn neighbors ... living in another country.

And sure enough, when I check the map, there's the dotted line all right. The border between the two countries not only runs through the middle of Beebe Plain, it runs through the middle of this residential street, just like the painted line on the tar says, right up to the old Post Office building by the square, split down the middle by the same running line.

The sky is overcast with dark-gray clouds, and frost covers just about everything with a thin layer of ice. This miniature town looks to be frozen in time. No other car driving down the street except for us, no one's out for a walk, not even a dog barking, or curtains twitching. Zilch. We're about to enter Canada through a microscopic outpost, and by the look of things, it's not exactly high season around here. This can't be the main entryway into Québec, man.

"How on earth did we end up here with an itinerary map?" I ask.

"Without one it would have been impossible to end up here," Éolie says back.

The tiny Customs house is probably smaller than the bedroom I shared with the guys at BIA, which is saying something. We have to summon the Customs officer by the press of a button from the car. And wait. In the car.

"We're probably the only ones coming through his gate in the middle of November, in the middle of the day, in the middle of nowhere ... If this doesn't spell suspicious, what does?" I smirk, drumming my fingers on the steering wheel.

"Red doesn't make for a good getaway car," Éolie says. I snort. And wait some more.

I cast a sly glance sideways at Éolie. Her aqua eyes are full with wonder as she stares out at the quaint ... What's smaller than a town? A hamlet?

A sharp but respectful knock on my window brings me back. I look over, and find myself staring straight up to a pair of bushy eyebrows and dark-brown eyes narrowed at me. I lower my window with a polite nod and hand over our passports, complete with my Electronic Travel Authorization, or eTA for short, the brand-new form of visas. The customs agent's piercing gaze sweeps by us, taking stock of the cargo bay with its labeled bins, then looks down at our papers. His face turns dispassionate, not a shred of evidence left there to give me a hint as to what he thinks.

"Do you have anything to declare?" he asks.

Looking deeply into Éolie's eyes, I solemnly declare, "I love her."

Rendered speechless for a few, the stocky officer recovers, seemingly undeterred by my fit of the crazies. Not that surprising really, he's the one who lives in two places at once.

The gentleman's mouth twitches, and he looks at Éolie with crinkling brown eyes. "Do you have anything of worth to declare?" he corrects.

Éolie, not missing a beat, reciprocates with, "I love him too."

Enchanted, I lean over, and kiss her for good measure. Guess the officer can't resist happy love stories either, as he waits a bit before clearing his throat. And Éolie's cheeks turn bright red. I grin. She wears thoroughly kissed so well, and wouldn't you know. The car's color is suddenly growing on me.

"Won't take long," he says, before stepping inside the Customs building. And true to his words, he's back within a few minutes.

"Mr. O'Shea of Ireland," the man reads from my passport, "welcome to Canada. Enjoy your visit, sir."

"Ms. du Maurier, welcome home." The agent hands over our documents, and the gate opens.

I drive on, but not even five hundred feet away from the Customs house, there's snow on the ground and sleet coming down. I hurriedly park on the side of the deserted road, madly going through option menus on the tactile screen, resisting the urge to curse Odyssey's space module console until I finally get heat, defrost, and wipers to work in sync.

Well, shit. Now the name's growing on me. "When did that happen?" I mumble to myself. Éolie looks up, her eyes swimming in tears. Holy...

"Hey, sweet, what's wrong?" I ask, releasing her seatbelt, gathering her trembling body in my arms. I nestle her head in the crook of my neck, waiting out the moment, murmuring a string of nonsensical words of comfort, just about ready to throw in a few Odyssey this, and Odyssey that, if it can make any difference.

"Silly me—" she tells my chest, before giving me a watery smile, wiping her eyes with the back of her hands. "It's just that, it took me by complete surprise ... It feels strongly like coming home, Liam. For the first time ever, I'm coming home," Éolie repeats with wonder, and her slow beaming smile mirrors mine.

"Home. With you. I like that," I say, as she settles back into her seat, buckling up.

I lower my window, and yell out, "*We're coming home!*" Éolie's face glows in beauty, her eyes take on the shine of a thousand stars, and I'm suddenly on top of the world.

For all of twenty-one seconds.

"No offense to your new Canadian sensibilities," I mention, willing my window to move up just a little more quickly.

"None taken. Why?"

"You didn't feel that blast of wind straight out of Antarctica just now?" Jesus Christ. "*It's freaking cold out.*"

"You're nuts." She lets out peals of laughter.

"Then why am I blowing on my fingers to warm them back?" I ask pointedly.

"It's your boundless imagination at work. We're like, two kilometers from the border."

"We've just crossed a line, I tell you. It's definitely colder on this side of Celsius degrees."

I'm dropped into a parallel universe. It's amazing how small details can alter your sense of direction. There's nothing quite like being abruptly plunged into metric once more, with a twist of French road signs.

"Um. Liam? You know when that last sign read Maximum 100?"

"Yep, what about?"

"It meant kilometers per hour, not miles per hour."

We stop for lunch in Georgeville on the shores of Lake Memphrémagog, and it's like stepping into a live postcard in a small Cornish village. Already held under its spell, we walk into La Maison MacBride, a former fishing clubhouse dating back to the 1900s, according to the commemorative plaque outside.

"Mais entrez, entrez, venez vous réchauffer. Je suis Robert, votre hôte, bienvenue chez moi." Robert, the inn's owner, a short skinny man as bald as a coot and of indefinite age, welcomes us to his place, and leads us to a pub table sitting four near a wood stove, cheery fire crackling, in what was once a sitting room, its shelves full of interesting Lake memorabilia. The wainscoting painted a yellow gold, and the mismatched painted wood chairs, add to the warmth of the place we have all to ourselves.

"You're coming in from Beebe Plains? I'll be. At this time of the year, you're lucky it wasn't closed for the day," he says, entertained by our quick retelling. "The main port of entry is at Champlain/Saint-Bernard-de-Lacolle further down in upstate New-York," he says.

And with the way he describes the busy multilane highway customs, the happier I am with where we ended up crossing by way of the Eastern Townships. Intrigued by the region, and as we wait for le spécial du jour to be served up, fish and chips for me, and special eggs and chips for Éolie, a quick search on the Internet yields loads of articles. We read the first one up, leaning our heads close together.

'Experience British history and Quebecois tradition in La Belle Province.

Look for the ancient Appalachian Mountains

Taking in the view from the top of Montreal's Place Ville-Marie on a clear day, a visitor could be forgiven for

gazing at a crumpled range of hills along the eastern
horizon and wondering, "What the heck are those?"

"Those" are the Appalachian Mountains, and they
form the scenic backbone of the Eastern Townships. In
less than two hours from Montreal down Autoroute 10,
the Eastern Townships (or *Cantons de-l'Est*) feature some
of the most breathtaking landscapes in eastern Canada
with distinctive roots from the British Isles.'

I program the itinerary into my phone, and it syncs with Odyssey's
computer. I relax back in my seat, taking a closer look around.

Éolie thanks Robert with a smile as he puts a cup of green tea in front of
her, and a cup of black coffee in front me.

"All of those were recovered from the bottom of the Lake?" I ask Robert,
pointing to a shelf half-filled with old bottles of Canadian Rye whiskey, reading
the writing on the wall.

During the Prohibition era, Lake Memphremagog
was a favourite route for bootleggers and rum-runners,
who used the cover of night to smuggle contraband
bottles into the United States. It is said that many a bottle
now lies ensconced in silt and seaweed, deep below the
surface, as bootleggers rid themselves of their precious
liquid cargo to avoid being caught by patrols.

"The Lake border into Vermont is legendary for it," he says. He wipes
his hands on his apron, taking one down for us. The glass bottle is encrusted
and filled with silt from decades of submersion, but it's still intact, if empty of
whiskey can be called that.

"It's a fun cruise in the summer time to cross over by boat and have lunch
in Newport," he says, as we give him back the bottle. "Come visit at *la belle
saison,* we offer daily sailing cruises on the MacBride, a nice forty footer. It's not
at all like winter when we're only open half-weekends."

"You mean, you're closed right now?" I ask, bewildered.

"Officially." He shrugs matter-of-factly

And Éolie slaps her hands over her mouth, red creeping up her cheeks. "We
didn't know, I'm so sorry for the trouble," she mumbles through her fingers.

"Mais non voyons, rien de plus normal. It's no trouble at all." He waves one hand in dismissal of Éolie's apologies. "Our door's always open to anyone in need of a warm meal, or a chat by the fire," he says, eyes twinkling, and Éolie and I share a buoyant look.

Back in the car, the Eastern Townships region we're currently passing through is truly breathtaking. Picturesque hilly farm lands, hidden valleys, and tucked-away romantic little villages, barren frigid freaking cold notwithstanding, which says a lot.

My incursion into Quebec so far reveals that it's definitely very different from any other place I've been to. It's like a unique blend of just the right amount of North America, striving for efficaciousness, sautéed with a rich serving of Old World charms and its natural cultural flair, flambéed with a generous dollop of easy-going laid back.

Maybe we do belong somewhere. I inwardly grin, happy.

Forty-Five

LIAM

The City of Montreal is an island sitting in the middle of the majestic Saint Lawrence River, and our first view of the City coming in from the South Shore, with le Mont-Royal surrounded by skyscrapers, is spectacular, the crossing of the Champlain Bridge, high over rapids underneath. Picture perfect ... and a perfect nightmare.

"Jesus, at this rate we'll still be here in a week," I grumble under my breath, turning off the GPS app before it blows a circuit trying to figure out where the hell we are, as opposed to where we're supposed to be by now. In the past hour alone, I don't think we moved more than a few hundred meters. I chug the rest of my water bottle, disgruntled.

"Circulation non fluide," the overhead panel reads.

"No shit, Sherlock." I shove my hands in my hair, leaning back on the headrest. That traffic panel's a joke. It states the obvious once we're already trapped. We've been basically parked underneath it for the past fifteen minutes, its blinking screen warning of major maintenance work taking place, closing up all incoming lanes but one. Mocking me. Talk about traffic jams, or more appropriately said here, *bouchons de circulation*.

"Could be worse," Éolie says, unperturbed, scribbling something into her notebook and then tucking it back into the passenger's storage pocket.

I give her a look.

"Not much can be worse than this, right now," I gripe.

"Really?" she challenges me.

"Really," I say in one stellar comeback.

Bending down to untie her hiking boots, she takes them off. And, for once, she keeps her thick wool socks on, heels coming up on the edge of her seat.

"See what I mean. You're settling in for a long wait," I say, totally vindicated.

"Sooo?" she replies in a patient tone, sorely lacking in mine. "We're just passing through, they daily commute." Her head tilts sideways, and her arms fold around her bended knees.

"We're not passing through, we're parked through." I huff. "I don't know how everyone stays so calm, they daily commute from hell." I let my forehead thump on the steering wheel. "I'd need to take chill pills."

"Or the bus," Éolie says as a South Shore accordion bus shuttle zips by us in a reserved bus lane, cordoned off. I shoot her a look.

Montréal is Éolie's birth place and for that reason alone, I started out favorably inclined towards turning a blind eye to any specific irritants, like let's say, atrocious road conditions in and around the city. However, that was before we got stuck on that bridge for more than two hours. Driving in Montréal is hazardous to my Zen. Potholes everywhere, some of which the size of craters the moon would be proud to own, getting stuck constantly, either by a flagrant lack of road signs leading you nowhere, or by an overabundance of road signs to nowhere.

A few hours later, we're finally speeding down the Metropolitan Expressway that will spew us right on Highway 15 North, on the other side of the city. And it's one big mess of elevated concrete, four lanes of speed crazies, a grid of city streets running underneath, some fifty feet down.

"There are so many cars, and trucks, and noise, and concrete, and towering buildings, it's giving me vertigo and ... I don't feel so good..." Éolie says in a small voice, and a quick glance sideways confirms her head's bent forward towards her knees.

"Hang on, I'll pull over," I say, my eyes searching for the stopping strip on the highway shoulder. I soon find out there's no emergency stopping allowed on this bloody highway. There's no shoulder. I've had my blinker on for the past few minutes, and no one leaves a bloody opening to change lanes to access the exit ramps either.

"I'm okay, I'm okay, I'm okay, I'm okay," Éolie repeats like a mantra, her breathing growing shallower by the minute.

With that, all patience is gone. I jam the car into gear and swerve into the steady stream of traffic rushing by on our right. I'm fairly certain they're all headed for the exit that is not ours, but now, I don't care. We just need to move.

"Just hang on for a little while longer," I say, jaw ticking, staying focused on the road, and the insane flow of eighteen wheelers and cars speeding by like mad. Montrealers stay calm in traffic jams, but once they get going, better steer clear.

Indication panels, side by side, give me no prior warnings of what's to come.

Autoroute 15 Nord Saint-Jérôme, gardez la gauche.

Autoroute 40 Est Trois-Rivières, gardez la droite.

And it's too late by then to do anything about the info; this suspended highway from hell splits in tentacles left and right, two lanes here, two lanes there. We're en route vers Trois-Rivières, in just about the opposite direction I was aiming for.

I manage to switch lanes in an aggressive maneuver, an eighteen wheeler tailing me, taking the first off-ramp down, only to land on a six-lane boulevard with No Parking signs plastered every five meters. "Hang in there, almost parked," I say, checking for a side street that's either not a one-way I'd need to switch five lanes to access, or if a one-way, one going my bloody way. Left.

I drive some ten blocks before turning left on the first side street that allows for it.

I curse under my breath as I drive around one-way streets up one side, down the other, for more than twenty minutes before finally finding a place to park the goddamn car already.

"Fuck," I mutter.

A sign reads in French, Snow Removal Operations October to May, No-Parking Zone from16h00 to 8h00 Mondays, Wednesdays, Fridays—my side of the street fast emptying of cars that will park god knows where.

Ask me if I care at this point. It's been too many hours since we ate lunch in Georgeville, I realize, and Éolie's hypoglycemia's probably acting up.

I step out, opening up the cargo bay, rummaging through the duffel, finding two bottles of organic beverages and some granola nut bars. Éolie's door is already open, and I crouch down uncapping one, and she sips, her color returning.

"Getting stuck in traffic happens a lot when driving around in cities, Éolie. New rule," I say, tipping her face up. "Green goop kale juice. Nuts. I don't care which. At all times with you. Got it?" She nods, shivering. I hand over the other bottle and the granolas, dropping the bag onto the backseat grabbing her coat, tucking her in, diving into mine.

"It's four, and it's past dusk already. I thought about staying overnight in Montréal instead, but it's so ... I don't know, different, overwhelming," she says, swallowing hard, watching street lights switching on in series.

Very Organized-Éolie already made online reservations in a couple of Bed & Breakfasts, up in the Laurentians, for the next week. The plan is to drive around back roads, getting the feel of things, combing through a specific village area one day at a time, and see what comes up. I pick the Log Book from her door's storage pocket, and check her notes. We're expected at Le Vieux Clocher in Saint-Sauveur-des-Monts, tonight.

I give her a quick kiss on the forehead. "Rest for the next few. I don't care how late it gets. We're getting the hell out of the city," I say reclining her seat. "Preferably not by way of Trois-Rivières," I mumble under my breath. We need to get back on track, and access Highway 15 North.

My breath comes out in puffs, and biting cold humidity seeps all the way through my bones, my jeans stiffening to a crisp from the frigid wind. I clamp down on the gust working its way in my sleeve and tuck Éolie away once again, before hurrying back to my seat.

Back inside the car, I rev it once, blasting the heater on, and moan out loud when the heated steering wheel and seats kick in.

"C'mon, Odyssey, get us out of here," I say, opening up the GPS app. I program our destination Saint-Sauveur, Le Vieux Clocher and put pedal to the metal, peeling away from the curb.

Forty-Six

ÉOLIE

I sit on my heels on the window seat of the ivory-themed attic bedroom under the eaves at our Bed & Breakfast, Le Vieux Clocher, hands splayed on the glass, my nose pressed to the window, absorbed by the amazing view.

A smooth blanket of snow has fallen while we were snuggled up in bed. I watch a flurry of snowflakes as they dance merrily in the wind, the new accumulation cocooning us from within in quilted silence. Enchanted, I trace with my fingers the spider web frost covering the bottom of the window in lacy patterns. The overcast sky heavy with swollen clouds, the steeple of the village church farther down in the valley, frosted apple trees from the backyard orchard, and adorned evergreens crumbling under their white mantle. I see beauty as far as the eye can see. And I know I'm right where I should be.

"What's keeping you out of bed?"

I whip my head around, finding Liam with his head propped on one hand, watching me.

"Come and see," I say, beaming up, jumping from my perch and hopping on the four-poster bed, tugging on his hand. He resists, eyes crinkling at the corner, pulling me down, and I stumble on top of him in a tangle of limbs.

"First, I need a good morning kiss. It's in the rule book of road trips," he says, and I laughingly comply, which makes for a quirky kiss full of awkward teeth nipping and giggling.

"You're showered and dressed? How long have you been awake?" he asks, groping around the nightstand for his watch in the gray light, and I knock his hand away.

"Long enough. Come on, you've got to see this," I insist, pushing up, pulling at his hands, walking backwards, and he follows, ducking at the last minute, narrowly missing the slanted roof.

Bracing his hands on the upper window frame, Liam leans over my shoulder. "It's magic," I say, and I feel wonder. "It's like waking up in a pristine new world."

Liam kisses the top of my head, but remains quiet.

My Log Book lies open on the window seat with my latest to-do entry, thermal clothes shopping for the winter challenged. He picks it up, scribbling on the next page.

The world is full of magic things
patiently waiting for our senses to grow sharper.
W.B. Yeats
The Enchanted Forest of Laure is near. I feel the magic.

I read on, inhaling sharply, eyes growing moist. He tilts my head up so our eyes meet. The soft look in his makes my heart turn over.

"I'll be ready in ten," he says, tickling my cheek with the tip of my braid.

We walk down the stairs together, stepping into the common room with another stunning view of the village below and multiple ski resorts farther away on the surrounding hills. The sitting room is cozy, with bookshelves filled to the brim with books and board games of every kind lining up all but one spectacular wall entirely made of natural stones, a fireplace hearth at the center of it, fire blazing, burning logs crackling.

Well-lived-in, dark-brown leather sofas are strewn about and red Vichy checkered cushions are peppered throughout invitingly. A few of them are occupied by older patrons quietly reading. One of them, a woman dressed in a cream turtleneck and assorted soft shell ski pants, hair styled in a sleek blonde chignon, looks up, giving us a brief nod in greeting before returning to her book.

Pachelbel's Canon plays in the background, and I softly bump my shoulder into Liam's, whispering, "They're into classical."

"And it rocks," he whispers back, lips twitching, and I almost snort out loud.

An antique refectory table sits on the other side of the rectangular room, laden with an array of sliced fruits, cheese, and charcuterie platters, baskets full of warm croissants and baguette, homemade jams and assorted condiments. I smell the aromas of wood-burning evergreens twined in winter wreaths, freshly baked bread, berries, hot cocoa, and coffee mixed together, permeating the air.

Two others occupy the table, an attractive middle-aged couple with hands interlaced, their murmured conversation animating their handsome features. The gentleman drops a warm kiss on his lady's forehead, and she leans into his touch before letting go, a loving smile curving her lips. They reach for their steaming cups, clicking them in a toast before taking sips, eyes aglow with warmth. Liam and I share a look, charmed.

"Not so close, leave them be," I say low, discreetly tugging on Liam's arm, trying to direct us towards the other end of the long table. But I'm not quick enough.

"Bonjour," they say, looking up, welcoming us with warm smiles.

"Bonjour," I answer back, biting my lip, and Liam nods in greeting, towing me behind.

Hélène, our grandmotherly hostess, peeks in from her kitchen door. "Ah, mes p'tits oiseaux sont debout," she says, clasping her hands over her heart. "Sit, sit, I'll be right back with ze eggz," she gestures expansively.

We plop down on the rustic bench gracing this side of the table, sitting opposite the other couple. I stare at the blue toile placemats with their neatly folded cloth, wondering if I'm expected to make small talk, and if so, what to say.

One of Liam's strong arms comes around my hips, and in a quick move, I'm slid nearer up to his side, surprising a half-yelp out of me. My fingers come up to cover my mouth. A roguish grin form at the corner of his lips, and I jab his thigh under the table. "Behave," I murmur through cupped fingers.

A peal of tinkling laughter rings out. "No need. I'm used to it," a mischievous young voice states from behind us, and my eyes grow wide. I still.

"Magali!" the lady exclaims.

Liam pours himself a cup of coffee from one of the carafes, an amused expression playing on his face, and I turn my head sideways.

A girl around my age stands to my right, dressed in black soft shell racers and bright-red coat, labeled Mont-Saint-Sauveur Ski Patrol in reflective white letterings. With her glossy curls of dark-brown hair held in a messy bun, highlighting her smooth complexion and the loveliness of her face, animated with barely contained joy, striking silver-grey eyes glinting with warmth, I find her beautiful.

"What? Holding hands, kissing, cuddling at all hours, you never behave, it's normal," she says in an affectionate tone of voice, and I track her warm gaze to the other couple. I release a breath, taking a closer peek at them.

The fiftyish man, in all likelihoods of Norse descent judging from his chiseled face, light-blond hair turning white at the temples, and piercing grey eyes, quirks up his mouth, one arm coming around to rest casually on the back of his sweetheart's chair. His fingers caress her upper arm in a lazy back and forth motion. The petite woman, probably around my height, wears her greying hair in a smooth French bob cut to frame her delicate jaw, and soulful dark-brown eyes enliven her features.

"Magali," the older woman warns softly, her tone belied by eyes glinting with merriment, her full lips fighting a smile.

"What? It is normal. I'm living proof—" She throws her arms up, looking our way, doing a double take, taking a step back, suddenly gawking. "Dieu du ciel!" she exclaims comically. "When Hélène mentioned she had two young guests looking over properties in Les Laurentides, I had no idea you'd be—" Her hands flutter around in Liam's direction.

Liam's shoulders stiffen, fingers clenching on his silverware. "And you're staying over in La Mansarde, and at winter solstice time too. Double Oh Mon Dieu. You're—" She sighs breathily, hands coming over her heart, her gaze darting between us, and Liam's jaw tightens.

I kiss his cheek and put my hand on top of his, thumb stroking gently.

"—truly, so lovely together. Hélène's idea of young is usually someone in their fifties. Please, please, tell me you're intent on getting pregnant, you'll make gorgeous babies," she pleads, clasping her hands.

"Magali," the lady utters, her voice torn between shock and laughter, and the gentleman shakes his head, clearly amused.

"What? I'm networking," she says. "They're in the honeymoon suite."

Liam gives a shout of laughter, shoulders relaxing. "Enjoying some practice makes perfect, aiming for a handful of them," he replies, shooting me a wicked look sideways. Right on cue, I feel my cheeks flush and burn.

"See? They're my new best friends." Magali bounces excitedly.

I blink.

Sympathetic brown eyes smile down on me. "Magali's just been accepted for her master's, and she'll be training as a midwife in Sainte-Agathe come next term, she's—"

"Enthusiastic, ecstatic, euphoric, over the moon, bouncing off the walls," Magali says, waltzing down to join the other couple on the other side of the table, hugging their shoulders tight and kissing both their cheeks.

"All of those, and then some," the man says in a dry tone of voice, clear affection written all over his face.

"Don't mind me. I'm suffering from 'running off at the mouth' syndrome. It's congenital, and I blame my papa," she deadpans, and the gentleman snorts behind his coffee cup.

Magali squeezes his shoulders, resting her chin on top of his head.

"We were just discussing not five minutes ago how hard you studied for this, and how happy we are for you," the lady replies warmly, offering her a tall glass of pulpy orange juice she poured from an earthenware pitcher.

"It's your moment, Lili. Enjoy it," the gentleman, Magali's father by all appearances, says over his shoulder, the sharp angles of his face softening.

"Babies! What's not to love?" Magali proclaims endearingly, arms opening wide, head thrown back, just before toasting up the ceiling with her glass of orange juice.

Babies ... A collage of lightning-quick moments and images comes to me. So clear in my mind though, I can almost feel Nicolas, Sébastien, Rose, Sophie, and Mathieu in turn, in my arms, their sweet little babies' faces cuddled up in the crook of my neck, nuzzling close, and my insides instantly melt into goo.

Magali's gaze connects with mine, and Liam drops a kiss on the top of my head.

"I know, right? Babies are my kryptonite too," Magali says, giving me a soft, all-knowing smile. "And in less than two short years, I'll be the one bringing them safely into the world around here. But for now," she makes a small moue, "I still have to wrap up my last semester down in Montréal. So in a few hours, I'll be trading all this fresh, pristine, new falling snow," she motions dramatically to the back of her, "for brown slush in the city, and miserable people because of it."

"Thirty-five centimeters are expected today. You're still taking the train back to Montréal, right?" Magali's father asks sternly.

"Of course, mon petit papa à moi, don't worry," she says, giving him a quick peck on the head. "I'm leaving you stuck with my jeep snowed in at the train station," she adds, a fun-loving smile tugging at the corner of her lips. "Who's crazy enough to drive around Montréal anyway, and at the end of November on top of it, even tourists wait for July." She shrugs, and Liam chokes on his coffee.

"Yeah, been there, done that," he says, recovering on a last cough.

"Congrats, that makes you officially one of us now." Liam and I share a sidelong glance. "Seriously, Montréal is the coolest city ever if you own a bike, or a subway pass. But a car? Seventh Circle of Hell," Magali says, pilfering some grapes from her father's bread plate, popping them into her mouth, checking her phone, eyes growing wide.

"Zut de flûte, I'm running late." Quickly leaning over the table, she grabs a cut croissant stuffing it with camembert wedges, lean fingers deftly rolling it into a paper doily she takes from the bottom of the platter. And her mom adds a blueberry muffin and a green apple, buffed to a shine, to her loot.

"Breakfast. Same time, next week," Magali says in a flurry of good-byes, giving her parents warm hugs and sweet kisses on both cheeks, receiving the same.

"See you all on the slopes." She waves to the few remaining readers by the fire, leaving in a blur of red.

I blink.

In the wake of Magali, our plump hostess Hélène rolls in a dolly with five plates filled with fluffy scrambled eggs mixed with fresh spinach and grilled mushrooms, with a dash of grated Parmesan cheese on top, served with a terrine de pommes de terre à la poêlée.

"Carefool, plates zare hot," she mentions in her thick French accent, serving them with a tea towel. "Magali?" she sighs, eyeing the skewed cheese platter.

"Eat and run, mayhem on the camembert, the usual," her father says unperturbed, taking the extra plate for himself.

And suddenly, my chest expands. Maybe, just maybe, I'll fit right in somehow, and make friends. Here. Not to mention babies somewhere down the line ... I smile softly, happy.

Forty-Seven

LIAM

"You mentioned a thirty-five centimeters snowfall, will they close down roads?" I ask Magali's father. That's more than a foot of snow in one drop.

"Up north? No, we have crews working the plows round the clock in ski country, and you'll see all wheel drive's pretty much across the board," he says, leaning back in his chair. "What are you driving?"

"A Volvo station wagon," I answer.

"Red," Éolie adds with a little elbow nudge.

"Smart choice, you want to be seen. Your red Volvo won't be mistaken for a banked snowdrift," Grégoire says, nodding, and Éolie tilts her head at me, raising a brow. I give her a sidelong glance. I may concede that red is an okay color for our car after all. Especially when she'll be driving it.

"Hélène mentioned that you're planning on living here full time," Magali's mother says, contemplating us over her tea cup. "The first thing you'll probably learn is that winter in Les Laurentides isn't exactly a season. It's more like a state of mind."

"Yeah, sneeze in July, and you will have missed summer," complains a dour-faced, balding man. One of the last patrons left in the common room. He huffs, taking one of the carafes to his reading nook by the fire.

"Not quite that fast, but close enough," Magali's mother says, eyes crinkling, hands around her steaming cup of tea. "Then again," she motions towards the view behind her, "we live in a proverbial winter wonderland so, I guess it evens out."

"It's truly breathtaking," Éolie agrees, getting lost in the view, and I lightly squeeze her hand, agreeing. The Saint-Sauveur valley down below takes on sepia colors, snowflakes dancing in the wind in a picture-perfect way, covering up everything in white fluff.

Magali's mother looks at me, and her face clouds over. "The only thing is..." she says with a sigh, fiddling with her teaspoon, and Magali's father glance at her sideways.

I rest my chin in my palm, and Éolie leans forward to rest her elbows on the table. "The only thing is?" I ask, prompting her.

"Where are you from? I can't quite place you," she asks instead. And I'm not sure if it's because she exudes a motherly vibe with her kindly voice and concerned expression, but her prying question doesn't bother me. "Your English sounds British. Your French is flawless, but clearly you don't have our thick, French Canadian accent, so maybe that's why you're not ... aware..." Her voice trails off on another sigh, before she asks me point blank, "Is this your first time up here in winter? I mean, anywhere in Québec?"

"It's our first time, yes," I reply, and Éolie concurs with me. "I grew up in Switzerland but I'm Irish, and Éolie is French Canadian, but she grew up out of country," I add, beyond curious now to see where this conversation is going.

"No wonder, then." Magali's father mutters, upturning his eyes. "Vie, you'll worry all night, tossing and turning, just tell him."

"Grégoire."

"She's worried you'll freeze to death in your smart-looking jeans, but she doesn't want to hurt your feelings," Magali's father, Grégoire, says, pinning me with a direct look. "Winter here has two seasons, cold and colder. So, no offense, but you won't last in those hipster pants."

"You really should consider thermal clothing with negative fifty degrees specs," Vie says, showing Éolie her own layered clothing and soft shells.

"*Negative* fifty," I repeat, unsure I heard her right.

"Wind-chill factor." Grégoire waves one hand in dismissal. "We have a few spots of extreme temperatures in winter, but nothing to it with today's high-tech clothing," he says with a sidelong glance at Vie, raising a brow. "And some good old-fashioned body warming techniques," he adds, and Vie shoots him a look, fighting a laugh.

"I promise you'll stay toasty warm," she says to Éolie, who is intently listening. "In comfort too. It's like wearing your favorite yoga pants."

They're soon lost in their own convo, and Very-Organized-Éolie starts writing down local outlets addresses with a board game pencil on a piece of doily, making lists of must have from boots and snow shoes, all the way up.

I absently brush my fingers back and forth on the small of her back, taking in the moment, letting it seep. On the outside, a fierce snow storm, yet on the inside, all the warmth in the world surrounds us.

"So, it's your first time up here. What are your impressions so far?" Grégoire asks, eyeing me.

"I admit to being agreeably surprised. It's like Old World charm served à la North America. The wide-open space, the easy laid-back, the cultural flair, it's like the best of both worlds, and I love it so far," I say.

"We get that reaction a lot, especially from Europeans visiting for the first time. Québec is more than eighty percent French, so we're less likely to be taken aback visiting France, it's like visiting closely related cousins, then we are visiting Ontario, another planet." He shakes his head on a low chuckle. "What kind of property are you looking for exactly?" Grégoire asks, refilling our cups.

"A vast track of forest," I say, shooting Éolie a look. "We visited one often when we were small kids. So, it kind of set the tone for what we want, and we'd rather drive around to get the feel of it rather than pouring down property listings."

Éolie gives my hand a light squeeze.

"Gut feeling buying. I like that, I'm the same. Vast track, hmmm."

Grégoire gets up, and comes back with a borrowed red pen and one of the paper maps displayed up front at the reception desk. "It's a mapping of ski resorts for tourists, but it'll do." He unfolds it on the table.

"Cross out Saint-Sauveur, Sainte-Adèle, and Mont-Tremblant proper. They're high-end resort areas, lots of condos and hotels," he says, circling both areas on the map crossing it out.

"Cross out Sainte-Agathe, it's a small town by Lac des Sables." He circles it, and draws an X on it.

"What do you suggest for a starting point then?" I ask, leaning over the map.

"Your best bet is to look within this area towards Mont-Tremblant, La Vallée de la Rouge." He circles a much smaller area on the map. "Beyond that is Route 117. Scattered villages, a few small towns, mostly lumber companies and outfitters' wilderness straight up to Kuujjuaq, and you don't strike me as the type so," he says, "depending on how vast you mean, it starts here, in my own backyard."

He draws an arrow on the map, turning it towards me, and I read the print of the town he's indicated as our starting point.

"Val-David," I say, repeating it a few times under my breath. A rush of excitement churns deep in my gut as, somehow, the name said out loud resonates within me.

"If you're into nature's simple pleasures, that area is a good starting point." Grégoire salutes me with his cup, his arm casually coming around the back of Vie's chair. "We have a place here, which isn't far. If you need anything, give us a call." He writes a phone number on the map and hands it over.

"Thanks for this." I pocket the map and grin into my cup, before draining the last of my coffee.

We're getting closer. I feel it.

And I can hardly wait to come home, at last.

Forty-Eight

LIAM

Thanks to Vie's life-saving advice, we're now outfitted head to toe to brave the wilds of Lower Antarctica, better known in these parts as Les Hautes Laurentides.

I love driving on these quasi-deserted back roads we've been crisscrossing for the past couple of days. We're on the look-out for something that will either look familiar, or for Éolie's internal radar to kick in, whichever comes first, telling us we have finally arrived. Home.

So far no luck though.

And it's already too dark out to see anything clearly. Dusk comes quickly in winter time, and night settles in as early as half past four. "Guess that's it for today," I say. "Where to?"

"We're booked at Le Clos Rolland in Sainte-Adèle for the next couple of nights," Éolie says, crossing it out in the Log Book before programming it into the GPS app.

The Volvo is made for this kind of weather, and the roads are better kept in the North Country in winter than anywhere else I've been before. I accelerate in the long winding curve, the softer rubber compounds and unique tread of studded winter tires adhering to the surface as the car climbs smoothly.

"C'est féérique," Éolie exclaims as we top the hilly mountain. And she's right, the view that suddenly spreads out in front of us from up here is truly spellbinding.

Far away from big-city lights, and under the heavy cloud covers, it's pitch black out, which, by contrast, renders the sight of so many illuminated ski resorts dotting the horizon even more dramatic.

"Wow," I marvel, parking on the shoulder, and we get out. I lean back on the car, running my arms around her waist, nudging her towards me. And she leans into my chest.

"It's like sprinkled cups of stardust that fell down to earth," she sighs, hugging my arms.

"Wait until the guys see this. Night skiing and dozens of resorts to choose from in one's backyard, they'll drool for months," I say.

"Won't they find these beautiful rolling hills sort of puny, though?" she asks, tilting her head up at me.

"Hey, you. Don't call my hills puny," I mock growl, tickling her side, and she dodges under my arm, gamely sidestepping my move.

"Oh? You'd prefer I call them well-rounded?" she says on a lilt.

"Well-rounded, curvy, both works for me," I reply on a roguish grin. "That's what makes them different."

"Different, my point exactly." Éolie loops her arms around my neck. "It'll be pretty different compared to skiing in the Alps, non?"

"Yeah, sure. But in Europe, you take ski trips, you don't have ski nights anytime you want," I say, remembering fondly the weekends I spent off campus skiing at Zermatt, St. Moritz, and Chamonix with the guys in our A-Level years.

"Will you teach me?" she asks.

"I'll teach you everything I know," I whisper in her ear. "We have plenty of time."

"Promise?" she says, her breath fogging on my lips. But it's so dark out I can hardly make out her features.

"*Promise.*" I angle my head for a scorching kiss, but my lips numb instead from the ice-cold air as we're suddenly buffeted by frigid gusts of wind whistling by us on top of the mountain. "Come on, let's take this somewhere warmer, and call it a day."

"Or a night," she says, fumbling in the dark until I open the driver's door, and light spills out.

"I like the way you think," I say.

We drive down the other side of the hill somewhere in the back boonies of Val-David.

Villages up here are so different than what I got used to growing up in much more densely populated Europe. There's no narrow streets, no medieval castles, no medieval plumbing ... They're sparsely populated and they cover huge territories. In the Val-David area alone, courtesy of the many glaciations that came and went, there's an incredible three thousand, two hundred seventy-three lakes within fifty kilometers, their staggering number gleaned from an article I came upon. And aside from a village center with a handful of streets, or the tighter clusters of cottages sometimes found around lakes, neighbors are few and far between on back roads.

"Stop," Éolie says on a sharp intake.

"What? You felt something?" I ask, heart thudding in my ears. No answer.

I turn the car round slowly. Its halogen headlights sweeping in a circle reveal sparkling snow abundantly covering an abandoned barn, roof caved in, and then open fields. Nothing else.

I turn on the interior light, making sure I'm not startling her like I did back in the woods in Bar Harbor, and wait for Éolie to come out of whatever visions she's seeing. She soon blinks, her gaze sweeping by the barn as her focus sharpens back.

"Liam, it's right here," she whispers, hands pressing on her chest.

I search her eyes. "How's that possible?" I ask, scanning the landscape again, and coming up empty.

"It's Leo's barn and fields," she says excitedly, eyes swimming in tears.

"Whoa. Back up. Leo's fields?" I ask bewildered. "What did I miss?"

"I saw Leo, right there." She points out to the ramshackle barn, half-laughing, half-crying. "That barn will become a greenhouse at some point or other, 'cause it's where Leo and I were discussing his latest cross-breeding results on soy beans. And Sébastien and Nicolas, age three or so, were kneeling down by a garden tray, pushing sunflower seeds into the soil. After which Leo picked both boys up in his arms to show them another tray full of green shoots, patiently explaining that their tiny sunflower seeds would soon be edible sprouts," she says, and a dreamy look appears on her face.

I stare at the barn. Man, Leo's farm...

"What about our yellow house?" I ask, twisting in my seat, trying to see past the fields, holding my breath.

Éolie furrows her brow, staring off. "We're just a bit farther down in the woods. I>m pretty sure of it ... I didn't see our house this time around, but in the vision I just had, after the twins ran out of questions over the sprouts, Leo winked at me, asking our little twins if they were ready for the trek back home. He even said that by now, baby Rose would surely appreciate being rescued from her papa poule's clutches," she says softly, and I get lost in the comforting vision Éolie's words create in my mind. Family. Roots. "Sébastien and Nicolas were already out the door at the word trek, running up the fields to the edge of the woods beyond," she says, my imagination supplying the rest ... Home.

A bit stunned, I look over the fields, or what can be seen of them by the car's halogens, contemplating Leo's experimental farm, the one he talked incessantly about having one day. Neighbors? Jesus, just like my long-ago stories told ... This is like something straight out of *The Tales from the Enchanted Forest of Laure*, where I would launch the six of us on quests to find Home in The Normal Kingdom.

My pulse leaps and my blood pumps wildly. Man, at seven, I didn't know how real it would all turn out to be.

Éolie grabs the tourists' map putting a big fat X on the spot, marking it on the road we've been following. She draws a dot on the village main street, la rue de l'Église, and then maps the back country roads all the way up with the highlighter color of the day, neon green.

"There. It's our treasure map," she says glowing, and I add little Xs around it in a sappy, loopy clover shape.

"Irish green. Our lucky charm," I add on a laugh, tugging her close for a quick kiss on the temple.

"If this is right, I'm so framing this," she says on a flash of teeth giving me a quick hug. "Come on." And before I can react, she's out the door, running down the road.

"Whoa," I cry out, taking off after her, leaving the car idling with the headlights on. "Éolie, come back here, it's darker than pitch out there."

"First light tomorrow, Liam, it's here." She jumps into my arms, her legs coming around my waist, kissing me all over. I walk us back to the car, stopping here and there to nibble her jaw between kisses, unwilling to break off our impromptu make-out session.

I briefly wonder how long it takes for a loaded-down Volvo to fog up in ski country as I turn off the engine, reclining my seat.

A record three point four seconds.

To defrost again...?

That's another story.

Forty-Nine

LIAM

This is surreal.

Every single curve and slope on this back country road are a remembered voyage from the village up. My chest expands, heart rate picking up. The fork to our road is just around this bend. I've been here before. It doesn't matter that it was only in my mind. I feel the magic.

"There's no road." I frown, parking the car on the shoulder at the spot where, according to Éolie, we're supposed to turn.

"Maybe it's snowed in," Éolie says, getting out. Her boots crunch over the packed snow.

"No way," I argue to the empty car, looking at the thick cover of trees where the road should be, getting out. "It just isn't there."

"Ssshhh, listen," she says. The early-morning air is rich and thick with the sound of splashing water. We walk a dozen meters up the road to where a hidden brook gurgles, white water rushing through a drainage pipe crossing on the other side. Éolie climbs down the shoulder. Squatting, she takes one glove off, dipping her hand into the swirling white-water, bringing back up a few shiny river pebbles. She stares at them without blinking for what seems like a long moment, before a look of wonder crosses her face. She puts them in her pocket, blowing on her fingers.

"So?" I ask, grabbing her hands and pulling her up.

"It's our brook by the meadow. I saw it clearly just now, and our road meanders by it through the forest and ends a few hundred meters from the house, on a small barn tucked into the undergrowth," Éolie says excitedly, putting her glove back on. "It has to be our brook, I feel it. It means the end of Leo's fields should be around the next bend in the road, marked by a two-hundred-year-old Acer Saccharum, a sugar maple tree missing one of its four main limbs." She hurries up the road, and I follow at a slower pace, in awe.

Sure enough, the end of Leo's fields is marked by a venerable maple tree, its trunk twice over the length of my arms, one of his limbs missing. We walk back down, each deep in thoughts. We stare a long time at the brook, both unwilling to venture forth, still reeling by the fact that there's no road where we thought there'd be one.

"Maybe there's another road branching out from behind Leo's farmstead that I haven't seen?" she suggests quietly.

"Let's go ask whoever lives there," I say, taking her hand. We walk back up, past the few fields, past the abandoned barn and another field until an old farm house appears sitting on a small hill tucked away, its driveway buried in four feet of snow. We stare.

"Looks like nobody's home," I say wryly as somehow, I don't think whoever owns the place forgot to shovel this morning.

"But our forest, it's here," Éolie insists, frowning.

"I know. I feel it too," I say, trying to walk through a snowdrift thigh deep. "Let's bring the car up here. We'll need snow shoes to take a closer look around. We'll take it from there."

We clip them on, starting the trek up the long driveway, through snow banks dipping and swelling, carved by the wind. Some more snow starts falling down in big fat flakes.

"Breathe that air," I say on a deep inhale, "it's so pure and engorged with moisture. I can practically taste the evergreens, and the view, man."

Éolie breathes it in, eyes closing. "You have good taste," she teases, sticking her tongue out, playfully catching flakes.

"Damn straight." I swing her over my shoulder, sinking to my knees into the snow, stumbling, dropping her. I help her up, dusting off a few tons of extra snow. "Guess snow shoeing isn't meant to be shared that way. Means you're on your own," I add, hardly able to contain my laughter.

"So obliging of you," she retorts drily, melting snow pearling on her cheeks and eyelashes as she beats her knitted cap on her legs to shake off the snow encrusted.

"Should have seen your face," I say in between chuckles, wiping her cheeks. "My bad." I hold my hands up, still grinning, as she gives me a long-suffering look and treks away from me.

From afar, the old farm house is charming with its gabled roof and covered front porch, but up close, what's left of the white paint peels off, and the exposed wood siding shows years of neglect. A faded sign labeled À VENDRE/FOR SALE hangs on one of the front porch pillars, twitching on a last remaining nail.

"Want me to call the real estate agent's number now, to get more info?" I ask, programming it into my phone.

"I'd like to check something first," she says, already rounding the house, walking toward the forest line. I follow her deeper into the woods.

"This trail is hauntingly familiar," I say, tingles shivering up my spine, my gut tightening with anticipation. Up ahead the trees are thinning out, and we soon stand in a natural clearing.

"We're home, Liam," Éolie says in a dazed tone, spinning in circles where a yellow house with red shutters … isn't.

My brows furrow because she's right. I can feel it. This is the spot we've dreamed on, right up to the meadow and the brook gurgling by. But where's the house?

Realization dawns slow.

"… and we're building it from scratch," I say.

Fifty

LIAM

I'm sprawled on the bed in La Flemmardise, our cream-colored room at Le Clos Rolland in Sainte-Adèle, head propped on the headboard, waiting for a return call from the real estate agent. "I can't find that property anywhere in the local listings," I say, stumped, putting my laptop aside, my Internet research coming up empty.

Lounging on the floor stretched on her stomach, Éolie's humming along to Bach's Brandenburg Concerto, leaning on her forearms writing in the Log Book, bended knees and crossed ankles swaying back and forth. Intrigued, I lean over, reading her latest entries. When I see what she's written, I grab the notebook.

"Hey, give it back," she cries out, jumping to her feet.

"Nope." I turn this way and that, dodging her arms, crossing out something.

"We're not camping out in an igloo in our meadow for what's left of the winter," I say, scribbling it out. "I like my creature comforts like hot showers and warm beds. I'm spoiled that way."

"Ice hotels are all the rage in Québec City during Le Carnaval. They have waiting lists," she informs me, motioning with her hand to return the notebook.

"Good for them," I say, dropping it on the bed, and lunging for my phone when it rings. "O'Shea."

"Monsieur O'Shea, Valérie Duhamel returning your call."

"Hi." I sit up straighter. "Thanks for calling me back. Is the land I referenced still available?" Éolie lowers the volume on Bach, coming to sit beside me.

"It is," she sighs heavily, her tone making it clear there's a catch.

"And?" I lean forward, impatient.

"Let me cut to the chase here. The woods you're interested in only look like a developer's dream come true. In actuality, it's your worst nightmare. Looking for a way to sell it to anyone has been mine," she says flippantly.

"I don't understand—"

"Look. Don't waste your time. You'll have to go elsewhere to develop. Good luck," she continues, ready to hang up.

"Listen, whatever the obstacle, I intend to live there," I say firmly, hoping I haven't made it worse with my "don't fuck with me" tone. "Can you give me a brief rundown on the conditions?" I ask more evenly.

She sighs once again, and I can practically see her rubbing at a migraine. "You must be from out of town."

"What if I say yes?" I answer warily.

"I'd do my good deed of the year, and show you residential listings," she says in a mordant tone. "In that price range, we have a few mansions in Mont-Tremblant I'm sure you'll love."

Christ above. "Ms. Duhamel, the conditions, if you please," I say, pinching the bridge of my nose.

"You have no idea what you're asking for. That property's been sitting on the market for more than five years, rotting away since Old Léon's passing. It's locked so tight by Léon Gaboury's last will's stringent conditions that not even the heirs could unlock them in court to auction it off to my six land developers salivating on it, so don't expect any better," she warns.

"Fine by me. Again, what are the conditions?" I repeat, shoving one hand in my hair, pacing the room.

She tsks. "For a cool million? You'd have to buy *all* of Old Léon's holdings, *or nothing*," she says, her voice turning saccharine sweet. "Meaning his two hundred acres of woods and farmstead standing in an agricultural-protected area, *plus* the one thousand acres beyond, he willed as a nature preserve, of which the *buyer* will become a *guardian*. And that guardianship? It's for life, thanks to his cursed attorney. Meaning you won't be able to rid yourself of the nature preserve because you'll be stuck with Old Léon's conditions to pass it over. You'll never get a return on your investment. Not even close. Still interested?" She oozes condescension.

"Yes, actually, it suits me," I say, giving Éolie a thumbs up and a wink. "What do we do next?"

She pauses so long, I wonder if she's hung up on me. "Could you hold the line for a minute?" she asks. I agree and wait for the inevitable tin sound of hold music, but instead, I'm startled by her office background noise. I cover the mouthpiece and motion to Éolie to keep quiet, and she nods.

"Valérie, come now," says another female. "Seriously. No one in their right minds with the means to buy that place would go for this."

"He doesn't know any better, you should hear him talk. He's not only from out of town, he's a foreigner," Ms. Duhamel mumbles in French.

"Just expose all the gory details up front then, and he'll run straight to your Mont-Tremblant's upscale listings, done deal, everyone happy," the other female in Ms. Duhamel's office says, and I can practically see her rubbing her hands.

Well, this is getting interesting. I almost snicker out loud.

I hear a click, finally putting me on hold. The soft music ends abruptly a moment later, and I hear another series of clicks.

"Monsieur O'Shea? Are you there?"

"Yes."

"Sorry. I thought I'd lost the connection," she says briskly. "Okay. I'll be perfectly honest with you. You don't want that property."

"I don't?" I ask, sardonic.

"No, trust me. The farm house comes as is, so you'll have to sign a waiver on the usual legal guarantees, and let's face it. It's a derelict relic, closed down for winter. The price is non-negotiable. Old Léon's last will fixed it, and worst of all? You'll be saddled with the neighbor from Hell, Maître Deslauriers, the attorney behind the Léon's Conditions. So much as look at a tree the wrong way, and he'll be on your back faster than you can say bird of prey. He's lethal."

"Seems like pretty straightforward conditions, and I like the way the neighbor thinks," I say, making a mental note to tell Theo that attorneys are attributed the title of Maître up here, just like in France. He'll get a kick out of that. Master, indeed, I shake my head. He swore he'd move to Calais one day on the other side of La Manche and his native Great-Britain, if just to get the appellation. "I'm ready to sign," I say to the real estate development troll. "Email me the documents for revision, *or transfer me to someone who will*," I say forcefully.

I hear a dull thud and a shuffling sound, followed by a muffled scream.

"Ms. Duhamel? Hello...?"

"I'm sorry, I dropped the receiver. Monsieur O'Shea," she replies on a deep, ecstatic breath. "We will be emailing you the documents, Monsieur O'Shea, and right away too. Anything else, Monsieur O'Shea?"

I end the call, and shoot a text to Theo.

Me: Found Laure. Spellbound. Watch for incoming paper trail.

Theo: No shit. For real?

Me: Not kidding. For real. Fun in three words. Ski.Ski.Ski. Gather the troops.

Theo: I like the way you spell fun. On it man.

Fifty-One

LIAM

The language of money is universal.

The real estate agency delivers the property within a week, probably afraid I'd change my mind at any given time. But buying Leo's old farmstead beats living in an igloo for now, anyway. I have to smile, wondering whether Ms. Duhamel will eventually recover from us. I thought she'd go into cardiac arrest when the papers were finalized and the money transfer came through, the way she kept blinking and clutching her chest.

The old farmhouse was thus opened up and cleaned under our daily supervision and assistance. Éolie and I, unable to stand still, lent a hand to Ms. Duhamel's crew as much as possible. The place is now spotless, and smelling lemony fresh after years of moldering, which was quite the undertaking.

Soft light spilling out from the kitchen windows, welcome us, twilight fast approaching.

We step on the porch, and I stop to take a moment. I let my gaze sweep over the land, my chest expanding, and Éolie burrows into my side. I'm no longer adrift.

"It's happening. We're sprouting roots," I murmur.

"Yes, we are," Éolie says resolutely.

I hug her tight before unlocking the front door with the keys we just officially received, notarized transaction completed.

"I wonder whether Leo will sprout roots here in a couple of weeks when all the guys come," I say. It's pretty easy to picture him both figuratively and literally, sprouting roots, concocting new strains of soy beans, or corn to feed the world.

"You mean you left him in the dark when he called last night to confirm?" she asks, her head darting toward me, and I know she's referring to her vision of him living in this very farmhouse, growing his plants.

"Yep. I figured it's something better experienced live, and totally clueless," I say, my voice low and amused.

"He might not recognize any of this, so don't get your hopes up," she says, her brow dipping.

"I want to see the look on his face if he does." I waggle my eyebrows, and she shakes her head at me. "Anyway," I continue, "we'll know soon enough if this place calls to him, or not."

The five of them are expected here in a couple of weeks over winter break, for a ski vacation. And I can't wait. The last time the six of us went skiing altogether we were still at Berlinger.

Éolie is already putting a match to the kindling wood shavings and logs neatly prepared in the fireplace. An old couch, an indeterminate shade of beige, sits in front of it, spruced up by some royal-blue wool cushions and throw blankets Ms. Duhamel's crew had the foresight to add as a welcoming touch after taking stock of the barren place on our first day of cleaning.

The windows are drafty, but with both the living room fireplace and the wood stove in the kitchen going full blast, the downstairs should warm up in no time. I figured out pretty quickly the reason why the only bedroom with a double bed is parked in between the living room and the kitchen. And for now, it's ours. Sorry, boys.

"I'll go unload the car," I say, breathing the Laure Magic in the air.

Old Léon's rustic house with what's left of its sparse furnishings speaks of a simple life lived, one that resonates within me. I enter the kitchen, and I'm zipped by the same jolt I get every time, ever since I first walked in there last week.

I brush the palm of my hand on its scarred wood table in passing, the desk of my future study. Sorry, Leo. Future bestsellers will be written on it.

I unlock the door to the mud room in the back.

With the last load of the Bar Harbor bins of clothes stacked up in our bedroom, I return to the living room.

Éolie is blowing out a match, tea light candles lit everywhere now, and it transforms the little farmhouse into a warm, mellowed, magical realm intimately our own.

I'm swept along by the sound of Dusty Sprinfield's 1967 rendition of the Look of Love softly playing in the background from one of Yann's old playlists Éolie must have found.

Heart rate stuttering, eyes locked on my forever, the lyrics are taking on their full meaning.

"Dance with me?" I hold my hand up. The answering glow in her loving eyes I see reflected in her smile light up the place.

Holding her close, I sway and twirl us around the downstairs rooms, soft jazz music following our every move.

I croon along, my lips murmuring the heartfelt words in her ear.

"So this is what magic feels like," she says, haloed by the crackling fire, stars in her eyes.

"No. This is what magic feels like." I cup her face, my lips melting onto hers.

And she kisses me back. Long, sweet, slow kisses, their warmth traveling through my body to my heart, getting me high.

We shed our clothes unhurriedly, one arousing, languorous caress at a time, warm skin brushing against warm skin.

I wrap my arms around her and pull her as tight against me as I can fit her, and it's still not enough. I crave more, much more...

Laure. Taking root. Forever. Mine. Happily ever after.

The thoughts swirl through my mind as we sink to the floor. The fire crackling in the stone fireplace bathes Éolie in a golden glow, as I give myself over, falling into her warmth.

I nibble the sensitive skin just below her ear, and a shiver ripples through her. I kiss her back. Hard, soft, tasting all the flavors in between.

Her taste, her scent, the feel of her sheathing me, her sex pulsing around my shaft, pulling me in, they all drive me wild, but this, I want to savor.

Éolie breathes my name as I kiss my way down the curve of her neck to her shoulder. Unable to contain myself, I thrust once, her breathing ratcheting up as she arches into me on a low whimper.

I shift, inhaling, closing my eyes against my own impatience.

But Éolie pushes against me, her hips coming up provocatively, demanding to unleash the beast or at the very least, giving him implicit permission to let loose...

My palms hit the floor on either side of her.

I pull out of her slowly, coming to a halt just before I pull free, and I push back in a little faster, a little harder. And Éolie wraps her legs around me, lifting her hips to meet each and every one of my forceful thrusts, each one piercing me with sharper pleasure.

I lower my head, and ravage her mouth.

She sinks her teeth into my shoulder on an involuntary shudder, moaning loudly as her ecstasy comes roaring, tightening around me, milking me on its journey over.

I growl deeply and give in to my release, enthralled once more by the ferocity of our joining as its orgasmic echoes bounce back and forth. Until the last of our tremors dwindles, and only quiet bliss remains.

"Happily ever after, Éolie-Jolie, it starts here," I vow in the afterglow, trailing the back of my fingers down the contours of her exquisite face.

She murmurs a reply, but it's soft and sleepy.

Wrapping us in throw blankets, I watch the fire slowly burn into embers. Éolie peacefully sleeping in the shelter of my arms.

A true sense of belonging settles down upon me, and I let it seep deep into my soul, anchoring me.

We made it Home, Éolie, together. We've found where we belong.

Fifty-Two

ÉOLIE

"This is ridiculously bright ... and early to be out and about on our first morning here," Liam grunts, swinging an arm around me as we step off the front porch on our way to the village for some grocery shopping. I woke up with a ravenous appetite, strangely enough, as I'm not usually hungry in the morning. Stuffing ourselves full on a box of granola bars for breakfast didn't quite make the cut for a feast, but at least it fed the hunger.

"Do you know what's missing in the picture?" I ask, blinded by the reflection of the sun on the snow, the brilliance making my eyes water.

"A warm bed?" he suggests slyly as he pulls on dark sport shades to protect his eyes from the glare, and I follow suit.

"It's too early to be this cute," I say. "Not my fault if we never made it to bed."

"Not my fault either," he quips. "I liked everything about that couch last night."

"So did I, last night." I fill my lungs, elation brimming over. "It's morning now. And it's obviously missing a snowman." I gesture to the empty fields as evidence, bouncing down the driveway. There must be something in the air up here that makes me feel different, lighter. On the other hand, it could be just this newfound peacefulness in growing roots, knowing we made it home.

He spins to face me. "Ever made one?"

"Nope, but I always wanted to. How hard can it be?" I ask.

"Famous last words," he says drily.

"And didn't we conquer laundry, groceries, and cooking since I last said them?" My head tilts to the side, daring him to argue.

"Yeah, but we had to go through the blob disaster we cooked up that first night in Bar Harbor in order to do so," he points out, crossing his arms, but one dimple appears. And I do send a quick, silent thank you to Monsieur François as I'm filled once more with gratitude for his invaluable lessons.

"Come on, what are you afraid of, a little snow?" I challenge Liam. "We'll even turn him into the coolest one ever with your mirror sunglasses, and one of your shabby hoodies," I say, my level of enthusiasm hiking up. "We'll pretend he's undercover, dodging coeds," I add, feeling mischievous, and he just snorts.

"The poor sod," he says, shaking his head.

But I only grow more enthusiastic as I visualize our *bonhomme de neige*, making a mental list of things to get for him at the village market.

"We could cut broccoli florets for curly hair? Oh, and for a toothy smile, we can get red pearl onions and—"

"Onions," he cries out, swiftly picking me up. "No way." He laughs, throwing me into a snowdrift, and I sink into it.

"Way!" I holler, jumping up. I clip him at the waist, but he only stumbles back a few steps, still laughing.

He swings me up over his shoulder, and I squeal, pummeling his back with my palms.

"Hey, no swatting the muscles behind this whole snowman operation," he says, dropping me from higher up into another drift where I sink even farther, pretending to pout.

"C'mon, let's make a real snowman before someone mistakes you for one," he chuckles anew, pulling me up by the arms. "We'll go shopping for details like food afterwards."

"Voted best idea you've had so far this morning," I say, regally walking back into the drift.

"Where are you going?" he asks.

"I'd like to see our snowman waving from the kitchen windows," I reply, sinking thigh deep. I drop down on all four and start crawling.

"Nice moves you got there," he snickers.

"You liked them even better last night," I say unruffled, picking up speed.

"Speaking of which, want me to share another idea I've just had?" he asks suggestively from behind me.

"I'll pass."

"Too bad, it's a good one." He tsks, sliding his sunglasses down a bit, shooting me a pointed look over them, but amusement dances in his warm eyes.

"Your definition of a good idea isn't the same as mine just now," I quip, gathering a mound of snow with my arms. "Start rolling."

However, I soon realize that under today's clear blue sky, the early-morning air's crisper, colder, and dryer than when it snows. And it sucks moisture out, giving snow on the ground the consistency of fine, fluffy powder that refuses to stick.

"Casimir is as flat as a waffle," I say, giving up.

"Casimir? Of course, you had to go and name the spineless thing, didn't you?" Liam cracks, kneeling by its side.

"I can't help but name things, it comes to me naturally." I shrug, contemplating the crumbling pile of snow a.k.a. Casimir the Spineless Snowman.

Liam's hit in the face by a blast of snow dust from a gust of wind, little ice crystals instantly forming on his stubble, and he wipes them clean with his sleeve.

"Did he just puke on me?"

I laugh. "Shouldn't have called him spineless."

I look at him, and start gathering fluffy snow with my hands.

"You like to live dangerously," he says, egging me on. "You sure you really want to go there?" he asks, dodging all of my countermoves. Until he stumbles backwards, one leg sinking lower than the other, and I let fly with my mini-avalanche of ice fluff, hitting him smack on the face.

"Victoire. All mine!" I cry out, hands over my head.

"You're so done!" he yells out.

I stumble and fumble in snow packed knee high in between squeals of laughter. My waist is grabbed from behind. The both of us freefalling into a deep cushiony bank, laughing so hard, we eat ice cold fluffy snow by the mouthfuls.

"Maybe we can try some fallen snow angels?" I tease, rolling over.

"Look at you two, laughing and playing in the snow. It will make Vie so happy when I tell her."

We turn as one at the sound of a man's voice above us.

"Grégoire!" we both exclaim, Liam pulling me up alongside him. We brush ourselves off and mounds of snow fall away.

"Vie has my undying gratitude," I say, breathless. "We found everything we needed on her list at the Saint-Sauveur outlets."

"And all under two hours, she's my hero," Liam agrees as we trudge our way over to him.

"She'll be glad to hear this," Grégoire says, a pleased look appearing on his face. "And she'll be as thrilled as I am just now, when I tell her you're the ones who bought Old Léon's place. Who'd have thought you'd find it to your liking." He walks down the driveway towards a dark-blue pickup truck, and we follow. "It's not exactly a residential listing as you know by now, and it's a bit more than a vast track of forest I'd say."

"You knew about this place all along then?" Liam asks.

"Everyone around here knows about this place, but let's just say we preferred to let well enough alone. I've brought some firewood to tide over our new neighbors," he says, motioning to the truck with his head. "You'll run out by the end of the week with what's left of Old Léon's."

"So, *you're* Maître Deslauriers? Both attorney and neighbor from Hell, we've been warned about?" Liam's lips tug up one side.

"Guess Ms. Duhamel still remembers me by. I'm touched, really," Grégoire replies with a sardonic twist to his voice, but his mouth mirrors Liam's lopsided smile.

Grégoire cocks his head to the side. "Magali mentioned to us that you're some famous author with an even more famous father, but that there was some sort of fallout between you two recently. What are your plans for this place?" Grégoire asks, his piercing grey eyes assessing.

Liam pales and his shoulders sag a little. "So, Magali did recognize me," he sighs heavily. "I've no other plan than to live here normally. Think that's possible?" he asks Grégoire in an even tone, but irritation clouds his features. I swallow to wet my throat, wondering if Liam's newfound peace of mind has just been shot.

"If what you're asking is 'will I be hounded everywhere I turn,' the answer is no. There's no pack of paparazzi lurking up north like in the States or Europe, for one. And no one up here will care if you're famous or not, for two. If you're looking for star-struck fans, look elsewhere, it won't be here. We'll care about what you do with the land though, make no mistake. But I see the answer I'm looking for written all over you," he says, nodding his head once. "And that's good enough for me."

Liam holds up his hand, and they shake on it. My breath swooshes out.

"You saved the Forest of Laure for us, a million thanks," I say gratefully, giving him a quick hug. His lumberjack clothes reek of *eau de woodsman,* and I almost gag. Overwhelmed by the pungent mix of smells, I instantly take a step back. I'm not usually that sensitive to odors, weird.

"I like the name," he says to me. "Care for it, no other thanks necessary."

"We'll take good care, promise," I solemnly vow, and he nods. *I know you will,* his eyes convey back. And I realize this land is just as special to him, or maybe Old Monsieur Léon was.

"So? How about that firewood? Ready to give me a hand here by moving your car outside?" he asks Liam.

"That's not a carport?" Liam asks, and Grégoire lets out a short bark of laughter.

"It's the woodshed."

Fifty-Three

LIAM

The three of us stack the last of the chopped wood into neat cords underneath the carport. No. The woodshed.

By the time we're finished, I'm shocked by the fact I've worked up a sweat. I unzip my coat, and wipe my face with my thermal fleece.

"Give me a minute," Éolie says over her shoulder. "I'll be right back with some water."

"How much do we owe you for all of this?" I ask Grégoire.

"Nothing," he says with some surprise, bracing his hands on the truck's bed. Dressed in lumberjack's thick, padded clothing that has seen their fair share of hard work judging by their rips and holes, he didn't even break a sweat.

"You're sure?" I ask, unsure what to do with kindness like this. People have always done a favor in order to get one.

"I'm sure," he says, eyes glinting with merriment, and I seem to be missing out on the joke. "You'll need about two more truck loads to see you through. I've got the wood covered, but you'll need to haul it in, though."

My eyebrows rise up and I'm about to argue, but he puts up a hand to stop me.

"Before you argue any further about paying for it, you should know that it's your own wood. I clear the dead trees out of your Forest of Laure to rejuvenate it, and it keeps me in shape. I left it cut, but you may have a time digging it out of these drifts."

"So you know the Forest of Laure pretty well then," Éolie says as she returns, offering us full glasses.

"Like the back of my hand," Grégoire says, putting a last piece of wood on top of a pile before accepting his glass, thanking her.

He leans his back on the wall taking a long drink of ice-cold spring water, his gaze quietly sweeping the land, and I prop one hip on his truck.

In a flash, Éolie's face turns from rosy, to green, back to rosy as she holds on to the truck's bed. I frown, staring at her with a question in my eyes, but she shrugs both shoulders, cringing. "I just drank two glassfuls of water. Bad idea. It almost came back up. I'm good now," she says low.

I pull her closer, and she burrows into me, her arms coming to rest round my waist. "There's a natural clearing and a brook further back into the woods," Éolie says, tracking her gaze to where Grégoire stares, at the edge of the forest. "It's where we'll live."

"I know where, nice spot. You're not going to revive the farm then?" he asks, pinning me with a direct look.

"No." I inwardly shudder at what Leo calls my black thumb, his medicinal plants and grafting experiments left all over our common room at BIA having suffered under it many a time. "We have a friend who's into agronomy research, so we're keeping it on the back burner for him," I add, and Grégoire's face brightens.

"Beats living in an igloo meanwhile," I murmur for Éolie's ears only, and she elbows me.

"Do you know why Monsieur Léon's holdings came subdivided into ten separate lots merging into The Forest of Laure?" Éolie asks, and I take a long drink of water.

"Long story short? A third-generation family feud that got settled out of court in the 1960s by Old Léon's buying the others' share, keeping the farmstead and forest lands you just became responsible for, whole," he says, crossing his arms and his ankle. "Old Léon never reverted back the land to its original division at the Registre Foncier du Québec. He hoped his three sons would take to the place, but they never did. Your gain if you intend to build this upcoming summer as it's already parceled off. Although, you have to keep in mind that aside from the preserve, which is untouchable, the one hundred fifty-eight acres left of the original fields are protected under an APA. You won't be able to build on these, you know that right?"

"Yes, no worries. Our vision is of a meandering road following the brook, and for the house itself to be built in the meadow opening up to the Enchanted Forest of Laure," Éolie says, her whole being fairly radiating joy one second, and the next one, her eyes grow wide. "Bathroom emergency," she grits, rushing by me, the mud room's door clacking closed behind her.

I briefly wonder if Éolie considered all the layers of thermal clothing we have on in her level of emergency.

"Do you know of anyone who opens up private roads without using heavy machinery around here?" I ask, not missing a beat.

"Not right off the bat," Grégoire says, rubbing his jaw, pondering the matter. "I'll let the word out, but in any case, you better start applying for the different permits. You're never too early to get through the usual red tape around here."

"Will do, thanks." I salute him with my empty glass, inwardly cringing at the words *usual* and *red tape* thrown in there as though they belong together in a normal fashion.

He squints up at the sky before giving me back his empty glass, thanking me.

"It's almost ten, have to run to a meeting, but next round, let's take a walk through this projected road of yours. There might be something we can do before spring, with a pre-approved permit," he says, giving me a one-hand salute, and just like that he's gone.

And Éolie returns, looking around for the missing truck.

"Grégoire had to leave," I state the obvious, and she squints up at the sky.

"Time really flies. It's already ten. Are you ready to go down to the village?"

I check my watch. Ten o'clock on the dot. I squint up at the vastness of the clear blue sky, and come up empty. Am I the only one needing a watch, a phone, a laptop, something or other to know what time it is, or what?

"So ... the village?" she urges.

I narrow my eyes. Is it me or is her face a shade paler than a minute ago. "You good?"

"Everything's good." She gives me a startled look. "Why?"

"You seem a little pale that's all," I say, watching her face flush a lovely shade of pink.

"I'm pale?" she squeaks, palming her cheeks.

"Not anymore." I raise a brow.

"Good. Cocooning groceries. Can't wait," she says, almost sprinting to the car. "Let's do this."

"If you're sure," I start, but she's already seated in the car, buckling up.

Fifty-Four

LIAM

The village is surprisingly not a sleepy little town, thanks to a very large community of artists. Out of every corner, arresting rock or recycled metal sculptures emerges. Interesting murals or wood carvings, inspired by nature, adorn all the shops, the grocery store boasting the largest one—a carved wood painted mural lending a 3D dimension to different flora and native birds that wraps around all four sides. The public bulletin boards at the old train station, now part of a vast two hundred some kilometers long linear park for cross-country skiing and cycling, are all about local exhibits, pottery, photography, custom jewelry, glass blowing, poetry readings, concerts, dance recitals, and the likes. Bistros with creative menus line up la rue de l'Église, alongside cafés with live music, and quaint little shops, offering staples so wide ranging it boggles my mind, the front windows displaying everything from handmade soap to micro-brewery beers, knitwear to hand-crafted furniture.

A short fifteen minutes' drive away from our place, it's like stepping into an art explosion anytime we feel like it.

And my roots shoot a growth spurt.

Our pit stop lunch at Le Petit Mouton Noir, a café bistro by day and live concert bar by night, is another great discovery. The gourmet poutine du jour, involving homemade French fries, curdled cheese and, well, anything you can think of to put on top of it, is served in a fun, eclectic decor on the shores of La Rivière du Nord. I could eat here every day forever.

All fueled up, our groceries are soon dealt with.

"Want to go see what they have in there?" Éolie tugs on my hand, motioning to the old presbytery house, now a permanent exhibit hall for local artisans.

"Sure," I say, my insides melting at the joy stamped all over her face.

We walk in, and Éolie steps away from me, already admiring the first display.

"Come and see," she says in a reverent tone, brushing her hand over raw stones twice the size of her head etched in some tribal designs. Her fingers stop on a particular one.

I take one of the pamphlets on the table, and read on with some interest.

"Vous aimez?" the artist, a young woman in her twenties with intense green eyes, and light-brown hair with golden highlights, asks Éolie. Her name is Anaïs Desgroseilliers, the bio reads.

"Oui, beaucoup," Éolie says, a finger trailing along a swirl of water carved within, her gaze enthralled by the stylized fossil fish etched to a dull polished shine onto the rock.

"You're the artist behind the boulder groupings standing in front of the village school?" I ask, looking up from the pamphlet.

"I am," she says.

"We love them!" Éolie exclaims. "Your snowy owls taking flight in twilight skies, spilling out of an open book, they're truly amazing." Anaïs's face glows with quiet pride.

"You're so kind, thanks. L'Harfang des Neiges is Québec's aviary emblem," she says. "If you're interested in indigenous art, I've etched larger ones that are part of Les Jardins du Précambrien." She reaches for her portfolio, showing us pictures of fifty feet tall scalable boulders etched with sleeves of different flora and fauna, one on top of the other like a layered totem. The rocks are part of a groomed forest with graveled trails inviting everyone in for a leisured walk.

"It's really impressive. That's in the village, right?" I ask, and she nods.

"They're closed in winter, but every summer, they showcase international art exhibits on site, besides the permanent ones like mine, and it's really worth the trip back to the village," she says.

"We'll make sure to." I look over Éolie's shoulder at something else that's caught her eye.

"You're designing jewelry too?" I ask, pleasantly surprised.

"Just necklaces for now, but working with pebble-sized granite is my new passion, scaling down," she says on a quick smile, pointing to the pictures Éolie's looking at. "I'm all out. Every single one sold early this morning." Elation is written all over her face.

"It's no wonder. They're lovely," Éolie says, giving back the portfolio, and Anaïs thanks her with a shy smile.

I fold the information pamphlet into the inside pocket of my unzipped jacket.

"You really liked her stuff," I say, pretending nonchalance while checking the next display over. Amber maple syrup sold in handmade glass carafes, each one unique in shape and size. I pick one up.

"I love her particular art form. It speaks to my soul," she replies, her voice still held under the spell. "Can you imagine? Those stones are more than five hundred million years old, patiently rounded to perfection one ice age after another..."

"Yeah, it's something else," I say in a neutral tone of voice, outwardly tampering down on my enthusiasm. My mind wanders, hatching plans, as I absently pay for maple syrup in a dainty glass carafe I'm not even sure is equipped to survive the farm. I thank the blushing school girl behind the counter, and move on.

"I'd like to commission Anaïs for an etched boulder, to mark our civic address by the future road," Éolie continues, her eyes staring off for a brief instant while her hands unusually fidget in her coat's pockets. "What do you think?"

"Love it. Voted best idea so far," I quote her back, swinging one arm over her shoulders. *Until I surprise you with mine*, I silently add.

"What's with the loony grin, you up to something?" she says, bumping my side, bringing me out of my thoughts. Her eyes search mine, her head tilting to the side.

Well shit, there goes my stealth operation. Will she guess out right? She says she can't read my mind, but sometimes I wonder...

"I'm always up to something," I say on a shrug, hoping to deflect her attention away from any talk of Anaïs and indigenous art forms, like custom jewelry made from pebbles.

"You're so busted," she teases. "Spill it, you."

"You want me to spill it?" I search for a quick, improvised diversion; otherwise, she'll likely put two and two together, and I'd really like to surprise her, for once. "Right now?" I stall some more.

"Why not right now," she says, giving me a suspicious look.

I look down at the carafe in my hand and flash her a wolfish grin. "You, me, maple syrup," I whisper in her ear. "You ready to hear the rest of it?"

"Liam." She blushes a fiery red before pushing away from me.

"What? You wanted details and I haven't even told you the best part," I say from behind her, and she throws her arms up, crossing over to the next room.

I follow at a slower pace, discreetly readjusting.

"Come and see," she sighs breathily, admiring a display of traditional handmade furniture, according to the wood sign above.

A wiry guy with scruffy cheeks, his dark hair held back in a leather tie, approaches Éolie, stumbling in his haste. The dude wears a long-sleeved brown tee with a French rooster weather vane logo reading, La Belle Aventure, Ébénisterie Inspiration Nouvelle-France. Saved by the shirt.

"Elle vous plaît?" he lingers, asking if she likes.

"I like everything you have in here, but we're just looking." Éolie says, timidly brushing her hand on a rustic farm table sitting eight, dyed a mustard-yellow color.

"We're not ready to buy furniture yet. We're building. But it gives us ideas," I say to the cabinetmaker, with a wink at Éolie, and she tilts her head at me, eyes luminous.

"Faites le tour, ne vous gênez-pas," he says, inviting us to take a look around.

We come upon a really nice piece in the back. A massive, solid wood, two-door wardrobe in a style I've often seen staying over in a few Mas de Provence in the south of France.

"It's beautiful!" Éolie exclaims.

I take a closer look, impressed by the craftsmanship and the attention paid to authentic details, like wood hinges. The wardrobe is antiqued in multilayered blue tints, their distinct shades coming through the patina, and one of them, I discover, is the exact light aquamarine of Éolie's irises. And just like that, I'm sold on it.

Éolie softly trails the fingers of one hand on the smooth, blue-hued textures. She grows misty eyed as she opens the doors, gently brushing one hand along the middle shelf.

The moment she touches it, she goes rigidly still, unblinking.

Oh shit.

"Éolie," I cry out, darting towards her.

"La demoiselle, elle va?" the cabinetmaker asks, looking from her to me and back, growing confused.

"Oui." Everything's peachy, under control, man. "We'll take l'armoire! And we'll just wait here while you prepare the paperwork," I say, sheltering her from the curious looks the cabinetmaker shoots our way, afraid to embrace her, in case I get zapped into her vision as well.

"Éolie?" I ask, but she doesn't answer, her open eyes unseeing.

"Elle a peut-être besoin de s'asseoir un p'tit brin," the guy insists from behind me, stating that she probably needs to sit for a bit, pulling up a chair behind us.

"Non. Non, ça va aller," I answer that it's not necessary. Man, I'm starting to sweat bullets in my jacket just picturing Éolie's upright body unbending on the chair; now wouldn't that be a sight. Both times I witnessed her having visions previously, her whole body had locked as is, and I'm not prepared to test in public if it will bend into a sitting position, or what it might do to her.

"Bon, alors, si vous le dites. Je prépare les papiers de l'armoire bleue et je vous reviens," the guy says, shrugging a shoulder on his way to prepare the paperwork, and mine slump in relief. I gently massage her stiff shoulders, kissing her temple, but she stays unresponsive for a minute or two longer. An eternity.

"Oh mon dieu." Éolie sways, grabbing my forearms as she blinks back into reality.

"Thank God," I say, enfolding her in an enveloping hug.

She goes limp as a rag in my arms, taking me by surprise.

"Éolie...?" I whisper frantically, holding her up, and she blinks, coming to.

She takes one look at me, and her already pale face leaches of all its remaining color.

I sweep her up in my arms. "C'mon, let's get you back to the farm."

"I can walk," she insists, her face wearing a stunned look, her gaze unfocused.

"Humor me," I say, and she snuggles into my chest, the cabinetmaker tagging along with us, following me to the car, making sure I sign on the dot.

Fifty-Five

ÉOLIE

In something of a blur, I'm driven home and soon put in warm fleece jammies, and tucked in by Liam, all curled up in our bed. In the downstairs bedroom at the old farmstead in the early afternoon, at nap time ... just like in my vision.

"You're awfully quiet. You sure you're good?" Liam asks, crouching down beside me at eye level. And I simply nod, cupping the side of his face, and he leans into my hand.

"I bought the blue wardrobe, Éolie-Jolie," he says, anxiously searching my eyes.

"I know. I saw it just there." I point to the wall behind him.

"You never went out like that before. Did you see something ... unusually sad?" he asks, eyes tinged with worry.

"What do you mean by unusually sad?" I murmur, bewildered.

"You see beauty, Éolie. Happiness unfolding somewhere down the line, not ... I don't know, the dramas, I guess."

I straighten on one arm. "I never noticed it before," I say, floored. "You're right. I only foresee glimpses of happy, don't I?"

"And I like it just fine that way."

"I just got zapped by a stronger jolt than usual, but I swear to you nothing bad happens with l'armoire bleue, promise."

I curl back under the covers, pulling them up to my chin.

"Sure takes a load off my mind; that guy insisted on delivering it here, tonight. I was ready to bury it somewhere," he says half-jokingly.

"I couldn't let you. It'd be a crime against beauty," I say, eyelids fluttering closed. I want to tell him what I saw, but I can't find the words. Later, I promise myself. I'll tell him later.

"Rest," he says, giving me a kiss on the forehead. "I'll put the groceries away, and go take pictures of the meadow while the sun's still up. We'll need them for the permits." My eyes pop open. Our yellow house. Liam is striding out the door.

I stare for a long moment at one of the empty corners of the room, seeing two cribs side by side, l'armoire bleue filled with neatly folded babies' clothes standing right beside them.

I close my eyes, my hands coming to rest protectively over my belly. How do I tell Liam the twins are coming earlier than even I ever thought? And that I don't know what happened to our house in the meadow, but it's not there either.

"And it's all my fault," I murmur.

Unused to having to keep tabs on any of this contraceptive stuff, time flew by me, my mind floating elsewhere. It's past three months already. And I just plain forgot about renewing my injection.

I'll find a way to break it gently to your papa, is the last coherent thought I have before sleep claims me.

Fifty-Six

LIAM

Leaving Éolie to her nap, I wrestle with the wood stove in the kitchen, the rusted hinges giving out on me when I yank too hard. I'm left holding the door in my hands. I put some more wood in and light up the fire, propping the skewed door up in front of it on the brick floor. It will have to do.

Sliding the chain to the mud room's back door free, I notice white frost covering the lock and the outward edges. I jiggle it a few times, but the door doesn't budge. I forcefully pull, and the bloody door knob comes off in my hand.

I grumble, and then shift direction, bringing the groceries in through the front door instead. Traipsing snow all over, I soon turn the wood planks' floor into a neat little slush trail. I make a few snowballs to show Éolie later on, leaving them in a suspiciously warm freezer. I shrug, could be my reddened hands from the cold misleading me.

I slip slide my way through the rest of the melting snow, sweeping it down with what's left of the sad excuse for a broom I find in the pantry, and our two meager tea towels that can't absorb the half of it. The rest of the puddles will have to dry on their own, 'cause there's just no way I'm willing to sacrifice for the greater good the two bath towels we have for now.

The upside is that food doesn't spoil if left a few hours in the car.

I pry open the warped doors of the wood cabinets, which leave my hands full of peeling paint chips in a god-awful green. One door keeps popping ajar when I close the other, and vice versa. Gives them personality, Éolie would say. And she'll probably name them too.

I may beat her to it with a few choice names myself...

I dump the contents of a few reusable grocery bags full of dry goods into the cupboard. One shelf caving in precariously, I distribute its load up.

In what I'd call horrified fascination, I watch the whole-wheat flour bag drop right through, cleaving two other dry-rotted shelves neatly down the middle on its way down the bottom.

I release my breath. The flour bag stayed intact, and I'm overflowed with gratitude for small miracles like sustainable packaging.

Grabbing my coat from the back of the chair, a persistent dripping sound eerily starts to break into the quilted silence, stopping me mid-motion. I stare at the kitchen faucet in front of me, and slowly turn on my heels.

The refrigerator's door is sporting a water rivulet running down its front, trickling onto the floor one fat drop at a time. The compressor chooses this moment to retch and belt its way to another cooling cycle noisier than Zac's Piper at a full throttle.

I almost rip the upper door off. The warm compartment clearly refuses to freeze like any good, normal, proper freezer should, as evidenced by the leaking, melted snowballs.

"Enjoy your last few hours, mate. You're about to be toast," I say to the offending thing, wiping with my hands what's left of my bright idea.

"We need a list in here," I mumble, my eyes searching for something to write on. "Alongside someone who knows their way around it." Hands on my hips, I look up the ceiling. I narrow my eyes. Is that a water stains around the light fixture?

Ripping a blank sheet off the Log Book, I tack it up on the wall, writing with the permanent marker.

TO DO:
Backdoor knob
Kitchen cabinets
Fridge
Wood stove

I leave the marker beside the Log Book on my table/desk, satisfied that I've created some order in here for the day.

I take one last peek at Éolie, peacefully napping, before heading out for the meadow, taking a few pictures here and there as I go.

I look down at the gurgling brook by my feet. Clear, pure, crystalline water rushes by in between sculpted ice formations. Taking off one glove, I plunge my hand into the swirling water, inhaling sharply.

Holy freaking shit.

Éolie made it look so easy the other day but it's colder than...

I put the handful of pebbles in my pocket, and go for more. By my second go round, I don't feel the cold as sharply anymore. On my third go, my pocket's half full, and I start to blow like crazy on my numb fingers in between slapping them in order to regain feeling.

That's when I see it. A small pebble.

I crouch back down and pick it up, mesmerized.

Years in the making.

Years patiently waiting for me to find you, Éolie-Jolie.

In a vision of my own, I see it all. Our yellow house with its wraparound porch, just there, underneath the maple trees, wild flowers in bloom, a warm summer breeze ruffling my hair, crickets singing their hearts' out, and me. Waiting in this exact same spot.

I'll look up, and a radiant Éolie will be walking towards me...

Staring at the heart-shaped little pebble I hold in the palm of my hand, beaming, I suddenly know exactly how, where, and when to make it official.

Fifty-Seven

LIAM

I chug the last of my second cup of instant coffee, by now quite cold, which either means I'm in dire need of caffeine this morning, or we're in dire need of small kitchen appliances. Probably both.

Éolie's quietly humming, sitting by the fire, scribbling notes. It's been a couple of days since her strange vision, and she still hasn't told me what she saw, but she's fine now. And I'm not about to stir her up all over again by asking her what it was, just to satisfy my curiosity.

"Grégoire must have been joking about red tape, you know some kind of local humor I didn't get yet, 'cause that looks pretty straightforward," I say, downloading the last of the municipal by-laws and permit applications from the municipality's website.

She puts her chin on my shoulder, her arms coming around my chest. "Maybe it'll be faster to process if you apply in person? You could even stop by the hardware store in Sainte-Agathe on your way back." She straightens, giving me a torn out sheet from the notebook.

I scoot back, inwardly rubbing my hands, pleased by this legitimate ready-made opportunity befalling me.

"Are you trying to get rid of me for a week?" I ask, looking down at the long list of tools and whatnots.

"No. Only the day, shoo," she deadpans, putting my wool beanie on my head.

"Shoo? Who says that?"

"I just did, shoo. I need those tools and the rest of what's on the list." She motions to the rotten cabinets, and waves me off.

"You know your way around those power tools you're asking for?" I ask, crossing my arms.

"Come on, I grew up on a sailboat not a cruise ship," she says, upturning her eyes.

I put my hands up. "All right, I get it. I'm off. Don't wait up, I may get lost somewhere in bureaucracy or worse, in between hammers and drills. Don't miss me too much."

I tie my boots and shrug my coat on, patting down my inside pocket, making sure my little pebble's there.

"If you're not back by nightfall, I'll miss you, promise," she says, giving me a peck on the cheek.

"That's not a kiss." I grab her by the waist and bend her backwards, kissing the stuffing out of her. "*That's* a kiss." I straighten, leaving her dazed-looking in the doorway.

"Bet you'll miss me now." I back away, and she closes the door on me.

"I will miss you," I hear her say through the door, "by nightfall."

"Your applications are duly completed." The skinny guy behind the counter at La Mairie returns after a disappearing act that lasted more than an hour. Talking designs for Éolie's ring and necklace with Anaïs was way more fun than sitting around waiting, or reading over and over again stale by-laws on their public notice boards.

"Before we can submit them to the town planning committee, however, we require Québec's stamped permission. Your land sits on an APA, Monsieur O'Shea. You'll have to fill out their applications," he says, his little beady eyes shifting twice behind his tortoise-shell glasses.

"Okay ... And where can I do that?" I ask pulling my phone, ready to take notes.

"Try le Palais de Justice in Sainte-Agathe, they'll know better than me." He shrugs, indifferent, giving me back my papers.

And off to Sainte-Agathe I am, a short fifteen kilometers down the road.

The courthouse in town is nothing more than a minute satellite of the mothership; the main courthouse for the judicial district of Terrebonne is located in Saint-Jérôme, le chef-lieu. According to the info written on the locked door anyway, which basically says they're only open once a month.

And off to Saint-Jérôme I am, some sixty kilometers away, down Highway 15 South.

"No, you're misinformed. We're from the Ministry of Justice. You will need to apply directly to the following Ministères in Québec City," one of the clerks at the information desk says. On a list of twenty different provincial ministries, he highlights four before sliding the paper over to me.

I read them over. Jesus, their names alone spread a mile long, and are quite the mouthful. "Must be fun to man the phones over there," I commiserate under my breath.

"So, Québec City?" I say, quickly programming into my phone the itinerary address of the Parliament House he just gave me. "You've got to be joking. It's more than three hundred fifty kilometers away..."

"You asked to apply in person, sir. You can also fill your applications online," the young man points out, tugging on his dark-blue uniform jacket.

"Will do, thanks," I say, staying polite. "What about my other request, a marriage license?"

"That's easy. Just go to the fifth counter, ground floor." He points down the corridor to my left.

I follow his directions, and I'm soon shuffled from one counter, to the next. And the next.

And once there, inspiration for a new book unwittingly strikes like a thunderbolt, hauling me out of my previous dry spell, or keeps me sane as I face yet another clerk, whichever. A full-length epic fantasy SciFi horror suspense neo-realistic novel that will take place on this nebulous RedTape Planet in a near galaxy, where the inhabitants are ultra-civil clones wearing white shirts, speaking gibberish in triplicates with license to kill time.

It will read something like this, loosely translated in English.

"No. You're misinformed. You must complete Form 273488 before Form 009765, Monsieur O'Shea. Straight through, take the elevator down, seventh underground floor, door D78, second counter," the fifth clone will say.

"No. You're misinformed. You must complete Form 009765 before Form 273488, Monsieur O'Shea. You will need to complete beforehand Form XYZ0083, to obtain Form 009765. Take the elevator up to the fifth floor, suite 53895. Ask for sub-department number 571458, reception area, third counter," the sixth clone will say by rote, and so on.

I grit my teeth.

I want this bad enough, and my stubbornness prevails. More than a few twists and turns later, I finally complete all the required forms, and the short interview with a *Greffière Adjointe*.

I'm duly processed into the grinding mill.

I just need to plug in a date, and we're licensed to be lawfully married.

Fifty-Eight

ÉOLIE

I wave goodbye from the kitchen windows, watching Odyssey's tail lights disappear down the winding driveway. I open my fist, and stare at the odd-colored, square-shaped little pebble I retrieved from our swirling brook when I plunged my hand into it that first morning. Was it less than a month ago? It's funny, really. It feels like I've always lived here. But then again, maybe I have. I admire once more its strange and unique blend of swirls, from the lightest blue grey to the darkest, charcoal blue grey. Seven shades of swirls to be exact. I can't help but smile, re-pocketing it.

I lock the door and take a deep breath. Pulling the strap of my empty duffel over my shoulder, I turn on my heels and start my trek down to the village. Hopefully, by the time I get there, Liam will be on his way to Sainte-Agathe and kept busy long enough with errands, so I'll have plenty of time to get back and prepare.

The hour-long walk is invigorating, and I arrive at the old presbytery energized.

Anaïs's brow furrows, and clears, and furrows. She's furiously sketching what looks like a band. Perfect. I wait.

She jumps when she sees me, hastily closing her sketch pad.

"Sorry, I didn't see you there," she says, squirreling away her sketchpad into a large tote bag.

"I'm sorry. I didn't mean to startle you," I reply, my fingers coming up to cover my mouth.

"No worries. I was just doodling away ideas."

"Actually, I'm glad you were doodling ideas for rings. I'd like to commission you for a band of my own," I say, showing my pebble, and producing a tie wrap with Liam's finger measurement.

She gives it a mischievous little grin, picking it up.

"You know if my 'Cutting Edge' rings take off, I'll probably start a tie wrap collection on the side. I'm already up to two just this morning." She tapes it to a piece of yellow paper.

"If you need more, just say the word. I found a drawer full at the house we're staying in," I enthuse, and she chuckles, turning the paper my way.

"What do you have in mind?" she asks, examining the small pebble from every angle.

"Do you think it'd be possible to cut seven slices and work it into a band, like this?" I ask, sketching a rough design of one continuous wave of swirling shades of blue grey, no beginning, no end.

"Yeah ... I think so," she says, growing even more enthusiastic, looking from my design to the pebble and back.

"Yes," I breathe out, just about ready to jump up and down.

"Wow. The colors are something else, where did you find it?" she asks, turning it, this way and that.

"Where it all begins, at the start of our road," I say, happiness flooding me.

"You're by Old Léon's farm, right?" she asks, her moss green eyes sparkling. "So cool. I can't wait to work on your piece. It'll be such a meaningful wedding band," she says excitedly, already sketching away ideas.

My eyes grow wide.

"Oh nonono, it's not for a wedding at all," I exclaim back.

Anaïs snaps her head up, the spark in her eyes dimming.

"Merde alors! That's not what—" She shoots me a queer look, clamping her mouth shut, and I watch her buzz fizzle out. *Uh-oh.*

"It's not formal or anything. It's just a little piece of—" *my heart,* I don't get to say.

"Look, the stone has to speak to me. I work with it, not against it, so I can only do stuff that inspires me," Anaïs says, and she looks crestfallen. "You're saying it's just some casual gift from a friend then?"

"Well, he's my dearest friend for sure, but there's nothing casual about it. Liam's always been in my heart," I say in earnest. "That band is a personal troth ... something to remind him at all times that he's the second half of a never-ending circle of love," I continue, my hands clasping over my belly. And Liam might need it sooner rather than later if he happens to keel over from my next reveal.

"Can I write that down?" she asks, already scribbling away.

"Um..." My cheeks instantly burn.

"It's for me. I like what I hear, and I'll put the love right back into the band. In a never-ending circle, I swear." She perks up once more, taking notes. Her whole face shines, and I let out a pent-up breath. "Give me about two weeks, maybe less, depends on how my other design goes," she says, and we smile on it, done deal.

I walk out with a new spring in my steps. Folding my insulated winter gloves into my pockets, I put on some lighter, knitted ones. I'm ready to browse through a few local shops looking for the things I need without touching anything directly, hoping the simple solution will work to prevent any other public episodes from happening.

I look up at the partially cloudy sky, noting the time. I have about four to five hours in front of me to prep our bedroom at the farm before Liam is due back.

Fifty-Nine

LIAM

Coming up the driveway, the little farmhouse on the hill appears welcoming in the early twilight sky. Mellow light spills from the living-room windows, white puffs of smoke billows out of its red-brick chimney, pristine snow abundantly covering its decaying splendor, a poem all by itself, reading like a picture-perfect postcard.

I park, and narrow my eyes at the condemned backdoor.

Well shit. I smack my hands on the steering wheel. I totally forgot the hardware store list. Guess I'll have to embellish a bit on the time it took me ... not to get the permits, after all.

I unlock the front door and step inside, shaking the snow off my boots.

No Éolie to greet me.

"Éolie?" I call out. No answer.

I frown, shrugging my coat off, taking a few steps in.

A winding trail of multicolored sticky notes spread out on the floor catches my eye. I peel the notes off one by one, and follow their trail to our bedroom.

> *Brace yourself*
> *There's something in the air*
> *Feel it yet?*
> *It's potent...*

By the fourth one, I'm pulling my fleece sweater over my head, chucking my soft shell pants along the way, letting them drop on the floor. By the fifth?

Ready to find out?

... the rest of my layered clothing pretty much follows.

My gaze tracks the last note on the bedroom door.

Live Magic Within

Wearing a wicked grin and more skin than thermal underclothes, I open the door ... and freeze in my tracks.

My jaw grows slack.

My eyes dart up the ceiling to a starry night constellation of mixed-sized LED light strings tacked to the age-darkened wooden slats, bathing the entire room in a soft bluish glow.

I turn on the spot.

L'armoire bleue shimmers, incandescent under the low light.

Éolie, wearing a Madonna smile, a rare messy bun, one of my tees and not much else, stands in one of the empty corners underneath a flurry of blue felt snowflakes coming down in all shapes and sizes, from the lightest azure to the darkest navy. They hang suspended on invisible threads.

She brings an open palm close to her lips and blows me a sweet kiss, releasing her breath slowly through the flakes, sending them fluttering about on a merry dance. My eyes follow their movements up. Some white gauzy material bunched into cloud formations mute the lights in that corner.

"Where did you find ... how?" I can't even begin to figure it out. She walked all the way to the village or what? "What happened to I'll just catch up on my reading?" I ask, my mind spinning on its wheels.

"Some catching up on my writing," she says softly, worrying her bottom lip as she points to some writings on the tee she's wearing, briefly closing her eyes. She wrote something with a silver marker on one of my black T-shirts, and I can't make out exactly what from where I stand rooted, my brain cells running as slow as molasses in the wintertime. Fitting.

Searching my eyes, she walks towards me, and stops a few short feet away. Her hands quiver as she smoothes the tee over her toned abdomen.

Finally, I read the Sharpie.

Magic Formula
1+1=2

My face scrunches up for a second there, unsure, but when it clicks, a slow grin creases my cheeks. By all means, Éolie-Jolie, let's add my body to yours, and come up with two ... tangled up in one.

"I like the way you think," I say reaching for her. "My kind of math."

Her lips curl and upturn by a fraction, but she backs away, looking at me from underneath her lashes, shaking her head.

Game on.

I motion with my hands for her to come closer, but she keeps shaking her head.

"Do I have to catch you first?" My grin turns predatory.

I take one step forward, and she spins on her toes, bowing her graceful neck. A few tendrils of golden hair tumbling down distract me.

Then I catch sight of a second equation scrawled across her shoulder blades. I blink, stopping dead in my tracks, caught off guard.

1 maman +1 papa = 2 bébés

Holy shit. I stop breathing.

I lick my lips, my mouth suddenly dry.

Are we talking let's try to get pregnant as of right *now*? Am I ready?

She turns and I catch sight of her expression .... and my heart tumbles. She's trembling.

"Come here, you," I murmur. One of my hands comes up, tenderly cupping her cheek close to my heart, the other rubbing her back in soothing strokes, and the rapid rise and fall of her chest calm down. Her shakings stop.

"I worried you'd be upset about the timing," she whispers, hugging me tight, her face burying into my chest.

I enfold her in my arms. "You're ready for some serious baby making already, is that what you're telling me, luv?" I murmur close to her ear, my heart two beats away from toppling over, seduced by the thought of Éolie round with our child. Guess it means I'm ready to go for it, full speed ahead and damn the torpedoes as Leo would undoubtedly say.

But her entire body locks for a good minute there, before her forehead starts to rub on my chest, going entirely in the wrong direction here.

She's saying no? My brow furrows. Something doesn't add up.

"If it's not that ... then what—" I still.

I replay the last few minutes, mentally rereading the notes from a different angle. Realization trickles in.

My mind turns sluggish, my face goes slack, my pulse skyrocket. Can we be—? No, can't be, aren't we still on contraception? *Holy shit* ... How long does it last for again? I cannot for the life of me articulate any words, a kaleidoscope of thoughts and images tangling them up in a whirlwind before they can exit.

Backing away from my loosened arms, she grabs my tee by the hem and pulls it over her head, placing both my unresisting hands on her lower abdomen. "Live Magic Within," she whispers.

And it starts to seriously add up.

"Éolie? Nicolas and Sébastien are on their way? Now?" I breathe.

She mouths, "Yes."

Soft, cerulean eyes meet mine, and my heart brims over.

I feel both lost in the moment and found within a stretch of eternity.

"We're pregnant!" I shout, amazed, swirling her once before delicately putting her down on the bed. I hover on top of her. "Am I *virily* potent or what?"

"Told you," she says, her finger shyly tracing my lips.

My chest's just about ready to explode. "I'm going to be a dad, a real one," I murmur to her belly, kissing it.

"Is this all right?" I ask, rolling her on top of me.

I relish the warmth and contours of her body against mine, heartbeat to heartbeat. To heartbeat.

Sixty

LIAM

It's been a couple of days since Éolie broke the news of our pregnancy and I'm frequently slammed by the notion that this is all for real. It's happening. Sébastien and Nicolas. The thought of me as a dad is surreal.

"You sure it's okay? What if you fall or something?" I say, growing unsure as we clip our snowshoes on by the woodshed. "Did you eat enough this morning? Do you have a nut bar with you?"

"You mean besides you?" she deadpans.

"Cute. So cute." I cross my arms.

"I'm sorry, I couldn't resist," she says, wincing, giving me sad puppy eyes, and Christ above, it works. The moon? Hey, no problem, yours.

She shows me a granola nut bar that she zips back into her sports waist pack. "I also have Açaí berry juice, an extra pair of gloves, an instant heat pack, a headlight with extra batteries, waterproof matches. We're all set."

"You saying I worry too much?"

"Well ... we're only going for a short walk, mapping the road," she says, her hands tenderly spreading over her belly in a loving caress, and man. It gets to me in such a warm fuzzy way. "Think of it as the first time they walk home with us, how's that?"

"I ... huh ... yeah ... I..." I stutter, the image just about slaying me, touching me like nothing else.

"You're chirping a text alert," she says, shaking me out of my twin trance.

"Chirping?" My lips tug up one side and she shrugs both shoulders. "P.O.'s worried about our lack of connection," I say, texting right back. "He's sending over a shipment of computer gizmos to upgrade us to high speed next week when they all get here," I read out loud. "He says Lucie will get the shakes otherwise." I let out a snort.

I hear Grégoire's truck coming up the drive, and we walk down to meet him.

"Come on, then, before I change my mind." I squeeze her shoulders. "But if you want me to downgrade the worry level to DEFCON 5, promise me no more walking alone to the village."

"It's good exercise," she says, zipping her coat higher up.

"Éolie, I'm not joking."

"What if I get a GPS chip implanted on my hip?"

"Hey, that'd be great. I'll ask P.O.," I say back, reaching for my phone.

She turns on one heel and crosses her arms. Not an easy feat with all the layers. "Liam. I was joking."

"Well I wasn't," I mumble.

"I swear, I'll tell you from this point on if I plan on walking down to the village, no more surprises," she says, moving past me to join Grégoire as he gets out of his truck.

"Not good enough," I reply, following behind.

"I loved every minute of my hour-long walk down to the village. It's energizing; don't worry so much," she says as I catch up to her. "Bonjour, Grégoire," she greets him.

"Did I hear you say you walked down to the village? By yourself? In winter?" Grégoire frowns, hands coming on his hips.

"Um ... that would be a yes?" she says, sporting a deer caught-in-the-headlights look.

"Visibility's dangerously reduced either by snow or glare, snow banks are twice your height, back roads are quasi deserted on weekdays, and the plow comes through like hell on wheels," he says, crossing his arms, staring her down with a stern look. "And that doesn't even cover the reason why night skiing starts at four."

I cross my arms as well, and stare her down with a stern look. "What he said." I motion with my head.

"I promise. I won't anymore," she blurts, her hands folding around her belly protectively. "Cross my heart," she adds quickly, her knitted gloved finger hastily making the sign.

"Is there anything else we should know about winter precautions up here?" I ask concerned.

"Don't think so. You have enough firewood. Keep ration packs and bottled water just in case of power failure, but those are few and far between. Roads are cleared, but just use common sense in blizzard conditions and stay put, unless absolutely necessary. Relax, enjoy, makes for the best cocooning time of your life," he says, grey eyes twinkling.

"And a slew of summer babies I'll bet," I tease under my breath, and she elbows me.

We walk up the trail to the meadow, discussing the curves and dips of the future road, mapping it to follow the natural contours of the terrain. I love it.

Éolie draws a rough plan in the Log Book identifying the trees to take out, writing down the genus and species, Grégoire spray painting a yellow dot on them as we go.

"Did you submit your permit applications for approval?" he asks over his shoulder.

Ha! Bureaucracy, the final frontier, where no man in his right mind has gone before ... I groan, recounting the part of my tale involving the property paperwork, and Grégoire huffs, crossing his arms over his chest. His eyes narrow.

"Leave the papers with me. The town clerk is taking advantage of your foreigner status, giving you a classic runaround. This subdivision was cleared ages ago for one residential dwelling. I'll enjoy giving him a heart failure by showing up to submit them."

"And they'll let you do that?" I ask, thinking about all the municipal by-laws and regulations surrounding the right of ownership.

"Damn straight they will. Didn't you just give Maître Deslauriers a clear mandate to do so?" Grégoire says, and I can't help but match his evil grin.

"By all means, they're all yours," I enthuse, about ready to drop to my knees in thanks. I've got twins under construction now, and we live in a house with just a little too much personality to my way of thinking.

We reach the meadow and I stand back, contemplating Éolie gesturing, tracing lines in the snow, animatedly explaining to Grégoire, who is attentively listening, her vision for the future kitchen, the future family room, the future porch, my future study, well, just about the entire house plan. And I like what I see; she glows.

"I like your plans," Grégoire says. "Okay, then. Cutting and clearing trees by hand so as to preserve the limited access to the meadow as it stands now, with roughly half a kilometer of road into the woods, my guess is you're looking at two years of construction," Grégoire estimates.

Bloody everlasting Hell. Two years of living in a disaster waiting to happen. As if to underscore this abysmal fact, the wind picks up in strong gusts, rustling through a few dried leaves still hanging on a tree limb, snow swirling in a mini vortex around us.

"You seem to know a lot about construction, another hobby of yours by any chance?" I ask, hopeful I might have found yet another time-saving miracle in him, and he gives a shout of laughter, clearly entertained by the notion.

"Vie will have a hoot over this one, she's the handy woman around the house," he says. "No, sadly, my in-depth experience of it comes from thirty-odd years of civil litigations. You'd be surprised at the number of unrelated subjects I know too much about."

"So, I guess you know all the good contractors around here?" I ask instead.

"And all the bad ones too," he says drily.

"Good to know."

"So, two years, then?" Éolie muses, nodding to herself as though it explains something.

"Looks like it to me. One for the road and barn, one for the house, or..." Grégoire squints at the trees up ahead, leaving the rest hanging in there.

I brace myself. Gloves are off. I inhale sharply. *Jesus.* "Or what?" I ask him, cracking my knuckles to limber up a bit my stiff digits.

Grégoire crosses his arms, and I detect a tad of reluctance there. Éolie takes an immediate step back, as though sensing what's coming.

"Or heavy machinery plowing through," he sighs heavily.

In the Log Book, I write on a new page, Bulldozing Option, or I try to. Is my Sharpie frozen?

"It would bring you to the end of the summer, beginning of fall for sure, leaving you the following winter to finish up the details inside," Grégoire concedes.

My fingers numbing from the wind-chill factor alone, I quickly change my mind about writing this down. It will have to wait, preferably for me to be roasting my toes by the fire, so I put my frozen stiff gloves back on.

End of August. Just in time for the twins...

Hmmm ... I start to scratch my jaw with a crusty glove, and end up scraping my runny nose instead. Never leave your gloves unattended in a snow drift, not even for two minutes, man.

"But it wouldn't be the same," Éolie cries out aghast, gesturing around. "It would destroy everything on its path on a much larger scale, and it would take about twenty years for the surrounding forest to recover from it, if at all."

"That's for sure," Grégoire readily answers. "Still, it's an option, something to think about."

What's two years in that bloody rotten house compared, I argue with myself. Éolie pleads with her eyes, and I grunt, unfortunately having to agree with her assessment on that one. I sigh, mentally scratching the bulldozing option out already.

"You two married yet?" Grégoire asks.

"What?" I cough out, eyes fairly bugging. Jesus, did he just kill my big demand in the works here by alerting her to what I've been up to? I snap the Log Book closed. How the bloody hell did we go from discussing logging trees and house building plans, to marriage contracts anyway?

"Married as in head over heels in love, or as in rules and contract?" Éolie asks, wrinkling her nose.

"As in rules and contract," he replies, twisting his mouth up a fraction.

And since when does Éolie need to distinguish between two kinds of marriage bonds? I glower at him.

"Oh. No, we're married as in head over heels. Ever since we were kids," she says, her face clearing up.

"No offense meant," he says to me, waving his hand in dismissal. "If you're not married, you'll need to apply for permanent residency to stay over, now that you've bought property together."

"Oh. I figured, thanks, my attorney's on it," I reply before turning to Éolie. "Theo and I had already planned to look into my applying for residency when he comes over next week," I say, and her face shines with quiet joy.

"While we're still on the subject of options available to you or not, applying for residency is not an option, it's an order," Grégoire says sternly, staring at me. "Overstay and you'll automatically be refused entry back. You're only allowed a total six months yearly visit, starting from your initial date of entry, no in and out resetting of the clock," he warns, his sharp eyes piercing me.

"I thought I could use some kind of extended visa to bridge over?" I say, a prickle of unease slithering down my spine.

"That would be a no. You're not eligible for an extended visa, students or special work permits only," he says, uncrossing his arms. "In any case, you'll have to work around a yearly schedule because you need to be out of the country to apply for residency, and we're talking in terms of months here, not weeks. It takes Immigration a certain amount of time to process applicants, and there's no express lane."

Éolie pales, I still. The twins...

"Lots to think about, so I'll leave you to it," Grégoire says, walking up the trail, disappearing round the bend.

I look at Éolie, and all my fears come crashing over me.

"Marry me," I blurt.

Sixty-One

LIAM

C hrist. For someone weaving words into stories for a living, not my greatest moment.

"I'm so sorry," she whispers through her gloved fingers, her eyes overflowing with misery. She looks devastated...

"Whoa there. Sorry for what?"

"That you have to marry me," she says in a small voice, her arms folding on her.

"I don't have to. I want to. I'm sorry for just blurting it out like that, but I want you to officially be mine to protect, to nurture, to grow with, be with—"

My heart's slamming against my ribcage while my mind is lagging three paces behind, wondering what the hell just happened back there. Or why Éolie hasn't answered me yet.

"I've always been yours! And we wouldn't have to marry if ... if it weren't ... I ... It's a signed contract..." she stutters, tears overflowing. "What if it changes everything in the way you look at me, and I become this obligation instead? It would slowly kill my soul. Perhaps we could ... I don't know, go abroad? You apply for residency like you wanted to in the first place, and maybe we'll be able to come back here before the—"

"Éolie, look at me." I grab her shoulders. "I've always wanted to make it official, no one's forcing me to. We're building roots here, not traipsing around the world with you pregnant. Let's do this now, please. I want this," I say, searching her eyes.

"What if you start seeing me differently?" she whispers, her eyes veiling over.

"You're being silly. I swear, no piece of paper could make me look at you differently." I drop a kiss on her forehead. "I love you to the moon and back."

"Promise?"

"Promise," I say, hugging her tight.

"*I can do this*," she breathes a few times, nodding on my chest. "Okay then."

Sixty-Two

LIAM

"Okay then what?" Theo asks over the phone.

"That's what she said ... Okay then."

I huff into the woodshed, throwing firewood behind me in a not-so-neat pile, all the while keeping my phone precariously balanced between my bended neck and twisted shoulder blade. I turn, checking the progression of my selection du jour. Just about two more logs should do it to keep the fires burning for the day, and my pile will be ready for the trudge back inside ... all the way around the bloody house using the bloody front door.

I throw two more out, and go lean on the evilly frosted mud room door, banging my head on it, sighing heavily.

"She looked so dejected, man."

"Just so we're clear, was that before, or after you told her you wanted to get married for legal reasons." His sarcasm drips over the static of the line.

"Heads up. If you're trying to make me feel better? It's not working, Theo."

"And we're supposed to copy your notes on love to use as cheat sheets? Christ, Liam. You didn't even get down on one knee."

"Yeah well, seems I don't do traditional," I say, pinching the bridge of my nose.

"No shit."

"Bloody hell, man. Even after three days of telling her otherwise, she's not totally convinced I really wanted to in the first place. She fears I'll see her differently from this point on, like some sort of obligation," I say, unzipping my coat to cool me off a bit.

I slap my gloves on my soft shell pants. There's a shadow passing through her eyes every time she thinks I'm not looking.

"Why do you keep telling her when it's obviously not working? Show her."

"Show her what? Nothing's going as planned," I say, disgruntled, but the truth is, I'm mad at myself. There was no build-up, no ambiance, nothing I'd envisioned when I plucked that pebble out of the stream. "I had it all figured out," I mutter.

"You're a fiction author for chrissake. Rewrites are what you do for a living."

"Imagine that," I retort, unimpressed.

"Isn't that what I just said?" he asks drily.

I straighten from my slouch. Imagine that.

"Theo, man, you're a genius," I enthuse.

"Agreed. Now tell me why exactly," he says, his tone cautious.

"Can't. Major rewrites in progress. Listen, I got to go. See you on Friday," I say, ending the call.

I shove my hands through my hair, my beanie flying off. I start pacing back and forth, ideas blooming at lightning speed, almost as fast as my shit-eating grin.

I'm not just planning ahead this time. I'm setting it in motion.

And the first thing on my To Do list is to go ask Éolie to forget all about it. Until I say when...

"So, basically, you're telling me your promise necklace has been downgraded to '*what's the occasion again?*', and your summer wedding has been upgraded to '*let's do it now*,'" Anaïs says, her lips upturning as she slides over the counter the necklace we designed together.

"It's still a promise necklace. Timeless, no downgrade." I smile back as she gives me my "let's do it now" ring to check over.

Masterfully cut and polished to opalescence, slices of the pink, hard stone are weaved into intricate little vines, set in platinum. It enchantingly holds all the pieces of my perfectly imperfect heart throughout its web, in a never-ending circle, no beginning, no end.

A stunning piece of eternity.

"You captured the exact meaning I wanted it to convey. Wow. Just, wow." Anaïs' rendition is exquisite, and I can't wait to see it on Éolie's dainty little finger. "It's the perfect representation of my pledge," I say, awed beyond measure by the end result.

"I have to admit that I was seriously inspired by the story behind it," she replies, her translucent green eyes alive with happiness as she picks up the necklace, admiring it. "I'll probably be out there looking for pebbles everywhere I go now."

"I know what you mean." I give her back the ring, and she wraps them both.

"Hey, could you do me a favor?" she asks, her face brightening on a sudden thought, reaching underneath her counter.

"I'll do my best, what's up?" I ask, pocketing my little packages, feeling lighthearted.

"Could you give this to Éolie the morning after?" She gives me a gift-wrapped box.

"The morning after?" I repeat, unsure what she means.

"The morning after your upcoming wedding," she says, eyes twinkling.

"Sure ...What shall I tell her?" I shake the box, intrigued.

"Tell her it's a little something she inspired me with," she reflects with a faraway look. "Freely given, nothing formal."

"Will do." I turn the small package in my hands. "But for the record, now I just can't wait to give it to her." In more ways than one, I add silently.

"Got any brothers secreted away no one knows about?" she jokes, playfully throwing at me a little pebble, visibly shaking herself out of her reflective mood.

I laugh and she joins in.

I do indeed have a few brothers, I tell her on my way out. And they'll probably never know what hit them over winter break, in two short days now. I inwardly smile.

I check my watch, and start on a light jog. I'm running late for my coffee date. Literally.

I cross the linear park and enter Le Général Café where, at this time of the week, only a few locals are reading books or typing away on their laptops, as they quietly sip a café au lait served à l'européenne in cobalt-blue earthenware bowls.

I immediately spot Vie, who waves me over near the back of the century-old house converted into a small café.

"Vie, thank you so much for setting this up," I say, shrugging out of my coat.

"Think nothing of it." She comes up for a hug and a peck on both my cheeks in greetings. "I can stay in there for hours. I had so much fun getting everything on Éolie's list," she says bright-eyed, passing along a couple of bags from the local hardware store.

"Better you than me." I shake my head, safely tucking my alibi underneath my chair.

"Grégoire's the same," she says, clearly entertained.

I order a black coffee and Vie orders a refill of green tea.

"We're both so happy for you two. Now tell me what you have in mind, I've been dying here."

I take my laptop out, and for the next couple of hours, we hammer down the details. Under Vie's input and suggestions, my vision grows by leaps and bounds, and I just can't wait.

"I think it's the sweetest thing ever," she gushes warmly. "And it will make a perfect counterpoint to the ten-minute formalities at the courthouse."

"I sure hope so, Vie. I don't want Éolie to freak for all eternity ... It's a pretty dry formality," I sigh. It's basically a read through by a Superior Court Deputy Clerk of a list of rights and duties of the spouses, prior to signing a legally binding contract solemnizing our civil marriage, my short interview with the Greffière revealed the other day.

So it's not really helping my cause here, to get married in such a rush in a courtroom, on the one day of the month the Sainte-Agathe Courthouse will be opened next. "She's truly afraid, deep down, that I'll see her from this point on as some form of obligation like her parents did, of sort. It's an irrational fear, but Éolie, well, she feels things ... deeply," I admit, fiddling with my coffee cup.

"Oh, Liam." Vie's expressive dark-brown eyes instantly soften with a world of compassion. "Her parents ... our generation, it stems from a French Canadian syndrome thing, most likely."

"What do you mean?" I ask, curious.

"It's from way back," she says, "steeped in our roots."

"Go on, I'd like to know more," I encourage, leaning back in my chair.

"I'll go with the quick, condensed version, then," she says wryly. "Otherwise, we'll still be here by nightfall, or you might run for the hills, whichever comes first."

"Try me." I pin her with a direct look.

"Upon the British conquest, the Nouvelle-France colony was granted permission to keep three things: its civil laws, its language, and its religion. Roman Catholic," she says, leaning forward to rest her elbows on the table. "From there on, in the French-speaking community, the Church ruled over every aspect of our lives up until the 1960s, be it education, health care, politics and so forth ... On one hand, it kept our language and customs alive, but on the other, it offered no other alternative than blind obedience, allegiance, piety, abnegation, self-sacrifice, duty. And for women, breeding children was the outmost sacred duty. You either became a nun, or married. Up until the 60s, French-speaking families of twenty-some children were common enough to be a norm, no matter the poverty and harsh living conditions that came with it. Men were resigned to their small lot in life and made do, and women quietly endured theirs. In either case, you can well imagine that buried, deep down, and better left unsaid, children were not quite viewed as the blessing they were and should have been ... but more like a curse. It's no longer the case, thank God."

"What happened to change all that?" I ask, riveted by this new insight.

"If I had to choose only one particular event? Bearing in mind that nothing is ever as simple, I would go with Expo'67, Terre des Hommes, or Man and his World. L'Exposition Universelle."

"L'Exposition Universelle? Like the one who gave Paris the Eiffel Tower in 1889, you mean?" I ask, fascinated.

"Yes, or the one that took place in Milan, just last year," Vie says, eyes shining, folded arms leaning on the table. "I was just a little girl of six that summer but still, I remember it vividly. The energy carried behind it all was so vibrant, there was such an explosion of hope and possibilities, that you couldn't help but be touched by it. The world opened up to us with more than fifty million visitors from all over. And suddenly, the future was ours for the taking. In a matter of weeks, churches emptied. Young men and women enrolled en masse in universities, and a lot of them refused to even consider having children, preferring careers, as if it had to be one, or the other.

"In Québec, the 1960s were dubbed the Quiet Revolution ... And my generation grew up as the first by-product of it, somewhere in between this huge shift in mentalities."

"Well, that explains a lot," I mumble into my cup of coffee. "You really gave me a whole new perspective here." Shit. It's no wonder Éolie's terrified of marriage.

I stare at the online confirmation on my screen. "I really hope it will be enough to show Éolie that her fears are just that—fears, not reality."

"Liam, it's from your heart, how can it not be enough?" Vie says, bumping her shoulder into mine. "Go for broke."

"I will," I say resolutely. "You provide the flair, and I'll provide the muscles behind the operation." With all the guys over here for our ski vacation, that part should be a breeze at least.

"And it's as good as done," Vie says.

Sixty-Three

LIAM

"**M**an, I thought you were playing drama queen in your emails but—" Zac begins.

"It's cold as fuck," I finish.

Zac's the fifth one to come out of the Piper exclaiming the exact same thing on the frozen tarmac at YTM Mont-Tremblant International Airport.

"Bloody hell. I just shrivelled up into nothing," Theo says stiffly, walking bow legged in the general direction of the terminal and I smirk at his designer jeans, remembering Grégoire's advice to me that first day.

"Didn't you receive Éolie's list of essentials I sent you?" I ask.

"Yeah, but we didn't think we'd need to travel geared up in our space suits. Our winter gear is stowed in the cargo bay," Zac complains, jumping back into the plane. "No way am I doing Theo's penguin walk, dude."

"Does that really say negative forty-two degrees on that digital display?" P.O. squints at the terminal, his eyes watering. "Holy shit. It just switched to negative forty-four."

"Yep. Shows wind-chill factor," I say breezily. "Your visit will separate the boys from the men."

"Zac, wait up. No shit, the air in my lungs froze solid," Leo says, disappearing back into the plane.

"Almost perfect!" Yann exclaims, his breath fogging as he slaps his hands on his back, shuffling his feet around.

P.O., Theo, and I give him a look.

"What? We're back in Celsius. Negative forty degrees is negative forty degrees."

P.O., Theo, and I grunt.

"C'mon, this is exciting. We're freezing up solid almost exactly where both Celsius and Fahrenheit meet at that perfect point on the axis conversion."

"Not on my watch." Theo swears a blue streak, grabbing Yann by one arm, shoving him back into the plane.

P.O. follows, blowing on his fingers. "My touch screen can't feel any of my fingers. That's fucking cold, man."

On the second go around, five happy campers strut their way into the terminal.

"Éolie, we all owe you big time," Leo cups his hands and hollers up upon spotting her sitting in front of the massive stone fireplace in the upstairs visitors' loft inside the posh, log cabin airport terminal.

"Leo!" she exclaims, looking down on us from over the loft's wooden ramp. "Hi, guys! I'm so relieved you got the memo, and dressed warmly. Wait up, coming down."

"No rush, hold the railing," I say sternly and the guys give me looks. "What? Those stairs are steep."

But the ribbing I get for my being overprotective of Éolie is nothing on the ribbing I get once Zac sees the car. The red car.

I stroke her hood once in passing before unlocking the doors. "No dissing Odyssey's color, she'll take it personally." I watch with no small amount of satisfaction the guys dropped jaws.

"Did he just call the bloody red car by name?" Zac asks, looking around. "Will the real Liam O'Shea please stand up?"

I snicker, and Éolie and I share an amused look.

We're soon stowing the last of their luggage in the car's rooftop cargo box and on our way to the Forest of Laure ... and clueless Leo's farmstead.

"This is it, Leo," I say under my breath, turning up the drive to the old farmstead.

"I counted at least eleven resorts on our way over," Yann says, closing the front passenger door.

"There's at least fifteen more on the way down to Saint-Sauveur," I add.

"How cool is that?" Zac says, getting out of the car, stretching. "C'mon, let's unload and hit the slopes."

P.O. checks his phone. "Only one bar, man. You need boosting."

"Have at it," I say.

"Éolie, you sure you don't want to come with us?" P.O. asks, picking up Lucie's backpack.

"Yeah, Éolie, come on. We'll have a blast, we'll all teach you," Theo says, coming out of the other side.

"Don't gang up on her." I frown, flipping the backseat to help her out of the jump seat.

"Thanks, but really, I'll pass this go round. I'll let you guys catch up on your skiing, and I'll ... catch up on my reading." Éolie looks at me, crossing a finger over her heart.

"Whoa," Leo marvels, coming out of the car, squeezing out of the other jump seat. He turns on the spot and an arrested look pops up on his face.

I brace my arms on the car's hood. "Crunch time," I say for Éolie's ears only, and her arms come around my waist, gripping me.

"This is some serious Kool-Aid, man," Leo says, his gaze landing on the barn. "You won't believe this..."

"We won't believe what?" I ask Leo, and the four others stop their bantering and turn our way briefly before picking up again where they left off in the unloading of the car's rooftop cargo.

"Did you send us pictures of this place before you bought it?" Leo's brow furrows as he stares intently down the fields at the old barn.

"Nope."

"When you bought it?"

"Nope."

"You sure?"

"Yep."

"Well, Christ. Either my brain is fried or ... it's real."

"Spit it out already, Leo," Zac groans, slumping face down on the hood.

"Skiing. Do you know how long I've dreamt of this exact moment while sweating it out in my jungle? Weeks, man, weeks."

Leo's baffled gaze sweeps past me to the farm house, and back to the fields and barn. "Who cares about weeks, Zac. I'm talking years, here. Ever since Liam's *Tales of The Enchanted Forest of Laure*, man," he says, clearly bemused. "This," he gestures, "is exactly how I imagined it ... This has got to be the weirdest déjà vu I've ever had. I swear this is my experimental farm. I can practically see my greenhouse, over there, by the barn."

"And *that's* the first thing Éolie saw when we drove by, the first time," I say, eyeing Leo. "You, in a greenhouse over there." I point to the barn.

"Get out!" Leo exclaims. "You really saw me? Here? In one of your visions?"

They all turn and stare at Éolie, and she turns bright red. "Don't ask. It just sort of happened..."

"Awesome," Leo says brightly.

"You do realize that it means *Liam* is your closest neighbor." I hear Theo drop the bombshell on Leo as I walk away.

"Bloody hell. I forgot your killer black thumb. Of all the possibilities and I end up with you as my neighbor?" Leo mutters, breathing down my neck.

I unlock the front door, unperturbed.

"No shit, Liam. You're not allowed within ten feet of my fields, you hear me? And my future greenhouse is completely off limits, got that?"

"Here," I hand him over the mud room's door knob and my list as the others file in, hauling luggage.

"What's that?"

"My housewarming gift to you, complete with a Honey Do list."

"We'll go put our stuff away while they yap it out; where do you want us?" Theo asks Éolie, and she points upstairs.

"You'll have to bunk in the three bedrooms—"

"Ten single beds upstairs, and counting," Yann hollers down.

"Éolie? How many kids Leo's having?" Zac hoots, taking the stairs two at a time.

She slaps her hands over her mouth, stifling a laugh at the spooked look Leo shoots her way.

"See yourself breeding lots of little farm hands?" I ask suavely.

He falters. "Don't tell me. I really don't want to know—"

A cavernous gurgling startles us from above.

"What's that noise?" I ask, instantly wary.

A loud burping shakes the rafters. My eyes dart up the ceiling. In a deafening clunk, the kitchen light fixture drops down, spewing water all over the place from the hole left behind.

"Fucking shit," I cry out and both Leo and I take off at a run.

"Goddammit!" Zac shouts. "A wrench, quick."

"Coming!" Éolie shouts back.

We find Zac sprawled on his stomach, in the one and only upstairs bathroom, laying in two inches of water, applying pressure on the pipe to limit the spread as best he can. And we both stumble back out to go look for something, anything, to mop the worst of it, but Yann, Theo, and P.O. beat us to it, rushing in with bedspreads.

Éolie weaves in and out, passing a wrench to P.O., who secures the pipe, cutting the water supply off, while Zac holds on for dear life as the rest of us make do with the old bedspreads to mop it up.

"A real gem of a fixer-upper you've got here," Zac grumbles, drenched from head to toe, holding the rusted-out cut-off valve in his hand as evidence.

"Yours, I believe," I say with a sidelong glance at Leo.

"No dissing my house," Leo states, a frown forming on his face. "She's..."

"Temperamental?" I supply.

"Sensitive," he says, hands on his hips.

"Ornery?" I reply.

"Full of character." He crosses his arms, challenging me.

I just snort. "Whatever makes you sleep better at night, man."

"I started a fire so you can go dry by it," Éolie says, squeezing in to give Zac a fluffy towel, taking stock of the disaster area. "Guess we'll all share the downstairs bathroom."

"Hope it's a bigger one. Seven in here's a bit crowded," P.O. wisecracks, and a ripple of snickers starts.

"Brings us back to BIA big time. Single beds, one bathroom, man," Theo says.

"Let the good times roll," Zac adds, dripping water all over the floor as he pulls his wet shirt over his head.

"No streaking past the commons into the yard, Zac," Yann orders.

"Yeah, bad habit to have up here," I say drily. "Things fall off in cold like this."

"I was nine." Zac upturns his eyes and rubs the towel over his head.

Éolie darts her head between us, wide-eyed.

"No worries," Theo reassures her. "He's house trained now." He ducks the flying wet shirt, which hits the wall and flops down on the floor with a suction sound.

"Debatable," I say.

"You got that backward. It's your bloody house that needs training," Zac comments over his shoulder, picking his wet shirt up. "Come and get me when you're ready to ski. I'll be the one in wet thermals standing in front of the fire."

"Hey, cool formula, Éolie," Yann says, reading her shirt front as we start to file out. We share a warm look.

"What's that you're adding up?" Leo asks from behind her.

I take her in my arms, sweeping her messy braid over her shoulder. "About time someone notices," I say.

"Notice what?" Theo asks and P.O. turns in the doorway.

Leo stares open-mouthed at Éolie's shirt and Éolie laughs. "We're having twins."

Sixty-Four

ÉOLIE

We settle into a routine of a sort at the old farmstead, if my being surrounded by six mother hens for the past week or so could ever be called that.

"Éolie, take another spoonful of vegetable broth, it's full of vitamins," Leo says, eyeing my half-emptied bowl.

"She needs protein, man. If you fill her up with vitamins, she won't have enough room left for protein. C'mon, give her some more of this tofu dish," Zac orders to Leo.

"Are you nuts?" P.O. exclaims.

"Nuts. Good one. An excellent source of magnesium, lots of magnesium," Yann adds, and Zac agrees.

"Don't give her that crap. It's not tofu, it's hummus." P.O. hurriedly scrapes my plate clean of it with a forkful. "It's on the Forbidden List."

"Why?" Leo asks P.O. in a baffled tone. "It's made from chickpeas."

"I don't know why," P.O. argues with him, showing him a webpage. "I just know it says so, right here, on the List of NoNo's."

I don't bother to argue. If it wasn't so touching it would be comical on an epic proportion scale.

"Is that apple properly washed and dried?" Theo intercepts it.

I join him at the kitchen sink, and pass along a request note. Theo reads it and gives me a low five, pocketing it. "*Done,*" he mouths, and I smile my thanks.

I haven't been able to reach Anaïs at Le Vieux Presbytère on my own yet. I'd like to keep the element of surprise for Liam, but I don't want her to think I've forgotten about his band either; it's been almost a month.

"What's the slopes du jour?" I ask them, biting into my apple, chewing. For the past week they've been skiing at a different resort every evening, and I conk out early every night. Pregnancy makes me drowsy. I can't seem to concentrate on anything for long periods of time. I'm pulled inward at the drop of a hat.

"Mont-Saint-Sauveur," Leo says, folding his hands behind his head.

"Didn't you ski over there last night?" I ask, puzzled. I'm pretty sure that's where they said they'd be skiing, as last night I went to bed remembering with fondness the very first time I woke to this winter wonderland in Saint-Sauveur, at Le Petit Clocher, and meeting Grégoire and Vie. Not to mention Magali, their beautiful, vivacious daughter, and one of Mont-Saint-Sauveur ski patrollers.

I inwardly smile thinking of her. Well, she did get her wish, we are making gorgeous babies ... *And I can't wait to hold you in my arms*, I rub my bump tenderly.

"Huh ... yeah ... no..." Leo stutters, interrupting my musings, his mane of shoulder-length hair held back in a leather tie showcasing his ears turning red. "Wasn't it, huh ... Chanteclerc last night?" he asks around, tugging on one ear.

"Chanteclerc? Wasn't that Wednesday night?" I ask unsure, plopping back down on my chair. I'm probably more distracted than I thought if I'm skipping on some of the fun details I'd normally absorb like a sponge, listening in on their daily recounting, and loving it.

"Wasn't it Mont-Gabriel?" Theo says, scowling, his pewter-grey eyes narrowed at Leo, who shoots him a strange, cut-it-out look.

"I guess we're getting them all mixed up by now. I think it was Vallée-Bleue, or could have been Belle-Neige, who knows?" Yann frowns on a shrug, picking a handful of chips.

"Yeah, don't mind me. What do I know, right?" Leo blurts, throwing his hands up. "I just follow where they go, down on my knees for all this plus-que-parfait French I've had to learn that's finally useful for something."

"Yeah, right. Like you didn't crush big time on mademoiselle Dauphinois." Yann snorts, throwing a chip at Leo, who catches it.

"I was thirteen. Get over it," Leo says.

"What's to get over, man. We were all crushing big time," Zac says. "I would have switched to French five times a day instead of Swiss German lessons with Herr Shönbächler, any time."

"True dat," Yann says, munching chips.

"What do you mean *Swiss* German?" I ask, mystified. "I've always thought Switzerland was a French/German bilingual country. Isn't German, you know, German?"

"Yeah, well, contrary to popular belief, no," Zac replies, shaking his head. "French is French. Swiss German has its own pronunciation, many different words, its own grammar, and most Germans have difficulty understanding this funny language. Remember Munich?" Zac chuckles under his breath, and they all share an amused look, except for P.O., who stays focused on his computer, typing away.

"Well, don't leave me hanging. What happened?" I ask.

"We'd just turned eighteen that year, legal drinking age, legal everything, invincible, on top of the world. And all of Berlinger's first year A-levels group was on a field trip, touring Germany. And it so happened we were in Munich at the same time as Oktoberfest," Theo snickers, leaning one arm on the back of his chair.

"Christ, you should have seen the look on the girls' faces, Éolie," Leo says wryly.

"Never mind those girls' faces. Zac's face?" Yann cheerfully says. "Now, *that* was priceless."

"Tell me already," I groan.

"I invited some pretty hot, twenty-something older girls over to our table for a beer, or so I thought," Zac says, and his eyes dance with barely contained laughter. "But with the differences in dialects, they thought I invited them to lick boogers, we later learned."

"Eww."

"Yeah, that's pretty much what they said," Theo says, and they all start chuckling.

"So, you all what? Speak three languages?" I ask, impressed.

"Not outside of Switzerland," Zac says drily.

"More or less. BIA's affiliated with Cambridge International so we mostly spoke English, outside of Liam's obsession with learning French." Theo winks at me.

"Mont-Saint-Sauveur it is, dudes," P.O. interjects, totally focused on his screen. "I just booked our five tickets online. Got to love Lucie."

Yann chokes on a piece of sweet potato chip, and Zac gives oblivious P.O. the stink eye.

"Five? Who's staying in?" I ask, taking another bite of apple. They're acting weirder than me, which is saying something.

P.O.'s head whips up over his screen. "Did I say five?"

A ding alert sounds.

Liam comes out of the bathroom knotting a towel at his waist, his chest and hair dripping wet, and my breath catches. He ticks his name out of the daily rotation schedule tacked on the door, and I watch his towel slip down, revealing his backside dimples, distracting me.

"Zac, you're next. In exactly twenty-three minutes, twelve seconds," Liam calls out, resetting the stopwatch nailed to the door, "and counting."

The ancient forty-gallon water heater needs this exact recovery time, as precisely calculated by Yann, to bring cold water back to lukewarm. With a quick prayer, and our fingers crossed. So, after the plumber confirmed the whole plumbing system was a lost cause, at least until spring, we started out our own version of a Scottish Shower Spa, warm and cold showers à la Swiss precision style.

"Nap time," Liam whispers in passing, and I scoot back from the table.

"Nap time alert, code red. I repeat, code red," Leo calls out after me teasingly. And right on cue, my cheeks burn, and Theo low fives Leo.

"Have fun, you four," Zac says on a sly grin, tipping his chair up on two legs.

"Oh, we will," Liam retorts, cupping my bottom, lifting me up.

"Aww man. TMI," Yann groans.

And Liam chuckles low as I bury my face in his neck, holding on.

"Yann? Just curious here," Zac says as we leave them behind, "have you ever kissed a girl without running an algorithm beforehand?"

"Zac?" Yann replies without missing a beat. "If you're telling me you never do ... it explains a lot."

Liam closes our bedroom door with his foot, and the guys' usual ribbing gets lost somewhere outside of our bubble.

He deposits us gently on the bed, hovering above me on his forearms.

"It's *when*, Éolie-Jolie," Liam says, the indigo of his eyes darkening to midnight blue, and I inhale sharply. I take deep breaths to calm my racing heart, he said the "when" word. The one I'm supposed to wait for so I know the time has come for a do-over on the whole proposal thing ... and a wedding.

Liam is not my parents. It won't be like my parents ...I won't let it. I can do this, I silently repeat as I go within myself, and connect to Sébastien and Nicolas for a brief instant. *You're not a mistake. You're both desired with all of my heart, and not one day will go by where you'll doubt. I love you so so much.*

"As in now," I murmur.

"As in right after nap time," he says, his wet hair glistening under the LED constellation. "I want you to close your eyes, and repeat after me. *I am Éolie.*"

I close my eyes, and repeat, "I am Éolie."

"*Liam's kindred spirit.*"

"Liam's kindred spirit."

"*Always was, always will be.*"

"Always was, always will be."

"And no piece of paper can ever change that. Not even a legal one binding me to you." He brushes my hair back with warm fingers, untangling my braid. I open my eyes. His are the deepest, bluest I've ever seen them. "I love you quite simply."

"Me too," I say, overwhelmed. "Je t'aime tout simplement." I hug him tight, listening to his steady heartbeats. Safe, I feel safe. My reservations melt away as I let Liam's loving warmth seep deep into my soul. I'm all in.

In the Sainte-Agathe courthouse lobby, Liam and Theo are busy revising the last of the documents with the court clerk at the counter, while the rest of the guys and I wait farther down the room. The huge doors of the courtroom at our back are closed, and two uniformed officers from La Sûrêté du Québec stand guard over them, at attention.

When Liam said he'd say *when* and not to worry about it meanwhile, I thought it'd take place in some bland office, or something like it. But Le Palais de Justice in Sainte-Agathe only has one room, the courtroom, nothing else.

It's imposing and stifling in here, more than probably meant to intimidate all parties, opposing ones or not, and it works. My heart is hammering, and my stomach is just about ready to drop. My nervousness hiking up, I swallow to wet my throat. "It's only a ten-minute formality, right?" I ask no one in particular for the umpteenth time, berating myself for asking again.

"Just under ten minutes," Yann says encouragingly and Zac, P.O., and Leo all give me thumbs up and a "no worries, you've got this" look.

I've got this? The ambiance of this place is starkly oppressive, and I've never been in such a formal place before. The many decades of court battles that took place, and still do within these walls, weigh me down. I shiver, rubbing my arms to shake the feeling away.

The walls are painted a slate grey and the only bit of color comes from the coat of arms, Les Armoiries du Québec, etched on them at regular intervals. I direct my attention on Les Armoiries instead of the vast, echoing lobby. On it, the Tudor Crown surmounts a shield divided into three horizontal fields. On the top one, three gold fleur-de-lis on a blue background, symbolize royal France. On the middle one, a gold lion on a red background, symbolizes English royalty, and on the bottom one, three green maple leaves on a gold background, symbolize Canada. The whole is accompanied by a silver scroll bearing the provincial motto, *Je me souviens* (I remember).

It's funny in its own way since no one remembers today exactly what they're supposed to remember, the subject up for debate. As always, the colorful anecdote makes me smile, and it defuses some of my nervousness.

A quick look around confirms that Liam and Theo are still engrossed in their discussion with the court clerk, while the rest of the guys are seemingly engrossed in a deep conversation of their own, P.O. busy texting something. My gaze returns to Les Armoiries, and refocusing my attention on it helps me breathe easier.

Some say the motto stems from a poem, and I think back on my favorite version of the controversy surrounding it. *Je me souviens que né sous le lys, je crois sous la rose.* I remember that born under the Lily, I grow under the Rose...

And it comes to me in a flash of insight. Remember where you're coming from, but don't let it hold you back. Don't forget it's okay to flourish under a new set of circumstances befalling you. And the last of my nervousness fades away. I can do this.

"Do you think I'll have to go on a witness stand?" I ask half-jokingly, readying myself for it.

"They wouldn't dare with all of us in there." Zac gives me his knuckled fist to bump.

"You're all coming in?" I ask, bewildered. Didn't the clerk say one witness only?

Leo takes me by the shoulders, looking me in the eye, "Éolie, that guy over there?" He motions with his head in Liam's direction. "He saved us all. When he came in at BIA, we had been imprisoned there three years already ... and he just swept us along with him on nightly quests for freedom in the Enchanted Forest of Laure. We had a grand time over there from then on. He showed us that it's okay to hope, and dream, and be. Just be. What you're meant to be, even when it's completely different than what's expected of you. And we are who we are today because of that spark you first inspired in him, then in us. So yeah, we're all coming in."

"You're about to become part of our family for real in there, that's all there is to it," Yann says, and I dart my eyes between them, overcome by a rush of feelings.

"And we all got your back," P.O. adds, bumping his shoulder into mine.

"Are you making her cry?" Liam frowns, hugging me, and Theo cuts them a peeved look, and we speak all at once in something that sounds like a *no* in surround sound.

"No, I'm not crying." I deny wiping my cheeks, surprised at finding them wet. "Oh. I am, but I'm okay. I'm more than okay," I say, my heart brimming over. "Our family," I murmur under my breath, tenderly rubbing my hand over my bump, sharing the warmth that comes with "feeling" the words with our little twins. "Thank you," I mouth, and the guys and I share a look of understanding.

"O'Shea, du Maurier," is called out in a monotone by the bored court clerk.

"Let's do this," I say, heart tripping. Liam takes my hand and winks at me reassuringly. I squeeze his hand back and square my shoulders. I am ready for this. More than that. I want it.

We step into the musty, high-ceilinged courtroom, my eyes sweeping the place. At the end of the long aisle, the Superior Court Greffière officiates behind an imposing desk sitting high up on a podium. The austere-looking lady wears a black robe pleated in the front with wide sleeves and a white frilly jabot. The only piece of costume missing is a white curled wig to complete the impression of stepping into another century.

Liam lets go of my hand, and pulls his wool sweater over his head. They all take their sweaters off, and the Judge's eyes widen.

My hands come over my heart. They all wear navy blue, long-sleeved tees with hilarious inscriptions, and I'm hard pressed not to laugh out loud. I shake my head at them, torn between crying and laughing.

'I make twins, what's your superpower?' I read on Liam's informal shirt.

"Thank you for this," I breathe. I grab hold of his hand in both of mine and walk a few steps backward, mouthing *"love you."* I turn on my heels, tugging him along as my feet dance the rest of the way down the aisle.

I crane my neck, take a deep inhale, and say to the Greffière, "Ready when you are."

She soon reads from a long list of "Neither Spouse May," droning warnings...

—Neither spouse may dispose of a family residence whether a main or secondary residence without the consent of the other spouse. The same applies to the furnishings and decorative elements in the residence that are for the general use of the family. A spouse who disregards this obligation could be sued for damages. This restriction, however, has no effect on the right of ownership. Neither spouse may—

"Isn't it normal *not* to do that? Why are they telling us all this?" I ask Liam, cupping my hand to his ear as the Greffière keeps on reading out loud.

"Beats me. Just waiting for I do," he side mouths.

—By law, both spouses will keep their birth names after marriage and will continue to exercise their civil rights under that name.

"By saying I do, you hereby solemnly consent to the aforementioned and will enter into the state of matrimony," the Greffière says, and waits.

Liam looks at me expectantly. "Oh—I still do." I answer the Greffière, bemused by the question, let alone the whole procedure.

"I do," Liam states clearly, and the Greffière check marks it on the document in front of her.

The guys cheer and a slow smile forms on Liam's lips as he dips me low, going for a playful kiss, swinging me back up.

And then we sign a gazillion copies of what's labeled a Declaration of Marriage stating that a civil marriage between Liam and I was solemnized on this day.

"Only one witness each," the Greffière scolds.

"There's one exception to every rule, and they are mine. They all sign as witnesses," I say, resolutely passing the pen to Zac, whose shirt reads, '**He shoots! He scores!**' and we bump knuckles.

"Please wait? Really?" I tease as P.O. kisses both my cheeks. His shirt reads, '**Coolest Uncle of Twins. Downloading now. Please wait.**' "Didn't you upgrade us to high speed?"

"Yeah, but your site is under construction," he deadpans, but his eyes glint with merriment, and I shake my head at him.

"Hey, ByteMan, did you make sure you're virus free before kissing them?" Yann asks, and P.O. gives me an eye roll.

"I knew we could count on you," I say, teasing Yann.

"Anytime," he tells me, as I kiss both his cheeks. "You can count on me." He brings my pointer finger up the formula on his shirt. '**Applied Math: xx + xy = xy^2.**'

"MathMan, you're such a geek," Leo says, before gamely shoving him aside.

"Takes one to know one, WeedMan," Yann snaps back, unperturbed.

The guys started slinging old BIA nicknames at one another a lot lately, ZeeMan, MathMan, WeedMan, among others. Single beds and shared bedrooms apparently have that effect on them. Or so they say.

"So? Visions, babies, they don't scare you anymore?" I ask Leo.

"Nope," he says, stretching the writing on his torso. '**You don't scare me, my nephews are twins.**' "Read and weep."

"I'm so happy. I didn't know how to tell you about the triplets I saw— or was it quintuplets, not sure," I say straight faced. I did see triplets. At the grocery store. Once.

"Seriously?" he asks. I uplift my shoulders but I can't hide my grin.

"Aww, man," he groans, tossing his head back. "You're dangerous."

"Now that the formalities are over with, let's go home." Liam swoops down on me, kissing the back of my hand. "Mrs. O'Shea," he says, cocking his head, eyes shining, and I didn't know it would give me such a thrill to hear, but it does.

"It's against the rules. I'm not allowed to change my name in Québec," I remind him, pointing to the Greffière. "She said so."

"Even better. You're *my* Mrs. O'Shea, not theirs," he says, giving me his heart-melting crooked smile, and I hug him tight, not letting go.

"You did it, KnightMan." Theo slaps him on the back. Liam signals him with his eyes, and Theo nods, texting something.

"So what have you done?" I ask Liam, reading Theo's shirt. **'The twins are presumed innocent. He.Did.It.'**

"I did this." Liam's warm hands cover my baby bump, and he beams up at me. "Ready for more of the same, Mrs. O'Shea?" he murmurs, sweeping me up into his arms.

"Mr. and Mrs. O'Shea, right this way." Theo bows, opening one of the huge doors, and we step out of the courtroom.

The bored clerk's mouth twists up a fraction as we exit the premises.

"What's going on?" I ask as Zac parks the car at the beginning of our mapped road to the meadow. It's past dusk and already quite dark.

"Trust me?" Liam asks, getting out, holding up his hand.

"With my life, and beyond." I take his hand, and he pulls me out of the car.

"I'm walking us home, just us two," he says, clipping on his snowshoes as P.O. gears him up with a powerful LED headlight. "Hop on."

Liam bends down, giving me a piggy back ride. I search the clear night sky. Polaris twinkles down on me. I smile up to it, happy.

As we enter the meadow from the woodland path, my eyes instantly glaze over from an overflow of emotions.

"Liam ... it's..." I blink back tears, and slowly lower down. He gathers me back to his chest, his chin resting on top of my head as I take it all in.

Hundreds of tea light candles set inside outdoor lanterns in the trees light up the clearing, casting a magical glow on the intimate scene. Logs crackle in a bivouac, welcoming us. A long bench, swaddled in fleece blankets and cushions, invites us to sit back and enjoy. And underneath the maple trees ... a winter yurt awaits aglow, its translucent dome shimmering into the night, its wood stove chimney puffing white clouds of smoke up in the air. This is a wondrous sight indeed.

"You've made me an igloo..." I say teary-eyed, turning into his arms, overwhelmed.

He sweeps me up. "Let's call it something else—anything else. I don't know why, but that word leaves me cold," he says drily.

"A magical kingdom, worthy of long-ago fairies and knights." I brush my lips to the corner of his mouth.

"Now we're talking," he says as he swathes me in blankets at the bivouac, crouching down in front of me.

"I choose you, a thousand times over, Éolie-Jolie." He pulls my gloves off one finger at a time. "Your loving presence in my life magnifies me to a sum greater than all my parts, day in, day out," he says, eyes aglow, sliding the most unique, most gorgeous band onto my unresisting finger. I stop breathing.

"Éolie? Will you wear my perfectly imperfect heart as a symbol of my freedom of choice, you? A symbol of the troth I pledge tonight as I vow to keep you in my heart, come what may, no matter what. As I vow to promote your well-being at all times, and at all costs. As I vow to cherish our time together, never taking any of it for granted, in communion of spirits. You in?"

I leap into his arms. I let my silent answer ardently pour out in loving waves, as I seal it with a kiss, falling into it. Our lips melt into one kiss, after another.

I lovingly cradle his face, and murmur deep into his eyes, "I choose to be yours, Liam. I choose you," I pledge. "Je t'aime, it's magic." I punctuate the powerful words with a kiss, repeating it over and over again...

The both of us cuddle up deep within the comfort of each other, love overflowing, until the last of the lanterns' light flickers out. The only sounds to be heard in our meadow are the cheery crackle of the fire, and the gentle song of the wind passing through, here and there.

My eyelids drift shut and I fight, losing the battle.

I feel Liam shift on the bench.

"I don't want today to ever end," I say sleepily as Liam picks me up and tucks me in a feather-soft bed in an enchanted tent palace, cozy warm, underneath a night sky white with stars, upon stars, upon stars.

"Shhhh, sleep now." He kisses my forehead. "Today never ends, Éolie-Jolie, it begins anew tomorrow," he says quietly into the night, and I let myself fall under, deep into slumber.

Sixty-Five

LIAM

I stir, blinking my eyes open. The morning sun shines down on me through the yurt's translucent dome. Recalling last night and Éolie's pure joy, my chest expands.

"Mon premier Bonheur du jour," Éolie says, kissing me good morning. Her radiant face appears above me and I take both her hands, extending her arms high above her head, rolling her underneath me. Best way to wake up, ever, is next to her.

"I've never seen anything as exquisite and as meaningful as the band you dreamed up for me. I'll cherish it," she says, looking dreamily at her finger, "a few hundred times a day. Forever and a day."

My thumb strokes her ring finger. "It truly is a gorgeous piece of eternity Anaïs concocted for you to wear," I say, adding, "Mrs. O'Shea."

I delight in her glowing reaction every time I say it.

"I love the way it sounds coming from your heart. It floods me with magic," she sighs lovingly, staring at my lips, tracing them with a finger.

"Want to play desert island?" I ask, leaning close, inhaling her.

"Aren't you worried we'll turn into popsicles?" she teases.

"I'm talking serious desert island play, here," I say, getting up to put some more wood pellets in the small woodstove, set in the middle of the circular structure, and she buries deeper under the comforter, sighing. I slip back into bed, propping my head on my hand as I take a good look around in the light of the day.

The guys really hit it off with both Vie and Grégoire the other night, and we all had a blast prepping everything in the meadow. Fortunately though, with Vie's input and flair giving life to my vision, we didn't have to build an actual igloo, even though I was ready to do it. So really, it's the winter yurt's plush accommodations provided by Aventures Hors des Sentiers Battus, a Mont-Tremblant wilderness outfitter, that blew me away, surpassing all of my expectations.

The portable structure is spacious, and set on stilts. The hard-surface floor is covered in a thick Berber carpet. The inflatable mattress, high up on an insulated platform, is covered in warm fleece linens and duvets, and cushions, big and small, abound all over the place. On the other side of the wood stove, breakfast awaits, already laid out on a traditional Provençal, red garden set, comprised of a round bistro table and chairs, made from wooden slats and metal legs. And an ingenuous bathroom system with a cistern filled with melted snow, stands behind a screen for simple ablutions. Robinson Crusoe never had it so good.

"The winter yurt is ours all weekend long. The catering service that comes with it will drop by once a day." I kiss her chin, before propping my head back up on my hand. "What do you say?"

"Honey, I'm home," she gamely says, and then she sniffs. "You really cooked up room service in the wilds?"

"My very own recipe, it's a specialty," I say, tweaking her nose.

"How did you manage all of this? I never suspected anything." Wonder blossoms anew in her eyes.

"Magic," I say with a secret smile.

"You have powerful magic at your disposal," she says, awed. "What's your secret?"

"I'll never tell," I tease playfully. "I'd rather show you." And she buries her face onto my chest, inhaling me.

"Thank you for this," she breathes, eyes intent, gently stroking my face. "You're rewriting my Oops story. I'll no longer doubt, promise," she says, growing solemn.

"Do you hear that, boys?" I ask Sébastien and Nicolas, my palms spreading over our baby bump. "She promised." I kiss them, looking at her. "I have two witnesses. It's too late now, you can't backtrack."

I produce the necklace from underneath the bed, spreading it over her heart and she scrambles to sit up.

Staring at it, her eyes immediately water. "I'm turning into a walking flash flood," she lets out. "Liam, it's too much—"

"No, it's not. It's so you'll remember, and never forget," I say, wiping her tears with my thumbs, and she leans her cheek onto my hand.

"It's the promise in us," I continue, staring at the striking purplish hue of the half-polished, half-raw pebbles. "There's me," I point to largest one knotted down on the left side. "There's you." I stroke the smaller one right next to it, knotted down on the other side. "And there's Sébastien, Nicolas, Rose, Sophie, Mathieu," I touch each little pebbles knotted down separately, decreasing in size, stopping on the little knots left empty on the thin leather string. "And all the babies in the world left to happen, so no worries," I explain as I secure the necklace behind her neck.

"I'm not about to forget, I'll always remember ... Je me souviendrai, promise," she says half-crying, half-laughing, and her fingers gently stroke the ravishing pebbles, their color dazzling against the rosy skin at the base of her neck. "It's us."

"Better believe it." I take her hand, closing her fingers around Anaïs's little wrapped package, and she inhales sharply.

"It's really—"

"Not mine to give," I say, holding up my hands. "I promised Anaïs I'd give it to you the morning after; she said you'd know."

"Anaïs gave you a gift for me?" A pucker forms at her brow. She shakes the little box in her hands, trying to guess.

"She said it's freely given, nothing formal, just a little piece you inspired her with," I say, and I watch her face clear, and her eyes light up the place.

She tears out the wrapping, her eyes suddenly transfixed. "Anaïs," she breathes out.

"Can I see?" I ask, and she locks eyes with me, wondrous sea-green eyes pinning me down, looking straight at me.

"It's so you'll remember, and never forget the story of us, choosing beauty, seeing beauty, creating beauty, being beauty, in a never-ending circle of love," she says to me lovingly, surprising me to no end with a band unlike any other I have ever seen.

She takes hold of my left hand, quietly waiting, silently asking. On my nod of approval, my heartbeats erratically beating all over the place, she slips the unusual band onto my heart finger, kissing it.

"I love you, mind, body and soul, love you. I belong with you, to you. Forever and a day," she vows earnestly, leaning in until I lay sprawled on the bed. She moves in just a couple more inches, her lips trailing down my jaw, my neck, my chest...

"Jet'aimejet'aimejet'aime," her voice incants in my mind over, and over again, spreading to the very depth of my soul as she lets her body speak, revealing the story behind the stone, one layer at a time, one caress at a time, seriously overwhelming me.

She devastates me.

Boneless and satiated, I roll her underneath me, my hands holding on to hers. "I was wrong, you know, when I said marriage couldn't make me look at you differently," I say. "It does." Her warm eyes search mine trustingly. I smile softly.

"You're suddenly twice as precious, twice as beautiful, twice as loved, Mrs. O'Shea," I say. And her fingers curl on my hands.

Sixty-Six

LIAM

Mid-afternoon, two days hence, finds the outfitter's crew busy folding in the yurt's outer shell when we leave the meadow for our short trek back. Both delighted by our twin news, Vie and Grégoire remained behind, insisting on supervising the last of the cleanup upon noticing Éolie's frequent bouts of drowsiness. A bit hard not to notice as I kept cutting worried glances her way as she curled up a few times to take quick naps on the bivouac bench, dead to the world. Vie affectionately reassured me it was normal in her condition, swaddling her in two more blankets, and I instantly breathed easier.

Vie and Grégoire are expected to drop by Leo's house with the bivouac cushions and blankets on their way back, and I didn't even need to call in the cavalry either, a.k.a. the guys, this go round, Éolie wanting to keep for now the lanterns up in the trees. So, for once, everything went according to plan, I can't help but mentally fist pump.

A few minutes later, we step on the porch of the old farmstead, still riding on the high of our yurt weekend.

"After you, Mrs. O'Shea." I sweep my arm in a grand gesture.

"Just so you know, it never gets old," she says, coming up on her tippy toes to kiss the corner of my jaw. "I love the way you say it."

"We aim to please." I trail a kiss down her jaw. "Mrs. O'Shea," I murmur the endearment, before swooping down on her lips for another aching kiss.

"Cancel search and rescue, Zac, I found them," Leo says. "They're making out on the front porch."

"They're at it again? Man," Zac says. "We're missing out on something there, I tell you."

"They're nuts!" Yann shouts from inside the house. "It's freaking cold out."

"Tell them to come in, or stay out, but close the goddamn door, Leo," P.O. yells out from the living room. "My keyboard's freezing up, and Lucie's allergic to cold fingers."

We fight not to laugh into our kiss, and lose it. Our teeth end up awkwardly scraping together, ending the moment. It's almost dark out now, so I guess it took us a little while longer than expected to make it back inside.

Leo closes the front door behind us, and we shake the snow off our boots, our cheeks flushed from the cold.

"Mission accomplished, I'd say." Leo leans on the door. "Frozen bliss is written all over them."

"Looks like we pulled it off, boys." Zac lifts his hand and high fives Leo.

"You really want me to answer that?" I ask, winking at Éolie.

"I'll never, ever, forget it, for as long as I live," Éolie says warmly, looking at each one in turn. "The meadow, the yurt..." she sighs blissfully, closing her eyes. "Pure magic."

And the guys and I share a pleased look.

She pulls her wool beanie off, hanging the rest of her outer gear on a peg, and I follow suit.

"Anyone for hot chocolate?" Éolie asks, giving me a peck on the cheek in passing, sauntering her way to the kitchen.

"I would have loved some," Zac gripes, following behind her. "But *someone* found your stash of Swiss chocolate, and we're fresh out."

"News flash, it wasn't stashed, dude. It was hiding in plain sight, and it begged me to eat it," Yann says with a quick glance over his laptop, from beside P.O. on the couch. "For your info, P.O. and I haven't been this near Swiss chocolate for over a year, man."

"Get over it, Zac. Lucie did," P.O. says, stretching and rolling his head from side to side, cracking his neck, which leaves Lucie precariously balanced on his lap. "She totally understands my love affair with Swiss chocolate and my dark addiction to it. But *unlike you*, she forgives me and my weaknesses."

"Unlike me," Zac states, staring them down, and Leo low fives him in passing, handing over a glass to Éolie.

She pours a glassful of milk, wrinkling her nose.

"You ate them all? Even the Cailler's," I say, double checking behind the peanut butter jar. "Man, on Friday we had like, ten of those."

"We didn't know it was the last of them," Yann mumbles.

"Want me to call Theo, and ask him to find some on his way back?" P.O. asks Éolie sheepishly.

"If Theo's out, don't bother him just for dark chocolate," she says on a huge, infectious yawn that, funnily enough, makes the round a few times. "I only have about five minutes left on my battery before I crash, anyway. Don't gang up on Yann and P.O.," she warns the three of us. "I'll drink the cow juice."

She squares her shoulders, pinching her nose just before chugging down the glass of low-fat milk. She swallows the last of it on a shudder, and we all cringe, more or less. "There. Done."

It's pretty safe to say that milk straight out of the carton is no one's favorite around here, largely due to the fact we were obliged to drink a glass of it at every goddamn meal in primary school, and we all feel for her. Dark, unsweetened Swiss chocolate, on the other hand ... Let's just say it has been out of stock at the village market for the past couple of weeks, and who knows when they'll restock. Probably not before the guys all leave in two days, though, their ski vacation almost over.

"So, Theo's out? Where to?" I ask, leaning back on the kitchen table, my fingers absently brushing over it.

"He commandeered the Volvo more than an hour ago for a recon mission down in the village," Leo says, peeling an orange, offering half to Éolie.

"A recon? In the village?" I ask. "For what?"

"God knows. He's probably off checking over some boring legal shit," Zac ponders, leaning a shoulder on the kitchen's archway. "You know how he is. He'll spill the beans when he wants to, not before."

"Oh no. It's because of me..." Éolie whips her head up.

I make an incredulous noise. "Theo's just being Theo," I say, pulling her to me, and she pops into my mouth her last piece of orange.

"No, it's because of me, really," she says a bit flushed, her hands looping behind my neck. "I gave him a note on Friday, asking if someone could drop by the Old Presbytery and seek out Anaïs without your knowing."

I watch the four others snap to attention in a chain reaction at the mention of Anaïs. Interesting.

"Oh?" I say, leaning back from her embrace.

She gives me a peck on the corner of my jaw before unlatching her hands to take hold of my left one. "I didn't know Anaïs had already given it to you," Éolie says, dropping her gaze. Her thumb lightly strokes the smooth edges of my band and I look down, shocked anew by the beauty of its seven swirls of color. We all belong together, I silently vow, touched once more by the rightness of it.

I kiss her forehead, folding my hands at the small of her back. And I make a mental note of enquiring about driving schools in the area at the first opportunity. If she can't walk down to the village by herself in the winter time, she should, at least, be able to drive down to it when she wants.

"I've been floating elsewhere all weekend and I totally forgot to tell him that it was no longer necessary," an apologetic Éolie says.

"You were supposed to be floating elsewhere," I reply, my voice dropping to a low rumble. But for an answer she yawns and sways a bit on her feet. Her forehead thumps on my chest and my attempts at seduction fall short. "C'mon, I'll tuck the three of you in." I kiss the top of her head.

"If I'm not up by the time Theo comes back, please tell him I'm sorry for the wild-goose chase," she murmurs, settling in bed.

"Will do."

But something tells me that he'll probably beg to differ. Not sorry. Not one bit.

"That explains that." Leo drops on me the minute I close our bedroom door, leaving Éolie sound asleep, napping.

"Explains what?" I ask.

"Éolie's note. Theo's been walking in a daze ever since he came back from the village yesterday," Leo says, pulling a chair from the kitchen table and straddling it. "Who'd have thought, man. Theo? On a girl recon? He never bothers. This Anaïs must be something else."

"You think Theo's got it bad?" P.O. scoffs. "I'll bet it's nowhere near as bad as our Italian lover boy, here."

Zac's Italian good looks are on a par with his reputation for being able to seduce any girl, any time, on a scale ten times over what mine used to be on any given day.

"Zac's got it bad?" I ask P.O., eyebrows shooting up.

"He still doesn't know what hit him," P.O. says, somewhat smug.

"Screw. You," Zac snarls at P.O., shoving two more logs into the hearth, squatting down to watch the flames flare up, and sparks fly up the flue.

"For whom?" I ask Zac. How long was I gone, two days?

"No one." Zac clamps his mouth shut, a dark scowl etching on his face.

"Zac, anyone ever tell you you're a shit liar?" Leo says.

"Piss off." His voice is low, warning. "I'll go check on Vie and Grégoire, and help fold up camp like we were supposed to in the first place," Zac mutters, frustration bleeding into his tone, shoving past me.

What the—?

"Okay, what did I miss?" I ask, crossing my arms.

"A first ever. He's been chewed up and spit out by a girl," P.O. says. "A brand-new species. Impervious to Zac's legendary charm."

"And it's not for a lack of trying on his part," Yann says.

"Sod off." The front door slams shut as Zac storms out.

"What's with him?" I ask, baffled. Zac's usually as cool as a cucumber.

"Zac's been in a snit ever since Mont-Saint-Sauveur," Yann says.

"Zac? In a snit? Over a girl?" I ask, making sure we're talking about the same guy here.

"Yep. A super-hot ski patrol chick that not only gave him an epic tongue-lashing but, get this, also gave him his walking papers," Leo says, propping his laptop on the kitchen table or my study desk, depending on which viewpoint.

"And to add insult to injury, she even out-skied ZeeMan," Yann adds.

"Really went downhill," P.O. deadpans behind his laptop screen.

"Really?" I ask, blinking.

"Really. No downhill skiing allowed." Leo struggles to keep a straight face and P.O's lips twitch up.

"Unlike Zermatt, it's against the rules up here, apparently." Yann shrugs, putting his feet up on a piece of tree log Grégoire brought over. A gift from the Forest of Laure we're using as a coffee table. "He took it a tad personal. He'll get over it. Eventually."

"Eventually?" P.O. snorts. "Zac's black listed for all eternity at Mont-Saint-Sauveur now, or so the chick said."

"For all eternity? Is that all?" I say, lips twitching. "It so happens I know a way to make time fly by, in no time."

"Funny you should mention that," Yann says, stretching his arms behind his head. "We were just talking about that very subject last night, sharing notes on you."

"And you're telling me this...?" I ask drily.

"Earth-shattering moment you missed there, man. Another first ever, you've made consensus," Yann says. "We defined that when you fall in love, bang, life happens at warped speed."

"Tell me something I don't know by now," I say, on my way to a hot date with a cup of instant coffee.

"You step into normal, and suddenly nothing goes as planned," P.O. says.

"Scary crazy shit," Leo concurs.

"And two of the strangest things happen. You wake up, and you're alive," I reply, waiting on the water to boil in the pan. "It's all in the way you look at things."

"Yeah, well, don't look at us, we're nowhere near normal," P.O. says.

"No shit," I say, and the four of us end up snickering. The usual.

"Sweet," I say, checking out the Honey Do List posted on the brand-new fridge we got last month, right after the snowballs incident. "I've been gone two full days, and there's no new disaster filed, a record," I say to Leo.

"My house's organic. She's allergic to you, and your black thumb," he wisecracks.

Outside, tires screech to a halt. A moment later, the door bangs against the wall and Theo storms in.

"It's fucking closed on Mondays and Tuesdays," Theo scowls, tossing the car keys on the kitchen counter.

"The Village?" I ask, but my sarcasm is lost as he breezes by.

"We know about Éolie's note and fascinating Anaïs. Busted, man." Yann smirks at Theo, then shrugs. "So what if it's closed? All it means is that you'll have to go back another time—"

"That's just it. I can't, you arse," Theo snaps.

"Whatever," P.O. mutters. "Two days, man. What's the big deal?"

"We fucking leave on Wednesday morning," he says, all Theo like, disappearing upstairs. We hear bits of jazz music, and the slam of a door.

Man, something's brewing in here besides water, I absently note, wrestling with the cutlery drawer. *Jesus.*

"Cool," Leo says. "I've just received confirmation. My thesis is up for presentation mid-May, so expect me back here from Cambridge early this summer," he adds, typing away. "Think my house will survive you until then?"

"The better question is, will I?" I mumble, looking down at the cupboard drawer pull knob I'm left holding in my hand, with the better part of a rotten plank still attached to it.

"Heads up. You better start applying now for residency, because this house becomes officially yours this summer," I say, dropping the knob in all its glory onto his lap on my way to check on Éolie.

"Christ, Liam," he cries out. "At this rate there'll be nothing left for me to buy."

"It's all in the—"

"Can I borrow your laptop?" Éolie comes barreling into me.

Sixty-Seven

ÉOLIE

"What's going on?" Liam asks as he joins me on the bed, pulling his laptop out.

"I ... I'm not sure yet. I need to do some more research on something first." I wince, slumping back on the pillows, rubbing my belly in warm soothing strokes.

"Something's wrong?" Liam asks instantly concerned.

No, yes, maybe, I don't know ... I refrain from saying, aiming for a somewhat more rational speech.

"I've always seen the children there, already born, not before they were there," I start to explain, scooting back against the pillows, sitting more comfortably.

"Oookay...?" Liam's face scrunches up, a deep V forming between his brows.

"I never questioned how they came to be," I try again. "They just ... are."

"You seemed pretty au fait on the birds and the bees this morning but hey, if you need a refresher course," he says, face clearing, "I'm all for it."

"I'm botching it," I mumble, and he stares at me with a question in his eyes. "I've never thought about my labor and delivery in vivid details. I vaguely thought they'd just come, you know, normally, at home—" His gaze collides with mine, his face turning a pasty color.

"You mean, like here at the house? No way," he says, alarmed.

"I heal quicker than normal, remember," I say. My breaths growing shallow; I'm ready to hyperventilate, once more, like when I startled awake from my nap earlier on. Not happening, Éolie, calm down, I sternly enjoin.

"You mean I'll have to ... to..." he stutters, a mixture of wonder, fear, and astonishment flaring up in his eyes. Mostly fear. I apply a finger on his lips.

"I'll have plenty of time to coach you. It's not that either."

Some of the color returns. He blows out a breath. "Then what?" he asks.

"It's ... the twins ... When I focus and go within, I see them both clearly, and they're—" I flinch to a stop. I have no idea what emotions are swimming in my eyes, but his? Instantly fills with worry.

"Go on," he whispers, voice rough around the edges.

"Our twins are monozygotic, which means they're identical and—" I take a few deep breaths to calm my racing heart. "They're also monoamniotic, monochorionic, which means they're developing in a single, shared amniotic sac with a single chorion. You can't get more identical than that," I say, my shaky fingers typing into the search engine, MoMo twins. "We're over the risky stage of development where their cells needed to completely separate into two distinct individuals, but I just need to check something else to make sure I've got it right..."

My gut tightens with worry as I quickly scroll down the first few articles.

"I have no idea what you just said. Mono ... whatever. But why would it matter? I saw them play. You saw them as well, many times over. It doesn't mean they're all right?" He frowns, sitting up on the edge of the bed.

"I've never lived it!" I cry out. Forcing myself to calm down, I say in a more even tone, "I think so, but I can't be sure."

Liam hardly breathes now. Forearms resting on his thighs, he looks down at the floor, waiting. The more I read, the more frantic I grow. "What if we're supposed to do something, and we don't, and they disappear from the visions if something happens before they can get here?" I swallow, throat tight.

For a split second panic flickers over Liam's face, probably reflecting mine, before he shoves his hands in his hair, and I watch the panicky look vanish only to be replaced by a shuttered expression.

I read out loud, heart in my throat, "Only about one percent of twins are MoMo, a situation that causes additional risk to the babies due to cord entanglement or compression," I say in a choked voice, lips trembling.

His jaw ticks. "Meaning?" he asks, his voice gruffer than usual, and I know he's holding his emotions tightly in check.

"Meaning, according to this site, they need to stay as calm as possible in there, complete bed rest from twenty-two weeks, daily monitoring, elective delivery from thirty-two weeks, or as soon as viable in the event of an earlier emergency," I read on, hyperventilating. "And a more than probable c-section."

"Holy hell."

He grabs my shoulders, locking eyes. "We can't do this here. Jesus, Éolie, you can't ask me to slice you up..." His voice cracks, and he goes as white as a chalk, his forehead dotting with beads of sweat.

"I won't ask it of you. If it comes to that, I don't know ... We'll go directly to the Sainte-Agathe Hospital," I staunchly say, more to reassure him. Yeah, and deal with the repercussions of my preternatural healing that are sure to make waves, I inwardly cringe. Not helping, Éolie. No need to go there for now, focus.

I drop my forehead to his, and slow my heartbeats. I center myself. My breaths grow even. I calm. He calms. Somewhat.

"Bloody hell." Liam rubs his hands a few times over his nose and mouth. "Give me a minute, I can't keep up right now," he says, staring up at the LED constellation with reddened eyes.

I squeeze his hand in support, and he squeezes back.

My hands fold protectively over my lower abdomen, and my gaze strays to l'armoire bleue, shimmering under the low light.

In my mind, I see it all over again, like I did the first time I touched it at the Old Presbytery. I see myself opening its doors, turning to the stacks of freshly laundered baby clothes, neatly folded down on this very bed I'm sitting on right now. I bring them up to my nose, inhaling their clean, sweet baby scent, before putting them down in neat piles on the middle shelf. I tiptoe to the cribs in the corner, looking down on Nicolas and Sébastien, snug as little bugs in their sleep nests. My heart skips and cracks wide open. Little bottoms up, pudgy little arms with dimpled hands peeking out, bowed lips parted on cherubs' faces abandoned to sleep.

I tenderly smooth back their dark-haired curls, giving them one last look before diving for a quick afternoon nap into the rumpled, unmade bed. In the farmstead downstairs bedroom. Right. Here.

"Okay, possibly Sainte-Agathe, and meanwhile?" Liam asks, unnerved, hopping out of bed. Pacing the room, he sends the flurry of blue felt snowflakes dancing madly in his wake.

"We stay calm," I say, willing myself to do just that.

He stops pacing, his shoulders tense. "Like that's going to be easy," he mutters, pinching the bridge of his nose.

My eyes dart back to l'armoire bleue, intently focusing on our twins.

"I'll begin right away a self-imposed rest regimen and help them fight the odds, one day at a time," I say with conviction.

I can do this. I'm going to do whatever it takes. Because even more than our desire to belong somewhere? I want these babies *to be*. Happy and healthy. A family. *Ours*.

Sixty-Eight

LIAM

I stumble out of the bedroom.

I need space to breathe and compose myself back into a semblance of steadiness. Otherwise I'll just keep on freaking Éolie the hell out.

"You look like you've seen a ghost, man. What's wrong?" Leo gets up, and both Yann and P.O. put their computers aside the moment I walk into the room.

"I just need to go ... breathe," I say, putting my hands up, and they leave me be.

I grab my coat and step outside, walking on autopilot.

I end up sitting in the woodshed, my back propped on the useless mud room door. I stare at my band and count out loud the seven different shades of grey blue, over and over again, repeating their names like a prayer. Nicolas, Sébastien, Rose, Sophie, Mathieu.

I see once more Nicolas and Sébastien playing knights and dragons, Lords of the Laure, in the forest behind my study. And in my mind's eye, I can easily imagine them at three, gleefully running back home to me and baby Rose, across these very fields, Leo and Éolie trailing behind them.

What if something happens before they get here and they disappear from the visions, Éolie said.

Now that they're on their way, it never even occurred to me that we might lose them. My heart skips. And I swallow a lump the size of a watermelon, shaking.

From down the lane, I catch the glint of headlights, a dark-blue pickup truck, and a minute later, doors slamming shut. The sound of boots crunching on packed snow rings in my ears.

Vie, Grégoire, and Zac appear above me.

"He's going into shock," I hear Zac say, and it sounds distorted, like when we talked underwater playing water polo, back at BIA.

Someone puts a fleece blanket around me and I recognize the red plaid as one of the blankets from the bivouac. I look up, and Vie tucks me into another one, briskly rubbing my arms, and my shaking eventually stops.

"Drink this, it'll make you'll feel better," she says, giving me hot tea from a thermos Grégoire passes along. I take a few sips, and I feel some of the numbness in my limbs fading.

I blink, wondering how long I've been sitting here.

"What happened, man?" Zac asks, his voice thick with concern, crouching in front of me.

"It's the twins ... Éolie just got the news ... They're MoMo, Zac," I say, watching him attentively for any telltale signs, and I see an immediate reaction, he blanches. And I choke.

"Shit," he whispers, eyes briefly closing, but when he reopens them, they're full of determination. "Are they distinctly separate?" he asks anxiously.

"Éolie saw them both clearly," I say, and some of Zac's tension swooshes out.

"We can fight the odds, Liam."

"I don't know what MoMo means, but are they at risk, right now?" Vie asks softly, gathering the blankets more tightly around me.

"No. Not now, later on." I shake my head.

"Éolie will go into bed rest to help the twins along," Zac tells me, and I nod, intently listening to his every word. "They're developing in only one amniotic sac with only one chorion, so they've grown past the biggest concern for now. They're separate, meaning no organs or limbs are conjoined. We'll be watching for cord entanglement and compression from now on," Zac says, and Vie covers her mouth with one hand, her eyes filling up. And I close mine for a second there, overcome. "But today their chances are better than average. With daily monitoring, there is a lot that can be done to increase the odds in their favor," Zac confirms. "And you can help by helping Éolie focus," he says to me, pinning me with a direct look.

"I'm worried sick," I admit, my eyes prickling, growing moist.

"Liam, listen up. Real or imagined, worries have the uncanny ability to taint away every minutes of your day. Case in point, it's already taking a huge toll on you," Grégoire says, crouching down in front of me. "Well, here's my two cents. You have a worry? Ask yourself if there's something immediate, anything really, that can be done to either eradicate it, or alleviate it, and go do it. If the answer is no, you're worrying needlessly. Define your when, Liam. When to think about it, when to act on it. And meanwhile? Forget about it."

"The *when* word," I echo, thinking of Éolie's imagined fears that I'd look upon her as some form of obligation after marriage that got shelved with it ... until it was time to act on it. I absorb the thought, my heart still integrating, catching up to what my mind is already quite relieved to grasp. I may survive after all.

"Believe in yourself. Believe in your strength, Liam. I guarantee you'll be able to overcome whatever's thrown at you," Grégoire says, searching my eyes. "You already did, just so you know. You made it here." His face softens, and, seemingly satisfied with what he sees on mine, Grégoire straightens.

"So, any immediate worries left to address tonight?" Grégoire asks.

"No, not tonight," I say, breathing in the crisp night air, and he squeezes my shoulder once, encouragingly.

"It'll be all right, Liam. I feel it in my heart," Vie says warmly, hugging me goodbye. "My thoughts will be with you."

She hugs Zac next, murmuring a few words, and Zac's face suddenly lights up, and he mouths "Thanks."

"Beautiful night tonight, boys, seize it." Grégoire says in a parting shot.

"They're pretty cool. I like them," Zac says, eyes fixed on the disappearing lights of the pickup truck.

"So do I."

I get up, bunching the blankets together, ready to go back inside, filled with strength and determination. I will be there for Éolie and our little twins. I'll do whatever it takes.

"I like it here," Zac says quietly, shoving his hands in his coat pockets, one booted foot shuffling snow around. His tone and words stop me in my tracks.

"So do I." I lean one shoulder on the mud room's door, waiting, knowing he's not finished. He stares up at the starry night, and I follow suit. The dark velvet sky is white with stars upon stars, just like last night and the night before last, up in our meadow. Home.

"So I've been thinking..." Zac trails off into silence, looking down.

"About..."

Zac's gaze darts up, glancing out toward the abandoned barn and fields as if contemplating how to begin.

"Life ... Roots to put down ... This long-ago Normal Kingdom we used to dream about..."

"Best place there is to live," I say with conviction.

"I'm ready for a change of pace I think, something a little more ... normal. I just don't know how exactly," he admits, rubbing the back of his neck, my self-assured friend seemingly at a loss.

"Does this have anything to do with that girl?" I ask with a sudden flash of insight.

"In a way. She said something that really got to me, man," he sighs heavily, a frown etching onto his face. "And I don't want to be that guy. I'm not that guy," Zac says to himself, his voice gruffer than usual. His eyes narrow and he nods once, determination stamped all over his face. "I have to go back to South America for a few weeks to tie loose ends and then," he takes a deep breath, "I jump, both feet, man."

And I just know that whatever that girl said to him had a profound effect on my pal, one that has nothing to do with being turned down for a quick lay.

"House mates?" I pull my hand down.

"House mates." He gives me a low five. "We'll make sure the twins make it out just fine."

Sixty-Nine

LIAM

For the next few months, my worry takes a backseat to the work. Grégoire takes me under his wing and we both end up with work gloves and helmets on almost daily, clearing road space to the meadow.

And, to my surprise, the intense manual labor, and seeing with my own eyes the dips and curves of our meandering road emerging daily from under my sweat, is the best therapy I've ever had. The close proximity to nature as well as building something for my family help me calm the hell down.

But how can time fly away and crawl by at the same time? Hands down, pregnancy does that to me.

I step into the bedroom, comforted by the sight of Éolie, eyes closed, propped by a sea of pillows, palms resting on her knees in the lotus position, headphones on our babies' bump, the three of them listening to Baby Mozart music. "Do they like it?" I murmur quietly.

She slowly opens her eyes, face aglow. "They love it," she whispers. "Yann truly discovered a gem there."

Éolie is pure beauty in pregnancy, and I once more revel in it.

I kiss her forehead, and kneel down next to the bed at eye level with my little twins, sixteen weeks, three days in the making, and counting. She takes the headphones off, and I stroke her skin underneath her shirt.

She brushes her fingers through my hair, and my chest expands.

"So, working up in the woods today, your papa started thinking that you were just about ready for your first Enchanted Forest of Laure Quest in there," I tell them, my open palms stroking soothingly, my lips feathering little kisses on her round belly, and Éolie's fingers still in my hair.

"Something like your own, long-ago bedtime stories, you mean?" she asks, intrigued, and I mouth, "*You'll see.*"

"Can I join?"

"Nope. Boys' night in," I whisper to them, winking at her. "But you'll be needed regardless, so stay close by."

I reach into my lumberjack's coat pockets, and take out one of the old preserve jars we found by the dozens in one of Leo's rotten kitchen cupboards. Along a small aquamarine ceramic bowl, one of the pottery artisans made to order, and a sealed bag full of brook pebbles.

"Listen carefully now, my little fireflies. It's the mission of your life," I tell them, and I swear a fluttering sensation ripples underneath my palms. "Whoa. Did you feel that?" I ask, awed, and she nods, eyes shining.

I swallow. "This is seriously awesome." I look down at my hands spread on her taut skin. My heart flips over.

"I think they agree with you. They're ready to officially become Fireflies of the Laure," Éolie tenderly says as she covers my hands over our bump.

"Should I plug my ears?" she asks, and I shake out of my stupor.

"Absolutely not, they'll need you to watch over them. You're the Laure Magic after all," I say, my voice thick with love, looking straight at her, and her eyes return my sentiments, like tenfold so it seems. "Hear that, my little fireflies, maman is watching over you," I murmur to them.

"And Papa is counting the days until we'll both be watching over you," Éolie says, and I feel my lips twitch. That's putting it mildly.

"Sure am, so pay attention in there. The most recent discoveries confirm that the journey you're on takes on average only two hundred sixty-eight days to complete," I say, my lips trailing down her rounded abdomen. "Fireflies of the Laure, you're doing so well. You've successfully completed the first one hundred fifteen days of your quest, already," I tell them. "And for each one of these completed days, an extraordinary pebble materialized into this special jar I have here."

I put the half-filled jar on the bedside table, another log gifted by the Forest of Laure.

Éolie picks it up, her other hand coming up her chest, pressing down. "*Extraordinary Within*," she reads the label out loud.

"You betcha." I put my hand up, and she high fives it.

"Listen up now. Your mission is to stay quietly put in there, readying to come out normally, and at the exact right time." *So Papa doesn't freak too much*, I silently add. "It means you still have one hundred fifty-three days left to complete your journey into the Light, Fireflies," I say and Éolie squeezes my hand.

"Gain a new day, and you get to transform one of these ordinary pebbles into extraordinary." I upturn the bag holding one hundred fifty-three pebbles into the ceramic bowl. "And by the time you're ready to come out? You'll get to see how filled with extraordinary your journey was. Got that?" I kiss them, and a ripple tickles my lips.

"They get it," Éolie's says, her fingers lovingly stroking my forearms, and we share a tender look.

"So? We all set to wait in there?" I ask, and two more ripples feather down my hands, enchanting me all over again, before a quiet settles back in. And Éolie's eyelids start to droop.

"Nap time for the three of you," I order, folding back the covers.

"That's a fun way for the three *of you* to learn patience." She yawns, settling in for her nap.

"Hey, I know all about patience, but it doesn't mean I'm good at waiting," I reply, staring at the pebbles in the bowl. "They inspire me, Éolie-Jolie ... I've all sorts of bedtime stories coming to me, New Tales from the Enchanted Forest of Laure," I whisper, my lips trailing down her jaw.

"They will love your stories," Éolie whispers back, running her fingers through my hair. "In fact, they already do. They love hearing your voice, and so do I."

"Love you," I murmur to all three, tucking them in for nap time, kissing her forehead.

"Me three," Éolie says, nestling down under the comforter, and I shake my head at her dorkiness.

"I'll go shower." I rise and begin to shed clothes. "I probably reek of eau de lumberjack."

"Not going back to work on clearing the road with Grégoire?" she asks drowsily.

"Nope. Zac was called in Sainte-Agathe for a last-minute interview just now, seems an internship opened up in the field he wants, so I'm the one staying in," I say.

"Hope he gets what he wishes for," she mumbles, more than half asleep, "it'd be cool if he stayed..."

"Yeah, for all of us," I say, bending low to give her one last kiss on top of her head.

She's fast asleep.

I murmur to Sébastien and Nicolas, "Guess what? Obstetrics is Uncle Zac's new passion, and he decided to specialize."

Seventy
... and a Couple Hundred Extraordinary Pebbles Later

ÉOLIE

Coming in from the shower, Liam shuffles his hand and randomly picks an ordinary pebble, and drops it into the extraordinary jar, almost full. "Only thirty-seven cocooning days remain," he says, softly palming my belly's roundness in a good morning ritual.

I watch him dress, grinning when he pulls on a pair of Bar Harbor one-sided bleached-up jeans.

"It feels like living in the Caribbean in this crazy humid heat. Who'd have thought that, when just six weeks ago we had a spring blizzard, and snow on the ground," I say, amazed by the extreme temperatures of July.

"You still good in here without air-conditionning?" Liam asks, concerned, pulling a grey tee over his head.

"I wouldn't know what to do with it. Feel that gentle summer breeze coming in from the wide-open windows," I sigh with contentment. "It's cooling us off perfectly."

"Yann's been tinkering with the old fan to get it going; they're melting upstairs. If it gets any warmer, we'll need to do something," he says, tying his construction boots.

Except for Theo, legally lost somewhere in the meanders of corporate lawyering down in Boston, P.O. and Yann joined the rest of us for their summer break, with Zac and Leo staying up here permanently these days. And the old farm house is once more bursting at the seams.

"We'll just laze away our day while you run yourself ragged between your two construction sites," I say as I watch Liam strap on a stiff leather tool belt. The building contractor we hired for our small catchall barn at the end of the road lets him watch, and putter around, helping where he can. And Liam loves every minute of it.

"Not happening," he says, voice low and amused. "You're shit out of luck on the ragged part, there's only one site that's physically demanding. *For now.*"

"Want to consign in writing some of your twisted thoughts in the Log Book for future use?" I say pertly, grabbing the notebook. "The 'Coming Soon' under the tab, Red Hot Monkey Sex, is open to suggestions."

His stare is hot as it roams my skin. "Can't, they'd be a fire hazard on paper," he replies. "I'd rather show you anyway," he says, leaning in, his stare burning a trail to my lips. His eyes catch mine, burning brighter than I've ever seen.

"Can't wait." I fan myself with the notebook, before letting it drop beside me.

"Stealing my lines, Mrs. O'Shea?" he asks, straightening, the playful glint in his eyes bringing us back down from a boil to a simmer. We avoid make-out sessions now, as we usually kiss until we're both shaking with need, the pitfalls of literal shared pleasure, so we're getting skilled at keeping it down to a simmer.

"Told you counting pebbles would teach you patience," I say.

"Some things are worth the wait." His eyes lock on mine, and the soft look in his makes my heart turn over. "How many pebbles again?" he asks.

"We're almost there," I say, briefly going inward, seeing them. They're doing so well, not even one tangle in their umbilical cords, and I'm starting to wonder if Nicolas and Sébastien have the ability to telepath.

"We good?" he asks, immediately growing concerned.

"We're doing great," I tell him, gently stroking my belly with my hands, and he instantly lets out a breath, eyes crinkling. *Almost there, my little ones.*

"I'll go build something then, while you guys keep at it," he says.

Before Liam can slip out, Zac pops in, uncharacteristically wearing a rumpled white dress shirt and wrinkled kakis, his dark brown hair all mussed up but his face lit from within like never before. "Good morning. We wish you a pleasant day filled with good food, napping, music, reading, and stretching. This is Zac, your babysitter du jour, reminding you to play it safe. Get any bizarre requests, like getting out of bed to use the bathroom, please buzz me for assistance. On behalf of all our crew, thank you for choosing our company to keep you safe today," he says cheerily in his best commercial airline voice, backing away with a bow, making me laugh and Liam comment on his over the top mood.

"Hey, I had a pretty awesome day, yesterday," Zac says, his head popping back in. "I'm ready to take on the world!"

"Good to know," Liam chuckles under his breath, adding that it must have been quite the night too.

My eyes upturn, "whatever you do, don't tease him too much about it. He looks... ready to take on the world," I say, a feeling of contentment washing over me.

"Yeah, he does, and I wasn't kidding. It's good to know," he winks. "See you soon then." Liam kisses me goodbye.

I settle back into the comforts of the sea of pillows at my back, and admire the view from the wide-open windows. Everywhere I look, beauty blossoming, and within? A miracle greater than me. The Log Book lies open to the very first page I wrote upon embarking on our Laure journey, and I reflect back on it. The destination ... I pick my pen and add to it.

~~Destination:~~

Happily Ever After isn't a destination, it's an ongoing journey that never ends and only gets better.

I get ready for my first of three daily sessions of yoga asanas, exhaling, relaxed. I inhale and lift my arm above my head, palm facing inward, and turn my head to look past my left elbow. I exhale and bring down my left arm, repeating on the other side when a bladder takeover hits me, and the strong urge cannot be ignored.

I roll out of bed, careful not to put any undue pressure on either Sébastien or Nicolas. Now, if only I can make it to the bathroom in a timely manner...

I quietly shuffle out of the bedroom and waddle my way over, praying I can bypass the lectures I'll more than probably get from Leo and Zac. No such luck. I sigh. Guess I'm in it for sure now, they're both sitting at the kitchen table over coffee, standing between me and bathroom salvation.

"No shit," Leo's tone is incredulous.

"Not kidding, I'll tell you when I get there," Zac says, staring off into his cup, a loopy sort of grin floating on his lips.

"Hell, yes! Full speed ahead and damn the torpedoes, man," Leo replies, his face wearing an arrested look, but they both snap back to attention upon spotting me.

Zut.

"What are you doing up by yourself?" They both jump up, taking me by the elbows, helping me shuffle the rest of the way to the bathroom, lecturing me along the way.

The sound of the shower running increases the strength of my urge to pee, and I fidget. They pound their hands on the door. "P.O., out, Now!" they shout, and almost immediately, he barrels out, holding a towel at his waist, streaks of shampoo running down his neck.

"*Sorry,*" I mouth, cringing as he takes it in stride, sticking his head under the kitchen faucet. "Won't be long," I say over my shoulder, latching the door closed behind me.

"Almost there," I repeat the encouragement a minute later as I wash my hands, my pressing needs dealt with. Sébastien's foot presses into one side and Nicolas' elbow on the other, no doubt feeling their cramped quarters too.

I rub my sides feelingly, repeating the words a few times like a mantra. "We're almost there." One minute I'm standing in the bathroom, and the next, I'm zapped inwards.

My heart skips, our first night home, in our yellow house up in the meadow. I watch the lean, muscled silhouette of Liam coming towards me against the golden light of the fading sun, gilding with its last glorious rays of the day the woodland path. In his arms, he holds Nicolas and Sébastien. Busy little fingers express, convey, assert, and I rejoice in their delight in everything and nothing.

Spotting me, waiting for them at the end of the trail, they giggle and squirm to be set free. Liam smiles and slowly lowers down, letting go of two squealing little toddlers on unsteady legs.

Kneeling down in front of them, outwardly identical yet so uniquely different, my arms stretch wide open as they stumble gleefully into my welcoming embrace.

"Hey! You okay in there?"

I startle and sway as the voice comes again, and I have to look around to remember I'm still in the bathroom. "Christ. It's too quiet in there, Leo. Éolie? Éolie?" Zac shouts, banging on the door.

I turn toward the frantic sound, moving too fast, and lose my balance. I reach for the first thing I can grab to prevent my toppling over, and my hand crashes through the antique glass cabinet, where the neat row of folded towels stops my momentum.

I blink, sure I'm going down now—but I'm still standing. No pain. "Huh," I say to myself as blood begins to pool along the cuts on my hand, up to the crease of my elbow.

Then everything slows.

My thoughts are disjointed as I stare down at the contents of the fallen shelf. Do we have red towels? I don't think so, but I can't remember. They're red now, and oozing with the color.

Outside, the guys are still banging, but their voices are far away, as if through a tunnel. I want to reassure Zac that everything's all right, but I can't articulate any words. I feel sluggish as I pull shards of glass free from my forearm.

I stare in shock at the deep gash, watching my blood pooling and then dripping—then running, but I'm uncomprehending of it.

Behind me, the door splinters and bangs against the wall as it's torn open. I blink, trying to focus, but there's too many of them. I see a few Zacs, Leos, and P.Os shouting, but I can't hear the words.

The pain kicks in, blindsiding me with its burning, and my mind screams for Liam.

Seventy-One

LIAM

Working on the barn's outside structure, I roughen the hammer's striking face with sandpaper to help prevent glancing blows that bend nails, and often find one's thumb. A cool trick I learned from one of the four grizzled construction workers this morning. They're working on the roof today so it's a little beyond my scope of skills, but they usually give me little things to do as I tag along. I try to stay out of their way as much as possible, picking up things on my own, but I do want the barn to be finished before the snow comes in October.

Swift and blinding pain slices through my left hand, and I drop the hammer. I lift my hand, inspecting my wrist and forearm for damage, but there's nothing. No cut anywhere to be seen, but I feel the nightmarishly familiar burn of sliced flesh. I stumble back in confusion until I hear Éolie' voice in my head screaming my name, and then turning into deadly silence.

"Éolie!"

In a panic, I start running. The usual five minutes' walk probably shaved down to a record one minute. I take the front porch stairs two at a time, almost ripping out the door, but once inside, everything is chaos.

Zac is shouting rapid-fire instructions to Leo, while P.O. and Yann are barely holding up, leaning on the wall, hands on their knees, white as sheets.

For a fraction of a second, P.O.'s eyes lock with mine and the haunted look in his shoots me straight past panic and lands me into frantic territory. They both try to stop me from barreling through but I shove past them and everything slows down at once.

"Éolie?" I cry out at the sight of too much blood all over the bathroom floor, wall, cabinet ... and Éolie... Jesus, Éolie, lying on the floor...

Crippling pain shoots through my arm all the way to my heart and I feel myself go down, lights out, no sound, blackout.

Delicate fingers gently draw circles on my wrist, the caress generously soothing.

I feel no pain.

Soft murmuring. I must be dreaming. What am I doing dreaming? There's something urgent I need to take care of, I just can't quite remember what it is...

If I could only wake up, I'd remember, I'm sure, but my eyelids refuse to cooperate, too heavy. There goes another soothing caress, my wrist tingling up to the crease in my elbow.

So much blood.

Éolie.

I scramble up, forcing my eyes to open.

I swallow hard, my mouth as dry as the Mojave desert.

"Liam?" She brings my wrist up to her mouth, kissing it.

It takes me a minute to understand where I am but still no idea how I got here. My shoulders sag in relief. I'm in our bed, staring down at Éolie propped up as usual, by her sea of pillows.

So much blood.

Just a bad dream? Or worse yet, a horrific premonition?

My heart leaps in my chest.

Still under shock, unable to utter a single coherent word, I study her. My hands lovingly brush on her roundness, a warm caress celebrating the three of them unimpaired.

I finally release the breath I was unaware of holding.

"Christ, I've just had the most awful nightmare," I say, grasping Éolie's arms, needing additional reassurances. Relieved doesn't even begin to describe how I feel, finding both unscathed. Until turning them over, I come across the jagged light pink scar marring her left palm all the way to the crease of her inner elbow.

"You slept for the past twenty minutes or so, but it wasn't exactly a dream..." she starts, looking down at the scar, swallowing.

"What the bloody hell happened?" I ask in a daze. My eyes transfixed on her scar.

"I lost my balance and toppled into the glass cabinet," Éolie says in a small voice.

"What! How could—"

"Fuck, man. You two just shaved ten years off my life," Leo says, leaning heavily on the doorjamb. "He's awake," he cries out over his shoulder. One by one Leo, Zac, P.O., and Yann silently file in our small bedroom, the lot of them looking a bit green around the edges, clearly quite shaken up.

"Where were you and Leo?" I demand of my friends. "Bloody hell, Zac, how—?"

As soon as I release the word bloody, both P.O. and Yann blanch. Zac and Leo look at each other, then at Éolie, then at the floor, trying to gather their wits, clearly struck mute.

"Aww. Man—" Zac's hands, oddly trembling for one usually so cool and confident, restlessly twitch as he almost succeeds in pulling his shaggy hair out, clearly disturbed, and I wonder absently if he shouldn't start shaving it back into a buzz cut. Leo fares no better.

A delicate hand reaches for mine, lacing our fingers and squeezing lightly as though bracing for what comes next. I take a peek.

"I have never seen anything like it—" Zac starts, and stops on a shiver while he glances out the window, clearly at a loss. "There was so much blood when I tore down that door. I went into medic mode by rote but I knew ... I just knew..." Zac pinches the bridge of his nose hard. "Gimme a minute..." He gathers himself back somewhat, and, taking a deep breath, looks me in the eye before continuing on.

"Leo and I were trying to staunch the flow, and stabilize the wound when you came barreling through, and we lost you both ... You both went into shutdown at the exact same time and then ... and then something incredible happened—"

Zac turns watery eyes to Éolie, and I know something incredible indeed happened. "Éolie's whole arm began to heat and glow with a bright-blue light ... and then, it just healed itself. And I'll tell you right now, if anyone had come up to me with that story, even knowing what we know about you, Éolie, well ... I wouldn't have been able to comprehend, let alone imagine ... But we all saw," Zac says with a fierce look, and the others choke. "We all saw Éolie's wound closing up as it healed itself at what felt like lightning speed, and then it was over. You were both breathing normally, peacefully sleeping." Zac exhales a long breath, deflating as his back slowly slides along the wall, his legs giving way.

I look at my still freaked-out buddies, then at Éolie. Éolie, who now fixedly stares at her arm.

"At a cruising speed of one hundred kilometers per hour, which is more than twice the speed limit of forty kilometers per hour, on dry roads, no traffic, no mountains, no winding roads, straight line across, we're still twenty-eight minutes away from the emergency room at the regional hospital," Yann says, breaking the prevailing silence, and we all stare at him with a question in our eyes.

Still a little grey around the edges, Yann wipes his moist forehead with his sleeve. "Under the best of circumstances, after a call to 911, the paramedics would only be coming up the drive right about *now*," he says on a forceful note.

"*Why* do you think I'm still freaking out here. I know it would have been too little too late!" Zac yells.

"Stop. Please, guys, just ... please..." Éolie pleads. "I'm so sorry. I—"

"We're all overreacting here, and losing focus. Who cares about the what if's and the how's?" P.O. interjects. "I, for one, will be eternally grateful that Éolie and our twins seem to be perfectly fine now."

I don't know what to say as I'm suddenly choking on gratitude. P.O. is right, who cares about the what if's and the how's? All that matter is that the three of them are doing fine. "They're fine," I repeatedly murmur.

"Well, sorry to burst your bubble there, P.O., but even if Éolie heals quicker, emergencies do happen all the same. So we need to hatch a contingency plan before these two are ready to make their appearance. One that preferably involves me nowhere near blood gushing," Yann says, only to turn green again at the mere mention. I may be turning a little green myself.

"We absoluty do need a plan," Leo agrees quietly, and we all shoot him a look. "Come now, aside from Éolie, am I the only one here clearly seeing that an emergency c-section at the regional hospital is out of the question?"

"Fuck..." My heart drops as realization seeps in. I can't believe I didn't think of this before. I was so caught up in Éolie's reassurances—and my worries—that I forgot about how strange it would be if we did actually present her at a hospital.

Zac stills, and my hand trembles in Éolie's.

"Cutting me won't be the problem if it comes to that, just do it ... quickly," Éolie says in a small voice as she looks pointedly at Zac.

"Hell," Zac says, his voice barely audible. "You're worried you'll heal before we can get them out, aren't you?"

"Yes," she murmurs.

"Jesus." I glance down to where her fingers touch mine, then back up at her face, and I feel mine leach of all color.

"Don't hesitate, Zac, as many times as it takes," she says, eyes intent on him. I inhale sharply, grasping her fingers.

"Christ, Éolie. Even without anesthesia?" he exclaims, horrified, and we all gasp and turn green.

"Humans endure much more for far less," she says, putting my hands on her taut, round belly, and movements, like a wave passing through, rumble underneath them.

I swallow, dizzying images spinning out of control, my imagination taken over by my fear.

"They're doing okay in there, right?" I ask nevertheless.

"More than okay. No worries for now," she assures us.

"Zac, is there any way you can help with drugs?' I ask, hating that I have to ask him to overstep but—this is Éolie.

"I'll find a way," Zac vows fiercely, his stare full of strength and support, and I breathe more freely. I don't know what I'd do without my family.

I briefly note the time, and realize I slept longer than usual. Beside me, my typical wake-up call is still sleeping away. Not that I'm complaining, sleep is good for them.

I bend down for a kiss, and don't even get one stir. With the night Éolie went through, constantly waking up, I'm quite happy that she's still out.

A quick text to Zac confirms that it's normal to get that restless on the last few miles. He's more patient with me than I am with myself.

I check the pebbles left in the ceramic bowl, like I do many times a day now. But it's not as though counting the remaining ones over and over can completely calm me the fuck down. I'm in a constant state of almost-hyperventilating. The lump in my chest is like a tumor of anxiety—growing larger the closer we get to the end.

Get a grip, man. They're all doing well. And I tamp down on my fear factor, hiking up through the roof every time Zac's away now, just the fleeting thought of the 'C' word enough to send me into a panic.

"Twenty-two left," I say, dropping into the jar today's addition. Beside me, Éolie's belly contorts. I press down gently on what looks like a knee, an elbow, a foot, god knows.

I step into the kitchen, preparing a tray of fresh fruits, yogurt, granola cereals and a tall glass of dark unsweetened chocolate milk.

"Aren't engineers bred for that specific reason, Yann? Man, go for it already," I absently hear P.O. challenging Yann to whatever video game is their flavor of the week.

Tray in hand, I turn on my heels, but a sharp pain kicks me in the gut, making me double-over.

The serving platter, the food, the milk, noisily crashing down at my feet has nothing on my yelp of pain. Footsteps running barely register. By the time they arrive, I'm rocking in the fetal position, sweat bathing my forehead. The crippling pain passes just as suddenly as it came.

What in the bloody everlasting hell was that?

"Did you trip on your foot, or what?" Yann grunts.

With cold milk dripping from my tee and yogurt staining my jeans, I tentatively open my eyes to the concerned looks of Yann supporting me while he pulls me up.

"I ... I don't know," I scratch the back of my head, looking around, my brain trying to figure out a rational explanation but finding none. Awesome.

"Man, glad you're all right. I thought you were dying. Those are some lungs you have on you," P.O. says, one eyebrow angling up. "Why don't you chill for a while. I'll get Éolie's breakfast."

"Where's Zac?" Leo frantically calls from the bedroom.

"Éolie?" Another kick in the gut, even more intense, brings me back down, momentarily preventing any other thought than survival. Just as before, the sharp pain pulses, stops, and recedes.

"Éolie." Scrambling up, clutching my shredded guts, I start yelling for someone to call Zac as I burst into the bedroom, closely followed by P.O. yelling something on his phone and, behind him, Yann.

Seventy-Two

ÉOLIE

In a fuzzy state of mind, I float. Not awake, not quite asleep.

I see Nicolas, head down, ready, inching along his birth canal aided by my body's contractions, and Sébastien's little bottom and kicking legs pushing him with all his might to hurry him out.

I whisper tenderly, encouragingly, reminding them they are not alone.

It's time.

And I hope it goes more smoothly than what Zac secretly fears, and that Liam is truly ready for whatever comes next.

I groggily come back to me, and the first thing that filters through my awareness is Liam. He's crouched at the foot of the bed, groaning. And I may or may not have given new meaning to shared pain.

But then the next wave hits, and I can't move or breathe or even—

"Liam, LIAM, LIAAAM..." I call out, coming fully awake on an intense contraction as moisture soaks the mattress underneath me.

It's time, *now.*

And I have a moment of panic. Isn't it supposed to go slower? I breathe in and out, already drenched in more than sweat, concentrating hard on helping my two little ones safely cross over to this strange new world.

On that thought alone a calm settles down over me. Sharply focusing my mind, I can feel the almost immediate results on Nicolas and Sébastien.

Seventy-Three

LIAM

"Listen up, man, and listen good," Leo says as he hurries by my side. "Éolie's having the twins, and they're coming out at terminal velocity. P.O. tells me Zac's en route, his ETA is about ten minutes. We're on our own until he's here. *You* need to breathe through her contractions. She's doing fine. You're not!"

Contractions. Éolie's doing fine. Contractions. I repeat his words until they sink in. I try to sit up. "I'm having contractions?" I ask, dumbfounded.

Is that what it is? I look down at my aching body af if it holds the answer. How's it even possible that women all over are willingly going through this? Repeatedly? In this very instant I'd willingly forego, renounce, forfeit, eschew sex. *Abstinence,* my prurient side screams at me.

Just then, the relentless pain recedes. Relief. Unabridged relief. Éolie's doing fine, doing fine, doing fine, I endlessly repeat, striving to calm down a bit as I get up, steadying myself.

"Liam, they're almost here," Éolie pants in between breath patterns, and the most blinding smile blossoming on her face slams into me.

The moment is surreal, but sharpens my focus on only one thing, the twins. Letting me jump into action.

"Leo, get the bath water ready," I say, picking her up.

"Yann's done it already. I'm your designated crutch," Leo says, keeping up with me, staying by my side. Éolie goes rigid in my arms, eyes closed, panting in a rhythmic pattern, and I only get a twinge of pain in my guts this go around.

"What's the ETA again?" I ask Leo, striving to keep calm and collected.

"P.O. tells me four minutes, and he's staying glued to his phone," Leo says, hovering in the bathroom's doorway.

I gently deposit her into warm body-temperature water, and she whimpers that she needs to push.

"Éolie, please, sweet. Zac's on his way, he'll be here any minute now, any minute, don't push. All's good, all's good." I softly massage her lower belly to promote a sort of standstill, buying us a few precious minutes ... or seconds. *Please don't let me fuck this up.*

"Christ, P.O, what's the ETA? We're out of time!" I shout, one small head crowning. She grabs my arms, panting. "Have to push—Nicolas."

Her eyes lock on mine for a fraction, her faith in me humbling.

And I suddenly know I can do this all the way. For her. For them.

Éolie pushes Nicolas, who, not a minute later, slides underwater into my waiting hands. I lift him out of the water and marvel at this tiny, rosy-pink miracle I'm holding, as he takes his first breath, smoothly transitioning.

I carefully deposit him on Éolie's chest and rub his back in gentle motions like Zac taught me, settling him to recover from his journey out of his aquatic bubble, whispering a string of nonsensical words of love.

"Sébast—" Éolie swooshes, closing her eyes, her hands anchoring a nuzzling Nicolas preciously in the crook of her neck. "Help him—breathe—"

On a final push, Sébastien's glides out into my hands, massaging him into his very first breath, taking mine away. I bend low over the tub, my hands cradling him. I'm on a high, feeling the rise and fall of his little chest against the rapid rise and fall of mine. Christ, they're so tiny, so perfect, so...

The muted sounds of a car driving up, the guys' excited voices calling back and forth, everything fades out but Éolie, Nicolas, Sébastien. My family.

Éolie's eyes are awash in wonder and love and devotion and infinity reflecting back at me.

She's never been more beautiful.

I gently lower Sébastien next to Nicolas, right over her heart, and she tenderly cradles my hands over them, protectively, softly murmuring words of love in a litany.

Devotion.

My chest hurts as I feel my heart expand.

Just then, they both open their eyes. Bluer than baby blue eyes stare up at me. All knowing, all seeing.

"I was wrong, you know," I tell them. My hands are trembling, and my face is wet with tears. "It's my journey you're filling with extraordinary."

I am lost with Éolie in euphoria, incandescently happy.

Dedication

To you
Who makes this story-telling journey, extraordinary.

Incandescently
(Liam's story)

By Design
(Theo's story)

Indigenous
(Leo's story)

Exposure
(P.O.'s story)

Apprehension
(Zac's story)

Gravity
(Yann's story)

Journey Into the Incandescent World
of Sylvie Parizeau...
The Forest of Laure

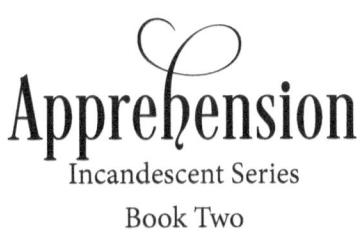

Apprehension

Incandescent Series

Book Two

Chapter One

Apprehension

noun

1.

anticipation of adversity or misfortune; suspicion or fear of future trouble.

ZAC

"Oh. Mon. Dieu. *That's it.*"

The girl's blissful cry reverberates throughout the ski chalet over the gurgling sound of the industrial coffee machine I'm milking for all its worth.

I blink.

For a reason I can't explain, that voice elicits a weird flutter in my chest.

With a will of its own, my finger slackens pressure upon the coffee lever. A trickling of smoldering dark brew inches its way up into my fifth cup to go, stopping at the three-quarter mark.

I tip my head to the side.

"Spot on," the voluptuous voice moans to the high ceiling of the café in what I'd call orgasmic enthusiasm. I look right and left, glad no other patrons are witnessing me ... witnessing her. And then I see her. Or rather, her appendages.

A nimble tongue licks a slender index finger, greedily lapping it up in exaggerated wet suction sounds.

My gut tightens.

I stare, torn between *what the fuck*, and *please don't stop*.

I give the girl the onceover. Facing away from me but bending low over the counter, her tight little body's hot all right. Her black turtleneck and soft-shell ski racers showcasing curves I'd like to palm. Interestingly enough, the fact that we're standing in the middle of a ski resort cafeteria, or that, no shit, it's probably colder than absolute zero tonight up in Québec's Laurentian Mountains, barely registers. Right this minute, I don't really care. My fingers twitch and warm up instantly, and so does my dick.

It's been a little while...

Lost in a steamy daydream, I find myself standing at the counter, coffees in hand.

"Will that be all?" the elderly cashier rudely interrupts me mid-fantasy, ringing up my five coffees to go, stowing them onto a disposable cardboard tray.

"I'd like to have some of what she's having," I deadpan as I hand over some money to the sugarplum fairy manning the cash register.

"You totally should. Mireille outdid herself. Here, have a taste." The splendid specimen of a girl turns to me, offering me half her cupcake.

I quirk one eyebrow, and her gaze tracks mine to the icing that's just about swiped clean. She shrugs sheepishly. "Tell me one of your guilty secrets, and we'll be even," the enchanting grey-eyed creature says, looking me straight in the eye. Her expression is guileless, which only adds to the tease in her words. My heartbeats pick up their pace.

"I think I will," I quip, bending low, trapping her gaze into mine. "Have a taste that is." I take a bite out of the offered cupcake still cupped in her hand without breaking our stare. Her impossibly large eyes grow by a fraction, and she stills. Well, that certainly caught her attention. *Good.* I shift, pinned by the clear silver color of her unwavering eyes. And suddenly, I'm the one who's caught.

Her creamy complexion stains rosy under my scrutiny, eyes wide and full of wonder locked on mine.

My pulse jumps in my throat.

That look. Those eyes. A déjà vu sensation washes over me.

We stare. Just stare. The space of an instant or an eternity, not sure which.

Why do I feel like I know you, like we've met before?

I reel back. Where in the bloody everlasting hell is that shit coming from?

I don't do involved. Ever. My usual type has a universal itch in need of scratching, and not much else.

My best friend Liam's new normality is messing with my head. It must be. After a lifetime of wandering, he's finally—and only recently—settled down with his new wife up here in these mountains. His pregnant wife. And all he can talk about is "normal." Maybe this is me being jealous. I have a sudden yearning for his brand of happiness, yet I have this feeling that I've just bitten off more than I can chew here.

The cupcake is delicious, though.

The girl's wondrous eyes flicker past me, and then back to me. "See? Definitely a keeper," she says with aplomb.

Damn, her smile is enough to knock a bloke off his feet.

"Are you sure?" a middle-aged woman asks from behind the counter, her tone of voice floundering.

"Yeah, pretty much," I say dumbfounded. She knocked years of suave right off me, so it seems, and scrambled my brains by the same token.

The girl, who's too lovely by half, studies me in the space of a second, before answering the timidly voiced question, addressed to her in the first place. "Told you so. A keeper."

Wait, *what?*

A keeper? Me? I inwardly scoff. "Worst pick ever, sweetheart," I say under my breath.

Shifting my weight on one leg, I cross my arms, feigning bored disinterest as I finish my taste of her baked concoction. Curiosity burns a hole in my gut, wondering what this bizarre conversation is all about. "What was that?" I angle a brow, challenging her.

The girl's exquisite face tilts in my direction. She raises her brow, challenging me right back. "A taste of something addictive. So worth keeping."

The woman's audible gasp from behind the counter pops our newest staring contest bubble. "Magali, seriously?" Blonde-haired and of the indeterminate age variety, her eyes dart between us, plump fingers fidgeting with her apron, clearly uncertain.

Ma Ga Lee, I murmur to myself, testing the French musicality of her name on my tongue, and liking it. A tad too much.

The girl stretches over the counter. Long locks of her dark-brown hair stick out every which way from underneath a rainbow-colored wool beanie. Adorable comes to mind. One of her hands clasps the other woman's fidgety fingers, giving them a gentle squeeze. "Seriously. This one above all the others."

I still. Six words. Like a vow. Unheard of. *This one above all the others.* What would it be like to be so chosen? My breath catches in my throat. She can't possibly be talking about me?

Magali. Soft lips … soft words … the voice of an angel.

"And … which one would that be?" I ask, a bit reeling from my wayward thoughts.

A small, delighted chuckle escapes Magali's lips, and I'm strangely pleased to be responsible for eliciting it. Mireille gives her a weird look, but Magali looks down before I catch her eyes.

"This one," Mireille informs me, motioning to the blackboard behind her where an elegant penmanship conveys the cafeteria's treat of the day under the heading *Decadent Bliss du Jour.* A damp spot underneath leaves the blank space wide open to interpretation. She points to Magali's half-eaten cupcake. "I just gave you a leftover diet cupcake I baked for Yolande and I; it's not meant as a special treat … It's so bland, non?" the middle-aged woman says in a hushed tone as though confessing to a great sin.

Bloody hell. My breath swooshes out, and I'm strangely disappointed. Of course, she'd been talking about the dessert. *Get over yourself, why don't you?*

"You did?" Magali's brow scrunches up in disbelief while her pearly whites take a tentative bite of the cake where a bit of frosting remains. "I don't know where you've put the diet in there; it melts in my mouth. The moist center is pure decadence with that frosting, and you know I can eat my weight in sugar. I'm telling you, this is your Avalanche Cupcake to top them all, and you'll have everyone coming back for more, guaranteed. *Definitely* worth keeping," she says.

"Don't you agree?" Her pale silver eyes light up on me as she smiles the most brilliant smile I've ever seen. Two dimples, cute as all hell, dance at the corner of her full lips.

My pulse jumps. Killer dimples. Kissable lips. *Definitely.*

"Definitely," I parrot. You'll have me coming back for more, I inwardly vow. *Where the fuck did that come from?*

Magali cranes her head above my shoulder. "Yolande, don't you agree as well?"

Three pairs of eyes swivel to the white-haired cashier. She grunts what can pass for a yes. Not quite meeting anyone's eyes, she starts fussing with the display baskets of whole-grain muffins and homemade energy bars arrayed temptingly next to the coffee machine, near the cash register.

I lean back against the counter, crossing my ankles, my ski boots at an angle, waiting for the outcome of this nonsensical debate about plain old vanilla cupcakes. In reality, I can't seem to make myself just up and go before I know more about this girl. She's fascinating.

"I'll be back for more," I say before I can stop myself.

Magali's eyes flick to my night ticket affixed to my left sleeve and the tray with five cups resting on the counter beside me. "See, Mireille? Everyone agrees on your newest treat, even visitors just passing through."

Just passing through. My chest constricts painfully upon hearing the words. What's with that? I've said them myself with a shit ton of relief to back them up more than a thousand times before.

Mireille twists her hands on her apron. "I'm not really sure that cake makes the cut for l'ardoise."

Magali leans closer, putting her hand on my sleeve. A fresh citrus scent worms its way into my sharp inhale. "Mireille's been trying to come up with the perfect Avalanche Cupcake ever since a local blog post mentioned that her Bliss du Jour wasn't worth the detour. Very bad form."

I'd like to wax lyrical on the goddamn cake if just to get on her good side, but for the life of me I can't think of any words; my mind's a blank slate. "Indeed." I rub my jaw, unnerved by the heady rush of warmth her nearness sends zipping through my nerve endings, firing me up. *Does she feel it too? This thing between us.*

"You can say it's a matter of pride now to prove that blogger wrong by the end of the season, and Mireille gets my vote on this one." Magali leans away and I mourn the loss of her hand on my sleeve. *Who's this guy?*

Mireille clucks her tongue on a soft head shake. "I'm still not convinced this afternoon's whipped chocolate berry mousse cupcakes topped with lemony frosting, weren't, I don't know, more ... *it*?" She dips a spoon into a stainless steel bowl, handing it over.

Magali's luscious lips part and she hums while her tongue takes a slow swipe of frosting, licking off the spoon.

Fuck, I can't breathe. I clutch the counter.

"That's funny." Magali's forehead furrows, her tongue getting in another slow lick. "I could have sworn I tasted this, plus a mix of maple and vanilla there, at the end, on mine. You know, less tart. Sweeter."

The grandmotherly cashier, Yolande, clears her throat, looking down at the floor. "I sort of ... spread another layer of frosting on Magali's cupcake."

Spread another layer of frosting on Magali's cupcake? The visual, man.

"Yolande," gasps Mireille.

Yolande shrugs both shoulders. "What can I say? It needed a boost."

Jesus. I don't need a boost. I'm sporting a boner from hell that not even the concept of a negative forty-something wind-chill factor awaiting me outside deflates. Never mind micro-fleece thermal layers stretched to the limits of endurance.

For an answer, Magali's eyes dance with something akin to mirth looking me over, and I wonder for a minute there if I voiced my thoughts aloud ... I grab the coffee tray, making sure it provides adequate coverage over strategic areas. The guys are probably freezing to death waiting on their coffees, and I can't stand here much longer without making a complete fool of myself.

"Time's up, Magaliiii. You coming, or what?" one of the ski resort dudes, in full patrol gear, hollers from the cafeteria doors, a few feet away from where I stand rooted in the quasi-deserted room, a huge bonfire keeping everyone on a ski break tonight out of doors.

Magali hands the bowl back over the counter. "Have to go. Cédric will have my head for sure but it was totally worth it. Here's to one of your tastiest collabs." Magali salutes both women with what's left of her cupcake before opening wide and shoveling it down in one swallow. "Keep it up," she says around a full mouth of baked goods.

Yeah, that's the problem.

My brain's stuck in neutral, my testis drawn tight, and my stomach's clenching in knots.

Great times ahead skiing this off.

"It's off the chart with frosting, you really should try it," she says to me in all seriousness, wiping crumbs from the corner of her lips as she spins on one heel.

"Off the chart with—" I choke, my voice barely audible. I'm struck stupid. What the bloody hell? I don't do tongue-tied. Ever.

"Enough. Come on, already," the hulking patrol guy shouts at Magali, grating on my nerves. My eyes narrow.

"I'm coming. I'm coming. I'm coming," Magali chants away.

Christ above, what's left of me to harden stiffens in a nanosecond. My blood pumps wildly, churning in my ears. The dude spares me a burning glance before pushing back out on his poles and skis, presumably on his way to the lifts.

My hands fist at my side. "Your boyfriend doesn't like you having treats?" I call out to her. I may have something against him if he gives her a hard time for enjoying herself. I may have something against him, period.

"Boyfriend?" She shakes her head on a small laugh. "Won't Cédric have a hoot over that one." The rhythmic thumps of her coordinated moves, heel to toes, make walking in these things sound effortlessly easy, which I know for a fact, is far from being so. "Guess I'll never hear the end of it now, will I?" she adds cryptically.

I clump my way over to her in my ski boots, managing to balance the coffees and myself in an effort to keep pace. "Meaning?"

Reaching one of the long tables a bit farther down, she shrugs on a bright-red jacket labeled Mont-Saint-Sauveur Ski Patrol in reflective white letterings, before grabbing her helmet, sporting the resort logo in front, with her name, Magali, tagged on the back of it.

She's a ski patroller too? Nice ... Maybe not a boyfriend, then. Even better.

She shoots me a smile that turns her from gorgeous to flat-out devastating. A direct hit to the Solar plexus. "You owe me one."

"What—?"

"Guilty secret," she says over her shoulder.

For the space of a moment, we fall into each other's eyes, a meeting of souls.

"Just so you know. What I said earlier on wasn't just about the cupcakes, either."
She winks.

I stare, slack-jawed, as she disappears in a blur of red, pushing her way out,
past Leo and P.O., who whistle low.

"Won't ask what's been keeping you." P.O. takes the lid off one of the cups
I've almost forgotten I'm carrying. His muddy, green-hazel eyes glint with
suppressed merriment, giving me the once over.

"He shoots! He scores!" Leo smirks, quoting the saying on the long-sleeved
tee I wore this afternoon at Liam's courthouse wedding. He ties back his
shoulder-length sandy brown hair before shoving back down his dark beanie.
I give him a look, unimpressed. Liam and Éolie are expecting twins, and the
shirt's only funny within context.

"I'd say it was just the usual shit," P.O. says, vastly amused, "but the mouth
hanging open's a new one. What'd she do? Say no?"

I shoot him a glare. "*She*," I uncharacteristically bark at P.O., "has a name."

Magali. Her name is Magali, I'd like to say, but refrain. I'm not ready to share
any details yet. I'm still reeling from the encounter and my unusual reaction to
her.

"I'm sure *she* does." P.O. smirks.

"Give over, man." Leo plucks the coffee tray from my unresisting hand.

"It's not like that," I grumble as I follow them out. I blink.

Shit. It's worse than that.

My eyes scan the crowd of skiers, dismissing one red coat after the other,
realizing too late that I've let her disappear on me.

"Of course it's not," P.O. says in an offhand manner, watching me.

"So, tell me again why you're *not* looking for a bright-red coat, and a pretty
fucking hot patroller wearing it," Leo says, annoyingly smug, and P.O. low fives
him.

I grit my teeth, my gut weirdly churning. "She's ... a friendly sort, that's all,"
I finally manage, irked to no end by Leo's comment as we approach Theo and
Yann waiting by the bonfire.

"Who's a friendly sort?" Yann asks, picking one of the cardboard cups. P.O.
sips from his, hiding a smirk.

"A girl, apparently," Leo says knowingly.

"Friendly as in 'just friends?' That's a new one." Yann's face scrunches up as though the notion does not even add up, his bright-green eyes blinking behind his wire-framed glasses. "Girls up here are a different species altogether if Zac can't even score one."

Theo scratches his blond scruff, his mouth twisting, fighting a laugh.

"Want a shot at me, stand in line," I mutter, my fingers gripping my own cup.

"About time," Theo says, snatching a cup. "Level out the playing field for the rest of us."

I cut them a look. "Aren't you guys regular comedians tonight."

"I could have made two more runs down the slope, man," Theo comments, struggling to keep a straight face. "Took you that long to wipe out in there."

The three others chuckle under their breath, and I'd normally join in the ribbing, dishing it right back, but for some unfathomable reasons I have no wish to explore right now, they're pissing me off instead. Big time.

"Wipe out, my ass." I guzzle down the lukewarm coffee before squishing the cardboard into a ball, pitching it into the bonfire. It lands dead center of the roaring flames.

Transfixed, I watch my cup crash and burn, a strange sense of apprehension washing over me.

Apprehension

on November 22, 2016
Zac is yours.

Acknowledgements

Curious about the pretty amazing people who contribute to my story-telling journey behind the scenes? Take a look :

http://www.sylvieparizeau.com/behind-the-scenes/

Book cover design provided *By Hang Le*

Copy editing provided by *Red Road Editing* 🖤

Coaching, story development editing, encouragements, hand holding and SO much more provided by *Heather Hildenbrand* (oh, BTW, Heather? I threw away the key. You are thus sentenced to life to hold a very special place in my heart). xo

Love, cuddling under the duvet, meals at regular intervals, and time-off work to write provided by my very own *Grégoire* (who discovered hidden depths of patience along the way). Know that you wear the halo with flair and that your unconditional support means the world to me, and then some (pour les prochains mille ans). xxx

If I did pique your curiosity and you'd like to know just a little bit more about me? Feel free to peek inside my head by exploring this website: www.sylvieparizeau.com

Curious about the real village my characters live in? Feel free to explore right here:

http://www.sylvieparizeau.com/sylvies-chronicles/

STAY IN TOUCH. Spread the love. 🖤

Sign in to my newsletter and get both, the Forest of Laure Map as a gift screensaver and your first email-tribe-only bonus scene, featuring Liam and darling little Sébastien.

Warning: May contain traces of Zac and become addictive.

Gift map, excerpts, teasers, bonus scenes, village news, upcoming releases, hugs.

Don't miss out!

My e-mail tribe gets it all. So can you.

http://www.sylvieparizeau.com/link-to-newsletter/

About the Author:

A paralegal by day and incurable romantic by night, Sylvie is a cross-genre, and she takes Happily Ever After very seriously. The End just isn't in her vocabulary.

An incorrigible daydreamer, she now feeds her obsession with epilogues by concocting stories in which heroes deal with the happy from the get-go. Ready, or not. And she confesses under oath to loving every minute of it.

Sylvie lives her own Happily Ever After in the beautiful mountains of Les Laurentides in Northern Quebec, alongside her whole set of characters.

In between treks in their backyard wilderness, you can find them hanging out at www.sylvieparizeau.com

https://twitter.com/SylvieParizeau
https://www.facebook.com/Sylvie-Parizeau-romance-novelist-526307707511745/
Come and say hello, they'd love to hear from you!

Lexicon

Page 18

Ton papa il est où? Where's your daddy?

Page 18

Je parle très bien français maintenant. I speak French very well now.

Page 42/43

Je m'appelle Rose. My name is Rose.

Je ne comprends pas très bien ce que vous dites. Je ne parle pas anglais. Je suis... Je suis attendue déjà...

I don't really understand what you're saying. I don't speak English. I am... I am already expected over there...

Merci mon dieu. Thank you god.

Page 47

Mais c'est quoi ce délire? Would translate into something like what is this madness?

Page 59

Mille fois merci. A thousand thanks.

Page 96

Bonne nuit is goodnight.

Sweet dreams is, fais de beaux rêves.

But Éolie takes matter into her own hands and *sends* Liam beautiful dreams, literally... ;)

Je t'envoie de beaux rêves. I'm sending you beautiful dreams.

Page 101

compote de coeur. Would translate into something like heart mush.

Page 106

à *la belle étoile*. To sleep out in the open under the stars.

Page 116

"Mademoiselle Éolie, je vous attends sans faute lundi matin."
Mademoiselle Éolie, I'll be expecting you without fail Monday morning.

Page 120

Je suis, tu es, il est, nous sommes, vous êtes, ils sont.
Liam conjugates at the present tense the verb 'être' in French, the equivalent of I am, you are...
Then he starts on the subjonctif plus-que-parfait.

Page 139

"Je t'aime, je t'aime, je t'aime,"
I love you I love you I love you.

Page 178

And my pièce de résistance, salade de poivrons doux au romarin.
And the best and most important part, my very own bell peppers salad seasoned with rosemary.

Page 183

"C'est mon premier bonheur du jour,"
(An expression we use frequently in our household =) meaning something like « it is my first happy of the day » - the expression is derived from a Françoise Hardy song, 1963 - Le Premier Bonheur du Jour : https://www.youtube.com/watch?v=CrHA9gA8qpE

Page 203

Incroyable non? A French expression meaning isn't it incredible?

Page 218

"Mais entrez, entrez, venez vous réchauffer."

An expression of welcome, meaning something like come out of the cold, come in and warm yourself.

Page 219

La belle saison. An expression typically Québecois used to convey something like when the weather gets nice, meaning summer.

Page 220

Circulation non fluide. Backed up traffic.

Autoroute 15 Nord Saint-Jérôme, gardez la gauche/Highway 15 North St. Jerome, keep your left.

Autoroute 40 Est Trois-Rivières, gardez la droite/Highway 40 East, Three-Rivers, keep your right.

Page 227

"Ah, mes p'tits oiseaux sont debout,"

A warm expression meaning something like my little darling lovers are awake. And not my little birds are up. =)

Page 230

Zut de flûte, conveys either something like drat or oops, depending (and is nowhere near a swear word as Zac will think, amused, in Apprehension). Magali is full of cute or tender expressions that do not translate all that well. Mon petit papa à moi is a cute and affectionate way to address her dad.

Page 236

"C'est féérique!" It's enchanting, magical.

Page 254

Victoire. Victory.

Page 261

Le Petit Mouton Noir. The Little Black Sheep.

Page 262

Harfangs des Neiges. Snowy Owls. Side note : Quebec's aviary symbol.

Page 264

"Elle vous plaît?" You like?

"Faites le tour, ne vous gênez-pas." You're welcome to take a look around.

Mas de Provence. Traditional farm house in Provence.

"La demoiselle, elle va?" Is la demoiselle all right?

Page 265

"Elle a peut-être besoin de s'asseoir un p'tit brin." Maybe she needs to sit down for a bit.

"Non. Non, ça va aller." No. No, everything's fine.

"Bon, alors, si vous le dites. Je prépare les papiers de l'armoire bleue, et je vous reviens."

Okay, if you say so. I'll prepare the papers for the blue wardrobe and I'll come back.

Pages 273

La Mairie. City Hall.

Le chef lieu. In a French country, administrative center. After the British conquest, Québec stayed under the French regime civil laws and legal administration structures for the civil side of things.

Palais de justice. Courthouse.

Ministère. Ministry of...

Page 316

Aventures Hors des Sentiers Battus. Off the Beaten Track Adventures.